To Jamie

THE RAVEN EFFECT

Thanks for
having me along
on this CBT ride!
(Hope we can work
together again.
Mike

THE RAVEN EFFECT

MICHAEL IPPEN

authorHOUSE®

AuthorHouse™
1663 Liberty Drive
Bloomington, IN 47403
www.authorhouse.com
Phone: 1-800-839-8640

First published by AuthorHouse   07/14/2011

ISBN: 978-1-4634-2945-4 (sc)
ISBN: 978-1-4634-2379-7 (dj)
ISBN: 978-1-4634-2378-0 (ebk)

Library of Congress Control Number: 2011910731

Printed in the United States of America

AUTHOR'S BIO

Michael Ippen has been writing all his life. He grew up in North Vancouver, BC, and attended Simon Fraser University and the University of British Columbia. While writing fiction has been his passion, Michael has worked in local government operations for over thirty years. He and his partner Stephanie live near Victoria, BC. and have raised three children whose love of books and writing rivals their own. The Raven Effect is his first published novel.

DEDICATION

In memory of Albert Forrester Black, my grandfather, who taught me that where people suffer in the midst of prosperity, nobody is free.

For my wife, Stephanie, and for my children: my Compass, my Moon, my Sun and my Star.

COVER ART

Chelsea Sundher is a recent graduate of the Camosun College Visual Arts Program. She lives and works in Saanich, near Victoria BC.

"All the world was in darkness . . . Raven plucked up the ball of light in his beak, flew through the smoke hole in the Sky Chief's lodge and disappeared into the dark sky. Raven stole the sun from the Sky Chief and gave it to all the people, though his snow-white feathers were burned black by the heat of the sun. And the people looked into the sky in wonder, for they could see their world for the first time, the trees, the rivers, the animals."

—Adapted from *Raven Steals the Light,*
Legends of the First Peoples of the Pacific Northwest.

BOOK ONE

Heat Stroke

The August sunrise blazed through greasy curtains thinned by age and careless hands. Maureen moaned softly, ground her palms into grit-caked eyes and crawled off the sofa bed, careful not to wake the man sleeping next to her. She snatched her clothes from the floor and locked herself in the bathroom. Her head hurt and her body ached. She shivered, scrubbing her bare arms with her hands. The face in the mirror was pale. Not just pale: old. Bloodshot eyes, craving sleep, stared back at her, begging for relief.

Or was it rescue?

She leaned into the mirror and probed the skin along her jaw. It was puffy and loose. Another disappointment. Her fingers trembled. She was surely coming down with something. Or getting over someone? She shut her eyes tight, longing darkness.

She needed a shower but couldn't stand the thought of the spray rasping her flesh. She settled for brushing her teeth—without turning on the tap—without opening her eyes. Not yet on speaking terms with her reflection. Sitting on the toilet she brushed her hair, pausing often to rest her head between her hands. If she barricaded herself in here—how long before they'd leave? How long before she'd have her room back, her solitude returned like a favorite sweater salvaged from the Lost & Found. But they wouldn't. They needed her. They'd gone miles out of their way to find her. Billy would break down the door if he had to, to prevent her from abandoning them.

She thought of slipping away—they were both still asleep. Maureen opened her eyes and stared at her dismal reflection. Hadn't she done enough? She'd showed Billy the Raven's hideaway. Let *him* take her on; let *him* be the hero. That was in *his* job description—*Big Time American Environmental Activist*—not hers. Just quit Victoria and go home to Vancouver; hadn't Helen and Anne begged her over and again? Today was as good a time as any to start cleaning up the mess. She'd made a damn fine one these past two weeks; it would take months—years—to fix things, to get back on track.

But which track? She stood back from the sink, unsteady on her feet. Her hand slapped the wall, struggling for balance. Which life could she reclaim? The one she thought was her own was now on life support, and the remaining options weren't great.

Her legs wobbled as she stepped into her clothes, rumpled khaki shorts and a cotton tee shirt that stank of cigarettes. She tossed her toothbrush into a cosmetic case bulging with shampoo and hand lotions and make-up and eye liners—stuff she had no use for, anymore—and opened the bathroom door.

Josephine was awake and sitting up in the double bed, her spine pressed against the flimsy, painted plywood headboard. She glanced at Maureen, sniffed, picked up the remote and turned on the television. "He'll fuck anything with a hole and a heartbeat."

"You're speaking from experience?" Three steps for Maureen to skirt the sofa bed. Billy slept naked, on his stomach. Maureen picked a rumpled cotton blanket off the floor and flung it across his back. She retrieved her suitcase from the corner beside the motel room door and tipped it over.

"Where's my boots?" Josephine watched the procession of channels as she stabbed the remote with her thumb.

"End of the bed," Maureen said. She tugged on the sloppy bureau drawers and dumped her clothes into the open suitcase. No folding, no arranging, just a pile in the middle heaped to overflowing.

"Leaving, Cage?" Josephine crawled the length of the mattress to fish her boots out from beneath the bed. They were black, sharp-toed and dusted with a fine, white grit. She used a corner of the top sheet to polish each one.

"Why do you care?"

Josephine spit on the leather, rubbing it angrily with the sheet. "Just making conversation. We're the ones what barged in here without an invite."

"Billy told me. About what you tried to do. I'm sorry. That it didn't work out, I mean."

"So am I." Josephine slipped her right foot into a boot. Intricate stitching outlined a large bird on the outside panel, its wings outstretched, sharp beak gaping. Thunderbird. She pounded her heel against the carpeted floor to force in her foot.

Billy flinched with each thudding blow. He rolled over but did not wake.

"What burns me is they're going to lie through their teeth."

"You got nothing in writing?" Maureen crouched over her suitcase, clenching her teeth at the knot of pain in her hip.

Josephine snorted. "Nothing. Not even a napkin. They shredded everything."

"Email?"

Josephine shook her head. "No chance. It was all arranged by phone. It's like none of it ever happened."

"Billy said you got them to agree to an inquiry."

"Before it all went for shit. Let's drop it, 'kay?" Josephine tucked her jeans neatly into her boot tops.

"I found the Raven," Maureen said. "I showed Billy."

Josephine stood. She unwrapped her braid and dragged hooked fingers through shiny plaits. "Show me."

"Want a brush?" Maureen unzipped her cosmetic case and stood to hand hers to Josephine. "I don't think that's a good idea."

"I'm going to jail," Josephine said, taking the brush and plunging it through rafts of black hair salted with grey. With each stroke her hair glistened, as if it, too, was emerging from slumber. "If I can't get official answers I'll get my own. This bitch knows."

"Leave it to Billy. Or the RCMP—Legare wants her too."

"No." Josephine tossed the brush at Maureen. "We need the truth. Not just those families, all of us. It's our story now, and it needs an ending, not a line in a police report or on some bigoted, lazy-ass newspaper editor's by-line. Then the Tse Wets Aht can move on. We always do."

Josephine's lips formed a thin, bloodless scar that ended beneath the deep hollows of her cheeks. The hot, white light of morning deepened the folds that radiated from her upper lip and at the corners of her eyes. Scalpel-thin lines etched into her skin. She looked older than her thirty-eight years.

Maureen hesitated, tapping the back of the hairbrush against her leg. She dropped it into the cosmetic case, snapped shut her suitcase and dragged it to the door. So much for the early ferry to Vancouver.

"I'm finished in this business," she said, sweeping her cigarettes off the table. She shook a smoke from the deck and offered it to Josephine.

"So am I when they catch me." The Chief of the Tse Wets Aht cupped her hands around the match Maureen struck. Her palms shone like warm honey at the verge of match light.

"I've lost my job, my house is next. The RCMP thinks I'm a criminal. I've broken every blood oath and promise I made to myself." Maureen plucked a smoke from the pack and waved it in the air between them. "Look at me! I smoke, I drink. Christ! I slept with *him* and I'm older than his fucking mother!"

"Stop feeling sorry for yourself, Cage. Makes you more pathetic than you are."

"Screw it." Maureen grit her teeth. She blew a plume of smoke into the air above her head and stuffed the deck into her shorts. "There's a place near here we can get coffee to go," she said, and her thoughts fled back to when this nightmare began, and where she'd gone so wrong.

This kind of silence had humiliation written all over it. She stood, exposed before her peers—lawyers, professors, scientists; the high-priced consultants. Being naked couldn't make her feel worse. Maureen scanned the document for its file number. Breathing was difficult. Her eyes read the heavy, black numbering in the upper right-hand corner but she didn't believe them. They had to be wrong. *FN010801.091.* So far so good. *Rev. 0408.1.* There. It's what she'd worked from; the version she'd prepared for. And they were telling her it was wrong? No way. She didn't know a second revision even *existed.* Her throat was as dry as ashtray sand. She reached for the water glass at her hand but it was already empty. Only nine-fourteen in the morning and she was perspiring already. Most days she could make it to noon before the stress sweats appeared as black crescent moons under her arms.

"You're working off the old proposal, Ms. Cage," Keith Templeton said with exaggerated patience. He smiled, picked up his copy and set wire-rimmed reading glasses across a wide, boxer's nose. He read to the assembled delegates who formed an uneven rectangle around the banquet room. "Pacific Coast Tribal Federation. Subsurface Mineral Rights. F-N-Zero-one-zero-eight-zero-one-point-zero-nine-one, revision zero-four-zero-eight. *Point two,*" he said, stabbing his finger for added emphasis. "First item on the agenda—unless today isn't Thursday."

Half-suppressed laughter rippled around the room. Templeton glanced over the top of his glasses. "We sent it out ten days ago." He let the report slap against the table and dropped his glasses onto the cover. He sighed, shaking his head like a weary grandfather whose well of patience had gone dry. "I suppose we could make copies here, if we have to," he said to scattered chuckles.

Maureen blinked. Her skin itched beneath her blouse, where her bra strap rubbed against her shoulder blades. She coughed. "May I see it?"

She stepped sideways, between her chair and the table, conscious of the dampness welling in the creases of her armpits, behind her knees, at the small of her back. Her hand trembled as it received the report. "Thank you," she whispered, her voice deserting her. Her tongue was swollen in her parched mouth. As she crossed back to her end of the conference table she kept her eyes on the pattern embossed into the carpet. A crimson spout of flame with orange sparks and yellow embers leaping from its tip. Maureen thought she would melt from the heat building inside her. A matching red haze fell over her eyes.

She scrambled behind the section of table reserved for Directorate staff. The Directorate for Aboriginal Settlement. *Dee-Faz,* as everyone in the land claims business called it. She snatched up her copy of the report and matched it to Templeton's. Hers was different, the file extension in the footer trumpeting obsolescence. Her briefing notes, analysis and supporting documentation were practically useless. She swallowed.

"Perhaps—while we wait for copies of the correct version—we could isolate the common clauses," she said, "you know, work off them." She heard the catch in her voice and a fresh, scalding rash bloomed across her throat. They'd never go for it. It didn't work that way.

"Ms. Cage," Templeton said, "my clients have put many hours of review into this document. I couldn't even *contemplate* summing up the changes. We've done everything *Dee-Faz* requires. Now I'd hate to waste the table's time negotiating the wrong information because your office isn't better organized."

"My apologies to the Principals," Maureen said. She didn't dare meet their eyes. From the pinched, dry features of Leonard Thorne, Senior Provincial Negotiator and Deputy Minister who, resplendent in his thousand-dollar Armani suit, commanded proceedings from the right side of the room, to Carole Simons, Ottawa's Chief Settlement Officer whose coif of spiked, platinum hair was matched only by the unconventionality of her wardrobe. They hadn't brought their teams to Port McKenzie to participate in Amateur Hour.

"We'll straighten this out," Maureen said. "The proper sets can be ready in an hour."

Templeton cleared his throat. "I'm sorry to belabor this, Ms. Cage, but that won't do. The analysis alone will take hours, days perhaps. I trust the Directorate hasn't changed course this far into the treaty process?" His smile tightened his jaw and made him appear—momentarily—younger than his sixty-seven years.

"No." Heat leaked out of every pore. She was dissolving before their eyes, like the Wicked Witch of the West: becoming a puddle of empty rumpled clothes. "We'll have supporting documentation ready by Friday's session."

"Better make it Monday," Templeton said. "Give the Principals some confidence your office has done its due diligence."

A lone, fat bead of perspiration tracked down the side of Maureen's face. It started above a faint, puckered scar at the verge of her hairline and at her left ear detoured toward her jawbone. She slapped it away with the fingers of her left hand.

"Excuse me," she said, clearing the shards of broken glass that lined her throat. "Cancel two days? It has already been a short week, what with the Monday holiday. We shouldn't lose more than one day over this."

Templeton shrugged, turning to face the room. He raised his arms. "What say you?"

Thorne nodded. "Monday. We'll expect copies emailed by Friday, to give us time to review them." He signaled his staff to gather their papers.

Simons smoothed the front of a green paisley vest. "We've come a long way for nothing," she said. "I'd prefer to sit tomorrow, but not if the paper's raw. I can live with a Monday restart if the Federation's counsel can."

"And we can," Templeton said as he sorted his papers. "Keep that copy for now," he glanced at Maureen, "but I want it back. The *Dee-Faz* copy is somewhere. I'm sure you'll find it. Eventually." He snapped shut his leather attaché and led three Brown, Martin and Houseman associates toward the exit. He paused at the door. "In all my years I don't think I've been party to such a performance," he said. His tongue made a clucking sound against the roof of his mouth. "Unforgivable, really. What with so much at stake."

Maureen pulled over to the side of Nelson Road, opposite the bird sanctuary entrance. Hers was the second car in line. The sun had climbed above the oaks on the eastern boundary of the marsh. It shone unchallenged into her eyes. She lowered the sun visor. The slanting rays caught a cloud of insects zigzagging through the air, rising out of the wolf willow and blackberry fringe. Birdsong as bright as morning drifted through the windows. She shut off the engine, left the keys in the ignition, picked up her coffee and cradled the cup in both hands.

"The red house. She's been there at least two days."

"But you haven't seen her?" Josephine leaned back to get a better view.

The place was small, more cottage than house, with faded white trim around old-fashioned windows. The curtains were drawn and looked worn and stained through the smudged glass.

"No."

"Why here?"

"Dunno. Candy's a friend, from awhile back. Raven's got a gig downtown, later this week. And she needs the cash."

"Let's get this done," Josephine said.

"Fine by me," Maureen said. "I still have a ferry to catch."

"Sarah!" Maureen inhaled through clenched teeth.

"Don't look at me, I don't handle courier shit." Sarah Cohen threw down her pen and raised her hands, palms out, like a shield.

"Well it's not me, if that's what you mean," Aaron Chen said from the other end of the table.

"Forget it," Maureen said. "Let's figure out what happened." She slid into her chair and with hooked fingers clawed at the itch in her scalp. "We're all wearing this. Why did I waste my time analyzing an outdated version?"

"*We're* wearing this?" Sarah glared at Maureen through thick, black-rimmed glasses. Her heavy blond curls quivered when she was offended, which was pretty much every time she spoke to Maureen.

"Yes," Maureen said. "Frankly, I think you tried to screw me. I think you tried to make me look bad at this table. Again."

"I got news for you," Sarah said, sweeping a loose strand of hair from her face. "I don't have to lift a finger to make you look bad."

Maureen shoveled the heap of papers in front of her into her open briefcase. She stood over Sarah, Templeton's copy of the latest report rolled into a club in her hand. "Here's how it goes. You and Aaron will break down the clauses. Finish the analysis. Then you'll make up twenty-six clean sets. You have until five tomorrow."

"I don't think we-" Aaron began.

Maureen's hand sliced through the air above Aaron's head, silencing his protest. The bottled rage from the morning session filled her lungs.

"It's been five weeks since Lee-Anne quit," she said, her voice climbing into a shout, "and I'm trying my best but I can't do everything and you're not giving me a chance. Nobody misses her more than I do. If I knew where she was I'd drag her back myself. You don't like it? Tough! Call RG. Cry to him, you've done it a dozen times since he promoted me! But until he fires me you both have a heck of a lot of work to do!"

Slamming the meeting room door behind her was the high point of her day.

Maureen stepped out of her car. It was a beautiful morning despite the pounding in her head and the acid in her stomach. She popped the rear hatch. The spare tire filled the well beneath the carpeted floor. She fished the jack handle out of its plastic case and laid it along the length of her forearm, its socket end cold in her hand. The hatchback door closed with a soft *snick*.

"What's that for?" Josephine nudged her door shut with her hip and ducked to avoid the trailing blackberry canes that lined the edge of the road.

"Crucifixes for the vampires," Maureen said, making a short, chopping motion with the jack handle. "Blunt objects for the crazies."

They crossed the road. Breathing became difficult, as if a solid mass had formed in Maureen's chest. The jack handle suddenly seemed too heavy to lift.

"I'll go to the back," Josephine said and disappeared around the side of the house.

Maureen eyed the front door. It was in dire need of fresh paint. Set at the back of a deep porch it lingered in a shade that morning had not yet vanquished. She set her right foot onto the lowest step and shifted her weight forward. The dry wood pinched, groaned and relaxed as Maureen climbed. She pressed the doorbell and waited. Nothing. She exhaled. Nobody home. If true, she could do it again, to be sure, with the same result. She held her thumb against the button. The chime brayed into the silence. Relief flooded through her, dissolving the weight behind her ribs. She was about to kill the doorbell when the walls shivered. Something inside had moved. Her thumb jumped off the button. Her hand tightened on the jack handle as footsteps pounded toward the door.

Sweltering. Muggy. Sauna. She'd used those words with Helen and Anne, trying to describe to two confirmed and stubborn city-born women too busy to travel what summer in Port McKenzie was like. The words had seemed wholly inadequate inside her drafty living room two blocks north of West Broadway, where they drank Earl Grey tea and listened to the rhythmic tap of a spring rain against the windows. She'd found Helen a sweater and draped the limp wool over the woman's bony shoulders and told stories of the hotel's broken air conditioning system and the airless meeting rooms on the Tse Wets Aht reserve. "'The mill makes the whole valley smell like a chemical spill.'"

Maureen hesitated under the hotel awning, scrounging her sunglasses from the bottom of her purse. "And it's dirty. No matter what time of year," she said aloud, to nobody in particular.

The acidic tang irritated her nose. It got into her clothes and under her skin. Her eyes itched. She stepped into an asphalt parking lot whose surface radiated stored heat. She bowed her head to minimize the glare. The scuff of car tires and the pock-marked dimples of stiletto heels scarred the sun-softened bitumous. The weight of the air made breathing difficult and reopened her pores, immersing her in sweat. She took quick, timid steps across the lot, her toes curling to grip the insoles of her shoes.

The parking lot was halfway deserted. Her 'ninety-four Subaru Outback was parked near the wide sidewalk that cleaved hotel property from Main Street. Maureen opened the rear driver's side door, turning away from the rush of oven-hot air. She placed her briefcase on the back seat and fished her keys from her purse. A blur at the edge of vision made her step back.

"Sarah."

"How bat-shit crazy are you?" Sarah's voice was strained, edgy.

Maureen shielded her eyes against the blinding light that encircled Sarah's face. Where she stood she partially eclipsed the sun. A dazzling halo painted by Michelangelo. "Who's stalking who?"

Sarah stepped closer, brushing against the Subaru's fender. She yelped and sprung away from the hot metal. "Lee-Anne never treated us like this."

Maureen tore open the driver's door. A river of heat swirled past her face. "Maybe because you weren't after her job," she said. "Maybe because Lee-Anne didn't have to watch her back every day."

The upholstery burned the backs of her legs. She slammed the door. Dust motes catapulted off the side-view mirror and hung in the air, so white they burned her retinas. When she looked at Sarah a film of tiny spots floated in front of her angry features. "I'll see you at eight-thirty tomorrow."

"Lighten up for fuck sakes. Stop trying to change everything."

Maureen twisted the key in the ignition. Her foot pressed too hard on the gas pedal and the engine howled. "Lighten up?" Her voice was laced with panic. She gripped the gear shift and wrenched it into reverse. The front wheels carved matching crescent moons into the asphalt as they scythed past Sarah's knees.

"You got no Goddamned clue," she said, biting her lower lip to hold back the Banshee struggling to tear free and plunge screaming into Sarah's throat.

"What the fuck do you want?" The door opened just wide enough for a pale face to appear.

"I need to talk to Raven," Maureen said.

"She's not here." The door started to close. "Fuck off or I'll call the cops."

"I already did," Maureen said.

The door stopped short on its arc. A woman's face emerged from the dimness. She blinked in the sunlight. Her streaked blond hair hung lank to her shoulders. She squinted and licked her lips. "What the fuck for? She hasn't done nuthin' wrong."

"I need to talk to her, Candy."

"How'd you know my name?" The voice became shrill. A sour smell leaked through the door, the ammonia smell of dirty diapers, cross-stitched with just-lit pot.

"A Raven told me," Maureen smiled. "Can I come in?"

Candy shot a glance over her shoulder. She shook her head. "This isn't a good time."

"She knows me from Port. It's very important."

Candy sniffed, rubbed a hand across her face. She leaned against the door frame, nodded once, then shook her head. "Just fuck right off, okay?"

"I can't, Candy," Maureen said. She inhaled. "I need to know what happened to those boys. Go ask her. I'll wait."

Candy began to cry. Her head sagged against the edge of the door. Her body shook. "I can't do this," she said. "Please, don't make me do this," she whispered.

Maureen grabbed the door. "Tell whoever's beside you to leave you alone."

The highway cut through downtown Port, past tired, Norman Rockwell storefronts lining a sorry main drag. Too many window signs *For Lease* or *Closing Out Sale*, lingering shadows from last year's layoffs. The mill might be busy again, but that hadn't brought everybody back. Too many downs and too few ups in the prosperity roller-coaster to put trust—let alone money—into a town so fresh into what the local paper had christened *A Fragile Mini-Boom.*

The big muscles in her shoulders began to ache, sent tremors down her arms, her wrists and into her fingertips. She gripped the steering wheel harder but that made it worse. She glanced over her right shoulder and swung across the inside lane, the front wheel blundering against the high, concrete curb alongside the *Exxon* gas station/mini-mart/Lotto-Centre. She leaned her forehead against the steering wheel. The skin around her knuckles was drum tight, translucent as greasy paper where it stretched over bone. She forced back her tears with loud, gulping breaths and raised her head, catching a glimpse of her face in the mirror. Red-rimmed eyes stared back above pale, blotchy cheeks. She swatted the mirror sideways and pressed the back of her skull into the headrest before twisting to stare out the driver's side window.

She was hoping for a view of the Slough—that slender, sharpened fingernail of Pacific Ocean where the Sleeping Man River tumbled out of the mountains, but in this place the mill obscured all clues to the water beyond. Its smudged stacks and metal-clad bulk squatted uncomfortably behind scores of halogen spotlights that blazed with amber light, even on the brightest, hottest day. Jewels in the sunshine. To hear the locals tell it there was a time in Port's living history they *could* have been real jewels.

Maureen wiped her eyes and with a darting glance over her left shoulder swung back onto the road. On the far boulevard an eight foot chain-link fence segregated the mill from the rest of town. Maureen raced it to the municipal boundary but the fence kept pace. One building followed the next: Admin, Fuel Storage and Marina, Physical Plant, Incinerator, Garage, Stores, and finally, the Timber Bins, where raw logs lay in two-storey high stacks. At a weed-choked ditch near the rocky bank of the Slough the run of chain-link jack-knifed away from the highway. It was a relief to be past the procession of asphalt and concrete, metal and wood. The fjord that had shouldered its way past steep-sided mountains from the open Pacific here narrowed to little more than a vigorous river, its adolescent tidal waters surging around rocks and the low-hanging branches of leaning hemlock, fir and cedar.

Maureen crossed the fjord at the Sleeping Man Bridge. It had been built where the Slough ended—or where the Sleeping Man River began—it depended on which locals she met. According to the Tse Wets Aht the first man had swum across the ocean and, exhausted from his efforts, fell asleep where the river met the sea. He slept so long that moss grew upon his body and his skin turned to rock. His sleeping form could still be seen from the highway, at the approach to the bridge.

When Lee-Anne quit Maureen had stopped asking about Port—its people, its history, its customs. It took too much out of her. When negotiating sessions ended—even those few sessions that had gone well—she emerged too spent to act on the curiosity that collected like crib notes on the margins of her day. The question marks, like thirsty, clutching vines, shriveled in the fever burning behind her brow.

On the other side of the bridge the highway branched. A right turn led to the West Coast and the open Pacific—at the end of another ninety-odd kilometres of twisting, rock-dinted asphalt. Through rain forests of towering cedar, giant salal, drooping hemlock and graceful fir to the posh, ocean-side resorts—built by consortia of ex-hockey players—promising miles of sandy beach, breaching grey whales and pounding winter storms.

She'd taken that road—once.

October thirty-first, nearly four years ago, the day of the official signing of the Agreement in Principle between the Pacific Coast Tribal Federation and two levels of Canadian government who combined to become the negotiating triumvirate that had toiled seven interminable years to cobble together a hallmark land claims deal worth half a billion dollars in land and cash. She was the only one on the *Dee-Faz* team who hadn't rushed back to Vancouver to celebrate. What did she know? She was just a junior research analyst, a rookie still finding her way after three months on the job. What nobody bothered to tell her was that she'd drive into a wind so fresh off a Siberian ice-field it would bite into the exposed skin of her arms like a spoiled nephew. She was forced indoors, banished to the five foot radius around the fireplace of her rented cottage. When she wasn't sleeping she nibbled on carrot sticks and spelt bread and watched through rain-spotted windows as foaming breakers pounded the deserted beach. She counted the hours to checkout.

Maureen now took the other road; the road that doubled back to stalk the far bank of the Slough. It was the road into the Tse Wets Aht First Nation Reserve—*the Only Rez Left on the Left* was an old joke in town. *Tse Wets Aht IR#1/1*: the Government of Canada's official land reserve catalogue number for the property; the only indigenous-held lands fronting the Slough that were accessible by road. This triggered another maxim she'd learned, one that the town fathers liked—off the record, of course—to remind land claims negotiators from Ottawa and Victoria: be generous with the land nobody wanted, the tough-to-get-to spots, but hold onto the good stuff close to home like it was gold or we'll put you down like a mad dog.

The pavement ended at the reserve boundary. It didn't end so much as expire. She steered between potholes larger than mattresses, some so deep they conjured images of bomb craters she'd seen on footage from Iraq. The houses here were close to the road as it curved upward, away from water. Sunburned grass and plastic buckets filled with exhausted geraniums or gangly rose bushes—the kind with flailing, thorny arms crowned with washed out pink blooms—were the prevailing landscaping features. The few windows that faced the road were like blinded eyes—lidded with limp, brown curtains or patched with sheets of creased aluminum foil—anything, it seemed, to repel heat and glare. Untended fires burned inside circles of soot-stained rocks and sent coils of limp, white smoke into the overheated air. The dried grass nearest the fires was scorched black.

Three hairpin turns later the road leveled as it entered the centre of the community. This settlement, almost a century-and-a-half old, was still considered new to the Tse Wets Aht. Their elders told of *The Relocation*—when their village on the Slough was sold off by the government in Victoria to the original owners of the Western Mill Company. It was late fall, a decade or more after the shouts of *Fifty-four Forty or Fight!* had faded, after the border was redrawn, receding north from the banks of the Columbia River to the forty-ninth parallel. After the last salmon had been dried and the oolican harvest had been pressed into grease the British soldiers came with the government land officers and the mill owners' representatives to escort the entire village from their homes. *To protect them*, was the official line. To protect the bespectacled and nattily-dressed bureaucrats was more like it.

Tse Wets Aht translated means *People from the Place at the Beginning of Things.* Yet they were forbidden to return to the only village they had known. Columns of soldiers led men, children and women to the new village, high off the water. For two months soldiers camped less than a mile away to make sure the Tse Wets Aht made no attempt to return. Even then, before the serious logging began and the belching smoke of the mill issued from polished brick stacks, it had been a dusty and dry place. When the Chief asked about water, the Senior Land Agent strode to the cliff edge. He jumped onto the remains of a fallen cedar giant and pointed, past the drooping tips of hemlock that blanketed the lower slopes, to the fine view of the Slough where the Sleeping Man River joined it. "There's your water," he said. Jocularity and contempt vied for mastery of his voice. "You have all day to fetch it."

It had taken forty years to get a well drilled and pump house built, but for a century the mill that rose over the trampled ruin of the Tse Wets Aht village remained in clear, full account, and on early mornings in the fall, when gluttonous rain clouds touched the hilltops and a grey mist filled the valley, the mill's steaming, bejeweled bulk seemed to float above the trees.

The Tse Wets Aht Council Office stood behind the new government-funded-and-built Community Centre and Elementary School, and from the road a faded sign propped against one of the towering cedar logs at the centre's entrance was the only clue to its location. The unanimous opinion on the reserve was that an opportunity had been missed when the Community Centre was built—one that would not reappear for a very long time. But if they couldn't tear down the soon-to-be-derelict Band Office the Tse Wets Aht were content to conceal it from plain sight.

The Band Office was a single storey, wood-framed house that rain and sun were gradually dissolving to its foundation. The roof needed repairs: blue tarps, long faded, had been draped over most of it, secured to each other and to the chimney with lengths of frayed rope and held flat at the corners with stones that threatened to roll off the roof given the least provocation. The windows were dust-streaked, their lower portions heavily caked in a rind of dried mold. When it wasn't blistering hot on the reserve it was oozing damp.

Maureen pulled on the doorknob. It wiggled like a loose tooth. The door shook on its hinges, locked. She'd half-expected it to be. She stepped off the landing onto gravel and moved to the nearest window. She leaned close, cupped her hands to either side of her face as she peered past the grime. A wood-paneled counter jutted from the near wall and cut the office into two, unequal parts. Nearest the door, in the larger share of the office, was a sofa as worn as the building in which it squatted. A couple of rough-looking armchairs were wedged apart by a small table buried beneath a stack of magazines. A fan hung from the ceiling, stirring the air above the chairs. Two desks filled the space behind the counter. Both were swamped under heaps of papers. Even the spindly chairs behind the desk had been enlisted to keep documents off the floor. On the counter—as bare and neat as the desks were cluttered—an answering machine winked from its round, red eye: three quick, three slow, three quick. A distress call to the nearby clunky computer monitor and boxy fax machine, but they were dark, unmoved.

Maureen got back into her car and drove further into the village. The few people who had reason to be in the open glanced up, then quickly away, as she passed. Every Tse Wets Aht, it seemed, had memorized Directorate staff and their cars. Most avoided her. That was what they paid their Chief for. She didn't blame them. On the contrary, it was a luxury she envied, most days.

The gravel on the next turn had never known pavement. It was grooved by spinning tires and gullied by the last spring rains, a fire-seared memory through most of British Columbia and Washington State. Her car bumped over the ruts and nosed down a sharp decline. On one side was forest, thick to the road's edge. The road took back most of the elevation she'd gained on the way in, insisting on the refund in half the distance. The houses here squatted on the waterfront half of the road, spaced as if proximity to water lessened the need of distance from encroaching neighbors.

Maureen turned into a driveway that ran toward a cedar shake house that someone had recently painted forest green; she could almost smell the paint in the hot, dry air. White trim, toothpaste bright around large windows, attracted sunshine as flowers attract butterflies. She parked behind a dusty Ford pickup. From its resting place beneath a single, gigantic Douglas fir, a dog charged, barking in rage even as the rope attached to its collar tightened. It maintained an eager tirade a dozen feet from her car door. Maureen hesitated only long enough to be sure of the rope. She stepped over a flowerbed whose bright yellows and alpine blues mocked the dull browns and dusty greens surrounding them. Marigolds, lobelia and geraniums sparkled from a recent soaking.

"Quiet," Maureen said as she walked a hand's span from the dog's snout. She'd never liked dogs, and this one confirmed her long-held suspicion that the species was at the core nasty as well as mentally deficient. This one in particular, with its blue-tinged coat and black ears, would not have been out of place in documentary footage of the hunting dog packs of the African savannah.

A girl burst from the front door and flew past her on the steps without a second look. She ran to the dog and grabbed its collar and dragged it back to the tree. The animal relaxed, its fight gone, and panting, followed the girl into the shade. It glared at Maureen once, over its muscled shoulder, but the girl scratched its chin as she scolded the animal and its ears came up, its tail wagged, happy to be attended.

"Good dog. Good Lady," she said. She looked back at Maureen. "You can go in, Gramm's out back. I won't let Lady go. Unless you come for money."

"No," Maureen said. "I'm not here for money."

"You're from the government," she said with a proud smile. Her fingers kept moving across the dog's dappled coat.

Maureen's jaw clenched. "Sort of. I'm from the Directorate."

"Same thing, Gramm says."

"We'll see," Maureen said and turned to climb the front stairs.

It was cool inside. It smelled of cigarettes and wood smoke. On the wall opposite the front door a sharp, curved beak thrust outward beneath black, almond-shaped eyes. The wood of the mask was smooth, the color of deerskin and as supple in appearance. Black feathers had been set into the rim above thick, red-painted eyebrows. Maureen moved closer and let her fingers caress the beak. The wood was new; she caught the lingering hint of cedar in the air around the mask. This was Raven watching her, not Thunderbird as she'd first thought. Raven the Trickster. Raven the Wise. Raven the Mischief-Maker. She squinted at the subtle facets of carved cedar, the thickness of the feather mantle. But ever her vision was drawn back to the flat blackness of the eyes. The hairs on her neck stood on end, as if taken by a sudden chill. She shivered, blinked and stepped away.

Bare wood floors, smoothed by time and traffic, creaked under her weight. The hall ended at a kitchen. Through the windows Maureen glimpsed the Slough and beyond it, the boxy structure of the mill.

"Chief David?"

Music played softly, she heard it as she crossed into the kitchen. Fats Waller. There was a low purring in front of the melody, on key, husky—a blues singer on her day off. It grew louder, heckled at by quick footsteps. A woman appeared at the back door. She was tall, very thin; her denim jeans fit snug across her narrow hips. The sleeves of her black cotton shirt were rolled to the elbow, revealing scarecrow-thin forearms the hue of oiled teak. Her hair was pulled back into a long, grey-streaked braid, so tight it teased the lines beside her eyes into razor-thin checkmarks. She could have been thirty or fifty. Her right hand held an open can of beer and a lit cigarette. In the other she clutched a small pail of potatoes, their lumpy, oatmeal flesh smudged with drying soil. She appeared untouched by the heat. When she saw Maureen she stopped humming and the house became, between the notes of the music, completely still.

"What are *you* doing here?" The music careened on without her. She put the potatoes down next to the sink. She leaned against the counter, took a sip from her beer and folded her arms across her chest.

"I'm sorry showing up like this," Maureen said.

"You will be if you keep me from making lunch. I gotta lot of work to do this afternoon and there's Council tonight. How'd you get by Lady? Taylor." She nodded in answer to her own question.

"Good watch dog," Maureen said. "Name doesn't fit, though."

"She's a mean bitch," Chief David said. She raised her cigarette. "Been that way since she was born. I figured a refined name might change her personality." Josephine shrugged. "Didn't take. Anyway, she's what we need around here."

"Protection?"

"Conviction, more like," Chief David said. "Can't change her mind no matter how many bones we throw her way." She propped the cigarette over the lip of a narrow shelf behind the sink and took another sip of beer. She set the can next to the cigarette and turned on the tap. Water splashed over the potatoes. "She reminds me to speak up for myself."

"Chief David, I-"

"Josephine. I'm not working. For a few minutes anyway." A wet sound, nearly a cough, lodged in her throat as she laughed.

"Friends call me Jo." She began to scrub the potatoes with a brush fished off the bottom of the sink.

"But Chief David," Maureen said. "I *am*. Still working, that is."

Josephine's shoulders straightened, but she kept scrubbing, her back to Maureen. "What do you want?"

"You're head of the Federation, so I'm coming to you. It's your negotiating team." Heat poured off Maureen's skin, settled under her arms and below the collar of her blouse. Perspiration collected like dew on her eyelids.

"My team?" Chief David turned, ignoring the water running in the sink. "Exactly what part? There are twenty-three bands from nine First Nations, each with its own representatives. How am I supposed to keep them together? Half of them forget to show up on their days and the others bitch 'cause they want all the meetings scheduled for Vancouver so they can stay in a good hotel and order room service and watch pay-movies all day and send their per diems back to their families. And I don't blame them—any of them. Not when you live in a house without running water or working sewers—some don't even have electricity. It all gets to be too much." She sighed heavily. "They forget there's supposed to be an end, a finish line. That there's an agreement to finalize. See this?"

She gripped the end of her braid and twisted it toward Maureen. She pointed to the pewter strands threaded between black. "I get more of these every bloody month. It killed Matthew. I'm trying to keep it from killing me."

"I didn't know him," Maureen said.

Chief David met her glance, held it for a long moment. Her right hand traveled toward the cigarette on the edge of the sink. Maureen thought she saw it shake as it hovered over the half-finished smoke.

"He was a good man, Matthew Watson. The best. Before your time," she said, exhaling heavily. The smoke curled above her head and broke apart in the breeze that came in the window. "He built this Federation out of nothing. That was how we got us a Framework." She shook her head, and the braid rippled. "I try not to let him down, but sometimes I think I should break us up and go it alone. Let the bastards win."

"Which bastards?"

Chief David's eyebrows arched. "Good question," she said. She found a knife in a drawer near the sink and carved the potatoes into chunks. "You got a decision to make, Maureen Cage," she said over her shoulder. The cigarette wagged between her lips. "Lunch's in fifteen minutes, if the damn stove works. You gonna stay or hit the road?"

Candy's head snapped back. She screamed; the door slammed shut. Something heavy hit the floor, made the thin walls shake. A scuffling sound followed, of the safety chain being set.

Maureen twisted the door knob, but it was locked.

"Maureen! Maureen!" Josephine's shouts ricocheted between the houses.

She took the stairs two at a time and sprinted through the weed-infested side yard. She rounded the corner of the house and glimpsed Josephine picking herself off the grass near the back steps as a shape barreled toward her. Maureen lowered her shoulder as the figure turned, wide-eyed, too late to avoid the collision.

The impact knocked the Raven backward, her legs buckling beneath her. Car keys flew out of her hand, striking the warped shingles on the house. Raven's landing launched a cloud of dandelion seeds into the air. Josephine tackled Raven, tried to pin the woman to the ground. Her bare legs thrashed under Josephine. Her left forearm was in a cast, and she was using it like a club.

"This bitch fights dirty," Josephine said, ducking under a second wild swing.

Maureen dropped the jack handle and fell to her knees near Raven's head. She grabbed the arm near the wrist and wrestled it backward to the ground. A black, jagged lightning bolt decorated the length of the cast. With her free hand Maureen cupped

Raven's chin and wrenched it toward her. She glared, tried to spit. Maureen released her chin and slapped her, hard across the face.

"Oww!" Raven went limp, tears welling in her eyes. The dark rings around her eye sockets had become sickly yellow bruises. With the bandages off her face looked different, familiar—almost.

"We need to talk to you," Maureen said.

"Fuck you. This is assault," Raven said. "I'm pressing charges."

"So am I," Josephine said. "You tried to break my jaw." She rubbed the side of her face.

"This is Chief Josephine David of the Tse Wets Aht First Nation," Maureen said. "She has some questions for you. About the boys who died on Pipeline Road."

Raven's nostrils flared. "Screw that. I got nothing to say 'cept fuck the both of you."

They dragged Raven upright. She did not try to run. She slapped at the dirt on her legs. Her hair stuck out from her skull in thick, stubby cords, greasy from sleep. Josephine twisted Raven's good arm behind her back. Maureen held Raven's left arm, just above the cast. It was adorned with smaller lightning bolts and blood-red crucifixes. At the end of the black lightning bolt someone had drawn a red tipped arrow that pointed at the middle knuckle of her hand.

"It matches the tattoo on her shoulder," Josephine said. She nodded to the spot above the Raven's right biceps. A single, jagged line—either a bolt of lightning or broken spear recalling one half of the Nazi *SS* symbol—was surrounded by a circle of red flames.

"Let's get her inside." Maureen glanced toward the neighbor's house. She expected curious faces in the windows. "It's too early for this."

It was a climb of a half-dozen steps to a small, covered porch and a back door with a ripped bug screen. Maureen had to release the Raven's arm to follow. She thought she heard sirens. Dandelion seeds drifted across the backyard, suspended in the sunlight that shone between the trees.

Maureen shared the kitchen table with Josephine, Taylor and a mountain of papers that had been pushed to the furthest corner to make room for everyone. Piles like square pancakes with sticky notes for butter pats threatened to topple into their plates. Taylor grinned at her between bites of potato and leftover pork roast. Maureen was convinced the girl was kicking the table leg to make one of the taller stacks fall.

Maureen ate her potatoes and beans in guilty silence, her back bent and shoulders hunched and her left hand wedged between her knees. It had started after she'd held up her hand, refusing the slice of meat Josephine offered. "I'm Vegetarian, sorry. Should have mentioned it."

Grandmother and granddaughter shared the same look—lips pressed thin beneath a single, arched eyebrow. Josephine forked over an extra potato and dumped a heaping spoonful of baked beans onto Maureen's plate.

"Wash it," Josephine said as Taylor jumped out of her chair clutching her empty plate and dashed for the kitchen door.

"I'm late," Taylor said with a protest in her voice. "I'm going to Shawna's."

"You know the drill. And take Lady with you," Josephine said.

The girl stamped through the kitchen.

"Don't argue. I've got Council and it'll go late." Chief David mopped up the last gravy with a crust of bread. "Just like her mother," she said without looking up.

"Where is her mother?"

The torn crust stopped as if stuck fast to the plate. Chief David raised her head and stared out the window. "Cynthia's gone. It'll be four years, this October."

"I'm sorry," Maureen said.

"Taylor keeps asking when Cyn's coming home." Josephine's eyes met Maureen's. They were hard, flat, like the raven mask in the hall. "I'm getting tired of making things up."

"Like what?"

Josephine abandoned the bread crust and drew the back of her hand across her mouth, twice, swiping at stray crumbs. "You're not a parent, are you?"

"I-"

"Cyn kept running away to Vancouver. Lived with hookers and addicts until she became one. She was on the street most of the time. Went through methadone treatment—twice—then vanished. Just when I was ready to believe that *this time* things might turn out good."

"That's got to be hard." Maureen set down her fork and pushed her plate away.

"Until the fires started it seemed every newspaper had nothing to report 'cept stories of missing women and that psycho bastard they caught. Every day I wake up and wonder if it's gonna be today they call and say they found her shoe, or something else of hers, under some pile of pig shit." Josephine turned and stared out the kitchen window, blinking hard.

"I had no clue. I'm sorry."

"Not as sorry as me," Josephine said, exhaling. She stacked their plates and hurried to the sink, Maureen following. She leaned over the counter, the slight crook in her nose parallel to the window as she turned.

"Did she take the dog?" Maureen asked.

Josephine wiped her eyes on the fringe of a dish towel. Her mouth creased in a sudden smile. "They're like sea and shore, never one without the other," she said. "No way Taylor would've gone without Lady." Josephine slapped the handle of the hot water faucet. "She deserves a better life than her mother had," she said over the stream.

"I think she has it," Maureen said.

Josephine did not turn around. "There's no guarantees, for us. *I* was lucky. Had enough to eat and a place to sleep. I worked in a cannery a couple of seasons, the money was there if I needed it. Then I went to secretary school in Nanaimo, my grandmother paid the tuition, forced me to see it through. Otherwise we lived off what this land gave us. You want coffee?"

"No, I should go."

"You haven't told me why you came, but I can guess. The recess. And only two months to the deadline." Josephine pointed to a scroll calendar hanging off the side of the fridge. From a Chinese restaurant in Port that displayed all twelve months on a single, rectangular banner. The top two-thirds bore the outline of a tiger charging from a stand of bamboo. "October thirty-first is marked on my calendar, too." A careless red oval encircled the last day of October. "And not 'cause I got a Halloween party to go to."

Josephine moved to the back door. "Let's go outside. There's a bit of shade now." She slipped through the kitchen door clutching her deck of smokes. "Was that your screw up?"

Maureen stepped onto a narrow deck, swallowing hard to keep down the denial that rose in her throat like a bad taste. The unpainted wood had weathered to a pale, smudged grey extending the breadth of the house. "*Dee-Faz* screwed up." She exhaled wearily. "Guess that makes it mine."

Josephine grabbed a pair of collapsed deck chairs and carried them to the far end, away from the stairs that led down to a sloping back yard surrounded by fir and cedar. "It's not the first, won't be the last," she said as the chair frames rattled against the railing. She set her cigarettes on the rail and pulled open the chairs as if pulling apart an aluminum wishbone.

Maureen looked over the rail onto a series of raised beds set in neat rectangles between pathways of crushed gravel. She counted six beds, each at least twelve feet long by four feet wide. They were brim full of staked tomatoes, runner beans that climbed cris-crossed poles and rows of lettuce whose leaves spilled over the cedar-framed sides. One bed was dedicated to potatoes.

"Can't grow anything else in that one," Josephine said, following Maureen's glance.

"That's not what I was thinking," Maureen said as she sat in the empty chair. "How can you keep up?"

"I don't. Too much work, it's falling apart," Josephine said, and made a gesture of surrender with her hands. "Taylor's father built them. Portuguese. But that's another story. They sure do love their vegetable gardens." She rolled her eyes. "This was how he tried to fit in. His way of fixing the world's problems is to fill every sunny slope with tomatoes and zucchini." She shrugged. "There's worse, I suppose, but it doesn't play here. After he left I took back my name and took over the garden, but I only get half the yield he used to. Thank God for my sister's family. If they didn't water the beds everything would be dead."

"Puts my sorry excuse of a garden to shame," Maureen said, her eyes sweeping across the yellow-green fruit of the tomato plants. She caught a whiff of mulch in the warm air.

"Then marry a Portuguese. Better yet, just live with one. Now what about my Federation?" Her left eyebrow froze at the peak of its arch like a cat stuck in mid-stretch.

"Not your Federation," Maureen said. "It's Brown, Martin and Houseman." She shifted in the chair, afraid for the aluminum frame beneath her. A weight in her chest made it harder to breathe. "They would be thrilled to miss the deadline."

Josephine scratched one forearm with blunted fingernails. "That was Matthew's biggest victory. They seem to forget, it was so long ago, but it was huge. The papers always leave out that part—that we're on the hook for *all* our legal costs. Matthew figured we could save thousands—millions—by forming a negotiating federation and using the same legal firm. Whatever cash we eventually get from a settlement, the first piece goes to repay the lawyers. With interest."

"You're not getting good value," Maureen said. She recounted what had happened in the morning session.

Josephine kept her eyes on the garden, or on something further away.

"I know I'm out of line here," Maureen said. "But the deadline is closing in. And Templeton couldn't get out of there fast enough."

"If we lose the lawyers we lose the Federation. I can't hold twenty-two chiefs by myself. As it is they are calling me every hour, emailing me a hundred times a day."

Maureen sat on the edge of her chair, her spine stiff. "You think the public is against you in this, but they're not. They're against lawyers getting rich with their dollars."

Josephine crushed the butt of her cigarette under her foot. She reached for another from the package on the rail. "Smoke?"

"No." Maureen held up her hand.

"Thought so," Chief David said. She struck the match head against the underside of the deck rail and held it off the end of the cigarette. "You don't like lawyers very much."

"Some of my best friends are lawyers," Maureen said.

"You don't seem the type to have a lot of friends," Josephine said, snuffing the match with a flick of her wrist. "No offense."

"To use your line—that's another story."

Josephine coughed, cleared her throat and spit over the railing. "Brown, Martin and Houseman have been ours since we filed for Intent. The Federation came along after."

Maureen stared into the shaded fringe of hemlock trees. Why had she come? What had she wanted the Tse Wets Aht chief to say? "We both want the same thing," she said after a long silence.

The lines around Josephine's eyes deepened. She plucked the cigarette from her mouth. The muscles at the hinge of her jaw bunched. "You have no clue what I want. Don't pretend to be better than the lawyers you trash."

Maureen recoiled as if she'd been struck. Josephine's outline seemed to swim in the heavy, afternoon air.

"People like you have been our biggest problem for more than a hundred years."

"That's not what I meant," Maureen said, but her tongue seemed to swell inside her mouth. "I meant the deadline. We both want a Final before the deadline."

"For you and every other bureaucrat it's a Final," Josephine said, rising out of her chair. "You want signatures and then you're done. It'll be bonus time, another trophy for your Goddamned display case. By now you should know that it's not like that for us. When you cross us off your To Do list we'll be here still, and our children will ask: *didn't you know they were taking all the salmon, all the herring, all the trees? Weren't you watching?* And we have to answer them. *That's* when the real work starts. Until you get that you can stay the Hell out of my house." Chief David drew hard on the cigarette and exhaled a plume of blue cigarette smoke. It hung in the air above her head, as if bound there by her angry words.

Maureen wanted to respond, but she could not think of any one thing to say that would mollify the Tse Wets Aht chief. Embarrassed, she ducked past Josephine and hurried through the house, avoiding the accusation in the raven's black eyes as she fled.

A string of profanity blistered the air. A body charged from the house and drove Raven backwards, screaming, off the top step. Josephine cried out as Raven knocked her into the railing. The two-by-four bulged and split under their weight. Maureen jumped backward off the third stair. Pain ripped through her knee as she landed awkwardly, stiff-legged. She rolled onto her side and brought one arm up to shield her head from the bodies pin-wheeling after her.

The Raven and Josephine crashed through the railing, landing hard. A cloud of milky dandelion seeds filled the air as a third body fell onto the women. Maureen scrambled to her hands and knees, her fingers sweeping through the tufted weeds around the house for the jack handle. She scraped the back of her hand on the corner of the foundation as she dragged the handle out of the weeds. Broken glass lined her knee joint. She used the side of the house as a crutch.

Larry Arnold lay on top of Raven. His bare, thin torso was covered with old tattoos, the designs long-since faded to tired blues and blotchy reds. He gripped a knife in his right hand.

Josephine screamed, masking Raven's unbroken string of profanity. Her fingers were claws in Larry's face. She clutched at his wrist as the knife arced downward. Blood sprayed Raven's neck and shoulder.

Larry twisted to shake loose from Josephine. His toes slipped and skidded across the grass, searching for solid ground. He could not break free. His hair hung in matted strips, handfuls of wet straw pasted to a bone-pale scalp.

Maureen swung the jack handle. It skipped off the top of Larry's head. Before Maureen could swing again the knife in Larry's hand reversed, slicing the air a whisper from her side. She struck again, harder, with two hands on the jack handle in her best imitation of a baseball swing. The metal bar connected just above Larry's ear with a sound like a boot crushing a snail's shell. The jack handle flew out of her hands. Larry dropped his knife and pressed his hands against his head, his foot twitching as his body went limp. Blood leaked between his fingers.

"You fucking killed him!" The Raven began to cry.

She stayed in the car, listening to the ticking of the engine and waiting to be sure her tears were done. She peeked in the rearview mirror and, with a wadded tissue, dabbed at the hot, puffy skin beneath her eyes. With two deep breaths she crossed the parking lot—briefcase in one hand tissue in the other—and ducked between the open hotel doors.

Carole Simons intercepted her before she reached the elevator. "You okay?"

"I'm fine," Maureen said.

Carole blocked her way. She wore a sleeveless white tee shirt featuring a wrung-out photograph of the Sex Pistols. It was tucked into a short leather skirt as black and shiny as her open-toed sandals. Her lipstick and toenail polish sported the same wet, apple-red enamel finish. "What gives? Your boyfriend dump you?"

"No. Not that it's any of your business," Maureen said. She sidestepped but Carole moved with her. "What are you doing?"

"Helping. You look terrible. We need to talk."

"This morning would have been useful. Right now it's the last thing I need," Maureen said. She tried to slip by but Carole's compact frame prevented her.

"I'll call security." Her voice was strained, an octave higher than normal.

"Do that. I'll buy them a drink too."

"I'm going to my room," Maureen said. "It's been a tough day and-"

"And you don't want to be alone," Carole said. "Trust me. I've been in this business too long. The bar's a dozen steps that way. Let's have a drink and maybe by dinner you'll earn your solitude. Or maybe I'll have to resort to more drastic action."

"Leave me alone."

"Methinks you've been alone too often." Carole grinned and, gripping Maureen by the elbow, steered her across the lobby, through an archway of tall, potted palms whose browning leaves drooped from thirst.

"I don't drink," Maureen said, balking at the lounge entrance. She was surprised at how easy it was to be led where she didn't want to go.

"Then don't," Carole said. "It's still early. Have a coffee. Or milk. Hell, have *Ovaltine* for all I care. I can drink enough for the both of us." She led Maureen to a table in the corner, behind a screen of small-leafed bamboo plants.

"Here." Carole dragged a rattan chair away from the table and pointed for Maureen to sit.

"Why are you doing this?" Maureen plunked herself down in the chair, her briefcase clutched in her lap. Her spine arched away from the chair back.

"You're like a cornered animal," Carole said. "Relax. I'm not going to bite."

"I don't need your pity and I don't need rescuing." Maureen gripped the handle of her briefcase until the flesh on her knuckles went white.

"You're in no position to say," Carole said. She tapped the glass-topped table with a scarlet fingernail. "Most people don't know when they're in too deep. When they need help. Or even how to ask for it."

"Not me," Maureen said.

"What? You don't need help or you don't know how to ask for it?"

Maureen's eyes fixed on the exit. "Neither. I manage fine."

"Not from where I sit—with all due respect."

Maureen turned to meet Carole's stare. "What does that mean? You think I'm lousy at my job too?"

"Yes, actually. I do." She glanced away to signal a passing waiter.

Maureen was half out of her seat when Carole grabbed her arm.

"Let me finish. It was cruel what they did in there. I should have said something. I wanted to. I expected your people to step in, but this morning convinced me. They'll let you dangle by your thumbs. You're lousy at a lousy job, but you're not incompetent. Far from it. You're just inexperienced. They're walking all over you and you've nobody watching your back."

A film covered Maureen's eyes. She brought one hand across her forehead and exhaled in short bursts, struggling to hold back tears. "And you're offering?"

"That would hardly be appropriate. But the federal government's a little more removed than the other two principals. We write most of the cheques, but we don't have to live here." Carole passed her a napkin. "It's been what, a month? Since Lee-Anne quit? Since you were promoted to Senior Analyst?"

"Nearly six weeks," Maureen said, snatching the cloth without looking up.

The waiter appeared beside Carole, appearing from behind the bamboo screen. Carole ordered a glass of wine. "A nice Okanagan red," she said.

"Soda water," Maureen said, pressing the napkin into the corners of her eyes.

"Bring the bottle and two glasses and we'll take it from there," Carole said with a dismissive wave.

Josephine pushed Raven sideways and scrambled clear. She was breathing hard, hands on knees.

Maureen bent to pick up the black-handled steak knife, but stopped short. Agony radiated from her knee, shot up her leg to greet the ache in her hip. She clutched at the splintered stair rail to keep her balance. Her stomach churned in a sudden, nauseous surge and she doubled over to vomit onto the carpet of crushed dandelions.

"He's stabbed her," Josephine said. She crouched over the Raven. Blood welled out of the dancer's left biceps, above the cast, but it was the right arm she cradled. She moaned in pain, rocking on her side, staring at Larry. He hadn't moved since Maureen's home run swing.

"I think I killed him," Maureen said. She forced her body to take slow, deep breaths to settle her stomach. A film of cold sweat formed on her skin. She wanted to kick him, to prove to herself that Larry wasn't dead, but when she released the broken railing her arms shook badly and her teeth began to chatter. She gripped the railing with both hands and leaned against the house. "There's a First Aid kit in my car," she said, but the words were messed up and Josephine did not react.

"In my car," Maureen said carefully through clenched teeth. "The First Aid kit."

"You okay?" Josephine said.

Maureen shook her head. "My knee. It's screwed."

"I'll get the kit," Josephine said. She stood. "Watch her. Maybe we should tie her up."

"You got no right." Raven rolled onto her knees and struggled to stand. She used her left arm to pull her tee shirt over her hip bones. Her right arm hung useless against her body. "You can't be doing this shit to me."

"You started it," Josephine said. She grabbed Raven's right arm, lifting it above her waist.

The dancer screamed and sagged to her knees.

Josephine forced Raven onto the stairs, beside Maureen. "Wait here. I'll be back in a sec."

"You need dessert," Carole said, laughing as she led Maureen between the crowded tables of a bar called Canal Slats to an empty table beside a stuccoed pillar.

"I can't feel my toes," Maureen said, falling into a chair. Three glasses of wine since two PM and she could barely stand. She leaned sloppily on Carole's shoulder. "This is a strip joint," she said, slurring her words.

"I think you're right," Carole said with a smile. "You know the drill. When in Rome?"

The music was loud, pounding inside her head. They sat near a stage, empty save for the flashing lights on each stubby wing. Random clusters of men leered at her as she scanned the room. She felt feverish and queasy. This was all wrong. She needed to get back to the quiet of her hotel room before things went totally off the rails.

"A red wine for me. Better make it soda water for the lightweight here," Carole said to the waitress.

"Sure."

The waitress wiped her hands on a short, off-white apron tied around her jeans. She leaned over the table to clear away the empties left by the previous occupants. She smiled at Maureen. "I'm Sandy, if you need anything." She slapped down a pair of cardboard coasters that boasted the crisp, clean taste of a beer made in a moose's head. Or so it seemed to Maureen.

"You're just in time," Sandy said. "Another five minutes and there won't be an empty seat." She winked and grinned, revealing the wad of chewing gum between her teeth. Her breath smelled of spearmint. She vanished in the direction of the bar.

One of the three men seated around the nearest table leaned close and nudged Maureen's shoulder with his arm. "Sorry, Sweetie," he said, and bumped her again to a chorus of laughter from his two companions.

Coarse, blond hair hung to his shoulders, spilling out the bottom of his ball cap like a spray of wind-blown, sun-blanched straw. He clamped a crooked cigarette between his teeth and waved. His lean face was smudged by a late evening beard that shaded a mottled, pasty complexion. Old tattoos decorated both arms.

Maureen skidded her chair closer to Carole's. As the bar filled it got harder to breathe. She couldn't move without bumping somebody.

"Don't mind us, 'kay?" The tattooed man lifted his ball cap, scratched a sparsely sown scalp and sent another lopsided grin in her direction. "We just come for the show. A real good friend," he said, gesturing toward the stage. He had to shout over the music and the swelling crowd.

Maureen looked to Carole for rescue, but she was busy lifting their drinks out of Sandy's tray.

"I'm Larry, FYI," the man said. He tipped back in his chair and stuck out one hand.

Maureen avoided both his glance and his hand. A roaring like the surf filled her ears.

Larry smiled as he tweaked the cigarette from his mouth and held it under her nose. "Hey Sweetie, gotta light?"

It happened too quickly—a reflex—or maybe it was the alcohol. It impaired her usually sound judgment. Her hand dove into her purse and came out with her lighter. Its gold case glowed in the smoky light. She ran her thumb lovingly across the engraved letters that marked the case with a fine, flowing script:

F. A. P.
June 1962
My Darling Angel

She kept it with her, everyday, filled with fluid, though it had been ten years since she'd last lit a cigarette with it. She used to leave it at home, safe in her desk, but she felt strange-lost—without it. Sometimes, away from home, alone in her hotel room, she would run her fingers over the butter-soft case, flip open the lid and roll her thumb across the flint to see if it still worked. It lit on the first try, every time.

"Nice lighter," Larry said. "Can I see it?"

His hot, damp hand enfolded hers. He seemed to will the lighter from her unsure grip even as he smiled at her muted protests. He opened the case, snapped his thumb across the flint and stuck the flame to the end of his cigarette. Two puffs of smoke rolled through the air toward her. He leaned into his friends to show them his prize.

"Hey, a *Zippo*. Gold, too. Where'd you get it?" Larry's companion said. He reached to grab it out of Larry's hand.

"It's mine," Maureen said, and put her hand on Larry's arm. His skin was hot yet slippery to the touch. She recoiled, shivering.

Larry turned and blew smoke in her eyes. "That's one nice *Bic* you got, Darlin'," he said, fondling the case.

"I need it back," Maureen said, but her words died against the crash of the sound system as the DJ began to shout.

"Canal Slats is proud to welcome our star entertainer of the evening! Put your hands together for last month's Men's Club cover girl! Star of seven hit films, Hustler Magazine's Adult Film Star of the Year and winner of Penthouse's *Up and Coming* Award! Gentlemen and Ladies, give it up for Raven!"

Larry and his friends were on their feet. They stomped and whistled and pounded the table as a tall, athletic woman appeared from behind the smoked glass of the DJ's booth. She wore tight, silver shorts and a sparkling silver halter too small for her breasts. She carried a folded blanket over her shoulder and tossed rolled up posters into the crowd as she climbed onto the stage.

Larry held up the lighter like he was at a rock concert. Raven saw the flame, stepped close to the edge of the stage, grinning at Larry. She crouched on her heels and reached for the lighter, her eyes fixed upon the gold case. Larry flipped the top, snuffing the flame, and shoved it into Raven's cleavage. His buddies hooted. Raven grabbed the lighter as she came out of her crouch. She stumbled as she stared at the engraving, grabbing onto the brass pole centre stage for balance. Larry and his buddies shouted, pumped at the attention Raven paid them.

The Raven retreated to the back of the stage, returned with a scrolled poster and aimed it at Maureen, but Larry leapt in front to intercept it. She slid the lighter beneath the glittering silver ball cap and jammed it tight onto her scalp. A single, jet pony tail sprang from the hole in the ball cap. It hung, thick, glistening, to the middle of her back. The soles of her boots flashed as she walked. An earthquake of hip hop music shook the beer bottles nearest the speakers.

Each time Raven circled nearer and met her glance Maureen had to look away. Beads of perspiration gathered on her scalp. She started to hyperventilate in the stale, clotted air. She had to get out, but she couldn't go without her lighter.

"That's my girl!" Larry shouted.

Raven blew kisses into the crowd. Maureen felt sick. She steadied herself, her arms planted on the table top. "My lighter. I need it back," she groaned.

Larry grinned and cupped one hand around his ear. "What?"

"Get it back." She had to summon all her strength to shout.

"I already did," Larry said, shaking his head with a sudden look of hurt and surprise. "Didn't I, Rick? I gave this chick back her fire, right?"

A hand touched her right leg. Maureen jumped. "Isn't this cool?" Carole shouted. Her face glistened under a sheen of perspiration.

"My lighter," Maureen said, but Carole either didn't hear or understand. She nodded and smiled and toasted the thickening air with her half-empty wine glass.

The music grew louder and the crowd rowdier as the Raven removed her halter. She swung the scrap of silver fabric at the end of one hand like a lasso. Her breasts proclaimed their purchased perfection with gravity-defying pride. She licked her fingers and fanned them across her nipples, then cupped each breast as she leaned over the stage to push them into the rapt faces of the men who crowded the rim of the stage. Her tongue became a prop. She let it roll slowly across shining, pouting lips.

Larry hammered his beer bottle against the table. Raven danced across the stage to squat directly in front of him, her gaze fixed instead on Maureen. His friends jostled each other for a better view as Larry leaned forward, one knee on Maureen's table, to get his face close to Raven's breasts. His boot flashed sideways and kicked over the soda water. Carole slid out of the drink's path. Maureen snatched up her purse and scooted backward, but the jam of chairs held her. Cold water flooded across her legs. Laughter erupted behind her.

The Raven sneered and moved toward a clutch of appreciative spectators at the opposite side of the bar, her glance locked on Maureen as she retreated.

The shock of ice water across her thighs cleared Maureen's head. She jumped, gripped Larry's shoulder and pulled him toward her. "Get it! Now!"

Larry stumbled, sagged to his knees. His tee shirt tore in Maureen's fist.

"Hey! That was my best shirt!"

"*Sit the fuck down, Larry!*" A voice called from behind Maureen.

"*Get your ugly head out the way!*"

"*Take off your clothes or siddown!*" That one was aimed at Maureen, who let go of the bunched fabric and dropped into her chair, into a puddle of cold water. Her face burned. "Let's go," she said but Carole was helping Sandy mop the table top, her glass of wine raised up against the flood.

"Shut the fuck up!" Larry wheeled toward his accusers, his fists waving in the sticky air. He squinted into the lights. "Me and the lady here are *negosheeatin'*. Ya know what *negosheeatin'* is dontcha? Sure ya do, ya fuckin' Rez Rats!"

Larry's friends hooted and pumped their fists.

A glass bottle pin wheeled out of the crowd and struck Larry on the collarbone. He staggered against the stage.

"Fuckin' dick-smokin' bastards!" Larry propelled himself into the crowd. His friends followed, diving across tables.

A roar filled Maureen's ears. She glanced to the stage. Raven had backed away from the crowd. She leaned against a speaker near the wall, an angry expression accessorizing her ball cap, silver thong and high-heeled boots. One hand rested on her flared hip, the other shielded her eyes from the stage lights. The white light accentuated the sinewy contours of her arms, outlining a tattoo high on her left arm: a jagged lightning bolt that ended in a plunging, barbed point surrounded by a circle of red flames.

"Let's get out of here," Carole said. She tugged on Maureen's arm.

"My lighter-"

"Now!"

A beer bottle crashed against the back wall. Raven ducked, swore and stalked to the stairs to gather her blanket and discarded clothes. The DJ cut the music. Three bouncers with arms like fence posts waded into the scrum.

"I'm going to be sick," Maureen said, her stomach heaving.

"Follow me," Carole said. She dragged Maureen past flailing arms and legs, past leering faces appearing like ghosts through the flash of strobe lights.

They ducked around the DJ booth as the Raven fled behind the smoked glass. Their eyes met once more. Maureen could not look away, transfixed by the pinpricks of light—tiny stars—that shone from the obsidian depths. Carole pulled on her arm and Maureen stumbled over an outstretched leg. Carole caught her, and by the time Maureen steadied herself the Raven was gone.

Carole leaned into the double metal doors under a glowing, red *Exit* sign. A chorus of *Why Can't We Be Friends?* crackled through the speakers as the doors swung shut behind them.

BOOK TWO

The Accident

Raven dragged herself onto the third step and leaned backwards, putting her weight on her left arm. Blood drizzled from the wound on her upper arm and stained her shirt. She stretched her bare feet toward the ground, lengthening the muscles in her thighs. Dancer's legs: they spoke of long hours in the gym. Sculpted bronze, under the streaks of dust and sweat. Not the legs of a girl who'd decided, out of boredom or desperation, to become a stripper. The breasts and tan might be accessories, but the legs? No, they'd been built years ago, the hard way.

"Am I getting you hot? You're a dyke, right? You were up front that night at Slats with your butch girlfriend."

Maureen blinked. "Nice try," she said, exhaling. The worst of the nausea had passed, but the pain in her knee infused every nerve.

"So you like them short and fat?"

Maureen laughed. She pointed to the prone figure near the steps. "That's no runway model you got there."

Raven reached forward to hit her, but caught herself short with a shriek and clasped her shoulder. Her breath hissed between clenched teeth.

Maureen let go of the railing and leaned over the dancer. She placed her hands on Raven's arm and pressed her fingers into the muscle, probing toward the shoulder. Raven's body tightened, her jaw set, but she did not try to avoid Maureen's touch. She moaned when Maureen's fingers reached her shoulder.

"Something's dislocated," Maureen said. Her fingers tingled from contact with Raven's skin.

"Fucking hurts," Raven said, her voice a child's whimper, and an expression of disappointment flashed across her features when Maureen removed her hands.

"I'm calling an ambulance," Maureen said. "For both of you."

Josephine reappeared and tossed Maureen a large roll of duct tape. "You got enough stuff to survive World War III in there."

"Nothing wrong with being prepared," Maureen said.

"OK, Ms. Girl Scout. We should get inside," Josephine said, and motioned Raven to climb the stairs.

"Candy's inside, be careful," Maureen said.

"Who's Candy?"

"How do you know so fucking much about me?" Raven glared.

"If I did I wouldn't be here," Maureen said. She bent over Larry gingerly to wind duct tape around his ankles.

"Anyone else?" Josephine said, following Raven onto the stairs.

"Yeah, a fucking army of Indian haters," she said.

Josephine pushed the Raven. She stumbled forward, crying out in pain as she reached out to catch herself. She glared at Josephine.

"They won't do you any fucking good," Josephine said. She pushed Raven again, this time through the open back door.

A baby's shrieks skittered across slabs of cold concrete. Careened off the drain pipes and the fenders of Toyotas and Fords and Hondas: the monthly, paid-in-advance vehicles that filled the parkade's lowest floors. It had to be as hungry as she was. The smell of shit mingled with the cheesy pall of dried sweat and antifreeze. A hand appeared through the oily light and struck the baby. It stopped crying, its eyes wide for the instant it took to register pain. It started to wail. Other hands lunged out of the darkness—fists swinging like hammers—until the crying stopped altogether.

Maureen sprang upright in her hotel room bed, her body soaked in sweat. She kicked off the blanket and hurried to the bathroom. She leaned over the sink, arms trembling as they tried to support her upper body. Her head hurt badly. Her stomach protested and she twisted toward the toilet and threw up.

At least a decade since she'd felt this sick, but not so long she'd forgotten what a hangover was. Her skin looked like cooked fish; her eyes were rimmed red from smoke. Dark patches had settled in the hollows of her face. She stared at her reflection, at the lines around her mouth. Old, she decided. Old and stupid and now sick as a dog. And her lighter was gone. Taken out of her hand, just like that. Stolen. It had been stolen once before, but this was different.

Last time *she'd* done the stealing.

Her finger traced the line that ran, more delicate than a snail's trail, from her left ear to the peak of her forehead. She pushed on the scar. It resisted. A seam—no, a watershed—it demarcated more than where her scalp ended and her face began. Twenty years had faded both the scar and the memory of driving head-on into a telephone pole, cleaving her life in two, along with the car and the bastard in the passenger seat. But the price of separating her past from her future was high: three months in hospital and too many operations on her hip and leg until she could walk again.

She ran her finger south, over the bridge of her nose, pausing at the place where the cartilage strayed off centre. Enough for an observant eye to notice that it had been broken, more than once. The other times were before the crash, but she'd fixed him so he would never touch another woman with his fists. She clenched her teeth and grimaced to expose her gums. Once, her teeth were as dazzling as celebrity. These days the dentist got to the plaque when she remembered to make an appointment.

She stripped, bagged yesterday's reeking clothes in plastic and put on a clean bra and underwear. She padded to the window and pulled back the curtains. It was still dark above the streetlights and fast food standards. She leaned as far as she could through the open window and searched out the Slough. The residual glow from the halogen lamps hanging off the mill's superstructure leaked around the corner of the hotel. The glare concealed all that lay beyond the water: the forested hillside, the faint lights of the Tse Wets Aht village—even the stars she knew existed were lost behind an amber wash.

She retreated to the table. As she bent to lift her briefcase a bolt of pain pierced her lower back near her hip. She grunted, the briefcase tight in her grip. The flare of an aching back came and went with dictatorial impunity, punishing her for missing too many workouts or doing too much in the garden. Last night's was a different kind of too much—one that didn't sit well with her body's regular routines. She set the case on the table and used both hands to lower herself into the chair. She removed two manila folders, one at a time. She placed the briefcase on the floor and slid the top folder toward her, mating its lower edge with the lip of the table. Then she opened it, chewed the inside of her cheek and plucked the topmost page off the pile.

"Your friend's in bad shape," Maureen said to Raven. She returned to the dingy kitchen from a circuit of the main floor—as fast a tour as her knee would allow. The joint was swelling and felt wobbly, loose, and any pressure or movement hurt desperately. "She shouldn't be left alone with that baby."

"I'll check on her," Josephine said. "Call me if this one starts talking." She offered Maureen her chair.

"Thanks." Maureen spared a grateful smile and lowered herself into the chair opposite Raven. "Tell us about the night the boys died."

"Fuck you," Raven said. She slumped behind a kitchen table heaped with empty beer cans and the stubs of burned out candles.

"Did the paper pay well?"

Raven lifted her head. Her dark eyes glittered.

Maureen remembered the mask in Josephine's front hall: the same black eyes that saw everything but gave nothing away. Trickster eyes. "If you'd stuck around long enough to collect you might have afforded a better hiding place."

"You'd have taken off too if-" Raven stopped and swatted the nearest beer can. It clattered into a dingy corner.

"If what?" Maureen said, lifting a wooden match off the table. The pale wood had been broken in two places below the match head and bent into the shape of a lightning bolt. The table top was ringed with dozens of matches similarly disjointed. They formed a sloppy border around the overflowing ashtrays and empty cans.

"Heritage League," she said, and nodded toward the markings on Raven's cast. "If what?" she asked again.

The Raven's lips thinned, turned white at the edges. "If you were scared," she whined.

"Of what? Why did you run from Port? Did somebody threaten you?"

Raven licked her lips but said nothing.

Maureen tossed the broken match onto the floor. "Larry, then. Or someone else from the Heritage League. They wanted you quiet, right? It's okay, they can't hurt you. The police will come-"

"I'm not saying nothing. Got it?" Raven said. "Shit. I can't take this anymore." She knocked over the First Aid kit, scattering the contents, and bolted for the door.

At the ring of the phone Maureen startled, lifting her cheek off a stack of papers. She grunted at the click and grab of uncooperative joints. "Cage." Her teeth clamped together against the soreness in her hip.

"Keith Templeton. Sorry to disturb." His voice was dry, clipped, as if every syllable cost him more than he was willing to pay. "Wasn't sure you were still in town."

"You're not disturbing me." Maureen jammed the receiver between her jaw and shoulder and gathered her travel alarm clock into her hand. It read eight-eleven. She was going to be late for her meeting with Sarah and Aaron.

"About the accident," Templeton said.

"Accident?" Maureen set down the clock and stood at attention, her feet numb. She was sore all over and her head ached.

"On Pipeline Road. I don't have many details. It appears a truck with young men from the Tse Wets Aht reserve went into a ditch. Three dead, two others in hospital. Central Island Regional."

"What accident?"

"Last night. This morning, rather. Chief David called me from the hospital. She's requested an extended recess. I thought it best to catch you, to keep *Dee-Faz* in the loop. In case you were putting in extra time on our report."

"Thanks." She was sure she imagined the low chuckle behind his voice. "How long?"

There was a pause at the other end. "It wasn't a good time to ask, but my estimate is two weeks, more likely three or four."

"Two days is too long."

"It may be less," Templeton said. "She's distraught. Her nephew was one of the casualties."

Maureen exhaled into the phone. "I'm sorry for that. But you know we can't afford a two week delay. I'll call her."

Templeton grunted. "I don't recommend it. The Tse Wets Aht are in mourning."

"Will you?" Maureen said.

There was a pause. "I'll call her, but I can't promise anything. Not this soon."

She stood and stretched the phone cord to the window. The sun had heated the sky to the color of old bones. A pick-up truck accelerated on the street, its cold, diesel engine knocking as it gathered speed. Had it been a truck like that one? It overtook a logging truck loaded with massive, fresh-cut timber. It miscalculated and raced through the intersection against the light. The logging truck followed, ignoring the red. Cars waited meekly on the cross streets, then gingerly passed through the blue-smoke wake. Maureen sniffed the air. She wondered how many rules of the road the Tse Wets Aht boys had broken before going into a ditch in the dark.

"Ms. Cage—are you listening?"

"Sorry?"

"I said, the RCMP are investigating the crash. Please don't disclose any of the details."

"Details?"

"Good Lord, Ms. Cage, are you still asleep? About the accident. Nobody was wearing a seatbelt. The alcohol at the scene. And the—um—entertainer."

"What *entertainer*?"

Templeton cleared his throat. "A *stripper*, to use plain English. Police discovered her fifty metres from the crash site. Unconscious. She might have been in the back of the truck, doing God-Knows-What when the crash occurred. I'm told she goes by the stage name of Raven."

Maureen tried to follow, to jump out of her chair, but a stab of pain froze her in place. The Raven vanished.

"Lose something, Cage?" Billy's large frame blocked the kitchen door. He held Raven by her left arm and led her back to the empty kitchen chair.

"Jesus," Maureen said, clutching her knee with both hands. "Where did you come from?"

"You were gone when I woke up. Where else would you be?" He threw Raven a warning look, then knelt to collect the spilled first aid supplies.

"She's been hurt," Maureen said.

"Let me see," Billy said. He unwound a roll of gauze and shifted to face Raven.

"No free shows," she said, pressing her knees together.

Billy grunted, glanced up at the dancer. "Then put some clothes on. Besides, you're not my type," he said, and winked at Maureen.

"Josephine," Maureen called, turning away from Billy. "Can you find some pants for our headline act?"

Maureen quit Port before noon. It took her ninety minutes to reach Central Island Regional Hospital. Making her way through the line-up at the Information Desk took half that time again. *Raven* didn't turn up on any admitting lists. The nurse on duty was angry, long overdue for a break. She clutched a cigarette in one fist and a disposable lighter in the other and suggested Maureen come back when she knew the patient's name and by the way, didn't she know there was a strike on?

Maureen planted her elbows on the counter and wondered, out loud, why so much public money was spent treating cancer when hospitals—strike or no strike—allowed staff to smoke on hospital property, in full view of grieving families and dying patients. The nurse flushed and punched up all admissions in the past twenty-four hours and yes, there *was* a car wreck near Port McKenzie early this morning. Two people had been admitted, a man and a woman. Jane Doe was in room seven-zero-three, but seeing as Maureen didn't know her real name she didn't qualify for visitor privileges.

Maureen thanked the nurse through clenched teeth and left. She walked around the side of the building to the Emergency entrance, squeezed between two unhappy, placard-wearing hospital staff who shouted *Shame!* as she hurried through the glass doors. She rode the elevator to the seventh floor and followed the wall-mounted directional arrows to the patient ward and eventually to seven-zero-three. The lone supervising nurse at the floor station was too busy to notice her slip past.

There were five occupied beds in a room built for four. Jane Doe was in bed three, the bed furthest from the door on the right side of the aisle. Her bandaged head was turned toward the open window. Flimsy, mustard-yellow curtains had been drawn back and their fringes flapped in a warm, playful breeze. The air smelled antiseptic, spiced with perspiration.

The woman in the bed bore no resemblance to the dancer Maureen had seen last night. Bandages covered the top of her head. Her long hair was gone: if she'd been wearing a wig last night it had been a good one. Her nose and sinuses had been taped and her left forearm was in a fresh cast. Her lips were dry and cracked. An intravenous drip stood like a coat rack beside the bed. Clear tubing connected a bag of equally clear fluid hanging off the rack to the inside of her right arm. Maureen squeezed between the bed and the window. There was no sign of her gold lighter.

Raven shifted slightly, looked at Maureen through blackened, swollen eyes. "More cops," she said, her voice a weak, croaking sound.

"I'm not with the police," Maureen said.

The woman's chest heaved with an attempted laugh. "Right."

"My name is Maureen Cage."

Raven's eyes were dull, flat, their mischievous glitter extinguished. Her face glistened from a recent flow of tears. "They cut off my hair," Raven whispered, and tears appeared in the swollen creases around her eyes. "Pass me my water," she said, struggling into a more upright position. The neckline of her gown pulled away from her shoulder as she moved. The fresh, red ink of a tattoo blazed in sharp relief against the over-laundered cotton. A lightning bolt set inside a circle of flames. Maureen remembered it from the bar.

"I work for the Directorate for Aboriginal Settlement," Maureen said, her gaze fixed on the tattoo. "I stopped by on my way from Port McKenzie."

"Whose Directory you with?" Raven took a sip from the glass on the stand next to the bed.

"*Directorate. Dee-Faz* for short. What's your real name? I feel silly calling you Raven."

"What's wrong with Raven?" Sparks flew from the slits of her eyes. "Can you draw the curtain? This doesn't have to be for the whole fucking world." Her voice grew stronger.

There were no other visitors in the room. Two elderly women watched from beds on the other side of the aisle. They blinked slowly, their eyes shiny beneath matted, grey hair. The curtain shut them out with a slippery, metallic whisper. Maureen was conscious of her bare calves showing beneath the curtain's ragged hem.

"Can I sit?" Maureen pointed to the chair wedged in the corner, between the bed and the window.

"You sure you're not a Narc?"

"Where are you hurt? Besides the obvious, I mean."

"Three broken ribs. Internal bleeding. Don't remember any of that. They told me I'm alive because I landed on the other guy they brought here." Raven's mouth started to curve into a smile, then stopped. She exhaled noisily. "Ironic, eh?"

"How so?"

"Never mind." Raven looked away. "Dense as a fucking cop," she said to the curtain.

"You were in the truck, not on the road when it happened?"

"Why do you care?" Raven's voice gained strength.

Maureen shrugged. "We settle land claims. We were making progress. Some, anyway. Now the Tse Wets Aht won't talk. Time is running out. If I find out how this happened, maybe it'll help get things going again."

"I don't follow any of that shit," Raven said.

"Did you know any of those men? Are you family?"

Raven laughed, a seal's bark that ended with a groan. Her breath hissed through her lips. "With that much cash it wouldn't matter."

"So they hired you? For what, a private show?" Maureen said. She crossed her legs and laced her fingers around her right knee.

Raven hissed again. "Maybe I felt sorry for them."

"You do this sort of thing often? Pick up men after a set?"

"Sure you're not a cop? Lemme see some ID."

Maureen plucked her driver's license and *Dee-Faz* identification from her wallet. She leaned forward and held them six inches from the Raven's eyes.

"I remember you," Raven said, lifting her head off the pillow. "You're the one with the lighter. You were sitting next to Larry. He dumped the drinks on you." Raven's eyes moved from Maureen down to her hands. Her fingers trembled as she picked at her nails. Her chest began to heave.

"Yeah, more on that in a minute. Are you okay?" Maureen said. "Do you need a nurse?"

Raven began to sob. She lifted her good arm and scrubbed away the tears as they flooded past the bandages around her nose. She cried so hard her breath came in desperate, heaving gasps.

"I'll get somebody." Maureen jumped up and bundled the privacy curtain against the wall.

Raven lifted her head. Despite the swelling and the bandages her eyes smouldered—the same, fierce glitter Maureen remembered from the bar. "Get the fuck away from me," she shouted. She drew a hand across her forehead, as if brushing away a phantom strand of hair.

"Sorry?" Maureen hesitated at the foot of the bed.

"Get out! Get the fuck away from me! Nurse! Help! This bitch is trying to kill me!"

Raven paced the length of the living room, stepping over broken baby toys and small piles of disposable diapers. Billy stood between Raven and the kitchen. Maureen peered out the window, pulled shut the cheap curtains and limped to a tattered sofa.

An infant's shrieks came from the bedroom off the front hall. Each wail was like sandpaper against her flesh.

"Your baby? Or Candy's?"

"Fuck off." The Raven dropped into a torn, sagging armchair opposite Maureen. She kicked over the coffee table, dumping two ashtrays onto a carpet that was no worse for the added mess.

"She gets you drugs, or do you supply her?" Josephine asked.

"Candy couldn't fart without an instruction manual," Raven said, and laughed at her own joke.

"Sirens," Billy said. He moved to the front window. He tweaked apart the curtains with one finger. "One of the neighbors must have called."

"I need a beer," Raven said. She pushed herself out of the chair, grunted at the pain, and stalked to the kitchen with Billy one step behind.

Maureen spent all day Saturday in her study. As a reward she passed the cooler part of Sunday working in her garden. At eleven she retreated from the advancing heat. The pain above her hip grew from a bee sting to an ache that spread halfway down her left leg. Ignoring the pain was not succeeding as a bona fide course of treatment.

She limped indoors to shower the smudges of earth and perspiration from her skin. She leaned away from the spray, letting the hot water massage a fist-sized knot beside her spine. The water softened clenched muscles and brought some relief. Avoiding the neighborhood walk-in clinic, whose melancholy, waiting-room decor complemented the coughing, pale-faced strangers who lined three of its walls, was a victory in itself.

She dressed as she would for any Sunday wedged into a record-breaking heat wave: khaki shorts, sandals and a light, cotton shirt. After a lunch of salad and iced tea with a recording of Puccini's *Tourandot* for company she shut herself in her study with the morning newspapers. Light entered from the south through large windows overlooking the front porch. No need for electric light. Maureen slid her hand across the surface of her desk. Blond oak, inset with a slate writing surface and nearly two centuries old. It dwarfed the nineteen-inch monitor that hunkered on the diagonal inches from her right hand.

The desk had come with the house when Mrs. Agripolis died. Her only son in London couldn't be rid of it fast enough. Maureen scraped together a down payment—with some help from Anne and Helen—and ten years ago had gone from room-and-board tenant to homeowner on Vancouver's pricey West Side. And not just a homeowner: her mortgage included a lifetime's worth of furniture, books and papers—all the possessions that Michael couldn't or wouldn't take with him. The desk had been her first successful project and she'd restored it where it sat, then repainted the room around the mammoth piece.

No, she had to correct herself: the desk had been her *second* restoration project.

She found an article on the Port McKenzie crash in both Vancouver papers. Not on the front page—that space was reserved for the latest forest fires that were threatening resort towns in every region of the province save Vancouver Island. The crash stories were short, and both were back-page items that divulged only the barest details: three dead, two hurt in a pre-dawn, single vehicle accident in Port McKenzie on the Tse Wets Aht reserve. No explanations, no allegations, no editorials—yet. She set aside the papers and pasted the articles onto plain printer paper. She dated each and set them into a separate folder on which she stuck a printed label with the words *Pipeline Road Accident-Port McKenzie.*

She set that folder aside and from her briefcase dragged the file with the latest Tse Wets Aht proposal on sub-surface mineral rights. She went through the document clause by clause, comparing Sarah and Aaron's analysis to her own work. She accessed *Dee-Faz's* online archives for the Federal Government's studies on ore deposit values, compensation to private interests and depreciation percentages for the proposed transfer of ownership rights. Every question or concern went into an electronic folder, one she named *C&C*—Cohen and Chen. She smiled, imagining their faces Monday when they opened their e-mail.

The doorbell's high-low chime booted her pen across her notebook. Maureen jumped out of her chair, sending it against the wall. Sudden movement brought pain. Through the twin lenses of discomfort and annoyance she saw Carole Simons on her front porch, smiling through her scarlet lipstick and carrying a bouquet of iris in her hands.

"It's barely six in the morning," Billy said.

"So? If you hadn't showed up I'd still be asleep." Raven returned to the living room with two cans, Billy the same generous step behind. She offered him the second, made a face when he refused. She set one can on the armrest, opened the other. The hand clutching the can trembled.

"Shit, this hurts," she said, wiping spilled beer off her chin and dabbing at the wet spot on her tee shirt.

"This is bullshit," Josephine said. "You walk away from a crash that kills my people. Young men. Good men. What're you going to do about that?"

Raven's chin trembled. She took another pull on her beer. "Nothing," she said.

Josephine lunged. Billy stepped in front of Raven and caught Josephine's hands. "Stop," he said. "She's garbage. White trash. Don't waste your time."

Josephine collapsed against Billy, pushed him away before his arms could encircle her. "Let's get out of here," she said. She scrubbed her face with her hands, ran her fingers through her hair, clawing at her scalp.

Billy opened the front door. "Hurry up, Cage," he said.

The sirens were closer, loud against the silence of the marsh. The birds had gone quiet, hiding in the brambles for the commotion to pass.

"I'm staying," Maureen said.

The others stared at her, shocked.

"Hi." Carole wedged the iris into Maureen's hands. "Is this a bad time?"

"No," Maureen said, "I mean, yes. Kinda." The cellophane crackled as she squeezed the bouquet between her fingers.

"I got as far as Vancouver, said *screw this* and called up an old colleague of mine. He couldn't stand Ottawa summers either. Or winters, come to think of it. Or anything at all about Ottawa." Carole's short laugh faltered. She cleared her throat. "I can leave, if you want."

"I was working. What time is it?" Maureen checked her watch, backing up to let Carole in. She shut the door quickly as Carole crossed the threshold.

"It's just past five. Nice house! You live here all by your lonesome? I thought maybe we could have dinner? I passed a couple of places on the way here. Indian and Greek, I think."

"Yes. I've heard both are good," Maureen said. She twisted her hands around the flower stems. "But I've still got quite a bit to do."

"You can't work all day and night," Carole said. "Even a workaholic needs to eat."

Maureen exhaled. "Let's put these in water. They're very nice." She led the way to the kitchen. She unwrapped the iris at the sink.

Carole sat at the kitchen table and ran her palms across the dark wood. "So much old furniture here. I like the feel of the old stuff. It's so smooth, so solid. Like a good friend you can always count on." Carole held Maureen's glance, then looked away quickly. "Modern furniture falls apart if you look at it wrong. It can't take the shit and abuse of real life."

"Who can?" Maureen said as she filled a cut-glass vase with water and used a pair of kitchen scissors to snip the ends off the fleshy stems. She plunged the iris into the vase and let them fan around the rim. She placed the vase on the table, between Carole and herself. "You didn't have to," she said.

Carole ran a hand through her bristle-brush hair. "Did so. I felt bad about Slough Flats, or whatever they call that bar in Port."

"Canal Slats."

"Whatever. I shouldn't have dragged you in there. I wasn't thinking."

Maureen felt the heat rise in her cheekbones. "Losing the lighter was my fault. To have it taken like that, with me right there. Stupid."

"You did tell the police?"

Maureen nodded. "They did up a report over the phone. They said they'd look into it."

"Then it's settled. Dinner's on me. To cement the apology," Carole said. "It won't get your lighter back, but maybe it'll help you forget what an ass I was. I promise, soda water only."

"You're not—I mean it wasn't your fault. I went to the hospital to see her, but never got the chance to ask for it back. And really, I don't think I can do dinner," Maureen said. "I'm so far behind."

"But the table's not sitting 'til after the funerals," Carole said.

"I know. This sounds silly, but I work best by myself, at home. If I get this done now, I'll be ready for the next disaster." Maureen shrugged. "It's just the way I'm wired."

"But you still have to eat," Carole said. "Peanut butter sandwiches and chocolate chip cookies don't count. My comfort food when I'm home alone."

Maureen hesitated. "I really need more time."

"How much?"

Warning sirens sounded in her skull. "Another hour," she blurted. It was wrong, but it quieted the alarm. Truth be told all night wouldn't be enough time to clear the work off her desk, but she had to admit she liked the sound of someone else's voice in her house.

"Tell you what," Carole said, fishing her car keys out of her bag. Soft-sided, a jumble of fuzzy rags stitched together. "That butter chicken is calling to me. I'll come back at seven and we can walk over to the Indian restaurant. That'll give you almost two hours. You'll have earned a break." Carole winked. "Really, it'll be fun. And I swear to have you back by nine."

Maureen glanced at the iris in the vase. The flowers were just opening, as sharp as new watercolor brushes dipped in paint pots of azure and gold then left, tips up, in a jar. "Okay. Sure. Seven is fine."

"Great!" Carole said. "But no dressing up." She wagged her index finger. "I want to see this *West Coast Casual* my friends are always bragging about."

Maureen raised her hands in protest. "Don't use me as a measure of anything even remotely current," she said, "but I promise, casual it will be."

"See you at seven. Don't get up, I'll let myself out." Carole vanished into the hall. A soft click signaled the front door's closing.

Maureen's hands shook like small, frightened birds. She leaned across the table and pulled the vase closer, her palms pressed against the cool, chiseled glass. She brought her face to the fan of iris. Their perfume was faintly sweet and settled her jangled nerves. She peered through the cris-crossing stems to the place where Carole had been sitting. The chair, the table—even the lopsided square of sunshine on the wall behind—seemed duller now she was gone.

Carole was back at seven as promised. Dressed in a brown, David Bowie suit and red short-sleeved shirt. Maureen wore her shorts and a fresh cotton shirt and felt under-dressed. They walked to the restaurant, slightly uphill toward Broadway and Maureen squinted against the sun in her face. It was hot, muggy, with no breeze to stir the leaves on the boulevard trees. With each step Maureen wished she'd stayed home; safe in the cool of her basement. She didn't enjoy being hot *and* outside her well established routines.

The restaurant was dim, but thankfully air conditioned. The food was hot, despite persistent pleas to the waiter for the mildest curries and extra *Raida* on the side. Blossoms of perspiration appeared across Carole's brow and coaxed salty tears into the corners of Maureen's eyes. They blew their noses on paper napkins and Carole giggled as she mopped the dampness off her forehead. Carole finished a half-litre of red wine while Maureen drained pitchers of lemon water. When they emerged two hours later the temperature had dropped and a careless breeze fanned Maureen's face. The insistent chorus of complaints inside her head had subsided into grudging silence.

She invited Carole inside. "Don't eat these," she said, making a face at a plate of coconut cookies she'd set out an hour before Carole arrived. "I think they've been in this cupboard since Confederation." She picked up the plate and slid the cookies into the trash. "I must have bought them with the house."

"I like the feel of your place," Carole said. "Not cluttered with junk like my apartment. How about a tour?"

"There's not much to see," Maureen said. She unplugged the kettle and filled the teapot. "Most of the furniture was already here."

"It looks restored. Who did the work for you?"

"I did."

Carole cocked one eyebrow. "I'm impressed."

"Don't be." Maureen poured the tea into a pitcher filled with crushed ice. The jumbled cubes snapped and cracked under the stream of boiling tea. "I started soon after I moved in. My landlady let me practice on the stuff in the basement." She shrugged. "It was therapy, really. Helped to get me past the cravings. There's still a few pieces left to do, but I don't have time, these days."

Carole followed Maureen through the dining room, into a spacious living room. She stepped around her and made a sweeping gesture that took in two book cases, the stereo cabinet, two straight-backed chairs and a sofa arranged around a coffee-black table. "You did all these?"

"Except for the sofa."

"If they fire you, I'll hire you," Carole said, then made a face. "Sorry, that didn't come out right."

"I get it," Maureen said, chewing her bottom lip. She set the tray of iced tea on top of the stereo shelf. "Maybe I'll just quit and take you up on that." The tea came out of the pitcher in an uneven, gushing stream.

Carole crossed the room. She reached one hand for the stereo cabinet.

Maureen stepped back and bumped the wall.

"Jumpy, aren't we?"

"Sorry," Maureen said. "I'm not used to having people over."

Carole ran her fingers across the blond wood. Her hand swept across the wood grain, an inch from Maureen's shoulder. "This is such a beautiful piece," she said. She looked up, held Maureen's eyes in her glance. "Really beautiful," she repeated, her voice a husky whisper. "Don't quit. It'd be tough to come to Port, knowing you weren't there."

"It's a pie shelf. Eighteenth century. Quebec." Maureen said quickly, looking away. She swallowed hard and brought her glass of iced tea to her lips. The ice cubes knocked against her front teeth as she drank.

"You know antiques," Carole said. "Why did you take this job?"

"Only the things Mrs. Agripolis owned," Maureen stammered. "Her husband loved prowling garage sales. He found a couple of gems, but a lot of junk. I guess to prove I can. Nobody gives me a chance."

Carole moved around the room, running her fingers across the polished oak of a bookcase, then over a burnished mahogany spindle chair. "Somebody must have. Who hired you? RG?"

"I think he did it to piss off Sarah," Maureen said. "She has way better qualifications."

"If you've been paying attention you'd know this kind of work isn't about the letters behind your name, or the diplomas on your wall." She stopped at the fireplace to examine a single photograph hanging over a rich, ornately carved mantel. "Who're they?"

"Old friends," Maureen said. "Convocation Day."

Anne and Helen sandwiched her in front of the university clock tower. The sky behind them was clean and bright blue. Maureen's eyes were closed; she'd half-ducked as Anne snatched at her mortarboard. Helen's thin fingers were a blur, diving into her purse for cigarettes. They were all laughing at the camera.

"You don't look much different," Carole said. "I hate you for ageing so well."

"It was only six years ago," Maureen said.

"Six years?" Carole twisted to face her. "You're not making this up then—this *Career Anxiety Shtick*."

Maureen felt the heat rise to her face. She gulped her iced tea, chewed on a stray ice cube between her molars. "It's no *Shtick,* I'm afraid."

"What the heck did you do before school?"

Maureen set down her glass and moved into the hall. "It's getting late. I really have more work to do."

Carole's glance pinballed between Maureen and the photo. "Something I said?"

Maureen shook her head. "No. It's the work. Really. Duty calls."

Carole set down her glass. "Thanks for the drink," she said. "Dinner was fun." She hesitated at the front door. "I had a terrific time." She stepped close, her hand settling gently on Maureen's hip.

A rush of heat ran up Maureen's body, from ankles to scalp. So sudden it itched. She raked her skin with her nails, raising scarlet furrows on her neck; on the tightening skin of her forearms. "Me too," she said, her voice faltering. She didn't know where to look.

Carole stepped closer. In perfect time Maureen stepped back. Like partners in a dance. Carole retreated, removed her hand, exhaling in a rush. Her hand fluttered to the lapels of her jacket, nervously straightening where no straightening was required. She held Maureen's eyes, her expression suddenly miserable. "See you in Port, Maureen," she said, and turning, stepped through the front door, shutting it carefully behind her.

"You'll get nothing out of her," Josephine said from the doorway. She turned to the Raven, her fists on her hips. "At times the Raven of our stories brings harm, but always there is good that comes of it. *You* bring only grief. In older times you would have been sent away, to live alone in the woods."

"Smoke this." Raven shot her the finger.

"Come on." Billy pushed Josephine through the open front door.

Maureen pulled herself off the sofa. She limped to the door, caught a glimpse of the jeep as it carved out a U-turn on the dusty boulevard and sped out of sight. She closed the door against the advancing sirens.

"What's your name?" she asked.

The Raven's frown deepened. "You bitch," she said. She drained the first beer and reached for the second can. "You mother-fucking bitch."

"Hear those? They're coming for you, too."

The Raven closed her eyes.

"For God's sake, tell me what happened," Maureen begged. "Then I'll leave. I'll tell the police this was my fault. You can get out of here and get on with-"

Maureen's cell phone rang. She yanked it off her hip, wanting to crush the plastic in her fist to make it stop. She pressed the phone against her ear.

"Yes?" She spoke through clamped jaws.

"Maureen." A woman's voice as soft and warm as honey in her ear. "It's Lee-Anne Carlyle. Got a sec?"

Monday morning and the air conditioning system at the *Dee-Faz* offices crashed. It surrendered unconditionally after five consecutive weeks battling temperatures in the low thirties. The heat wave had officially begun the week Lee-Anne quit. Maureen imagined air conditioners all over the city—triple-teamed by heat, dust and cloying humidity—expiring, their overworked compressors done in by an atmosphere so dense that by mid-afternoon it verged on syrup.

She desperately wanted to strip off her jacket; to shed at least one layer of clothing, but RG was winding up to another of his rants. She fixed her glance past his shoulder, to the glass trophy case full of photos and hardware from six seasons in the NHL. When he was *Bulldog Bob* Braithwaite. God! Maureen hated hockey. She re-crossed her legs, took shallow sips of air and dreamed of Vancouver winters: of dull, bruised skies that—from November to March—sieved out the sunlight and leaked a cold, gnawing rain onto the heads of city dwellers week after dreary week.

"You *do* know what two days of facilitation costs?" RG said. He leaned toward her. When he talked his hands moved in tight, quick circles. "What do we have to show for last Thursday and Friday?" His fingers, tanned, thick, with knuckles like knotted hide, curled around the far edge of his desk.

Maureen shifted in her seat. "The accident. Friday wouldn't have happened regardless," she said. It was a feeble defense she was selling and RG wasn't buying any of it.

"You weren't ready for a major counter proposal."

"I would have been." Maureen looked down at her hands, folded in her lap. They were hot, clammy, and would have suffered less apart, but she needed to hold onto something. They gripped each other tightly as if expecting a blast of wind.

"So you say," RG said. He straightened, tapped a pair of reading glasses against the leather of the desk blotter. "It's a sorry state of affairs when a captain can't rely on his team. But let's leave that for now. How do you explain this?" RG pushed a sheet of paper across the desk. "Read," he said, and he picked up a second page. He grunted, slid the glasses over the bridge of his nose and tilted his head to focus on the text.

Maureen uncrossed her legs to climb out of the low, leather chair. Her back still ached when she moved. "*Vancouver Star?*"

RG waited, watching her uncoil as she retrieved the paper. "Terry Edwards was kind enough to email me an advance copy. I told him I wouldn't comment until I got the full story from my staff."

Maureen settled back in her seat. The backs of her legs were damp from the heat. She pressed her sensible shoes flat against the carpeted floor.

"Listen to this," RG said, reading from his copy of the email. "*The two survivors of a serious single-vehicle crash outside Port McKenzie Friday morning remain in Central Island Regional Hospital,* yadda, yadda-" His voice jumped an octave for emphasis. "*-In another twist, the Star has learned that one survivor, an exotic dancer from Vancouver who goes by the name of 'Raven', was interviewed by a senior representative of the Directorate for Aboriginal Settlement. While details are pending, it appears that Dee-Faz may be interested in the accident in some official capacity, fearing its impact on the troubled land claims negotiations in Port McKenzie. Only eleven weeks remain before the Agreement in Principle, signed with much fanfare nearly four years ago, expires and still they have nothing to show the taxpaying public. Robert*

Gordon Braithwaite, Chief Executive Officer of the Directorate, has declined comment."

RG put down his copy and took off his reading glasses. "So far," he said. "What the hell is this about, Cage?"

Maureen ran her tongue across her upper lip, tasting the saltiness of her sweat. She was certain RG could see it oozing from her pores. "I stopped by on my way home." She said, restless in her chair. She tried to sound casual, but the squeak in her voice betrayed her.

"You visited a crash witness? The RCMP are still investigating!"

"I was trying to do damage control. I-" She could not bring herself to mention her hope of recovering the stolen lighter.

"Damage control?" RG came out of his chair and launched himself toward the window, straightening his tie as he walked. His silver hair was immaculately groomed, untouched by the heat, and brilliant against his suntanned skin. Wintering every year in Palm Springs will do that to a person. "The media will eat this up. Why should *Dee-Faz* care about a stripper who fell out of a truck? Why do you care, Ms. Cage?" He spun to face her.

"They didn't think she was even *in* the truck, at the start. I hoped the facts might get the Federation back to the table." It had sounded weak on her way to the office as she explained it to her reflection. Now, out loud in RG's office, it was worse than weak, it was pathetic.

"What'd you expect her to say? That she wasn't *really* there to give blowjobs, she was going to help them with their church garage sale?" RG's face was red. "Jesus Tap-Dancing Christ!"

"If she'd said—I don't know—that it was *her* idea—that *she'd* talked them into taking her with them then maybe the Tse Wets Aht wouldn't be so distraught." Maureen sighed, surrendering. "I don't know, RG. It kind of made sense on Friday."

"Maybe *you* should call Terry Edwards and tell him what you just told me. See what *his* reaction is. His readers love this crap. Another chance to attack the *Indian Industry*. Throw in a messy car crash and a whiff of *Dee-Faz* interference and it'll be front page news, something to print besides another Goddamned fire raging out of control, forcing another town's evacuation, or a bunch of senior citizens expiring from heat exhaustion in their unventilated apartments."

"What do you think I should do?" Maureen's face blazed.

"Lay low." RG said, waving his arms. "No, wait. You have to attend the funerals tomorrow. I'd be there, but I'm meeting with Premier Hargrove and Henderson, the Aboriginal Affairs Minister. They've got something they want to run by me. *High risk, but high reward*, they're calling it. My sense is it's just more bullshit but Hargrove is on borrowed time anyway and desperate men will try anything once. No, Cage, show up for the service, then get out. Even if the table reconvenes early, I want *you* out of Port. Off the Island altogether. Cohen and Chen can handle things for a few days. We're OK on this. Let's hope a couple more million dollar homes in Vernon or Kelowna go up in flames and this crash is on the back page. Or out of circulation for good."

"I was just trying to get an edge," Maureen said. She slid the copy onto RG's desk.

"You wear the *C*, Cage, and a captain's gotta take charge to win games. But this," he strummed the article with his fingers, "is a five minute misconduct. The team's got some serious penalty killing to do. I'll call Edwards, give him some bull for filler. All vanilla. This'll blow over soon enough. So long as we don't add any fuel to the fire." RG's hands transformed into a pair of pistols pointing directly at Maureen. "But you're out of Port after the funerals. Got that?"

"I got it, RG."

"Don't make me look bad, Maureen."

He pulled one imaginary trigger. "It's like in 'seventy-two. We were up three games to one against the Rangers, but couldn't get it done in game five. We pulled it out—a lucky one—in game six but it was dicey, right to the end. I wouldn't have given much for our chances had it gone to game seven. Cage, this is your game seven."

Maureen prayed he was done. With his hockey stories, all his *Captain* bullshit. She prayed that the sweat condensing on her body hadn't puddled onto his leather chair. She stood, refusing to look down. "Thanks, RG," she said, hurrying for the door.

"Anytime, Cage," RG said. He jumped from behind his desk and raced to intercept her at the door. He grinned. His arm encircled her waist and for a brief moment rested on her hip. "A good coach always has quality time for his star players."

"Are you there? Maureen? Can you talk?"

"You better make it fast," Maureen said. She limped into the kitchen.

"Where are you?"

"In Victoria. Look, Lee-Anne, I'm not with *Dee-Faz* anymore."

Maureen locked the back door, then leaned backwards into the fridge and felt the rattle of its overworked motor vibrate up her spine.

"That's why I called. I can change that."

"I don't think-"

"I'm back," Lee-Anne said. "The Minister called me last night. Hargrove needs a wheelbarrow load of damage control." Lee-Anne's voice tripped into a brittle laugh. "Maureen, you're talking to the new CEO of *Dee-Faz*."

Maureen glanced at the window set into the back door. Months—years, maybe—of cigarette smoke, grease and dust caked the glass. A yellowing rind, thickest near the bottom, tortured the sunlight that passed through it. She found a cloth in the bottom of the sink. It was clammy, wet and cold. She turned on the hot water and let it run across her hand, soaking into the cloth. Her skin turned a mottled red from the heat.

She couldn't help herself. It was a craving, an addiction of sorts: she could not just let her lighter go. Five minutes off the ferry she passed the highway sign that guarded the exit to the Central Island Regional Hospital and she had to turn. Two minutes later she was parked and past the ragged line of picketing support staff and through the main doors. She rode the elevator to the seventh floor and retraced Friday's steps. But the Raven was gone. Gone or she'd aged forty years over the weekend. The tiny woman beneath the white sheet returned Maureen's frown with a shy smile.

"Sorry," Maureen said. "I was looking for somebody else."

The expectant smile collapsed.

Maureen turned away.

"They took her downstairs," a voice behind her said. "They're giving her the V.I.P. treatment now."

"Sorry?"

"I heard the suits talking." The woman in the bed across the aisle lifted a hand to straighten her limp hair. "They've taken her to a private room. Five-twenty, I think. The memory's not so sharp, these days." She touched her temple with an arthritic finger.

"Thank you."

"You one a them reporters? They been 'round like flies on rotten fruit."

"I should go-"

"Wait. I got some ripper yarns for ya, I do. I bet they're worth money, too. Worked in the factories during the war, I did. Helped build the bombs that burned up Dresden and Berlin."

"That's interesting, for sure but I'm not-"

"One day it'll be you in this bed," the woman said, her voice suddenly angry, "and some *Shiny Bum* will be standing right where you are now. Then you'll be wishing you'd stayed and listened to me."

Maureen hurried from the room, cursing the woman's family, but secretly pleased to be mistaken for a *Shiny Bum* by this forgotten crone. She suppressed a shiver of foreboding as she sprinted for the elevator.

The Raven was in room five-twenty-one. A single room with television, DVD player, and private bathroom. Next to the bed there was enough space for a small sitting area with two comfortable chairs. The air conditioner hummed energetically in the window frame.

"You. I'll call Security," The Raven said as Maureen entered. She shut the magazine she'd been flipping through. "I'm not supposed to talk to you."

"Funny. The same goes for me," Maureen said. She sat in one of the high-backed chairs. It had been turned to face the window. The highway was heavy with afternoon traffic. Beyond it the mountains of the mainland stretched across the horizon. The tallest, most distant peaks were shrouded in a dull, brown-tinged fog. Smoke from the biggest fires, heavy enough to stand against the wind currents blowing off the Pacific. "How are you feeling? Better?"

"As if you cared."

"Terry Edwards at the *Vancouver Star* pay for this?"

The Raven glanced up from her magazine. "None of your fucking business," she said. Her voice, at least, had recovered.

"I was here first," Maureen said. "That should count for something."

"Did you set me up in this room? I don't think so. Are you gonna pay for what I know?"

The bandage around her head had been replaced by a smaller version, a gauze skull cap that gave Raven the appearance of a strung out skater groupie. The tape across her nose remained, underlining a pair of deeply blackened eyes. The intravenous drip was still attached to her good arm.

"So you're selling a story. What's your angle? *Peeler with a heart of gold?*"

"Fuck you," the Raven said, snarling. A thin, calculating smile formed under her black eyes. "How 'bout the accident? Like it wasn't one."

"Wasn't what?" Maureen leaned forward in her chair.

"Accidental." Raven's smile turned nasty. "And I'm not telling you nothing more. I got my future to think of. *You* never helped me. *You* never did anything for me."

"What are you talking about?" Maureen climbed out of the chair. "Give me my lighter back."

Raven's features darkened. "You miserable bitch! You lying, cunt-licking dyke. If you come back I will fucking well kill you!" She grabbed for the water glass on the bedside table.

Maureen was only half out the door when it shattered against the wall behind her head.

"Maureen?"

"I'm here." Maureen squeezed the cloth in the stream of hot water until she'd wrung the stink of sour milk out of it. She shuffled to the kitchen door. The hand that held the cloth hovered inches from the encrusted pane. "About that damage control thing? You might need a bigger wheelbarrow."

"What did you do?"

"I'm with the Raven, the dancer from Port. The only witness to how Henry Jackson and the others died. She's going to tell me what really happened."

"Now I am confused," Lee-Anne said. "Didn't the RCMP call that an accident?"

"You've heard of the Heritage League?"

"Yes. Unfortunately," Lee-Anne said.

"One of them's laid out in the back yard. Some time back they started a cell in Port. Somehow they tapped into our negotiations. They killed those boys to blow up our talks. I brought Chief David here. She's been hanging around an American shit-disturber who's big into conspiracies."

"Christ, Maureen."

"You may want to rethink your damage control strategy."

"I'll call the police."

"Don't bother, they're here," Maureen said. "I have to go. The paramedics are taking Larry the Nazi away. I don't think we've much time."

"Negotiate. Buy me some time. What's the address?"

Maureen told her.

Lee-Anne gave Maureen the number she was at. "Don't do anything stupid."

"Too late," Maureen said.

"I'll call you back."

"Since we're starting fresh, there *is* one thing. In case we don't get another chance to talk." Maureen exhaled into the phone. "Why did you quit?"

The hiss of Carlyle's indrawn breath was like a needle in her ear. "RG made things—difficult."

"No doubt. He made you sleep with him?" Droplets of hot water zigzagged down her wrist. They trickled off her elbow, cooling as they navigated the fine hairs along her forearm.

"It was easier to say yes. Around the time the AIP was signed. I wanted him to stop, but he wouldn't let me. From that moment on I was finished."

"You could have reported him. You didn't have to quit."

"I could say the same to you."

"Except I didn't sleep with him and I didn't quit," Maureen said.

There was a short silence. "Details, Cage, details," Lee-Anne said. "Coming to *Dee-Faz*, you knew what your biggest challenge was going to be. And it wasn't the work."

"It never came up for me—'til the end."

Lee-Anne laughed, a short, sharp bark. "RG thought you were queer, Cage. For the longest time so did I."

Maureen squeezed the cloth. A surge of entrained water flooded through her fingers onto the floor. "Wrong."

"Well congratulations," Lee-Anne said. "You'd be the first to escape from RG and his Seduction Express. So you'll have your job back?"

"Which one?"

Lee-Anne snorted. "Senior Analyst. I'll give you another shot."

"If I walk out of here."

Lee-Anne laughed. "You're not like any negotiator I've ever met, Cage. There's something about you, can't put my finger on what it is, but you're different. *Worldly*, underneath all that nice as toast exterior." She sniffed. "Try to stay out of jail," she said, just before she hung up.

"Not bloody likely," Maureen said and she pushed the wet cloth against the soiled window hard enough to bulge the glass.

The night before the funerals and she couldn't sleep, even in the familiar confines of her regular hotel room; she didn't know why she'd thought going to bed early would help. Her body was tired but her brain was restless; it flooded her muscles with chemicals, internal pinpricks in the shapes of the Raven and Carole. She dressed and walked to the Port McKenzie waterfront and from a spot against the timber railing watched the running lights of the last returning fishing charters glide over silky, black water to the marina. The breeze out of the west was cool, its salty tang easy to inhale. Every breath soothed her dry throat. She wrapped the deepening night around her shoulders and hoped for rain.

It was after eleven PM when she hiked back to the Queen Anne Hotel. As she passed reception she had the urge to ask if Carole had checked in, but she resisted and stayed the course to the elevator. Once in her room she peeled off her clothes and showered. The water was cold, raising goose bumps upon her flesh. She toweled off, pulled on a tee shirt and boxers and slid under the rumpled sheet. She lay on her back and counted the muscle spasms in her arms and lower legs.

At twelve-thirty she set up the ironing board from the closet and re-ironed her funeral clothes. A black skirt and jacket in the Port McKenzie heat: just looking at them was enough to trigger an anticipatory sweat. She hung her clothes, collapsed the ironing board and in the dark paced the breadth of her hotel room. She prayed for an attack of food poisoning—any plausible excuse not to go.

At two AM she showered again. The bathroom filled with steam. She stood beneath the flow until her skin turned a violent red. Her muscles were so weak it was a struggle to shut off the water. She clambered out of the tub and nearly slipped on the wet floor. Leaving her clothes where they lay, she closed the door on billowing steam and stumbled to the window. She turned circles next to the air conditioning unit to expose her skin to the flow of cold air, then fell onto her bed and begged the darkness for the grace of sleep.

Her first thoughts were all Carole. Memories of her smile, the warm hand on her hip, coaxed a glow that started below her belly and spiraled into her limbs. Neither scalding blast nor smothering heat, just a gentle, buzzing warmth that summoned her hands from the edges of the mattress. Her breathing deepened, her chin dropped and her lips parted, and as her fingers played her hips began to rock until the building heat bubbled through her pores, covering her body with a fine, sweet sheen of perspiration. A tropical sea surged beneath her. She was lifted on the crest of a towering, warm wave.

She waited for her breathing to slow, dragged the sheet off the floor and wrapped it around her body. She rolled onto her left side, tucked her knees to her chin and finally slept.

The cloth hurtled toward the sink. It splattered against the wall, clung for a moment, then slumped limply around the faucet. A single shaft of sunlight pierced the kitchen with a lustrous, white light. Through the glass Maureen watched uniformed police take up positions in the backyard.

"You're cleaning?" The Raven stood at the entrance to the kitchen. "The cops surround the place and you're cleaning the fucking windows?"

"That was my old boss," Maureen said. "She's giving me my old job back."

"Swell. This is turning into a fucking Julia Roberts movie." The Raven walked out. "Except in this one, Julia's gonna lose some teeth."

Maureen clawed the fabric of the bench seat when Sarah hesitated at the highway, missing another chance to merge into oncoming traffic. Fifteen minutes until the funeral service started and they were still in town. She bit her lip when Sarah missed a gap long enough to fit a tour bus. She swiveled in the backseat at the sound of a car horn. Vindication—somebody out there shared her opinion of Sarah's driving. She exhaled as the Honda leap-frogged onto the highway, her bones shaking with the shifting gears. Aaron sat next to Sarah, rigid, silent, his eyes glued to the highway ahead.

She had only herself to blame. If she'd taken her own car she'd be there by now, but when Aaron had called at breakfast and suggested they car pool she'd said yes. It had seemed like an olive branch of sorts and RG had it wrong—she was a good team player. She picked at the buttons of her blouse and berated herself for giving in. Sarah was doing this on purpose, making them late. Maureen covered her watch to resist counting the seconds.

Two PM on a Tuesday afternoon and the Tse Wets Aht reserve was deserted. Nobody on the road; even the dogs had vanished, but they were most likely hiding from the heat, not the visitors. The sun baked the exposed earth into a thin dust that hung in the air like a shimmering veil. It coated the houses and parked cars, ageing them. Branches of hemlock and fir hung limp at the road side, the green seared from their needles. Everything had the same, run-down look.

Maureen dreaded that first step out of the air-conditioned car.

The church lot was full. Plywood signs with spray-painted arrows were propped on the road edge, directing them past the driveway to an unfenced construction site. A faded, pockmarked billboard welcomed them to the future home of the Tse Wets Aht medical centre: *A Proud Joint Venture Between Governments Committed to a Brighter Future.* The sign was punctuated with bullet holes that clustered neatly around the Provincial Coat of Arms. Sarah bounced the Honda between tracks gouged by heavy equipment when the earth was wet and soft. She settled on a spot at the end of a row of parked cars, parking the Honda on the rutted earth at a spine-wrenching angle.

Maureen lunged from the car before the engine died. She struck out ahead, across the construction site. It was difficult to move quickly when each high-heeled shoe had to be deliberately placed. She stumbled past an idle bulldozer and tank-tracked excavator parked to block a steep cut into an unfinished foundation. The bare, earthen walls were covered with torn, plastic sheets. The excavator's windows were broken. Fragments of safety glass looked like oversized grains of salt on the ground. Neither machine appeared to have moved for a long time.

Ten past two and a crowd milled on the steps of the United Church. One wing of the twin doors was shut and young men—ushers—guarded the open side. They pointed late-comers toward the tents: four Arabian-style pavilions erected on the burnt grass in front of the church. Open-sided, the mold-spotted canvas was held taut by nylon ropes staked into the flattened ground. Each tent was wired for video and sound and surrounded with baskets of flowers. The carnations were starting to wilt in the heat. Mourners gathered in the shade. The older women sat together and fanned themselves with the Order of Service. Small children ignored the afternoon heat and chased each other around the ropes. When one of them tripped over a line the canvas ceiling shivered. Youth clustered in the back rows, at the verge between shade and sun. They turned the chairs to face each other and smoked cigarettes and laughed at jokes their elders could not overhear.

Maureen needed to complain. She was hot, her shoes were covered in powdered earth and she was late. She did not attempt the crowd on the stairs, ducking instead under the fringe of the nearest tent. She twisted between rows of metal folding chairs to a seat securely in the shade. She avoided the stares of the women in front of her. She took off her jacket, draped it across the chair back and pressed the soles of her feet into the dead grass. She tried not to think about her air-conditioned hotel room, where a cool shower and locked door beckoned.

"Hey."

One of the women leaned backwards in her chair, tipping it onto its two back legs.

Maureen took off her sunglasses.

The woman pointed to the church. "See that kid? On the stairs? He's got seats saved for you." The woman smiled and pointed with a tightly rolled Order of Service.

Maureen looked over her shoulder—there was nobody behind her. She raised her hands in an unspoken question. The woman pointed to a skinny youth dressed in a black suit and white shirt too tight for his neck. He was talking to Sarah and Aaron, who nodded, pointed at her and with a shared smile climbed the stairs. They disappeared into the crowd. The youth jumped down the church steps. He held up a sheet of paper as he shinnied between the seats.

"I got your names on this paper," he grinned. "They got seats inside."

"See?" The old woman laughed as she let her chair fall forward.

Maureen grabbed her jacket and followed the youth. He led her to a side door, much smaller than the front. The door was closed, but unlocked. "This way." He waved her inside.

Maureen stepped into a heated fog. It was as if the room had been pumped full of steam. The weight of it pressed against her—she opened her mouth to drag the oppressive air into her lungs. She felt dizzy. A tired fan rotated from a long shaft suspended somewhere in the rafters. It was no help. Neither were the small windows that ran around the building's perimeter, just below the eaves. Their single panes drooped inward, impotent against the stifling heat.

The usher closed the door behind them and gestured to the crowded pews. She blushed as rows of pearlescent faces turned toward her. The assembled fanned their reddened cheeks and wiped at the sweat with cloth handkerchiefs. Her escort's grin never faltered as he led her to her seat. As they passed in front of the altar she was struck by the perfume of roses and lilies. Three large bird of paradise anchored the floral display. The aroma mixed with perspiration and a fainter, waxy scent rising from a lake of burning candles. Inside the amber glow lay three closed caskets, each overlaid with a spray of white flowers. Behind the caskets there was barely room for the double row of choir members. They sat shoulder against shoulder, their hands hidden beneath thin, black gowns.

"Here," he said, and gestured to the empty space at the end of the third pew.

Aaron flashed a weak smile and shifted his body to make room.

"Thanks," Maureen said to the boy. She squeezed into the narrow space between Aaron and the wooden armrest.

"I picked you for the first one here." Keith Templeton tossed the comment over his right shoulder from the pew ahead. "Good thing nobody would take my bet."

The blood pounded in her ears. Her fist crushed her sunglasses onto her jacket where it lay folded on her lap. "Would've been nice to be early," she said. Aaron shot her a sympathetic glance but said nothing.

Maureen leaned into the armrest. She closed her eyes, but the heat stalked her even in darkness. When she opened them Josephine David was in front of her, in the aisle, speaking to Templeton. Their voices were too low to be heard over the hum of the crowded church. Templeton's hand rested lightly on Josephine's back. The Tse Wets Aht chief wore a black shirt, its two top buttons undone, her sleeves rolled to the elbow. It matched her snug black denims and stitched, black leather boots. A silver *Harley Davidson* belt buckle completed the outfit. It gathered and magnified the light of the candles. A miniature sun burned at her waist and still her narrow body showed no hint of discomfort.

Maureen pushed against Aaron's leg. "Can you slide over a bit?"

"Sorry, it's like sardines in here," he said, and pushed back. "You were better off outside."

A drop of perspiration rolled from her brow. It burned her skin as it followed the scar at her hairline, negotiating the line of her jaw. She swatted at it with her palm. It took all her strength not to scream.

Chief David detached from Templeton. "Nice that you could make it," she said, and her eyes jumped from Maureen to Aaron, to Sarah and back. "The flowers were appreciated." She nodded toward one of the two dozen or more bouquets that lined the front of the altar. Calla lily with salal. The callas were already drooping in the heat.

"Please accept our condolences," Maureen said. She held out her hand. She was conscious of how clammy it was.

Josephine squeezed Maureen's hand and released it quickly. "Thanks. They were good boys."

She turned away and hurried to a seat on the dais.

The baby stopped crying when the sirens ceased. Maureen remembered early summer mornings in her bedroom, when the silence peeled away, layer by layer: first by the birds in the trees outside her window, then the tramp of early-morning joggers and clinking dog collars as they passed on the sidewalk. By then the hum of traffic became so constant one forgot it existed: a continuous drone; white noise that saturated the city. Finally, the slap of a newspaper on the porch, the signal to get out of bed.

A surge of homesickness rose in Maureen's chest. She pushed herself off the sofa and tottered near the wall, gritting her teeth from the pain in her knee. "I gotta go," she said. "I came here hoping you'd tell me what really happened on Pipeline Road, but I don't care anymore."

The Raven tossed her second, empty beer into a corner. She belched. "See ya."

Maureen limped to the front door.

"Better put up your hands. Don't want 'em to shoot ya by accident," Raven called after her.

"By the way," Maureen said, hesitating at the door, "Elektra's looking for you. Something about being evicted."

"Fuck you."

"Good luck, Raven. I hope you make it."

"I *already* made it, Bitch. I don't need *your* sympathy. Any day now I'll be working again, making more in a week than you'll see in six months. *You're* the one who needs good luck."

Maureen pressed her back into the wooden pew and stared at the caskets, each inside its own halo of shimmering candlelight. The *whuff* of the fan mocked her from the rafters. She closed her eyes, willed scorched air into her lungs and searched for a feeling appropriate to the occasion. She found only the heat of an oven, dissolving her from the inside.

The minister appeared through a door carved out of the back of the dais and the noise sank into the withered floorboards. Tall and rakish, his white robe ended in sleeves that draped past his wrists. Veins like knotted cords scarred the backs of his hands. He carried a thick, hardbound book riddled with sticky notes to mark the pages. The choir sang a version of *Closer to Thee, My Jesus* that was much longer than Maureen remembered. Their voices were pleasant to listen to and the time standing brought minor relief to the creases of her body. The minister nodded to the choir. Everyone sat. He adjusted the microphone and pushed his glasses up his nose, then sipped from the water glass at his right hand.

Maureen licked her lips and stared at the back of Templeton's head.

"We have come today as a demonstration of our love for these boys," he said and his large, open hand swept toward the caskets. "To remind ourselves that though they have died, they are not gone from us. Henry Jackson, Donald Tom and Leonard Tom have been called by our Lord, Jesus Christ. It is not for us, no matter how important we think we are, no matter how intelligent others tell us we are, no matter how close to their lives we once were, to question this most reassuring, this most simple Truth: our Lord has need of them. There is much work to be done, even in Heaven, as there is much work to be done here on Earth. Let their deaths instruct we who remain to complete the work that they can no longer do. Until it is our turn to be called."

The piano struck the first notes to *Onward Christian Soldiers* and when she stood Maureen had to grab onto the edge of the pew to keep her balance.

The service lasted forty-nine minutes and thirty-six seconds. Maureen's body was drenched. Her skin itched. She had to wait for the minister to lead the families of the deceased from the church. She counted off the seconds before it was her turn to rise; sure she would either drown in her own perspiration or be driven mad by the heat rash. As the remaining pews began to empty she stood, stepped into the aisle, wedging herself behind a tall man in a tight-fitting sports jacket that was heavily stained with perspiration. His black pony tail ended its graceful arc just below his collar. It was tied close to his skull with a knotted, leather cord strung with small grey feathers that reached the middle of his back. As they passed through the double doors of the church he shrugged off his jacket as if it were on fire. His groan of relief drew modest laughter from those around him. As he reached behind his back to pull at the shirt plastered to his shoulders he bumped Maureen's arm.

"Sorry." He turned to face her. "That was almost lethal."

"I took mine off before it started," Maureen said. "Didn't help."

At the bottom of the stairs he stepped out of the river of mourners passing from the church. "You're Maureen Cage," he said, motioning her to join him.

"I am," she said, stepping beside him, "but if that had gone any longer I'd be the late Maureen Cage." She tugged at the damp fabric clinging to her arms. "Excuse me. That was in poor taste. You are?" She squinted against the glare that came off the church siding. She unfolded her sunglasses and perched them across her eyes.

"Billy," he said. His teeth were straight behind a generous smile and very white against his russet skin. "William Last Man Standing, but only my mother calls me William." He stepped close enough to offer his hand.

"Last Man Standing. You're American?" Maureen took his hand. It was cooler than hers and his long fingers completely encircled the back of her hand.

"Lakota."

"You're a long way from home."

"Not really. I live in Seattle."

"You know the families?"

"No," Billy said. "This is my first time here. The Tse Wets Aht most generously granted me permission to enter their lands to attend the service. I've spent time with their cousins on the Olympic Peninsula. They've been struggling to resurrect their whaling tradition. It's been in the news."

"I've followed the story," Maureen said. "It got pretty tense."

"It's not over," Billy said. "It's setting the Makah and other indigenous peoples against environmentalists. That was unexpected. Some of us had a tough time choosing sides."

"Which side did you choose?"

"I only work for the NFDI." He folded his arms across his chest.

"The Network for Direct Intervention," Maureen said. "I've seen their website. Do they care about land claims in general or just this one? There are forty-one active tables in BC at this moment."

"Just this one, for starters," Billy said. "We got wind of the situation and thought a quick recon was in order. Given my background I volunteered."

Maureen's eyebrows arched behind her sunglasses. "What *situation*? And what *background*?"

"This isn't the place to talk," Billy said. He nodded toward a clear space in the shade of a large arbutus, a short walk from the tents. Billy leaned against the smooth bark. "Chief David told me about you. Somehow I pictured someone older."

Maureen bit off a laugh. "I am older."

"You look hot," Billy said.

"Excuse me?"

"I mean: You. Look. Hot." Billy flashed a lopsided smile. "You need some water. Before you pass out."

"Shade is good. Air conditioning would be better."

The crowd moved in a line four abreast toward the families waiting beneath the tents to receive their condolences. Sarah and Aaron were in the thick of the throng, not yet halfway to the first tent. Carole Simons waited a step ahead, her eyes hidden behind oversized, aviator-style sunglasses. Her pale face glistened in the heat. She turned toward Maureen, tilting her head to see over the top of her sunglasses. Maureen waved. Carole jammed her glasses into place and looked away.

"Who's that one?" Billy said.

"Carole Simons. A Fed," Maureen said.

"What's she trying to prove? Punk might be enjoying a revival, but not with the over forty crowd."

"She always dresses that way. It's her *thing*."

Billy grunted. "Somebody should tell her it's time to find a new *thing*. What d'ya do to piss her off?"

"Nothing," Maureen said. She turned away from the line of mourners. "She's probably jealous."

"Yes, I have that effect on women," Billy said. He grinned. The muscles of his bare forearms stretched the fabric on his rolled-up cuffs.

"I meant of the shade," Maureen said. "They're dying out there. I feel guilty."

"Guilt is one of your culture's biggest exports," Billy said. "God help us when all the world's indigenous peoples become addicted."

Maureen lowered her sunglasses. "I know this sounds pushy, but do you have a car?"

Billy's jeep hugged the curves as it raced through the Tse Wets Aht village, plowing through the heat. The rush of air cooled Maureen's face and neck. She could breathe again, despite the dust kicked up by the jeep's tires.

"Thanks for the rescue. Driving with Sarah is like riding with your Grandmother."

"My grandmother's dead," Billy said.

"Not *your* grandmother, *anybody's* grandmother," Maureen said.

"I get it."

"Oh."

"Chief David told me you work for the Directorate," Billy said. Beneath his wrap-around sunglasses a sharp chin summarized a lean, elegant profile. He was handsome, and not much over twenty-five. His pony-tail bucked each time the jeep careened through a pothole.

"I know *Dee-Faz* is a necessary evil for most First Nations. Josephine has her share of concerns, but no more than any other."

Billy snickered. The jeep hit a sharp turn and skidded.

"What?" Maureen had to hold onto the door handle to steady herself.

"You have this entire industry around treaty making," Billy said. He waved his hands as he talked. "The Tse Wets Aht and the others have to make an appointment to talk about how they're going to live on their own lands."

"It may seem frustrating to an outsider, but it's a good process," Maureen said. "Better than not talking at all."

"Unless you talk them to death. How many of these forty-one tables are settled? Or close to settling?"

"None. Yet."

"Meantime who's keeping the profits from those timber trucks that I passed on the way here?"

Maureen felt flushed, despite the wind in her face. "That's *why* we're talking. Those resources are on the table, formulas are being worked out. It's complicated. You can't just hand over a tract of land and say *here you go, you look after it.*"

"Why not? They looked after it for ten thousand years. Did a pretty fair job of it, too."

"Can we change the subject, please?"

Billy shrugged. "Sure. Pick one."

"Why are you here?" Maureen said. The muscles along her jaw rippled.

The jeep swerved onto the highway, leaving a cloud of dust hanging in the air. Billy flipped his sunglasses onto the top of his head. "Three young men die, right as treaty negotiations are in a critical phase. Only ten weeks plus from the expiry date of the most ambitious Agreement in Principle ever signed in this province. Coincidence?"

"It was the Tse Wets Aht who wanted the recess, not *Dee-Faz,*" Maureen said.

"A couple of weeks off to bury the dead isn't going to kill the deal. Their lawyers don't stop working. Your office doesn't close. But what if that crash wasn't an accident? What if it was a warning?"

"*That's* why you're here?" Maureen rubbed her face, pressing her fingertips into the flesh below her eyes. "You think those boys were murdered? Why?"

"To arouse suspicions. To fan the flames of misunderstanding—I read that line in one of *your* newspapers recently. To eliminate what little common ground exists. I don't know, yet."

"*Yet*? You're seriously investigating this angle?"

Billy shrugged and shifted gears. "NFDI thought it was worth following up, whether your police do or not. It's typical in a race-based dynamic for authorities to ignore evidence that points to hate crimes, even when *they* commit the crime. Remember Saskatoon? Your police force here is mostly white. It sees and reacts to situations through that filter. When Kenny Jacobs comes out of his coma I plan to interview him. So far it's just hints."

"I don't believe this. What kind of *hints*?" Maureen watched the sunlight sparkle off the Slough. The mill stacks stood reflected in the flat surface, reaching for her like the fingers of a giant hand.

"Denial is another hallmark of racist cultures," Billy said. "The majority can't see the obvious. They're blinded by color, by their history and by their shared experience, even the most liberal among them. It's not your fault. I've seen it everywhere I go and no, I don't think the RCMP are involved. This time." He shot her a quick smile. "I'm also willing to give *you* the benefit of the doubt." His teeth were dazzling bright.

"Don't do me any favors," Maureen said. "If it wasn't an accident where's the media clip claiming responsibility? Where's the manifesto? Why hasn't anyone come forward?"

Billy's smile vanished. "How do you know they haven't?"

Maureen rolled her eyes. "You're quick with riddles because you have nothing else. Stop this Goddamned SUV and let me out."

"That's low," Billy said. He looked hurt. "This jeep is a back to the land vehicle. I can go anywhere, it runs on bio-fuel, gets great mileage, and only puts out half the greenhouse gases of those monster SUV's."

"Congratulations. Just let me out. Here is perfect." Maureen pointed to the sidewalk.

The jeep braked to a stop opposite Canal Slats.

"See you around, Cage." Billy waved as the jeep sped away.

She avoided crossing the highway until she was past the Timberman Hotel and its neon, zig-zag arrow that telescoped toward the side door entrance to Canal Slats. She stopped and watched the light show and saw the Raven's tattoo in neon relief. Halfway up the hill she had to stop again to dig a stone out of her shoe—a tiny ovoid of gravel that had insinuated itself under her big toe. For support she rested her hand against the nearest brick wall. Heat rolled off the building. She held her shoe like a hammer and struck its heel against the wall repeatedly—long after the pebble had fallen out. The heel came off on the fifth blow. She hit the wall twice more—cursing out loud—pulled off the other shoe and resumed her hike toward the hotel in stocking feet.

At the Queen Anne she wrestled her suitcase from her car. She dragged it to Reception and dumped the broken shoe on the counter. "I need my room back," she said.

The desk clerk handed her a new card key, his glance wandering from the broken shoe, dusty, perspiration-soaked clothes to her flushed and over-heated complexion. "Need a tow truck?"

Maureen ignored him, bundling her possessions into the elevator. As she dragged her suitcase along the carpeted hallway to her room she rehearsed what she was going to tell RG—once he figured out she had no intention of leaving Port McKenzie.

Maureen pulled open the front door. "I'm coming out-"

The black-clad shapes of Victoria's *SWAT* team tackled her, knocking her backwards. Their strong arms twisted her arms behind her back and pushed her face into the floor. At the extreme edge of vision more riot-geared officers appeared; she heard shouts as they pinned the Raven to the living room carpet. Their arms rose, their riot sticks hovered, as if momentarily suspended by the thickening air.

"Stop," Maureen said. "She didn't-"

For an instant she was off the floor, rising, lifted by many hands until all motion reversed and the left side of her face slammed against the floor. A pit opened—to a sound of an old bed sheet tearing—and blackness swallowed everything, even the diamonds floating above her head.

BOOK THREE

Mother's Day

A lone, female police constable escorted Maureen down the length of a bare, brightly lit corridor. She walked slowly, with a hitch in her step, so that Maureen had enough room to use her crutches. She stopped at the last door and tapped the business end of her nightstick against its dull, metal surface. Trip hammers went off in Maureen's skull.

She had no memory of arriving; didn't know whether this was hospital, jail or someplace in between; whether she was still in Victoria or back in Vancouver. Through her squinting, weepy eyes the walls, the ceiling, the floor—everything looked runny. Not long before there had been nurses and a needle, but her head still throbbed from the sickening pain and it hurt to think, to remember. As it hurt now, recalling the narrow, sagging bed in a cramped, windowless room. She'd thrown up into a steel bowl they'd set on the table beside the bed. She could still taste Demerol and stale cigarette smoke.

The door in the hallway opened inward. A second officer stepped aside to allow Maureen an entrance. The door latched shut behind her with a painful snap.

"You can leave us alone, thanks," Inspector Legare said.

The officers waited for Maureen to lean her crutches against the table and lower herself into the chair opposite Legare before vanishing into the hall. Maureen cringed as the door swung shut, but the knob twisted, mated with the frame without a sound. Maureen exhaled and slumped across the table.

"They'll be watching us anyway," Legare said. He gestured over his shoulder to the mirror on the wall behind him. A smile made him look younger—rookie-clean in his white, short-sleeved shirt and butterscotch paisley tie. His hands settled—the left nesting on top of the right—onto a closed, manila folder. They were soft hands, scrubbed pink to match his doughy, eager face.

"Good to see you again," he said.

Maureen found a free booth in the Millhouse Coffee Shop. The place was the tail end of busy—the day shift at the Port McKenzie mill was mostly through breakfast or already lining up to pay. They came for the huge plates of eggs and bacon, sausages and slabs of buttered toast and bottomless mugs of the best coffee in town—all for the same four ninety-nine they'd been paying since ninety-nine—the start of the last big bust. Maureen ordered fruit salad and coffee, though on rare, extravagant occasions she'd been known to splurge for a boiled egg and side order of dry toast. The cooking smells were hard to resist. How many other converted Vegetarians were haunted to the edge of despair by the aroma of frying bacon? Giving in to an order of fried tomatoes was to court disaster.

There had been another diner—long ago—where plates clattered against Formica-topped tables and the cutlery jangled like spilled pennies. The air was laden with sweet cooking smells. It was winter—all her memories were winter—and she was in her too-small snowsuit. Her mother set her thick, awkward body into the corner of the booth and helped her unzip her mittens and hood. The coffee came, for them, and a white china mug of hot chocolate, loaded with miniature marshmallows, for her.

They went every Sunday after church. The place overflowed with hungry parishioners, their souls renewed; it was time to replenish their bodies. Every week the same booth. She would ignore her porridge and play with a tear in the vinyl seat, pulling out tufts of matted, grey fibres while her parents ate their eggs. Another six months and the shallow split would become a hollow large enough to fit her whole hand. Her father never used a napkin until he was completely done. Always a droplet of egg yolk or a spray of toast crumbs or jam on his sharp chin. He looked nowhere but at her mother. He couldn't breathe if she wasn't in view and he barely drew breath when she was. Only after he'd scraped his plate clean, licked his fork and knife and laid them across his plate like he was constructing a capital letter *Q* would he pull the napkin off his lap and scrub his mouth, his jaw and finally, his hands, and dump the crumpled paper onto his plate then reach over to take both of his wife's small hands into his own.

After her mother got sick he never used a napkin. He barely remembered how to use a fork. He was useless without her. He would weep into his rye every night. Maureen heard him from the bedroom; from the middle of her hard bed, where she lay, doll-stiff, unable to sleep. While she stared at the ceiling through the eyes of a five year old he drank and explained it to the both of them in a loud, broken voice that blew through the flimsy bedroom door that separated them.

Your mother's body plain burned up, like paper in a campfire. Run dry of the stuff of life. You and me, we took too much out of her, needing her so much. The cancer never killed her: we loved her to death.

We killed her.

Maureen shifted her weight, but the chair was hard and straight and knuckled into the bruises on the backs of her thighs and around her kidneys. Where the *SWAT* team had landed on her. A cushion would have been nice. She wiggled the chair closer to the table and propped her elbows in front of her. It was an awkward position, with her bandaged leg stretched forward, but it was less painful. She used the back of the chair like a splint, forcing her spine straight as she rested her head in the cradle of her right hand and blinked to avoid the light.

Legare pushed a box of tissue across the table. Maureen yanked three from the box and dabbed at her eyes. The left side of her face was swollen and the ache pulsed through the bones, into her teeth and ear. The ringing, though fainter, never ceased.

"Where's my lawyer?" She spoke in a weak voice through clenched jaws. The hum through her vocal chords sent darts of pain into her head. Her body teetered on the verge of sickness.

"That I don't know," Legare said, swatting her question aside. His hand settled back onto the folder. "I'm sure someone's taken care of it. Just a few answers, Ms. Cage and I'll be on my way." He smiled as he opened the document folder and held the first page at the top corner, as if it were something fragile.

"I want my lawyer—any lawyer," she said, "before I say a word." Every syllable transmitted pain through her face.

The hospital trip came back first: waiting hours for a nurse to come and clean her up, wrap her knee in ice and give her drugs for the pain. Another interminable wait for a doctor to examine her face. He'd ordered an x-ray, diagnosed concussion, dispensed a handful of painkillers and given the bottle to the police officer assigned to stay with her. No broken bones in her face or jaw. Her knee was going to need surgery, but that could take weeks, what with the strike and the wait lists. Then another ride in the back of a police van and a feverish night in the tiny room down the hall. The drugs were wearing off and the morning wasn't looking any better.

"That's right," Legare said. "You're not a lawyer are you?" He pushed the top two pages from the manila folder across the table. "Still, you don't need a lawyer to read. Take it. It's a draft of my final report. Consider this an advance screening."

Maureen drank her Millhouse coffee with both hands wrapped around the mug. The heat eased the dull, arthritic ache in her knuckles. Her hands hurt all the time, summer and winter. It was worse in the middle joints of her fingers. Sometimes, when she stretched them out and looked closely, she could chart the progress of the arthritis: the gentle, insistent twisting of the bones; her fingernails angling toward each other like small, buffed paving stones heaved by invisible roots. Since she'd turned forty the process seemed to be accelerating.

Aaron came out of nowhere and threw himself onto the opposite bench. He ordered the House Special, eggs over easy, and apologized for being late.

It took Maureen a moment to back out of her memories. "I was early," she said. "Where's Sarah?"

Aaron shrugged and dumped four teaspoons of sugar into his coffee. "Haven't seen her since yesterday afternoon. You missed the food. Good spread. Who'd you take off with?"

Maureen held out her mug under the waitress' pot until the coffee splashed against the rim. "What do you know about the NFDI?"

Aaron made a sour face. "They got all the headlines in Seattle and Quebec City. Did most of the damage in those riots, from what I read, but who knows, right? Is he one of them?"

Maureen nodded.

"Why's he in Port?"

"I don't know," Maureen said. She looked away. She spotted Sarah entering the coffee shop. "He seems to know a little something about our treaty process."

Sarah slid next to Aaron. She signaled the waitress and leaned across the table, squinting into Maureen's face. "Have a good time? I should have remembered how great funerals are for picking up younger guys."

"Shut up. He knew me," Maureen said.

"O yeah, from the papers," Sarah said. A faint smile danced at the corners of her mouth.

The waitress returned with Aaron's food and waited for Sarah to order. *The Fastest Breakfast in Town,* the Millhouse menu boasted. Sarah asked for a toasted bagel and orange juice. "Why would William Last Man Standing want to talk to you?"

"So you know him?" Maureen said.

"I know he goes for older women," Sarah said. Aaron cringed.

"Go to Hell," Maureen said. A vein in her neck throbbed.

"Just kidding, Boss." Sarah put all the emphasis on the last word. "RG called this morning. He asked if you were on your way back."

"What did you tell him?"

"Relax, Boss," Sarah said. Her smile grew. "I told him you'd been tagged by the NFDI and were conducting some detailed research. He was okay with that. As long as you're outta here today."

"I know," Maureen said. "The timing sucks."

Sarah tossed her a dismissive wave. "That's nothing. RG says Templeton called. The Federation is down for the count."

"It can't be," Maureen said.

"It's done. Last night." Sarah snapped her fingers. "Templeton's faxed a preliminary submission for establishing Interims with each of the Federation members, one at a time."

"Then the AIP's dead," Aaron said. "We'll never get a Final without the Federation."

"Templeton's hands are tied, and he's loving it," Sarah said. "The crash has made the Tse Wets Aht jumpy. So we go with the flow. RG wants us to switch gears and begin the side tables right away." She glanced at Aaron. "Well, my brother from another mother, we are going to be here a very long time."

"I'll stay," Maureen said. "I need to speak to Chief David. She's over-reacting. She's being dictated to by outsiders with private agendas."

"We don't exactly come across as the Swiss," Sarah said. She held up her hand and pointed to the window. "RG said it more than once: you're done in Port. 'til the fuss over the accident dies down. Don't screw things up any worse. It's always Aaron and me who have to pick up the pieces."

Maureen slid across the bench and stood over Sarah. "It's the conscientious, caring staff around me that makes this job such a joy," she said. She turned her back and stalked out of the coffee shop.

Maureen reached for Legare's folder. She dragged the document between her elbows, opened it. The words were a black blur, like spilled ink. She squinted, leaning closer. She deciphered the word collusion and sat back, exhausted. She pushed the report toward Legare. Nausea rocked her stomach.

Legare made a disapproving sound with his tongue against his front teeth. He snatched the pages off the table and held them at arm's length in front of his face. "I'll summarize," he said. His smile gave her the impression he was enjoying this very much.

"This was looking like a random act—an accident, not a hate crime—until I heard about a fight at a strip bar a few hours before. It seems that there was bad blood between the victims and a group at the club who, I discovered, have a connection to the stripper who survived the crash. And wonder of wonders, I found they all belong to the same illegal, racist organization. I checked out each of them and, aside from a truckload of assaults, theft and petty crime, one of the most interesting things that stood out was a complaint, filed by a Ms. Maureen Cage for the purported theft of a gold lighter. As it happens, I was fortunate enough to interview Kenny Jacob, during his short window of consciousness. He was difficult to understand, but I pieced enough together to learn that he'd seen that lighter less than four hours before the accident. I then followed up with Mr. Arnold and his Heritage League associates. Both he and a Rick St. Clair acted like they'd seen it before, though they denied it. They were protecting you as well as themselves."

Legare removed a plastic bag from his pocket. It contained a slim lighter. Her lighter. Without removing it from the bag he turned it over. "*F.A.P. June 1962, Your Darling Angel,*" he read. "It's beautiful," he added.

He used both hands to open the lid and pull the fuel chamber out of the gold case. He set down the bag, carefully. It glowed with buttery warmth, even through the plastic bag.

Port McKenzie was not a big town. The roads were wide—almost highways—and the paved driveways that led to each residence that Maureen passed were large enough to store a boat and trailer, a camper, a second—even third—car with room to spare. Since the last slump Port had the feel of an elastic drawstring stretched too far: unable to snap back to its former vigor it sagged, with nothing but the smell of an ageing mill to fill the void.

The waitress from Canal Slats lived in a cluster of apartment buildings that surrounded the hospital—a smaller, poorer cousin to Central Island Regional, more walk-in clinic than hospital. Maureen had got her name the day before from the clerk at the front desk of the Timberman Hotel. The Port McKenzie phone book had supplied the rest. She parked at the curb in front of a three storey wood frame apartment block. She double-checked the address and triple-checked her reflection in the rear view mirror. She rubbed at the oily glow on her forehead. She crossed the sidewalk and followed a concrete path between two squares of dandelion-infested lawn. While the grass had long ago died, the weeds still flourished. Hundreds of yellow, pancake flowers covered the scorched flats.

A glass door was propped open with a wooden block. A lopsided *Vacancy* sign had been taped to the glass, invisible from the street as long as the door was open. Maureen ignored the intercom and took the stairs to the second floor. The once-white walls were deeply smudged two-and-a-half feet off the floor: it seemed that children were as invasive as the dandelions.

Maureen stopped in front of apartment two-fourteen. The door opened quickly, as if she'd been expected. A woman filled the space between the door and the frame. She held a small, dark-haired girl in her arms. The child's round face was blotchy and red, with the puffy, rubbery fullness of fresh tears.

"What is it?" The woman spoke quickly, her voice a hissing whisper.

"Sandy Harrison? My name is Maureen Cage. I'd like to ask you about the accident."

"Again?" The woman's expression changed. The twig-thin line of her eyebrows arched. "I get it."

Maureen frowned. "Can I come in?"

She shook her head. "My boyfriend's trying to sleep. It wouldn't be good to wake him twice." Sandy began to rock the girl. The baby laid her cheek against the woman's collarbone and stared at Maureen.

"Can I come back later?"

"I work the lunch shift today. Eleven-thirty to four. I can talk to you then."

"Fine." Maureen stepped back from the door.

Sandy threw a hurried look into the depths of the apartment, then stepped into the hall and shut the door behind her. She beckoned for Maureen to come closer. "Let's get this over with. I saw you at the funeral too. How is Kenny?" she whispered.

"Unconscious, from what I've heard," Maureen said.

"Those boys were regulars," Sandy said. "Good customers. Harmless."

"Weren't they underage?"

"Only Kenny. The others—a year either way. Up 'til last year every customer counted."

"Did they always try and buy dancers?"

"Never," Sandy said. She snorted. "They worked hard. Maybe one or two beers on Friday nights. Henry told me he was going be rich after October, when the land claims deal got done. He'd saved to buy his uncle's fish boat, was going after the license. They wanted to celebrate."

"They came back at closing time. After the fight."

"You know about that. Yeah, it wasn't their fault," Sandy said. She leaned back, letting her flexed hip take the child's weight. The arms that circled the girl's body were lean and strong.

"The guys who started it, are they regulars?"

"They work at the mill, or used to. They're assholes."

"I know. One of them stole something from me."

"Let me guess," Sandy said. "Larry Arnold. A right prick. Racist bastard and a thief. He grew up here. Moved away a few years back. Rick St. Clair and Gordy MacMillan aren't much better. Did you tell the cops?"

"I filed a report," Maureen said, "but I don't think it's one of their higher priorities."

"The good thing is they won't be back awhile, not after the damage they caused."

"You knew the Tse Wets Aht boys well?"

Sandy smiled, turned her head toward the child's face and kissed her on the forehead. "Yeah. Henry was an old friend," she said. "We were always in the same classes in high school—the dummy class—'til he dropped out. Henry was smarter than all of us." Her voice trembled. "We kept in touch, though."

"Sorry," Maureen said. She looked away.

"I just hope Kenny makes it."

"The men from the mill. They're connected somehow?"

"Sure. They're all losers. We all know each other, been to school together, you know, Port's a small town. Larry says that stripper, Raven, she's his girl. She's a Mainlander. Never seen her in Port before."

"How can you tell?"

Sandy smiled. Her glance ran the length of Maureen's body. "Easy. Clothes, hands, the way they walk, the way they talk."

A muffled shout leaked through the door. The child's head lifted up off Sandy's shoulder. Sandy caressed the girl's dark hair and made cooing sounds into her ear.

"I gotta go." Sandy winced, and slipped into the apartment, both arms tight around the child.

Maureen waited for a moment at the closed door. Silence leaked through the walls and the tightness in her chest eased. She followed the greasy smudges to the exit. She dumped her map—the *McKenzie Valley Chamber of Commerce Tourist Map* with its participating businesses shown in exploded view—onto the passenger seat and shifted into drive. Her foot jumped to the brake. Billy Last Man Standing spread his hands across the hood, blocking her way.

She leaned her head out the window. "You're following me."

"Who's following who? Whom? Who? English was never my best subject."

"Whom. You just talked to her, didn't you?" Maureen said.

Billy made a face. "Aren't you the one who told me there wasn't anything unusual about the crash?"

"There isn't. This is the second time you *happen* to bump into me. Have your people bugged my hotel room?"

Billy laughed. "Which people? My brothers and sisters, or my comrades in arms?"

"Your NFDI trouble-makers," Maureen said. "Or have the Tse Wets Aht hired you?"

"You're playing detective," Billy said. "The papers say that's not in your job description."

"My job is research."

"You're helping the RCMP?"

"I was visiting a friend."

The muscles in Billy's neck stretched as he laughed. "I think we should work together," he said.

"We're on opposite sides," Maureen said.

"No, we both want the truth," Billy said. "Where were you going?"

"You tell me," Maureen said. She took her foot off the brake. The Subaru started to roll forward.

"Okay, then. The shit-holes from the mill," Billy said, jogging to keep level with her. "The ones that started the fight. I think they followed Henry and Kenny. Maybe to get the girl back."

"I was there," Maureen said. She watched his eyebrows arch. "Right up to when the fight started. You're just guessing about what happened after."

"So you're going to check them out," Billy said. "I'd pay to see that. But you're coming with me instead."

"Why?" Maureen jammed her foot onto the brake pedal.

"Kenny Jacobs just woke up."

"I found it nearly half a kilometre from the crash. I ran fingerprints. The case was smudged, it had been handled too much. But I got one, perfect thumb print off the inner sleeve. It belongs to a Theresa Marie Pistilli, born November sixteenth, nineteen-sixty-five in Windsor, Ontario. Daughter to Françesco Alberto Pistilli and Marjorie Anne Whitelaw. You're still with me, I assume."

A roaring noise filled Maureen's head—a sound like a tower of stones collapsing—and her lungs leaked air in erratic, gasping spurts.

"Theresa had a tough life," Legare said. He set down the report and leaned back in his chair to stretch his legs. "At five her mother dies. Cancer. Her father, Françesco, drinks himself to death, but it takes him twenty-odd years to finish the job. In the short term things get so bad at home our Theresa is shuffled from one foster home to another until she runs away and lives on the streets. She's arrested in Toronto seven times for theft. They bring her back twice, put her in different homes, but she keeps disappearing. So they stop trying. She finally shows up in Vancouver in the 'eighties and is arrested again. This time for theft *and* prostitution. The last arrest report is in 'ninety-one. Please, feel free to stop me if I'm missing anything," he said and paused long enough to crack a wide smile.

Billy's jeep pulled into the hospital parking lot a little after noon. The skeleton picket line offered no resistance and they bypassed reception to take the elevator to the sixth floor. A wilted paper sign that warned patients about the broken air conditioning system curled in the humidity around the stick of tape that pinned it to the elevator wall. The air grew noticeably warmer as they ascended and was no cooler in the hallway.

"She's not welcome," Josephine David shouted. She stood across from the elevator at the nurses' station. "I invited only you, Billy."

"She's with us," Billy said. "She knows this was no accident."

Josephine squinted at Maureen. "I don't believe that."

"Good. Neither do I," Maureen said. "Billy said he could convince me."

Josephine blocked the hallway. "She's looking for a promotion. Not at our expense."

"I want a Final," Maureen said. "Get your Federation together and restart the main table before it's too late."

"Don't tell me what to do," Josephine said. She stepped close to Maureen and stuck a long finger under her nose. "Federation members can negotiate as many Interims as they want. We need to protect our fish and forests. Remember the Nisga'a? Their agreement got passed around to every social engineer with a hard-on. The papers tried to make it look like they were stealing, like they were spoiled kids. With their own land and resources. Screw that. The Tse Wets Aht will look after themselves, with or without the Federation."

"You still need a Final Agreement," Maureen said. "There's no time for games."

"We have been here longest. We know what games the White Man plays," Josephine said. "An election's coming. Hargrove's term runs out a week before our deadline. Think that was an accident? We knew when we signed the AIP that we were walking into a set-up. Matthew warned us of the risks, but it was too good to pass up, so we signed the deal. But he was right, and it's taken three deaths for me to figure it out."

"There was no set-up," Maureen said. The pounding of her heart echoed in her ears.

"You're saying the note's a fake?" Josephine turned on Billy. "What have you been telling her?"

Billy held up both hands. "She didn't hear from me," he said.

"What note?" Maureen said. "*Dee-Faz* can help you, but you have to cooperate."

"*Cooperate?*" Josephine's eyes flashed. "There will never be a Final," she said. "Victoria and Ottawa won't let it happen. Since the AIP was signed we've lost three years worth of timber, not to mention countless tonnes of salmon. All for trying to piss up a rope." The muscles at the base of her jaw bunched and released. "It's over. We won't bury any more of our children without guarantees. Not while the crazies are out there."

"Nobody gets guarantees," Maureen said. "Not until there's a Final."

"Easy, Cage," Billy stepped between them.

"Get her out of here, Billy, or go with her." Josephine spun on the soles of her boots and stalked down the corridor.

Maureen's legs were weak. "You covering my cab fare?"

"Take the bus." Josephine hurled the retort over her shoulder.

Billy laid his hand on Maureen's arm. "Wait for me. I know this is low, but wait."

Maureen shook off his hand. She retreated to the elevator. Her finger jack-hammered the *Down* button. As the doors slid shut with a sigh she pushed *G*, raised her hand and quickly held the button for the fifth floor. The doors opened one floor down.

She slipped between wheelchairs of heat-struck patients arranged the length of the hallway like backlogged valet parking. Giant fans were positioned at opposite ends of the corridor and blew air over the slumping shapes, some shiny with perspiration. Others clung to glasses of ice water and sucked noisily on bent straws. One or two fanned themselves with magazines. All of them ignored her as she passed.

There were no wheelchairs outside Raven's door. Only a chrome and vinyl chair, filled by a neatly dressed young man. He thumbed through a magazine. He looked up as Maureen approached.

"Sorry, Ma'am. No one but family allowed inside."

"But I am—family."

The man let the magazine slide onto the chair as he rose. He was large enough to make a living playing professional football. He stepped between Maureen and the door to Raven's room. "May I see some ID, please?"

"Who are you?" Maureen countered. She did not open her purse.

"Security."

"She hired you?"

"Your ID, Ma'am."

"Forget it. Tell her Maureen came by. She wants her lighter back." She turned and in full retreat dodged the wheelchairs lining the corridor.

The Nanaimo bus station waiting room was an add-on, tucked behind the Lucky Strike Hotel and the Cold Beer and Wine Store. The carpet looked like a giant rust stain, and its vanilla walls were matched by equally vanilla *muzak* piped through speakers in the cracked ceiling. If it weren't for her car still parked in front of Sandy Harrison's apartment she'd have bought a ticket for Vancouver, but instead Maureen paid sixteen dollars for a ticket on the four PM bus back to Port and slumped onto a cracked vinyl chair. Her head bumped against the wall. At least the air conditioning worked. It rattled noisily on the far wall.

Maureen fought the temptation to cross through the hotel lobby to the pub. That first glass of wine with Carole had been delicious: she'd shivered as it coated her lips and mouth. It had burned going down her throat. She'd read somewhere that every cell in a healthy human body was replaced each five to six years. If that were true it was likely that not a single one of her cells had known alcohol until Thursday evening. Could memory alone bring back a craving with such gnawing persistence?

She stared outside at the shimmering asphalt. The air conditioning's sputtering cough taunted the waves of heat rising out of the pavement. She needed to be home. She needed to lock herself inside her house; to slow things down and regain her grip. She had to pull herself tighter, like the string on a guitar in need of tuning. She was coming undone from the persistent, prying fingers of circumstance and the weight of awkward memories. She imagined a bus rolling into the space between the faded white lines of Bay Number Two. Over and over, she pictured the incoming bus. One of these times she'd be right.

"I should have looked here first but I didn't picture you as bus riding public," Billy said as he strode through the door. His teeth were even brighter under the fluorescent lights.

"Bugger off," Maureen said. She shifted in her chair to look the other way.

Billy dropped into the empty seat beside her. He stretched his legs and wiggled his bare toes through the straps of his Birkenstocks. Strands of curling, black hair dusted the knuckles of each toe.

Maureen shifted again.

"You never answered your phone," he said. "Look. I'm sorry. It wasn't my idea," Billy said, "but I couldn't miss out on the chance."

"You don't owe me any explanations."

"No. But I owe you a ride back to Port." He snatched the bus ticket out of her fist and ran to the ticket window with a whooping cry.

She swallowed the protest forming in her throat. She inhaled his long legs, the inverted triangle of shoulders and hips and the black swan-neck of his pony tail. She let him cash in her ticket. She let him arrange the money in her palm, his cool fingers closing hers around the cash. She badly wanted him to drive her back to Port.

"No more police records. But there's a hospital admissions report attached to the end of her police file. Apparently Theresa nearly died in a car wreck on April sixth, nineteen ninety-one. She was the driver. The lone passenger, a Bradley David Stewart, whose police file is ten times as thick as Theresa's, was killed. A downtown pimp, pusher and all-round low-life, until Theresa separates his head from his body using the closest telephone pole. His head ends up half a block from the wreck. Tests find no alcohol or drugs in Theresa's system. Murder-suicide, they figured. Only the suicide part got botched."

"Or not," she said, but it came out a weary moan.

"Sorry?" Legare's eyebrows arched. He raised his arms and laced his fingers together behind his head. "Anyway, soon after she gets out of hospital our Theresa becomes a stripper. Signs up with A&H Agencies. They're still around, by the way, but they don't seem to remember her.

Legare smiled, a wide, ingratiating grin that looked like he'd kept the best for last. "Funny thing, though, soon after our Theresa vanishes. Poof. Gone. No credit cards, no car insurance, no medical, no tax returns, no bank records. It's like she died and nobody noticed."

They were better than halfway back to Port when Billy mentioned Kenny Jacob. Maureen had refused to ask and he'd not volunteered until they reached a stretch of winding highway that clung to a bare expanse of rock. A narrow strip of shale below them glistened wet where the waves of a tiny, splinter-shaped lake slapped the shore. Boats drifted as their lone occupants waited for a bite, bound to the lake by arcs of taut fishing line.

"He's in pretty bad shape."

"Who?" Maureen said. She lowered her sunglasses and squinted at Billy.

Billy glanced at her, licked his lips and turned away to watch the road. He kept the jeep tight against the yellow line. The cliff face flashed past, streaked by dark water stains. "Kenny. He was only conscious a few minutes."

"Is he going to make it?"

"I don't know." The silence returned. "He says there was another truck."

Maureen stared across the lake. They had come to the place where open water ended, to a marsh full of reeds and skunk cabbage and mud. It smelled of rotting plants and slime. She saw herself sinking into the muck, her arms useless, her legs immobilized. She went very still, slowing the inevitable, but there was no way out of the ooze. Days ago a Final Agreement had been close enough to touch: there, just beyond the reach of her outstretched hand. No chance, now. Every move she made sank her deeper into quicksand.

Billy raced the jeep through a tricky chicane. "It pushed them off the road."

"He said so? He's sure?" Maureen held onto the dash to keep her body in the seat. The skin across her knuckles flexed and stretched as the jeep sped through the turns.

"As sure as anyone pumped full of morphine with a brain the size of a melon."

"Maybe he's delusional."

"Maybe," Billy glanced her way, "you're in denial."

"I think not. Do the police know?"

"Jo called them. She was ranting at somebody when I left to look for you."

"They'll never come back," she said to the spikes of skunk cabbage. "I'm finished."

"Maybe this homicide's more important than a settlement right now. It was a deliberate hate crime."

"Homicide! You can't prove that!" Maureen pounded the dash with her fist. "Nobody knows anything, you especially! Even if he is remembering—not imagining or repeating what you and the others have whispered in his ear—it still could have been an accident. Maybe the Raven's jealous boyfriend followed them. Or a drunk from another bar."

"Then explain this," Billy said. He leaned across her, opened the dash and pulled out an envelope. "Open it."

Maureen pulled a single white sheet of paper from the envelope. It was blank on one side. She threw Billy an anxious glance as she unfolded it. "Where did you get this?"

"Have you read it?"

"'*Jack fell down and broke his crown and Jill came tumbling after. The closer you get the worse it will get. The Pure will reclaim what is rightfully Theirs. Death to every Savage and Their Indian-loving Friends.*' Where did you get this?"

"Josephine got it the day before the funerals."

"Do the police know?"

"Are you kidding? We're handling it."

"Billy, the police need to know. Josephine needs police protection."

Billy shook his head. "Cage, you just don't get it. More natives have died at the hands of the police than by any other group, association, army or gang. The Tse Wets Aht know what they're doing. They know how to protect their own."

"Who sent this? Did Kenny know?"

"He didn't say, exactly. He's in pretty rough shape. What the pavement didn't damage Raven did. She landed on him pretty hard."

"What do you think?"

Billy blew air through his pursed lips. "Me? Heritage League. Gotta be. They're active in Western Canada again. They're no social club."

"Never heard of them," Maureen said too quickly, fixing her stare on the forest fringe along the highway's shoulder. The odor of skunk cabbage and standing water was behind them.

"They're a White Supremacy organization. Strong in the States, in Idaho, Montana and Colorado, connected with the *KKK* and *Aryan Nations*. The Canadian version of the Heritage League started in Alberta."

"You knew they were in Port," Maureen said.

Billy exhaled. "We had suspicions. I'm still putting it together. Kenny said something I have to check out."

"What?" Maureen held on tighter, though they had left behind the curves of the lake shore.

"He kept going on about a tattoo. *Circle of flames,* he said. He went under right after."

"Circle of flames?" Maureen said. Her mouth was dry.

"Yeah. Sounds like Heritage League. Their symbol is a flaming globe surrounding a broken spear or lightning bolt. It's supposed to be the Wrath of God, punishing those who threaten the purity of the Aryan race. Pure crap is what it is. So many of these groups use mystical Christian images with no clue about their real meaning."

"The Raven has that tattoo on her shoulder," Maureen said.

Billy shot her a hard look. "You're sure?"

"I've seen it. Twice. A lightning bolt surrounded by flames. It looked new."

"Jesus."

"That's why you're here, isn't it?"

Billy avoided her glance. "Maybe," he said. "But I wish it wasn't."

"But now it gets interesting," Legare purred.

Maureen hid her face in the palms of her hands. The smell of sweat in her nostrils had a pungent, sickly sweetness to it, like when she was feverish with flu.

"There's no trace of Theresa," Legare said, "until this lighter shows up. I figure she's passed the years as a stripper, dancing in the Boonies. Maybe got married to a logger somewhere, lived happily ever after. But then I check Theresa's file again and I find that the last foster family she lived with went by the name Cage. Just outside of Windsor, Ontario, across the line from Detroit. Imagine my surprise when I find out they had a daughter named Maureen."

They drove in silence. Maureen wrapped her arms around her sides as the jeep raced through patches of deep shade thrown up by stands of fir, hemlock and cedar. A chill touched her skin, raised goose bumps on her arms. She actually missed the itchy heat. Maureen unfolded her arms when they came out of the trees and began their descent into the McKenzie Valley. She pressed her palms into the dashboard. She inhaled the warm air, the mill smell hung lightly on the upper rim of the valley.

"Do you want to catch a meal?" Billy said.

Maureen blinked. "Are you asking me out?"

Billy laughed. "Okay, I'll bite. Sure. But I've gotta eat and so do you."

"How old are you?" Maureen said.

"Twenty-nine. Look, I know you're older than me. But I'm good with that."

"How old am I?"

Billy raised his shoulders and let them drop carelessly. "Thirty-five, thirty-seven at the outside." He winked.

"I'm nearly forty-five. Way outside."

"No shit! My mom's forty-six," he said.

"Terrific," Maureen said. "I can't figure out which one of us needs counseling more."

When Billy laughed strands of his dark hair fell forward, grazing his forehead. He swept away the stray locks, tucking the longest pieces behind his right ear. He shifted gears as they took a sharp turn and began the steeper descent. "Both. But we still have to eat."

"I'm leaving Port," Maureen said. "I'm in enough trouble with my boss without hanging around some under-aged, radical, fringe-funded, Nazi-chasing, eco-freak activist from the U.S. of A. No offense."

"None taken," Billy said with a grin and a shrug.

Maureen studied the columns of evergreen bordering the highway. Their downswept branches caught the sunlight and threw deep shadows into the forest behind. "It's time I figured some things out," she said.

"If you ask me, you're trying too hard. I know meditation, healing touch, massage. I had the best teachers: Oglala Sioux, Cheyenne, Ojibwa, Zen Buddhist."

"Thanks, no," Maureen said. "I'll do this my way."

"Physician, heal thyself!" He chuckled to himself as the jeep accelerated past the cemetery. After a minute of silence he looked at her. "No one can truly enlighten oneself. It requires a teacher. A Spirit Guide."

"So says you."

Billy smiled. "I sense resistance, Cage. I am not just wise in Native American Spirituality. All civilizations have their own wisdom, and the means to achieve it. Most have lost the connection to their source wisdom. Look, even your ancestors had their shamans. Odin, the Raven Master, was a great teacher. He seized the runes from the void. He discovered the secrets of the Universe locked inside them."

"What makes you think I've got Scandinavian roots?"

"Only your name. It's Old English. Most of those names began as Norse or Germanic. Out of the northern tribes. Look at you: tall, big-boned. I can picture you in furs and silver armbands."

"Am I wearing anything else in this fantasy of yours? Perhaps wielding a massive sword? You watch too much wrestling on TV."

"I'm trying to be serious," Billy said. "I can help you attain the enlightenment you so desperately seek."

"Now you really are dreaming," Maureen said. "And you're way off about my roots," she added. "Just get me back to my car."

"Good. You're setting boundaries. We're getting somewhere," Billy said. The jeep turned onto the block of Sandy Harrison's apartment. "I had a teacher, an old Buddhist monk in California. He told me-"

"Save it, okay?" Maureen held up one hand. "I got it. It's nothing I haven't heard before. I'm more enlightened than you think." She pushed on the door of the jeep and jumped out. Her hip tweaked. "Thanks for the ride, I suppose it was better than the bus."

Billy grinned at her through his perfect teeth. "Anytime. We still good for dinner?"

Maureen jumped. The shaking in her hands was getting worse.

"Maureen Elizabeth Cage died in Windsor in May 'seventy-five. She was killed by a car as she hiked home the night of her graduation party. One year later Theresa Pistilli came to live with the Cage family—a foster child, a runaway. I spoke with Maureen's brother. He still lives in Windsor. He's divorced, living on social assistance. When I asked him about Theresa he closed up, wouldn't say much, only that she stole his parents' car and some money and was a compulsive liar and that if I found her, not to believe a word she said. He'd heard she was a hooker in Calgary or Vancouver and was probably dead by now."

Maureen pressed her hands to her face. She wanted to peel away the flesh like a mask, to reach in through her eye sockets and pluck out the stones that ground against the inside of her skull. Watery, choking sounds bubbled in her throat.

The desk clerk at the Queen Anne Hotel had to chase her to the elevator to make sure she got the message. Maureen opened the envelope and frowned at the outline of the retreating clerk as the elevator doors whisked apart. A single row of tight, slanted letters formed the words *When you get in. Room 320.*

RG's handwriting. She crushed the note in her fist as she stepped into the elevator. So much for her dinner date.

She knocked on RG's door. It swung inward with enough force to snuff a candle flame. RG waved her inside. He shouted into a cell phone, stuck like a shiny tumor against his ear.

"No, Emily, that's not good enough," he said. He gestured at one of two chairs beside a table, then paced to the open window.

Maureen slid into the chair and pressed her sandaled feet into the carpet.

"This wouldn't have happened if you'd kept your promise." Tension gripped his voice. "Maybe we can pretend to be a family for what's left of this Goddamned summer! Or am I asking too much?" He snapped shut the phone and pitched it onto the bed. He leaned out the window, arms angled to support the weight of his chest and shoulders.

"Sorry," he said. He straightened and faced her. "Family matters."

Maureen nodded, but said nothing, preferring the momentary silence.

He dropped into the chair across from her, flipping it around so that his forearms lay one across the other atop the seat back. Nearly thirty years retired from hockey and they were still thick, heavily muscled. He rested his chin on the white cotton of his shirt sleeve. His sagging features reminded her of a tired bloodhound. "My daughters are as spoiled as their mother. Whose fault is that?"

Maureen looked down. "I wouldn't know."

"Well," RG said. He attempted a smile. "That's a story for another day." His expression changed. "Mind telling me why you're still here?" A storm was brewing behind his eyes.

"Templeton's broken up the Federation," Maureen said.

"That much I know."

"I spent the day figuring out how to get them back." She avoided eye contact. "I think I know how-"

"You went to see the stripper." RG's voice gathered pitch and tempo. He lifted his head off his sleeve. "Edwards called. He's paying a security guard. I was thinking of giving you the benefit of the doubt, but I can't do that now, can I? Not after disobeying me—twice. I'm suspending you, Cage. Without pay. I haven't decided for how long." his eyes narrowed. Thin lines collided at the corners of his eyes. "Maybe forever," he said. "Cohen will take over until this is resolved."

Maureen met his glance. "Since she's done such a great job keeping you informed."

"Don't turn this on its head, Cage," RG said. He levered his body out of the chair. "She's not the one flaunting my directives." He paced to the far wall and back. "I trusted you, Cage. Intimately. You repay me like this. I can't tell you how hurt I am."

"I understand." She had to get out of this place.

"*Dee-Faz* has spent over a hundred million dollars since the beginning," he said. The volume rose. "Not a single treaty has been signed. The Pacific Coast Tribal Federation was our best shot at undoing our shitty reputation."

"And I jeopardized that. I *said* I understand." Maureen folded her hands and set them on the edge of the table. Tremors raced up her arms.

"Jeopardized?" RG's voice jumped its track. "You've driven a stake through it! Not only the table, but other initiatives more sensitive than this. Go home and wait this one out. Understand?"

"Perfectly." She didn't mean to slam the door behind her.

She was halfway to the ferry to Vancouver when she remembered Billy and dinner. She pulled onto the shoulder and scrambled for her phone. The desk clerk at the Queen Anne said a young native man had hung around awhile, acting suspicious, but he had long since departed. She hung up and dialed his number. No answer, just a tinny message in a voice she didn't recognize. She threw the phone into the back seat. It bounced off a seat belt buckle and tumbled to the floor in two pieces. She jammed the accelerator and the car shot back onto the highway, peppering the road with gravel.

"Why did you change your name?" Legare stood. He planted his small hands on the table and leaned forward. "*I'll* tell you why. During your years as a stripper you'd made the acquaintance of Larry Arnold and others. You traveled to Port and other towns like it. As part of the Heritage League*'s* continental strategy you gained employment with the Directorate under fraudulent circumstances. They put you in a position where confidential and sensitive information came your way. You then re-established your former criminal acquaintances and fed them information regarding the swift progress of the treaty settlement with the Tse Wets Aht. They reacted, sending operatives back to Port. Larry Arnold was perfect, having grown up there. He, in turn, recruited others like Rick St. Clair and Gordon MacMillan. You were the perfect mole. Straight. Boring. Nobody had a clue about your past. These hate criminals used information from your progress reports to take direct action—lethal force—as a means of disrupting, delaying or permanently sabotaging the land claims settlement in Port McKenzie. This makes you guilty of conspiring to commit murder, Theresa Pistilli."

Maureen crawled out of a sleep abbreviated by nightmares and twitching pains in her shins. Though the images vanished when she opened her eyes, sadness clung to her like a bad smell. Even the birds in her next door neighbor's cherry tree sensed it. Doleful birdsong leaked through the open bedroom window. She rolled onto her back and stared at the long, gaping crack in the plaster where the ceiling met the wall. It had been at the top of her list of chores when she'd bought the house. She exhaled softly into the quiet of the room and waited, listening. The birds, unseen in the reaching branches, seemed uninspired. Maybe this long heat wave was getting to them, too. She blinked away the dregs of sleep and allowed the map of a new day to unfold over the remnants of her nightmares.

A well-tramped path, this lull between bad dreams and wakefulness.

Maureen pulled on yesterday's clothes. She had to convince herself to go downstairs, to greet her first *Morning-With-Nowhere-To-Be*. The staircase groaned under her weight. She made coffee and was pouring the first cup as the newspaper thumped against the house. More fires, more drought, hints of a looming provincial election, more economic misery, the headlines promised. She carried it back to the kitchen, plucked her mug off the counter and stepped onto the sundeck. A little past five in the morning and the air was already oppressively warm. Even her hardy daisies sagged. She sipped her coffee and promised herself time in the garden to repair the neglect.

The phone rang as she set her mug and paper onto the patio table. She jumped, jostling the mug, spilling coffee across the folded newsprint. She shook hot coffee off her thumb and caught the phone on the third ring.

"What?" She barked into the phone as she wiped her hand on her pant leg. The coffee left a thin, mocha stain near her hip.

"Maureen Cage? Inspector Daniel Legare, RCMP. Sorry to call so early. I wanted to catch you before work."

"Who?" She swallowed the cold lump in her throat.

"Daniel Legare." He pronounced it *Luh-Garr*.

"What do you want?" Maureen glanced at the splash of coffee on the outside table. She aimed herself at a roll of paper towels.

"I'm with RCMP Special Investigations Branch in Ottawa. I called your hotel in Port McKenzie but they told me you'd checked out yesterday. Can I meet you this morning? I'm in Vancouver now."

Maureen made a face into the phone. "Why?"

"The fatalities on Pipeline Road," Legare said. "That crash seems to have changed things, don't you think?"

Her legs felt suddenly weak. She sat down at the kitchen table and propped her head on her arms. "Not for long," she said, but her voice wouldn't fool anyone.

"Maybe not. But I'd still like to have a few words with you. I won't take up a lot of your time," Legare said. "I can come to your office if it's easier."

"I'm not at work today," Maureen said.

"Vacation? You're lucky," Legare said. He mixed a light laugh into his words.

"I'm not on vacation."

Legare cleared his throat through the phone line. "Right. Look, I saw a coffee house on Broadway, near Trafalgar. *Java Jive*, I think. Could we meet there?"

"That's close enough," Maureen said.

"How's seven-thirty? I know it's early, but I need to get to Port this morning."

"Now is early. Seven-thirty's fine. How will I know you?"

"I know you," Legare said. His voice changed. "Ms. Cage, I take it you haven't seen this morning's paper?"

"Only the headline."

"Then I won't keep you. See you there."

Maureen put down the phone, tore off a handful of paper towels and hurried back to the deck. She sopped up spilled coffee as she flattened the paper against the table. She chewed her lower lip at the bold print on the front page: *Hardcore Diary—the Life of an Adult Entertainer—Page 2 of the Attractions Section!* A frightened sound formed low in her throat as she flipped pages. A full-page story of the Raven's life as an *Erotic Artiste* followed the color photo, discretely cropped. She learned how Raven had, as an unhappy teenager, run away from home. Maureen noticed the article on the opposing page. Beneath the headline *Dee-Faz Snoops into Accident Probe.*

She had to look twice to recognize the woman in the small photograph set into the middle of the story. They'd used a photo she'd given RG her first summer with *Dee-Faz*. Her hair was shorter, more severe, her face much leaner than now. The photo's graininess obscured her crow's feet. She squinted at the photograph. She didn't have many to hide back then. She closed the paper and pressed her knuckles into her eyes. When she blinked and looked down wet, inky circles from her tears had soaked into the newsprint.

The *Java Jive* was full of customers as earth-toned as the walls and the Italian tile floor. Maureen ordered a small regular coffee from a rainbow-hued, chalk-board menu that filled the wall behind the cash register: a menu where a designer coffee and chocolate-drizzled *biscotti* required a double-digit commitment. When her coffee was set on the granite counter she added skim milk and retreated to a stool at a bar that mimicked the convex curve of the street-side window. She surveyed the room. A clutch of professors from the University (what did one call them—a herd, a pod, a murder? She settled on *bore*—a bore of professors) occupied the café's best corner, the one with the leather sofa and chairs. Their empty mugs and napkins indifferently crumpled onto dessert plates gummy with vestiges of date squares and flax cakes seemed the epitome of an unhurried, privileged existence. She blamed careless grants of tenure.

Three cyclists—not one of them younger than fifty—clacked across the floor in custom—fitted shoes and Lycra bike shorts. They, too, annoyed her. It was their casual leanness, their ropy limbs, their bony bums. Two women entered in business grey. Their small hands flew in and out of their slim handbags like frightened starlings. They moved quickly, by seven-thirty acting as if they were already hopelessly behind an impossible schedule. Their thumbs assaulted their *IPhones* with relentless determination. Maureen scowled at their well-tailored shoulders. She chewed the end of a plastic stir stick to dissuade the growing urge to cry.

She emptied her cup as a man entered, alone, dressed in a light blue golf shirt and beige, cotton pants. He was younger than she'd expected, and much shorter. He aimed directly for the counter without a second glance, and stood absolutely still as he waited for the Barista to whip his latte. He did not look over his shoulder, nor scan the room. When he cradled his bowl of coffee in two hands and walked toward her, she looked away. She jumped when he climbed onto the stool next to hers and set his RCMP identification precisely in front of her.

"Inspector Daniel Legare." He threw her a probationary smile and extended his right hand. The arm to which it was attached was pale, unmarked by the sun.

"Maureen Cage," she said, and lifted her hand off the counter. His hand jammed into hers and chewed into the tendon between her thumb and index finger.

"I'm late," he said as he withdrew his hand. "I don't remember this city being so busy." He shot her a quick smile beneath eyes as blue as an April sky after a rain. Intense, eager—a blue this city hadn't seen above the horizon for many, parched weeks.

"You're from here?"

His head rocked from side to side, stretching out a kink. "Born and raised. My parents still live in North Van."

Maureen tucked her sore hand behind her left elbow.

"I still miss it. Vancouver's way better than Ottawa. They say I'll get used to it, the heat and the humidity and the winters." Legare shrugged. His shoulders were thick. An athletic build despite the lack of height. "We've been there five years and we're not used to it yet. At least, that's what my wife will tell you." He stared into his coffee cup. "She can't wait for me to be transferred back. You *look* like you're on holidays," he said. He tossed her an eager, hopeful smile.

"I really am," Maureen said. The muscles around her jaw rippled. "How can I help you?"

"There's been a rise in hate activity in the West. It's disturbing. And it's getting worse."

"The West is a pretty big place," Maureen said.

"True. We mostly track the big guys, the *Aryan Nations* and *White Canada Forever*. But when we get a call from our Vancouver contacts that the Heritage League has been mentioned together with a truck crash on Vancouver Island, I thought it worth a closer look-see. So I caught a plane."

Maureen stared at her coffee mug. "Have you spoken to Terry Edwards?"

Legare shook his head. "Newspaper guy? Not yet I haven't. You know him?"

"We've spoken a couple of times. But not about this. He's paying a stripper for a story—her life on the circuit, some such nonsense, I guess it sells papers."

"You think he's got wind of something."

"She needs money, that's all."

Legare shook his head doubtfully. "Maybe, but we'll check it out."

"Edwards is paying for an exclusive. What can you offer her?"

Legare smiled. "We're the RCMP. We can be fairly persuasive when we need to be." He glanced at Maureen, his smile suddenly gone. "If the Heritage League has resorted to violence it means they have targeted your land claim effort as a threat. That means you are at risk, as well as your colleagues." He sniffed. "Any situations that have struck you as strange, out of the ordinary?"

Maureen flushed, pressed her lips together and shook her head. The brief urge to tell him about the note Billy showed her passed. "No," she said.

Legare stared. "Fine," he said after a long pause. "But make sure you report anything. And pass this on to your associates. They need to be careful."

Maureen picked up her cup and drained the last of the coffee. She wiped her hands on a paper napkin and cleared her throat. "I can't believe it's coming to that. Not in Port. Protests from sports fishers and commercial license holders, sure. Union forestry people—they feel threatened all the time. But to kill somebody over a land claim?"

"I wouldn't be here if we thought different. Apparently the NFDI share our sentiments. You've talked to their people?" Legare slurped his coffee, wiped the foam off his upper lip with the side of his thumb.

"I've talked to Billy, yes. William Last Man Standing," Maureen said. "But you're wrong. Port isn't like that."

She watched the cyclists depart, the bore of professors in their wake. As if on cue, a clutch of BMW's and Saabs nestled in front of the coffee shop, the first wave of West Side housewives gathering for après-workout chai lattes and non-fat fruit smoothies. She was stuck on the wrong side of an invisible divide. And the wall was getting thicker and taller with every word Legare said. If she didn't get out soon it would be insurmountable; she'd be trapped forever with Legare and Billy and Josephine and the Raven. "Half the town was at the AIP signing. Why now, more than three years later?"

Legare shrugged. "They're terrorists. Fear gives them the opportunity they crave. Killing innocents gets them the most attention, causes the most shock. They feed off fear and suspicion. As each side blames the other, the cycle not only continues, it deepens. Result? No treaty, no certainty, no future. They win. Just like that." He snapped his fingers for emphasis.

"Just like that," Maureen said. She slid off the stool. "Sorry, but I have to go. Nice meeting you, Inspector."

"You'll keep your eyes open?" Legare stood, rummaging in his pants pockets. He handed her a business card. "If anything changes," he said.

Maureen held the card between her thumb and index finger, reading the print. "This is crazy. Four young men tried to get lucky with a dancer who was only in it for the money. They weren't targets, they were horny. They didn't expect her to say yes." She hoped her words were even a little convincing. It was hard, especially when you doubted them yourself.

Legare pulled a thin notebook from his pants pocket. It was spiral bound, with a stubby pencil the kind golfers used to keep score tucked in the coils of the binding. He flicked open the notebook to a half-filled page near the middle. "She's missing," he said as he pulled the pencil out of the coil binding.

"Who is?"

"Your dancer friend. The Raven," Legare said, scribbling furiously without looking up. "Any idea where I might find her?"

"The Heritage League has infiltrated every province from Quebec to BC," Legare said. He set his hands onto the table and formed a tent with his fingers. "Our files on them fill a room. This organization exists to spread hatred and to sabotage relationships between ethnic groups. You are the perfect mole, you fit the profile perfectly. White. Mid-forties. Uneducated. From a broken home. Susceptible to mystical rhetoric and propaganda."

Maureen took the long way home from the café. She dodged pedestrians and crossed Broadway by reflex, as unconscious an act as breathing. She surfaced once at the sound of a car horn, then slipped back into her thoughts, her brain churning. The Raven, Billy, Sarah, RG, Josephine, Kenny, Carole and Legare: their images buzzed about her like angry mosquitoes. Singly each was an annoyance—worrisome but manageable. Combined they mobbed her, threatened to overthrow her sanity. Movement offered partial relief.

She avoided her street and kept walking towards the water. She crossed Fourth Avenue, struck the sidewalk that paralleled Kits Beach and headed west. The beach was already packed with bodies and blankets and umbrellas. Coolers, like oversized bricks dropped in the sand, anchored family groups and clusters of youth already stripped down to swim gear for the day. Maureen rested her eyes on the horizon; that seam where the forested knuckles of West Vancouver dove into the Confederate-grey waters of English Bay. A bank of cloud obscured the distant silhouette of Vancouver Island. Tendrils of grainy haze groped across a sky stripped bare of color by the heat, but still she felt the pull of Port McKenzie through the haze. The town barged into her head, knocking the reel of clear, rational thought off its sprocket.

After two hours Maureen looped back to her block. The sun was above the boulevard cherry trees and beat on her brow. A hint of breeze tickled her shoulders and when she glanced up the clouds had moved nearer. A storm approached, carrying rain, perhaps. If it fell where needed it would bring relief from the fires. A pang of shame stabbed her, for she wanted to keep the rain to herself, to feel those first, fat drops on her skin. She was tired of thinking, tired of walking. She climbed her front steps, house keys in hand.

"Maureen."

RG's rapid stride carried him from the sidewalk to the bottom step. He held a cylinder of tall, orange lilies in his right hand. "I've been waiting quite some time." He nodded toward the BMW convertible parked a dozen steps away.

She'd walked right by it without noticing, without seeing him in the driver's seat.

RG climbed until his eyes were level with hers. "A peace offering," he said and stretched the flowers toward her.

She hesitated. "Thank you," she said, because she couldn't think what else to say. She was sure he could see the drumbeat of her pulse on her neck. She reached for the flowers, the monstrous lily heads bobbing before her face. Their perfume overwhelmed her. Her eyes and nose began to itch. She wrapped her arms around the bouquet and crushed the flowers to her chest, holding them like a shield before her.

"You look great. And I have big news. Can I come inside?" RG gestured toward the door.

"What kind of news?" she said. "I'm running late." She brushed past him as she climbed the top three steps to the porch. Her fingers gripped her house keys.

"Not for work, surely," he said, and laughed at his joke.

"No. Not for work."

"Sorry," RG said. "That was in poor taste." He looked down at his manicured fingernails. He brightened, flung her a smile as pink and smooth as his cuticles. "We're done in Port. Shut down. The Tse Wets Aht refuse to negotiate at any level until there's an inquest."

"How is that a good thing?"

"It's not *good*. But it's concrete. And realistic. The Federation was an ambitious dream. It created a lot of unrealistic expectations. On all sides."

"A signed AIP's not bad for a dream."

"Sure," RG said. "In a way I'm kinda glad about the accident." He frowned. "You know what I mean. Gives us all time for sober second thoughts."

Maureen pressed her spine into the front door. "Sorry, I don't feel that way. Guess that's why I'm in my weekend clothes."

RG moved to collapse the space between them. His white shirt brushed against the flower stamens. Faint yellow exclamation points dotted his chest. "I came because I need you to know how much this suspension thing upsets me." The leathery skin around his mouth drooped in sudden sadness. "I'm here for you," he said.

"I need to go, RG." Maureen twisted, the hand holding the keys trembling as it searched out the lock.

"Together we can turn this thing around. You're the one I want. To lead my team. But you have to help me first."

Her head ached from the perfume. Her eyes began to water. She dropped the flowers onto the mailbox next to the door and stuck her key into the lock.

RG stepped beside her, perpendicular to the door, as solid as a wall. "You've learned your lesson, I can feel it. Let's go inside. We can talk this thing through." His hand came up to stroke the side of her face.

"Don't." Maureen recoiled from his fingers. Her face burned. She backed away until her hamstrings pressed against the wooden railing that framed the porch.

He moved fast, his hands on her hips, his weight against her. His breath was mouth-wash sweet in her nostrils. He kissed her, but she turned, and his lips mashed against her cheek, plastered across her jaw.

"Get away! Get off my property, RG."

His glazed eyes—as blue as a Delft saucer—narrowed, seemed to hunker down onto the bridge of his nose. A massive vein in his neck began to throb. "Come on, Maureen. You need me. Now more than ever." He licked his lips with a wet, vigorous tongue.

Maureen sidestepped closer to the front door. She swept the lilies off the mailbox and swung them like a baseball bat against his chest, peppering his shirt with a shotgun spray of pollen.

"Stay away from me," she said, her voice a low, menacing growl.

RG hesitated. Fear danced across his features. He crushed the bouquet between his hands and threw them off the porch. He straightened, smoothed his shirt and tie and held up his hands, palms outward. He backed down the steps. "Cohen thinks you're queer. That's okay, I'm a liberal guy." His laugh was cruel. He retreated down the steps two at a time. "But queer or not, you're one slow learner."

Only after he was inside his car did she turn her back to the street to twist the key in the front door. She set the deadbolt and dropped her keys on the floor as the BMW's engine roared to life. She caught a glimpse of silver as it lunged from the curb. With her forehead pressed against the door frame she pushed shaking fingers into each eye socket until a searing white light filled her head.

"I *am* educated," Maureen said. Her head pounded when she spoke.

"*After* your indoctrination," Legare said, dismissing her words with a careless wave. "You were a prostitute and an addict for years. Before you even knew what an education was."

"This is a joke. How can you-"

He cut her off. "If I dig deep enough I'm sure to find evidence of payments from the Heritage League to cover your education. Did they use A&H to channel the funds? Brilliant, really: creating your mole instead of buying one."

She had the sensation of a heavy, rusty screw being cranked into her sinuses. Shutting her eyes made only a marginal difference to the pain. "If I was their mole," she whispered, "why would I file a police report over a stolen lighter?"

Legare's smile was as thin and translucent as pond ice under a late winter sun. "You got greedy. Or you got cold feet. Or had second thoughts, got worried somebody might make a connection. Figured we'd return it without checking for prints. Maybe they tried to stiff you. There's no shortage of motives."

"No," Maureen said. She struggled to hold down the wave of nausea, the strong taste of bile at the back of her throat. "You've got it all wrong."

The coolest part of her house was the basement. A cement foundation had been poured against the original bricks some forty-five years ago. Together they kept the space a dozen degrees cooler than upstairs. Small windows, set high in opposing walls, allowed air to pass unchecked. They were open now and a breeze which two hours ago could barely merit a whisper now made a brazen trail through the room. Maureen caught a whiff of thunder and a tang of salt in its trail.

She shared her workshop with a clunking, wheezing oil furnace that stood near the chimney in place of the original sawdust burner. Alianna Agripolis had told her about the time the furnace had been installed—how Nick, her husband, had gone to the neighbors to show off how modern they were. He'd been so proud: no more shoveling sawdust to keep them warm. Fifty years on and Alianna still considered it new. She'd refused to make the switch to natural gas when every other home on the block changed over. Since taking over the house Maureen thought it important to keep the tired oil burner going for as long as possible; tearing out the ancient, temperamental heater would be disrespectful to her former landlady and late husband. But every October, when the furnace shook the floor beneath the living room as it rumbled to life with the first cold spell and the smell of burnt dust and heating oil tickled her nose, she wondered if this would be the winter when she finally and forever said goodbye to Nick's furnace.

Maureen always wore a dust mask when she refinished furniture. The solvent gave her a headache if she didn't wear it, though how the mask filtered out the chemicals she couldn't tell. She was working on a boy's five-drawer dresser—nineteenth century for sure—she'd stumbled upon at a neighborhood garage sale last spring. It had been painted and repainted by successive owners until the birch from which it had been made lay entombed beneath decades of generous coats. The topmost layer of dull, blue enamel had been badly defiled by a black felt marker, as if the dresser's last owner had needed a fencing partner more than a place to keep his socks.

She worked through morning into late afternoon. She stripped off the paint, coat after stubborn coat. An abandoned mug of coffee grew cold at the edge of the rough circle of newspapers spread across the cement floor. Coffee quickly wicked up the solvent fumes from the air, making it undrinkable but she couldn't resist taking a cup into the basement with her. Maureen wore kneepads strapped to her legs and rocked back on her heels to examine her progress. With a fine brush she applied the stripper, working it into the piece from top to bottom. She used short, easy strokes and loved when the old paint bulged off the wood before the insistent push of the scraper. Fine steel wool and a naphtha wash was enough to restore the true wood grain.

She was nearly done, already thinking about oiling and polish when the phone upstairs rang. She hesitated in mid-stroke, the steel wool pressed against a drawer front as she out-waited the answering machine. A male voice started to speak and she clenched her jaw and finished the motion, forcing the steel wool pad into the birch panel. It was the fourth time since mid-morning she'd ignored Terry Edwards and his promises.

As the phone line disconnected she heard footsteps on the back stairs. Two visitors. She recognized them both by their footsteps: Helen's quick, light, scuff and the heavy, measured footfall a moment behind that was Anne's. She put down the steel wool and peeled off her dust mask and set it on the workbench. As it returned to its original shape it teetered off the edge and fell onto the newspaper. She watched it fall, half-turned to retrieve it, then spun to race up the stairs. She emerged from the basement as Helen's narrow outline appeared in the glass of the kitchen door. She unlocked the door and heaved it open so that it struck the wall and rebounded, shivering on its hinges.

"Easy, Girl," Helen said. She stretched a long, sinewy neck forward to offer her left cheek. Her fists were full with the stretched white plastic of overstuffed grocery bags.

Maureen kissed Helen quickly and lifted the bags out of the woman's hands. "Great to see you," she said.

Helen sidestepped to get away from the door. "Come on, Annie. I can't start dinner if you don't hand over the main course."

"As long as I'm not the main course." Anne filled the doorway. She hugged a large wicker basket that she set onto the table. She spread her arms and closed on Maureen. "Always in a hurry, isn't she?"

Maureen slipped between Anne's thick arms. She let them gather her up and squeeze the air out of her. She was immersed in lavender, tinged with the musky warmth of perspiration. Anne's smell. She hoped Anne would never let her go.

Anne patted her between the shoulder blades and stepped out of the embrace. Her thin, white eyebrows crept upward as a smile tightened her chins. She tipped over the basket and heaved out a newspaper-wrapped missile. "This baby was swimming in the salt chuck less than six hours ago."

"Salmon? I don't remember asking for handouts," Maureen said. She took the fish out of Anne's hands. It was heavy, easily fifteen pounds or more in her hands. "What will I do with a monster like this?"

"We gotta eat too," Helen said, protesting. "Plus it'll keep forever once it's cooked. We noticed the old pizza boxes under the stairs. We were down at the Steveston docks today and couldn't resist."

"We read the paper, Honey," Anne said, making tsk-tsk sounds.

"She was so pissed," Helen grinned. "She made sure they wrapped Old Moby here in the front section of the Star."

Anne folded her flamingo pink arms across her chest. Her bare skin glistened in the heat. "You been stripping in the dungeon again." Her vowels were salted with traces of a persistent Dutch accent. "Get cleaned up. We'll do the supper. Then we'll talk."

Helen glanced at Maureen and smiled. "Go on, Mo," she said and waved her out of the kitchen. "Do as she says or none of us'll have any peace. I'll make sure she doesn't steal the silverware."

Maureen fled. As she climbed the stairs she pictured them in her kitchen: like dancers, so close, so at ease, never in the other's way. Their years together had forged an understanding—an instinct—of cause and effect. Without resorting to words each knew what the other needed. Maureen closed the bathroom door, aware of a tightness forming in her chest. It was a familiar ache, one that cried out from a lifetime of form-fitting loneliness.

She ate too much of Anne's salmon, drank too much of Helen's wine as they watched her, open-mouthed. Helen wondered out loud what other old habits had crept back into Maureen's life? Anne scolded Helen and refilled Maureen's glass. They left as the sunset dappled red the underbellies of encroaching clouds. Maureen lay on the sofa and watched darkness creep across the landscape. First the trees outside the living room window fell into shade, then the front porch, the walls and lastly, her island sofa. Her glance drifted to the photograph taken at her graduation ceremony; to the immodest joy in Helen and Anne's faces. She remembered the day she'd told them she was going back to school.

"You can't quit," Helen said. She stayed in her chair behind her desk as Maureen approached.

"I have to. I'm going full time."

"You been going to school forever." Helen waved a thin hand. "Night school, day school, correspondence school." She pried a cigarette out of the pack on her desk and brought the butane lighter toward her mouth. She offered Maureen the deck.

Maureen shook her head, folded her arms across her chest and flung out her hip. She hadn't had a smoke since breakfast and it was driving her nuts. She was ready to scratch out somebody's eyes. Anybody's, even her own.

"Anne, put down that phone," Helen said, and exhaled a fat fist of smoke into the air above her head. "Mo says she's quitting."

Anne lifted herself out of her chair and hurried to Maureen's side. Her Hawaiian print dress hung off her like an oversized umbrella. "Smoking?" She pried apart Maureen's arms and smothered both hands between her own meaty palms.

"I can't do the part-time stuff anymore," Maureen said, backing out of Anne's touch. "All these years, I got only half the credits I need. I have to go for it, or forget it."

"Then forget it," Helen said. "What will you do for money?" She cracked her knuckles.

"You taught me to save," Maureen said. "I've done the math. I'll rent out a room if I have to. Two rooms. The university's real close, there's always students looking for a place to live."

"I need a drink," Helen said. The drawer at her right knee rattled open. "Want one?" She held up a square bottle of Jack Daniels. She ignored the ringing phone at her elbow as she filled two glasses. She offered one to Maureen.

"No thanks. And it's not just the dancing." Maureen began to count on her fingers. "Smoking. Drinking. Pot. Even meat. I need focus."

"You giving up sex too?" Helen said. She snorted and emptied her glass.

"That's the easiest one," Maureen said. "I gave up on men a long time ago. When they gave up on me."

Helen reached for the second glass on her desk. "Listen to her, Annie. She's crazy. Except for the giving up on men thing—that's just good sense."

"If I find one who doesn't think two-way communication requires a fist, I'll reconsider," Maureen said. "So where do I sign? What do I have to do to quit this damn business?"

"As stubborn as ever," Helen said. She toasted Maureen and downed the second shot in one swallow.

"Besides, thirty-six is too old for this business," Maureen said. "How long before you cut me, or drop me down a circuit?"

"Psssht." Helen dismissed her with a wave of her bony hand. "Without their rubber tits and Botox injections the girls today are nothing," Helen said. "They think doing aerobics and spreading their legs is stripping. It's not dancing, its porn set to music."

"I remember when I started with A & H," Maureen said, pointing to the color photos that lined the wall behind Helen's desk. Behind Anne's desk hung many more framed photos, many of them black and white. The retired gallery. Anne liked to call it her Hall of Fame.

"I'm older now than you were back then," Maureen said.

"That was different," Helen said. "Anne's back forced her to quit, and I—well, you know when it's time to get off the stage." Her grey eyes glazed as she stared into her glass.

"Then it's settled," Maureen said. "Take my picture down. After ten years it belongs on Anne's side."

Helen dragged herself out of her chair and lifted a photo off the top row. It was the last black and white in her gallery. She rubbed at a spot on the glass and carried it to Anne. "You were one of our favorites," Helen said and she handed the photograph to Anne.

"One of our family." Anne beamed at the photo. She held it up like a prize.

"You say that to all the girls."

Anne shook her head slowly. "No I don't. You're *our* girl, isn't that right Helen? Our Mo. Our Angel."

The woman in the photo smiled from behind a wave of dark hair. The shot had been taken from behind, the girl looking at the camera over one bare shoulder. The makeup around her eyes screamed 'eighties excess. A tattoo of a shooting star trailed along the inside of her shoulder blade. The photo was signed *Hugs and kisses, Angel,* in thick black marker across the left border.

"Live fast, live for the moment. That's what the shooting star meant," Maureen said. She pushed the frame back into Anne's body. "Not anymore."

"Just because you're quitting don't mean you can't see us any more," Helen said. "I expect a regular call, Mo. Once a week at least."

"You checking up on me?"

"Sure," Helen said with a laugh. "I wanna know how long before the *new* you begins to look like the *old* you."

"No chance," Maureen said. She hugged Anne and waved to Helen. "By the time I'm done school I'll be so damn good you won't recognize me."

"Wrong?" Legare slid the report back toward Maureen. "I don't think so. Your associates substantiate my evidence."

"What *associates?*"

"Larry Arnold, for a start." Legare picked up the lighter, still inside the plastic bag, and turned it over in his hands.

"He's alive?"

"You sound disappointed."

"I didn't mean to—to hit him that hard."

Legare frowned. "He's got a fractured skull. Nothing life threatening, but forensics say it took a determined blow. Deadly force, some might say. Your prints are all over the jack handle."

Maureen dabbed at the corner of her left eye. It wouldn't stop leaking.

"Larry and I go way back," Legare said. "He's been in our custody before. But until now we've had only pieces, fragments of information. Their leadership we know—they're constantly meeting at survival games and boot camps in Montana and Idaho. But they use sleepers, mostly. They rarely ever meet." He smiled widely, genuinely pleased.

"You've led us into new territory, Theresa Pistilli."

She slept through the day. The end of the work week, for some. She drove the five short blocks to the grocery store. The sky threatened rain. The store was crowded, and every customer wore the same, reckless expression above their carts: desperate to find the shortest line through the checkout and the parking lot and the quickest way home. The ritual start to a typical Vancouver weekend. She ducked into the liquor store and grabbed the cheapest bottle of French red wine she could find. She used the same principle to choose a white. She paid with cash and felt a stab of guilt as the cashier stuffed each bottle into a plain, brown bag. It was that easy, turning her back on abstinence. She fled into the swelter of the parking lot, embarrassed by the flush spreading across her cheeks.

She parked in the garage and carried her supplies up the back steps. She grunted at the nettle of pain over her hip as she bent to place the bags near the door. She unlocked the kitchen door and ferried the bags to the counter, then hurried to bolt the door. A pile-up of battered clouds threatened to shoulder their unruly way inside.

She tossed her keys onto the table. She found last night's wine glass in the living room, on the floor next to the sofa. She set it on the counter, not bothering to rinse the dried wine off the bottom. The groceries settled lower in their bags, the brown paper creaking like an old foundation. Maureen set the bottle of white wine on its side in the fridge. It rolled from one end of the wire shelf to the other as the door swung shut. She unscrewed the cap off the red and filled her glass.

She carried both glass and bottle into the living room. She punched a button on the stereo and Dame Sutherland's voice filled the room. The Flower Duet from *Lakme,* one of her very favorites. Maureen straightened, exhaled in a loud, long sigh and closed her eyes. Outside were clouds that tasted of rain and the frantic tempo of a Friday evening. Inside was music, the quiet weight of her house, and wine. She brought the glass to her lips and inhaled—the aroma bordered on acrid but she didn't care. Her tongue danced across the rim of the glass. It was warm, smooth. She tipped the glass.

The front doorbell rang, its discordant blast tearing through the house. Wine spilled.

"Shit." Maureen set the dripping glass on top of the stereo cabinet, shook droplets from her fingers and stabbed at the stereo's power button. Sutherland's *Lakme* died in mid-lament. Maureen leaned to peer through the living room window.

Carole Simons shifted from one high-topped black boot to the other as she waited. She turned to face the street, hands fiddling with an oversized, silver belt buckle.

Treaty negotiator by day, ageing, punk rock lesbian by night, Maureen thought. She moved toward the door. The combination didn't seem that far out of line, all things considered. "You're back in town," Maureen said as she tugged open the door.

"Nobody's staying in Port," Carole said. "I heard what they did. Thought I'd check in, see how you're holding up. Those yours?" She pointed to the discarded lilies on the front sidewalk. "Have a fight with your boyfriend?"

"Ignore them," Maureen said. "I am."

Carole touched one hand to the points of her stiff hair. "Can I come in?"

"As long as you're not bringing salmon."

"Pardon?"

"Never mind." Maureen batted the question aside. "Can you grab that?" The morning paper lay undisturbed in the furthest corner of the porch.

Carole crossed the threshold holding the paper like a relay runner's baton. "The Tse Wets Aht are beyond angry," she said as the door closed behind her.

"About what?" Maureen said. She retrieved her wine glass from the stereo and led Carole into the kitchen.

"You haven't heard? About the election? Jesus Christ, Maureen, what have you been doing?"

Maureen tore the paper out of Carole's hand and stared at the headline. *Hargrove Calls Snap Election!* "In four weeks? They'll be killed at the polls."

"And with them all opportunity for *any* agreements. Interims, Finals, AIP's. We see the whole of it heading into the toilet. Bennett's boys have promised voters a complete review of the treaty-making process in BC. They want to shit-can *Dee-Faz* and hand the entire responsibility over to Ottawa." Carole took the full wine glass from Maureen's hands. "Here's to you. At least you got a head start on finding a new job."

"But why now? Premier Hargrove must know he can't win."

Carole swallowed and made a face. "Next time let me choose the wine, 'kay? We think he's either given up or got something big up his sleeve. Some monster giveaway to make everyone forget about the mess he's made. By the way, what happened to the not drinking thing?"

"It's my new hobby." Maureen refilled her glass. "Cheaper than refinishing furniture, a lot less work and the payback's much quicker. Cheers."

Carole touched her glass against Maureen's. "Just this once. I'll bring a nice Argentinean Malbec next time. Puts this stuff to shame." She smacked her lips as she lowered her goblet. "We were surprised as hell about your suspension." She laughed. "Even Templeton seemed upset. I sent you an email."

"Thanks. I haven't bothered to check today. Couldn't see the point. No chance you ran into Billy Last Man Standing?"

Carole's eyebrows—as blond and stiff as her hair—formed a pair of arches flanking the bridge of her nose. "The handsome

American? Saw him this morning at the hotel. He asked me if I knew where you were. First words he's actually said to me." Carole sniffed. "How would he know to ask *me* about *you*?"

Maureen cringed. "At the funerals. I might have mentioned our stint at the bar," she said. "Then I stood him up for dinner."

Carole frowned. "*Dinner*? You mean a date? Of course, you realize how young he is?"

"I do, and it wasn't a date."

"I didn't think you were his type."

"I'm not. I'm old enough to be his mother," Maureen said.

"Can't blame him for trying," Carole said. She shrugged, set down her glass of wine.

"Thanks." Maureen emptied her glass. A warmth welled inside her, one that made her hips rock and her palms itch.

Carole moved closer. "You're gorgeous," she said, in a voice so low Maureen had to hold her breath to be sure she'd heard right.

"My name is Maureen," she said, dabbing at the tears in her eyes. The words emerged as a half-whispered croak.

"I'm no shrink, but I'd say you genuinely believe this fantasy you've created," Legare said. "Ingenious, really. Using strippers as operatives. Why not? They're on the road a lot, they move in the same criminal circles. Drugs, prostitution, sure, but race crimes? It's perfect."

Legare walked around the table. His voice attacked her from behind. "You want to know what *I* think? You were planning to kidnap the chief. Josephine David. You have contacts, know her movements. We know she was there, at the house near the bird sanctuary, so maybe you did. There's signs of a struggle outside. Did she escape? Larry blamed you. You screwed up, right? He got angry, you got into a fight. Or were you just jealous? You wanted his girlfriend. Nothing surprises me these days. You wanted that stripper, right? The one called Raven?"

A pair of half-empty wine glasses stood side by each on the bureau near the window. Forgotten. The quilt lay on the floor, kicked off the bed onto their discarded clothes. Carole's body was heavy on top of hers. Her scent was strong on the sheets and in the pillow cases. Carole's fingers released liquid fire from Maureen's pores. She cried out. The voice was not her own. It begged, swore, rebounded off the shadowy walls. She knew it as hers by the rasp of hot air escaping her throat.

"I need a smoke," Maureen said as the tremors in her body dwindled to intermittent aftershocks. Her fingertips caressed Carole's cheek.

Carole kissed her stomach. "You don't smoke." Her finger traced a faint, puckered line, two inches long, below Maureen's navel.

"Like I don't drink," Maureen said. Her hand steered Carole's hand away from the scar.

"You're giving up vegetarianism, too?"

"I think I already did," Maureen said.

"That's enough!" Carole said. She pushed Maureen over onto her side and snuggled behind her. Her toes tickled Maureen's calves. "Nice tattoos, by the way," she said. "A bit out of character, don't you think? You don't seem the tattoo-wearing type."

"Hear that?" Maureen lifted her head off the pillow. She squinted at the window, but the shuttered blinds blocked her view. Blue-white light flashed into the room. Maureen counted off the seconds. Thunder boomed before she reached six. "It's coming closer."

Carole kissed the back of her neck. "I can't believe we're doing this."

Maureen fell back against the pillow. "I've seen more women without their clothes than most doctors," she said, "but you're the first I've made love with."

"I don't understand," Carole said.

Maureen took a deep breath, her gaze fixed on the narrow gaps between the blinds. She exhaled. "I was a dancer once. A stripper, to be honest."

Carole became very still. By the time Maureen had finished her story Carole was sitting upright, her knees tucked close to her chin, her shoulder blades pressed against the wall. The lightning storm had passed.

"Listen." Maureen sat up. The first drops of rain struck the roof, a strumming of nervous fingers. "Come on," she said, leaping out of bed. "It's raining."

She hurried downstairs. She shut off the kitchen light and pulled open the door. She couldn't see past the deck rail. Thunder from the passing storm trailed out of the north. A warm breeze hissed through the branches of the neighbor's trees. She smelled ozone and a rare freshness in the air as rain pelted her skin. She took tiny, cautious steps to the railing and pressed her body against it. It was cool tucked under her bare ribs.

The rain came harder, splashing onto the deck. It bounced off the railing into her eyes. Then it poured. A cloudburst rattled the gutters and played her garbage can lids like cymbals. Maureen stretched out her arms. She tipped her head back so the hard droplets struck her face. She had to close her eyes as the rain overwhelmed her. It hammered her mercilessly, as loud as the applause of a multitude.

"What are you doing?" Carole shouted from the darkened doorway. She wore one of Maureen's tee shirts. It hung loose off her shoulders and fell all the way to her knees. She wrapped her arms tightly around her sides. "The neighbors . . ."

"Screw the neighbors," Maureen shouted. She raised her arms and shook her fists at the sky. "This is *my* storm. I can do what I want."

"But they'll *see* you."

Maureen clapped her hands and the rain stopped—not gradually, but instantly—as if on command. Water sluiced down her arms, over her breasts, along the contours of her belly and hips and puddled on the deck. "I'm done," she said. She laughed and tripped inside, leaning close to kiss Carole as she splashed past.

"You're getting me wet," Carole said, recoiling.

"I'll get a towel," Maureen said, ignoring the thunderclouds in Carole's eyes.

"I never met Raven or Larry until Port. The night of the crash," Maureen said. Her face throbbed.

"Let me remind you of some basic facts." Legare darted into view, returning to his chair opposite her. He flipped the chair backwards and sat with his arms draped across the backrest. He glanced down at his documentation. "Her real name is-"

A muffled knock on the door interrupted him.

"What?" Legare glanced over Maureen's shoulder, toward the large mirror behind her. He nodded, the door opened.

A nurse carrying a tray entered ahead of the officer who had escorted Maureen from her room.

Legare folded his arms. "As I was saying. Born Windsor, Ontario, March twenty-ninth, nineteen eighty-two," he repeated. "Ran away at sixteen. Drugs, prostitution, hardcore movies, exotic dancing. Made her way to Vancouver in two thousand and two, spends half her time in southern California. More drugs, more arrests, yadda, yadda, yadda."

Legare lifted his head, his features crunched into a mock frown. "You people work out of the same handbook? *Striptease for Dummies?*" Then he cracked a toothy grin.

"I made a fresh pot," Carole said as Maureen entered the kitchen. She stood next to the coffee maker, dressed in yesterday's clothes. She read the newspaper with one index finger looped through the handle of her coffee mug.

Maureen rubbed her eyes. Yawning, she slid into a kitchen chair. Everything was different. It was strange to sit and not have to reckon on the morning sun in her eyes. Outside it was cool, overcast. The two low spots on her deck held the collected remains of last night's rain. It was even stranger not being alone in her house.

"How long you been up?" She yawned again, unable to shake the weariness that clung to her bones. She could have slept hours more.

"Not long. But then, I wasn't dancing naked in public."

"I wasn't dancing. I needed to feel the rain."

"You actually lived this life, didn't you?" Carole held up a section of the morning paper. She pointed to the headline: *Hardcore Diary Part II—The Grind of an Adult Entertainer.*

"Can you pour me a cup?" Maureen said, looking away.

Carole brought her a full mug of black coffee.

"I take milk, never mind." Maureen pushed her body out of the chair and shuffled to the fridge. "That one does everything, movies, her own web site, Facebook page," she said as she poured milk into her coffee. "She gets fucked for money. I just danced."

"*Just danced*?" The paper slapped against the counter. "It's like I went to bed with one person and woke up with someone else. When we were in that bar in Port. What were you thinking?"

"That I didn't want to be there," Maureen said. "I worked hard to put all that behind me. I don't like being reminded of it."

"And here I am just figuring you for uptight. A prude, a librarian," Carole said. She shook her head slowly. "What a dope."

"How could you know? I don't go around telling people I used to be a stripper." The weariness vanished. It was the same sensation as at work: she was guarded, on the defensive.

"That I can understand," Carole said. She stared down at the paper, her arms folded. "I should have known the moment I saw the tattoos."

"What's that got to do with anything? Lots of people have tattoos. Hell, every fifteen year old has barbed wire on her arm or a pagan sun above the crack of her ass. It's private. I don't tell people that I don't eat meat, or I don't smoke." Maureen cradled her coffee mug in both hands. She took a sip and set down the mug. "I don't volunteer the details of my personal life."

Carole held up a finger. "But it would come up the second you went out for a meal or when you're offered a cigarette. This is different, Maureen. Way different."

"I shouldn't have told you. I just thought you, of all people, would understand."

Carole's jaw fell open. "What, because I'm queer I have to accept everything? Tolerate anything?"

"Yes. I think so. Your entire image is permissive."

"*Permissive*? I'm a *civil servant* for Christ's sake. I spend my weekends calculating my pension! Look. I don't want to get into this now. I've got a plane to catch."

"I thought you were staying."

Carole put her mug in the sink and filled it with water. "Last night was fantastic," she said, without turning around.

"For me, too."

"Let's leave it like that, okay?" Carole dried her hands on a dish towel and moved toward the front hall. "I'll call when I get home."

Maureen sensed something hard settle between them. She lowered her glance to the coffee mug on the table. "I don't want to leave it like this."

Carole licked her lips, tossed a quick glance at the ceiling. "I'll call you soon, 'kay?"

"I'll be here," Maureen said to the bottom of her mug.

She prowled through the late afternoon, waiting for the phone to ring. She went down to the basement, once, with the idea of working on the dresser, but she walked away without picking up the steel wool. She tried to read, but novels were too thick and her stock of magazines was too thin and long overdue for the recycle bin. She was edgy. The muscles in her legs twitched when she stretched out on the sofa.

She paced.

By seven PM the restlessness had taken control of her body. Her hands shook. Her breathing came in rapid, shallow bursts. She needed medicine. She plucked the bottle of white wine from the fridge. She opened it and had to remind herself she owned glasses. She carried both glass and bottle to the living room sofa and drank. She muted Joan Sutherland, choosing instead the random, muffled sounds of the neighborhood. Cars passed once in a while, people less frequently. She adjusted the window blinds to see better the front porch and street beyond.

She remained on the sofa, staring through the window, dozing fitfully for a few minutes at a time. Evening settled around the house. The sun made one brief appearance, emerging red-hued from behind the clouds. It splashed the house with an angry, fitful glow before vanishing behind the houses across the street. As it disappeared her restlessness turned to unease. She had the sense that RG was near. Very near. He was in her backyard. She was sure of it—a splinter of fear was working deep into her mind. She held her breath, listening. She waited for a sound—a creak, a rattle—anything to confirm the suspicion pulsing in her veins.

She slid off the sofa—one foot all pins and needles beneath her weight—and limped around the main floor, checking the locks. They were secure. There was also a basement door to check. She snapped on the light at the top of the stairs. The lone, sixty watt bulb that hung over the bottom step wasn't strong enough to banish the deepest shadows. She hurried down the steps, inspecting the windows. They were locked. The basement door was shut. Everything was as she had left it. She reached out her hand as she approached the door, rattled the doorknob and pushed home the deadbolt. Locked. She approached the window next to the door, her hand ready to push the curtain aside and survey the backyard. She hesitated, suddenly aware of how rapid her breathing had become. She lowered her hand. Either the act of reaching out had altered something, or the chemistry of the silence had changed. The sensation of a nearby presence was less now, leaking away like a retreating tide. The mouth-drying fear was gone.

She ran to the stairs, her knuckles white on the handrail. A neat stack of shoe boxes on the shelf behind the stairs caught her eye. She stepped off the riser and pulled each box off the shelf. Dust floated above the cardboard lids. She re-stacked them, tucked the top box under her chin and carried them upstairs, her spine as straight and stiff as a good habit.

She dumped the boxes onto the kitchen table and sneezed. A pair of red high heels tumbled out of one box as it spilled across the table. Maureen picked up a shoe and a cassette tape fell from the wadded tissue paper. She sneezed twice more. She licked her fingertip and rubbed the red leather. She unlocked a rich, crimson sheen. From another box she produced a knot of shiny, slippery fabric as red as the shoes. It fit easily into her hand. In the bottom of the box were two joints, as dry and weightless as mummified caterpillars.

The tape still played. She was afraid it would stretch and break or ruin her tape deck, but the song sounded just as she remembered it. A crashing Bossa Nova beat shook the walls. Maureen pushed the coffee table against the sofa and twisted closed the blinds. She turned off the lights and lit the volcanic stub of candle on the dining room table, then with the same match ignited one of the joints and inhaled it, hard, like she used to. A hot, harsh smoke assailed her throat. She coughed once, then could not stop. She had to bend over, hands on her knees, to wait for the coughing fit to pass. She took a second drag, coughed—less this time—and hurried into the bathroom with the shoes and bundle of fabric. She emerged, adjusting straps and pressing rolls of pliant flesh into place.

She finished the first joint and closed her eyes and began to move her hips to the music in a rhythm that was once as familiar as breathing. Her knee and hip joints were wooden and sore. Movement came back slowly. As she swayed she ran her flattened palms upwards across her body, over her hips until they met at the sequined bra. They skimmed past her throat; fingernails grazed her cheekbones and came to rest in her hair, much shorter now than it had been. Back then, her fingers would vanish into thick, dark plaits as she piled her hair and winked into a sea of shiny, upturned faces. Her shoulders ached, her back was sore. The costume was too small—it bit into her ribs and shoulder blades. It surprised her how little of her it covered. And it was so red. As rich and deep as communion wine.

The first song faded into to a slower, melancholy guitar riff. Maureen's breathing quickened as she adjusted to the rhythm. Her hands whisked a sheen of perspiration off her skin. The scent of her sweat mingled with the dry, hot reek of pot. Her hands disappeared behind her back and unhooked her bra. It fell away from her breasts in a single motion. She let it hang off the end of her outstretched arm, held between thumb and forefinger. She tossed it onto the couch and brought both hands to cover her breasts. Her nipples hardened beneath her fingers. Her breasts were softer, heavier than she remembered. She could do this, still.

As the song—now a 'nineties cult favorite—flowed into its opening verse she dropped to the carpet. Her muscles seized before she reached the floor. She had to lower herself, in stages, onto her knees, then—groaning—onto her back. It had been a graceful thing to see, once. Elastic, effortless. She giggled, coughed as she stretched her legs, toes pointed. Her heels traced a red arc that framed the living room window. Hamstrings tightened, refused to stretch. The sinews that ran from her knees to her inner thighs screamed. She arched her back, sweat in her eyes, and pressed her shoulders into the floor. The carpet burned her flesh. The knot at her hip flared. She gave up, curling up onto her left side, breathing hard.

This was supposed to be the part where she lost her thong: as the chorus began she'd sweep the g-string off her hips, past her knees and over her heels in a single motion that brought down a crowded house on Saturday nights. As her legs imitated the old Timex commercial—ten and two o'clock on the watch dial—the drunks on Gynecology Row would shout *I love you!* or worse and beg for her phone number. She rolled onto her back and stared at the ceiling, chest heaving, to wait out the end of the song. She had to use the coffee table to stand. A fresh coughing fit seized her on the way to the bathroom.

"Pathetic," she croaked, after the last guitar chord died.

The nurse stood next to Maureen. She rubbed her arm with a cotton swab. She prepared a needle, watched as the fluid squirted from the point.

"Her name. You never told me her name."

Legare frowned. He jammed the plastic bag holding the gold lighter into his pants pocket. "You don't know? But the two of you are such close friends."

"She's no friend," Maureen said. She winced at the sudden sting.

"She'll need to sleep," the nurse said.

"I'm nearly done," Legare said, nodding. He turned toward Maureen. "Theresa and Frances. Such good, wholesome, Catholic girls. I'm sure your mother would have been so proud."

The phone's ring ripped through the house like a fire alarm. Maureen scrambled to stop it. "How was the flight?" she said. Her hands were all over the phone, juggling the receiver.

"Flight?" A man's voice rode a carpet of static on a bad cell phone connection.

"Who is this?" Maureen said, a flush of disappointment spreading across her face.

"Inspector Legare. Maureen Cage?"

"Sorry, I was expecting someone else."

"I've completed my interview with Chief David and others of the Tse Wets Aht First Nation."

"I know who she is," Maureen said.

"I'll be back in town tomorrow, briefly. I have to make a trip east, but I need to speak with you again. I know its Sunday."

"What about?"

"Can it wait? Cell phone signals wander."

"Anything to do with treaty negotiations should go through *Dee-Faz*. Sarah Cohen is in charge of things in Port." She sank into a chair at the kitchen table. She grimaced as her elbow touched the table top, and gingerly felt around the rug burn with the fingers of her free hand.

"I've spoken to Ms. Cohen," Legare said. "Quite honestly, though, my business is with you."

"I've been suspended," Maureen said. She propped her forehead in the palm of her hand.

"Yes, Ms. Cohen mentioned that. The fourth boy died tonight," Legare said.

"Kenny. Kenny Jacob." Maureen sagged. "I'm sorry."

"The stripper Raven is missing," Legare said. "I was planning on interviewing her once more."

"I wouldn't know-"

"The newspaper doesn't know where she is," Legare said, speaking quickly. "She still has a mild concussion. Larry Arnold is also missing. Our office thinks he's in Vancouver."

"I don't see how I can help you." Maureen stood and circled her kitchen.

"The Heritage League is claiming responsibility for the crash. Two known members are fugitives. *Dee-Faz* personnel may be targets. Have you friends that can check on you, drop by from time to time?"

"You're saying I could be in danger?" Maureen spun to look out the window. The sensation of fear she'd had earlier returned.

"I'd say the risk is low, but it doesn't hurt to be sensible. I'll call you when I'm in town." The static fell away as the line went dead.

Maureen swore into the handset. She punched numbers from memory. She moved out of the kitchen, away from the windows, and sat at the dining room table. The candle sputtered, nearly drowned in its own melted wax.

"Queen Anne Hotel," the receptionist said.

"Sarah Cohen."

"One moment."

Maureen chewed her lower lip. "Sarah, its Maureen."

"What do *you* want?" The voice sharpened, instantly on guard.

"I think it's time we faced facts. About the accident. It *was* the Heritage League. Arrange a meeting with David and her Tribal Council."

"Let it go, Maureen." The television was loud behind her words.

"They've got to get back to the main table, as soon as possible."

"Have you got shit for brains?" The loud television noises in the background vanished. Sarah's voice was harsh. "We're past that, now. How stupid do you think I am?"

"It's what they wanted all along."

"Who's *they*? Look. Stop calling me. I don't appreciate your demented ravings."

"Talk to Inspector Legare!"

"Harass me again and I'll tell RG. Never mind, I'll tell him anyway." Sarah hung up.

Maureen set down the handset and hunted down the open bottle of wine. Her hand was unsteady; the bottle neck kept knocking the rim of the glass. She used both hands to fill the glass and drained it in a single swallow. Her hands were cold. She returned from the study with her Rolodex and set it on the dining room table. It took the last of the wine to convince her fingers to dial.

"It's Maureen," she said after the answering machine had played its message. "We need to talk. Can I meet you-?"

"Maureen—Ms. Cage," RG said into the phone. He sounded out of breath. "Sorry, this isn't the best time. We seem to be in the middle of a crisis here."

"I know, that's why I called."

"You know about Rachel?"

"Your daughter? No. What's wrong?"

"Nothing, no problem," RG said. "Nothing to worry about. What can I do for you? Why are you calling me at home?" A hint of threat lurked beneath his casual tone.

"Business. Convince the Tse Wets Aht to return to the negotiating table. Before it's too late."

"Too late? Ms. Cage, we've already been through this," RG said.

"Can we meet? There are some things you need to know. I tried speaking with Sarah. She hung up on me."

"Well," RG said after a moment's silence, "I've canceled my twelve-thirty tee time tomorrow, with all this fuss over Rachel. Plus it may rain again. Can you come by the club?"

"How about the library?"

"The *public* library. I understand," RG said. "I'll have to dig out my card." He chuckled as he hung up.

Maureen exhaled. She shivered rubbed her bare arms. One more call to make.

Helen answered on the first ring.

"Hi. It's me."

"Mo. What's wrong?"

"I'm fine. I need a favor."

"How much?"

"No, that's not it. I need to find someone. A dancer."

"You mean Raven."

"Yes."

"Leave her alone," Helen said, her voice brittle. "She's done you enough harm."

"She's the last witness. The Tse Wets Aht boy died. There's nobody else who knows the truth. I have to talk to her."

"Haven't you already tried? She'll never tell. She's trouble. They'll end up dragging your name through the papers like you're some criminal. Stay away from her."

"Things are getting out of hand, Helen. I need to know the truth before I go crazy. I think this afternoon someone came to the house."

Dance music played in the background. They were previewing a new girl's routine. The rookies asked for Anne's opinion: what accessories went with what costume, what makeup worked best if you sweat heavy, was there enough pole work in the routine? Anne had the artistic eye; she was forever helping her dancers improve their routines. Her opinions were like gold, in a business where girls always needed an edge. Helen was the business half, the dotted *i*'s and crossed *t*'s, the movie deals and investments that earned double digit interest when others settled for less.

"Who? A burglar?"

"I don't think so. I know this sounds dumb. I never *saw* anyone. It was just a feeling. Maybe I'm getting paranoid. It was probably just my imagination. Can you get me her address? Please?"

"I'll ask around," Helen said. "I know she's with High C. But you're asking me to break the rules, Kiddo. A client's personal stuff is . . . personal."

"Thanks, Helen."

"No promises, hear? I said I'll look into it."

"You're a life saver."

"Anne says to lock your doors and take no chances," Helen said, and hung up before Maureen could reply.

Even in dreams he shouldn't have been strong enough to hold her down. He was smaller—just a boy, and she a grown woman, but his weight was like a stone on her chest and she could not move. His breath was sickly sweet—he stank of her mother's hospital room and of hay and manure and it was in her nose, on her skin. She could not fight him. He grinned as he lifted her nightie, forced her legs apart. Something hard and cold, like ice, touched her. Two soft, pink hands covered her mouth. She should have tossed him off her like a doll, but her hands were pinned beneath the sheets. He finished quickly, rolling off her, slapping her face. Warning her. Then he vanished, running past the door of the foster parents whose snores jack-hammered through the house. The phone rang and the paralysis passed, she could move. She picked up the receiver. It was her mother. Impossible, but it was and she wept, but then she was gone and now it was her father's sloppy voice, whining for money, ordering her to steal when the others were at work on the farm or at school. She begged, no more, but his laughter grew louder, an alarm, a clanging bell that wouldn't stop.

Maureen stumbled from the sofa to the kitchen for the phone.

"Mo. It's Helen. Got a pen?"

"What time is it?" she said.

"Who cares? I got you the address you wanted."

"Hang on."

"And I'm not happy about this. I feel like a criminal."

Maureen rummaged through kitchen drawers for a pen. "You're not," she said, cradling the phone between her ear and shoulder. She wrote on her skin as Helen recited the address.

"Shares the place with another dancer. Elektra. I don't know her. Another High C girl."

"Thanks," Maureen said. She tossed the pen into the gaping drawer.

"Nobody's seen her," Helen said. "She might be in L.A. by now. I didn't wake you up, did I?" Helen said.

"Just another trip down memory lane," Maureen said.

"Sorry. I didn't know they'd come back," Helen said.

"They're getting worse."

"Anne's got great pills, if you need them."

"Good night, Helen. Thanks."

"Take care, Honey."

Her eyelids were sticky with sleep and her arm ached from being pinned beneath her weight as she slept. She felt the coarse pattern of the sofa on her cheek. She padded upstairs to the bathroom and splashed cold water on her face. Her reflection, lit only by the glow of a street lamp scattered through the frosted glass, startled her. Her skin was paper-white, and shadows filled the hollow under each eye. Her lips were dry and chapped. In addition to the herring-bone design of the sofa on one side of her face, deep lines had been chiseled into the skin around her mouth—lines she'd not noticed before.

She retreated to her bed. Still no word from Carole. She stared at the ceiling, watching pinpricks of light float above her head. She was sure her eyes were still open when the spots merged, coalesced into the cold glow off the neon sign at the Dominion Parkade and her bed hardened into the unforgiving cement ledge she'd once called home.

"This is the first time the Heritage League has caught us with our pants down," Legare said. "Thanks to you."

The nurse gathered the empty vial and used needle on a small, steel tray. "I'll come back in five minutes to help her back to bed," she said as she hurried from the room. The door swung open, anticipating her, and closed behind her.

"Frances. Born in Windsor?" Maureen said. Along with the sudden nausea her skin was sticky. It was hard to breathe.

"Frances Marjorie Elderton, if you want her full name," Legare said.

Panic surged through her body, but the drug was already working, slowing her down, turning her arms and legs to dead weight. The throb in her sinuses was ebbing toward a dull, form-fitting ache.

"Can I see her? I have to see her." Maureen heard her voice as she spoke—it was already thicker, sloppy. Her tongue was too large for her mouth. She tried to stand, but her legs would not obey. The panic drained out of her. Her body, wanting sleep, refused to help her.

"I'm sorry," Legare said. He leaned forward, his forearms flat on the table. "I can't make out a single word you're saying."

"Where's Frances?" Maureen said, but it was just a single, undecipherable moan. Darkness was coming for her. The truth, even as it registered, was siphoned off with her strength, her reason, her senses.

"Nurse, I need a nurse," Legare said from far away.

She rested her head on the cold tabletop, barely able to mouth the words.

"I need to see my baby."

BOOK FOUR

Reformation

"Did you pay my bail?" Maureen retreated from Anne's hug and eased herself into a chair.

The reception area in RCMP headquarters consisted of a throw-away end table whose sole purpose was keeping a stack of two-years-stale magazines from hitting the ground, four faded teak chairs whose upholstery was long-expired, and a wall-phone installed when the station was built. Maureen, Helen and Anne were its only occupants.

"Don't worry about it," Anne said. "Helen says we're in good shape."

"I'll sell the house."

"And where will you live? Rents in Vancouver are criminal," Helen said. She gave Maureen a gentle peck on the top of her head. "Anyway, gold and energy stocks are doing well right now." She snapped her thin fingers. "There's no bail we can't raise. How're you feeling?"

"I'll live. Everybody should spend a weekend in a Victoria jail." She leaned forward, both hands cradling her bandaged knee. "So as not to take stuff for granted. Man, this still hurts."

"Those are impressive," Anne said, examining the bruises on Maureen's face. "Have you talked to a lawyer? With all the bad press the RCMP has had, I can't believe they're that stupid. Are you still getting headaches?"

"Not as bad. But it hurts when I turn my head too fast," Maureen said. She sat up straight and touched the flesh under her left eye.

"They get your car?" Helen said.

Maureen shook the car keys. "It's around back, in the impound."

"Anne can drive. You're riding with me."

Maureen smiled. "The rest of my stuff is still at the motel."

"Not anymore," Helen said. "We stopped by there yesterday, squared things away."

"Helen-"

"Shhh," Anne said, holding a plump finger up to her lips. "Done is done."

"Frances," Maureen said. "I have to talk to her."

Helen shot Anne a quick glance.

"What?" Maureen said.

Anne sniffed. "We shouldn't talk about it here, Mo."

"What's happened?"

"Nothing's *happened*," Helen said. She looked down and fiddled with her car keys.

Anne heaved a mighty sigh. "She's gone."

She dressed in her good clothes—*Sunday clothes* her mother would have called them—and drove downtown. She wasn't sure when the idea of going to church had seeded itself into her brain—perhaps during another night of bad dreams—but once germinated it would not leave her in peace. She parked at the back of a half-empty lot and walked to the front doors of St. Patrick's Cathedral. Organ music piped through massive open doors set into a thick wall of cut stone. Maureen stepped into the dimness and inhaled cooler, musty air. She listened—as her eyes adjusted—to an organist rehearsing a hymn she thought she recognized. Music tumbled down the twin aisles that divided three banks of pews. A row of stone pillars soared into darkness. Her eye followed their chiseled surfaces into the upper gloom, where only the spiders and bats could appreciate the fine scrollwork.

She slid into one of the rear pews. The wood was dark and polished. For decades worshipers had slid, shuffled or scooted the length of the benches, buffing the wood grain with their coats and dresses and slacks. Maureen moved to the middle of the pew and leaned into the backrest. The bench creaked and groaned.

Other early arrivals, singles or pairs of elderly women, arranged themselves in various groupings throughout the sanctuary. Some whispered greetings, others read from the hymnals resting on the narrow shelf jutting from the shoulder of the next pew. Mass did not begin for another forty minutes. A youth choir began to practice. They coughed and giggled and fidgeted under their white smocks while their black-suited director flapped like a scrawny crow to get their attention.

Maureen closed her eyes. Footsteps on the stone floor clipped across the children's voices. The surrounding pews chafed under the weight of fresh arrivals. Candle wax, old incense and a hint of mildewed stone reminded her of her of another church, many years ago. She wrapped her arms tightly to her sides. A sudden shiver coursed through her body, spawning an overwhelming urge to cry.

She made it through the entire service, kneeling, standing and sitting on cues from priest, organist and choir. She rarely opened her eyes, and for one moment near the end—when singing voices pierced her body with one of her mother's favorite hymns—she was certain the pew shifted gently under the weight of a latecomer, and a surge of joy and warmth filled her and she had to command herself not to open her eyes lest she spoil the dream and find only an embarrassed stranger hunched, penitent, beside her. At the conclusion of Mass she hurried outside, her eyes lowered, fearful of having to speak to anyone.

Maureen parked the Subaru with its nose aimed up the steep, West Vancouver hillside. She smoothed her skirt, checked her shoes for scuff marks. She tugged her briefcase off the back seat and locked the car. She crossed the street to the library, dodging boxy, concrete planters set before the doors and overflowing with miniature spruce and periwinkle. The wrought-iron benches that lined the entrance were empty. She re-checked her watch. She was five minutes late. Perhaps the pall of low, dark clouds had chased RG indoors. She passed beneath a rainbow-colored, canvas banner celebrating the library renovation project. Its corners slapped loose against the building in a precocious breeze.

The glass doors opened, automatic and soundless. She hesitated where the foyer divided into two, forcing visitors to choose between the new wing and the old. She chose the path to the new. RG was outside the varnished fir and etched-glass doors, occupying one of the tables in the new cafeteria. He had positioned himself beneath a sky light, looking relaxed and unhurried as he drank his coffee. The bright, new notice boards as backdrop showed off his tan.

"Want a coffee? Lunch? I hear it's pretty fair," RG said. He stood and offered the chair nearest his own.

"No thanks," Maureen said. She took the chair opposite and folded her hands across her lap.

RG leaned into the chair's backrest and crossed his legs. Everything about him was Sunday casual: his brushed, cotton pants sported a scalpel-sharp crease from mid-thigh to ankle and his expensive golf shirt was a green somewhere between olive and jade, framing a triangle of deeply tanned chest adorned with tufts of curling, white hair. His brown shoes caught the filtered light through the skylight and seemed to glow like well-polished wood.

"You look like you're ready to go to work," he said.

"Church," Maureen said.

RG's eyebrows twitched. "Church?" He shrugged. "Didn't take you for the type."

"First time in forty years," Maureen said.

"Hope it wasn't anything I said?" He grinned.

Maureen glanced across the open foyer. A steady stream of visitors moved through the doors, coming and going. Most carried bags of books. She couldn't remember the last novel she'd read. "Probably," she said.

RG leaned toward her. "You wouldn't be tape recording our conversation? Not without telling me?"

"No," Maureen said. *Moby Dick.* The last novel she'd read, cover to cover. The year the AIP was signed. She'd taken it with her to Long Beach and finished it while the rain lashed the cabin windows. It was either read or go stir crazy.

"It wouldn't be the first time," he said, and settled back in his chair.

"How's Rachel?"

"Still not home. Emily thinks she's gone back to McGill."

"You don't think so?"

RG shook his head. "Rachel's a lot like me. Pigheaded." He attempted a light smile, but quickly gave up. "She's gone off on another one of her causes. I know it. Always trying to save the planet."

"That's a good thing, isn't it? Acting on the strength of one's convictions?"

RG stared at her over the rim of his coffee cup. "Depends on the convictions." He sniffed. "We tend to disagree on what they should be." RG spun his cup on its saucer. It made a soft, grinding sound, like wet sand on ceramic tile. "You called me for a reason."

"Have you spoken to Sarah since my call?"

"No."

"I talked to her last night, before I called you. She didn't appreciate it."

"I wouldn't either, to be honest. She's got a million things to do."

"Like what? I was half-expecting she and Aaron would be out of Port. Especially since the election call."

RG shifted in his chair. "How 'bout we change the subject."

"Fine. Inspector Legare called. He's investigating the hate crime angle."

RG's glance jumped from the saucer to Maureen, but he remained silent.

Maureen opened her briefcase and withdrew two stapled documents. She held them to her chest to hide the text. "He thinks the crash was no accident. We're making a big mistake ignoring this."

"I don't understand." RG frowned and a crease appeared, splitting the rippled parchment of forehead.

"They call themselves the Heritage League," Maureen said, handing him the first document. "I got this off their web site. They operate out of Alberta. Legare says the accident was arranged to stop us cold, to sabotage the negotiations."

"What evidence does he have?" RG flipped his glasses out of his shirt pocket and draped them over the bridge of his nose.

"Some. The Tse Wets Aht have more. A note. Claiming responsibility for the accident. Threatening them."

When RG made no reply Maureen pushed on. "Several known members were in Port the night of the accident. In the same bar as the victims. One of the crash survivors made some accusations—that there was another truck, that it drove them off the road. Now those members are missing."

"Missing? What, kidnapped?"

Maureen shook her head. "Nobody knows. Legare thinks they skipped town."

"So you contacted Sarah because?"

"Because if he's right then they've won. No Final means the status quo—or worse—for years to come. Everyone knows Hargrove will lose the election and-"

"Not necessarily," RG interrupted.

"How can you say that?"

"Forget it," RG said. He reached for his coffee and as he sipped a thin smile appeared. "It's like in sports: it's never over 'til the fat lady sings."

"Here." Maureen handed him the second document.

"What's this?"

"The Heritage League's manifesto for British Columbia. I highlighted something on page two."

RG turned over the page. He held out the document at arm's length. "*It is the God-sworn duty of all Brothers and Sisters of the Secret Flame to hinder, harass and prevent the media-sanctioned pillage of our rightful inheritance by Indians and their sympathizers,*" he read. "This sounds like science fiction."

"It's not."

RG shook his head as he set down the documents. "The RCMP said the truck went off the road because of speed and alcohol. They found open beer in the cab. And the stripper? Hell, everyone knows strippers are drug addicts and prostitutes. She's taken off to feed her habit." He dismissed the documents with a quick wave. "I see nothing *conspiratorial* in all this. Coincidental, more like. This inspector's just looking for a promotion."

"The police closed the investigation before it began. Before the Heritage League connection was discovered. I don't think they even know about the note the Tse Wets Aht received. At least call Templeton. Let him know the situation. Better yet, tell Chief David. If she knew she'd have the Federation back together and pushing harder than before."

"Forget it. They'll think *Dee-Faz* arranged the accident if you keep up with this conspiracy bullshit."

"It's still not too late to get a Final," Maureen said. "Whether this has legs or not, it's what we need to restart the table. *Dee-Faz* needs this agreement, RG."

"We've got bigger fish to fry," RG said. "Don't ask me because I won't say any more about it, except it's big. Big enough to blow all this away." He waved his hand over Maureen's papers. "Now then, let's get down to business. In light of the demands on our resources and with the individual Interims starting the team needs you back."

Maureen blinked. "You're offering me back my job?"

"No," RG shook his head. "Not exactly. But I need you in Port. Sarah's stretched to the max. She can use you with TAC, they're up in arms."

"But the Treaty Advisory Committees work through Thorne's people."

"Thorne's been recalled to Victoria. All Provincial teams are shut down, pending the election. Mayor Conconi has hit the roof. I've been fielding calls from the mill ownership group and from Gilliam at the Chamber of Commerce. They're hearing rumors; they think the whole ball of wax has come off the rails."

Maureen made a noise in her throat. "You're mixing your metaphors, RG. Besides, even if I wanted to Sarah will fire me the first chance she gets."

"She can't. She'll be too busy. Besides, I'll call her."

"So just what am I negotiating?" Maureen said.

"Time. Stall the TAC. Keep them happy a couple of weeks. Hell, a week would be good." RG wiped his hands on a napkin. "Think you can handle that?"

"Sure," Maureen said. She was confused and dizzy. He'd kicked her feet out from under her. "But what does one week gain us?"

RG smiled and scratched at the side of his cup with a perfectly rounded fingernail. "More than you could ever dream. We're working on a slam-dunk here, Cage." He looked up, held her glance. He looked more like a schoolboy an hour from summer vacation. "Look, I'll call Keith; show him what you've given me. Hope like hell he doesn't laugh me out of town. In the meantime, I suggest you prepare for TAC."

"I can be in Port tomorrow." She closed her briefcase.

"One last thing." He coughed into his closed fist. "About last week. I apologize." RG stared into his empty coffee cup.

"Sure." Maureen rose, both hands on her briefcase handle. She needed to be someplace quiet. Someplace RG wasn't.

RG tossed his napkin on the table and stood. "Great. So, we're back to normal again."

Maureen did not answer. She hurried to the library exit. RG followed a step behind. He pulled up as the glass doors opened with a sigh and waved as she passed over the threshold.

"Thanks, Cage. I appreciate your flexibility." He was almost jovial. "By the way, not that it is any of my business, but I wanted to tell you, I am one hundred percent behind you."

Maureen hesitated, half turning, her eyebrows arched in confusion. "Sorry?"

"You know," he said, grinning, "it's not your fault you're queer."

"Gone? Where? How? Wasn't she charged?"

"She's out on bail, like you," Helen said.

Maureen followed the glances rebounding between them. "*You* posted her bond? Why?"

"Let's go, Mo," Helen said. "It's too stuffy in here. The car is air conditioned and we can make the next-"

"I'm not going anywhere until I see Frances," Maureen said. "Jesus Christ, I must be losing my mind! Frances is my daughter! What am I supposed to do? After three days locked up can I think of anything else?"

"We never wanted this for you, Mo," Anne said.

"How long have you known?"

They stared at each other, their lips pressed thin.

"Four years," Helen said. "It was my idea, not Anne's. I'm not proud for it, but I'd do it again if I had to. We did it to protect you."

"From what?" Maureen's voice stretched thin. "The truth?"

"She's bad news," Helen said.

"How did you-" Maureen's eyes widened. She tasted bile as it burned the back of her throat. "She auditioned for A&H, didn't she?"

"You'd just got a decent job," Helen said. "We figured you'd dump it, lose it all, if you found out."

"Time passed," Anne said. "We never got the right moment to tell you."

Maureen grabbed a plastic bag off the passenger seat and locked the car. She hurried to the building that matched the address Helen had given her. It belonged to a twenty-storey high rise, all concrete and glass, near the Vancouver waterfront. She hung around the entrance, rummaging through her purse. When the heavy doors swung open she grabbed the edge and held it.

"Thanks," she said to the couple leaving the lobby. "Can't find my damned key."

The pair exchanged hurried glances but did not stop.

Maureen rode the elevator to the seventeenth floor. The doors opened onto a narrow hallway decorated with heavily textured wallpaper and low-wattage wall sconces. The walls, ceiling, doors—every exposed surface—were sea green, down to the expensive, plush carpet. Save for the vague hum of an air-conditioning unit it was uncomfortably silent. It seemed to press against her body. She was drowning in a green hush. Maureen looked both ways, reversed her direction and headed for suite seventeen-thirteen.

A lean woman with straight, peroxide-blond hair opened the door to the limit of the safety chain. "What do you want? How did you get into the building?"

Maureen gripped her bag tighter. "Is Raven in? I wanted to return these," Maureen held up the plastic bag like a shield. "The front door was open."

"She didn't say nothing to me." The woman's voice brimmed with complaint. "What's in the bag?"

Maureen partly withdrew a pair of scarlet heels. "I've had these the longest time," she said. "They saved my life."

"Never seen 'em. She's never loaned me nothing, and *I* live with her. Who're you?"

"Maureen. We go way back. Is she here?"

The woman shook her head. "I don't know where she is." She looked ready to cry.

"Can I come inside then? I wanted to write a card, you know, to thank her, but ran out of time. I'm always running late. Can I borrow a pen?"

The woman shut the door. The safety chain rattled off the track. She opened the door and stepped backward. Bony fingers played with the hem of a limp, grey tee shirt, the kind football players wore beneath their pads. "Just for a sec, okay? I'm kinda busy."

"Thanks." Maureen said. "What's your name?"

"Shannon." The fingers quickened as they pulled on the fabric.

"Hey, aren't you Elektra?" Maureen slipped through the crack in the door and shut it behind her.

The woman's thin face brightened. "You've seen my act? Where?"

"Gosh, I don't know, at the Icehouse maybe?" Maureen said.

"Yeah, maybe," Shannon said, "that was last winter, but I don't remember you."

"Cool lava lamps," Maureen said. She walked into the living room and set the plastic bag onto a cluttered coffee table. She pulled a blank card from the bag. "Do you have a pen?"

Shannon looked around the room. "I'll be right back." She disappeared behind a door off the hall.

Maureen picked up the top DVD from a stack next to the shoe bag. *Sexxx Down Under!* listed Raven's name on the credits. Maureen sniffed, set down the plastic case and followed a trail of empty Diet Pepsi cans into the kitchen. She noticed an address book on the counter next to the phone. She picked it up and flipped through the pages. *Candy, ExxxStacey, Jewel*: most of the listings were dancers. She stuffed the book into her bag, her heart thumping against her ribs.

"I hope I'm not interrupting," she called out. "I'm leaving town and when I was packing, I found these shoes. Raven loaned them to me ages ago. I figured she was going to chew me out."

"You dance—I mean—still?" Shannon asked as she re-entered the living room. She held out a ball-point pen. The expression on her face was half suspicion, half disbelief.

"Not anymore," Maureen said, her hand executing a dismissive wave. "I quit. But it helped pay the rent."

"Which agency?"

"A and H," Maureen said. She tried to keep her voice calm as she scribbled *thanks for the loan—call me* in the card.

"I heard those dykes were okay. I wanted to change but Raven talked me out of it. Said that when she tried to sign with them they screwed her around."

"Really?" Maureen looked up from the card.

"Yeah. Everything was great, they loved her act, the contract was ready to sign and then one of them goes all weird and they disappear into the back and when they come back they rip up the contract and tell her to get lost. Bizarre, eh?"

"Very. That's not like them at all. I'll have to ask." Maureen handed Shannon the pen. "You sure you don't know where Raven is? I really wanted to thank her in person. Cards can be, you know, distant."

"I said I don't know, alright?" Shannon threw the pen against the kitchen wall. Her voice trembled, close to tears. "We're *supposed* to be pulling off a fucking duo set this week. The only reason I'm stuck *here* listening to you babble on like some mental defect is because if I knew where the bitch was I'd be kicking the shit out of her myself. She's cost me a week's wages and if she doesn't show by the end of the month we're gonna lose this place. When I find her even that psycho boyfriend of hers won't be able to help her." She yanked the door open and glared.

"Thanks-" The door slammed in Maureen's face.

She rode the elevator to the ground floor, clutching in both trembling hands the bag with the address book. She ran to her car, tossing the bag into the back seat as the engine started. She had a million things to do before heading back to Port and somehow had to find a way of convincing herself she was not resurrecting foresworn, criminal tendencies.

"Does Frances know?" Maureen leaned forward to cradle her face in her hands. When Anne touched her shoulder she pushed it away.

"Legare showed her the lighter when he interrogated her. She knows it was you who filed the report on it. I think Legare's the only one who *doesn't* know."

"You paid her off," Maureen said. Her voice cracked. "Is that what you did the first time, when you wouldn't give her a contract?"

"That was different," Helen said. "She wanted us to represent her. We said no. She's not going to run away now. She's facing charges."

"Bull. She'll take off. California. Montreal. You're counting on it. Did you give her cash, too?"

"Mo." Anne's cheeks were flushed. "What Frances does isn't up to you. It never was."

She caught the seven PM ferry out of Horseshoe Bay, wedged into the back end of the car deck. Sunday evening ferry rides in summer were always chancy—the boats were usually full. Until Labor Day, when the tourists going to the Island dwindled and the ferries carried only regulars: bus tours of seniors, commuters who lived in Victoria but worked in Vancouver and loaded commercial rigs. Maureen stayed in her car, thumbing through the address book. Opening it was an admission of guilt. She *was* a thief. It was an admission, too, that another thread had been broken—one of the remaining few that bound her to the life she'd remade.

As the ferry rounded the headlands and churned past Gambier Island she dialed numbers out of the address book. There was nothing to confirm whether the book was Raven's or Elektra's, save by calling and finding out. Each entry took up two lines, written in the same square, childish script. She started with an entry for *Alexa,* a Vancouver number that had been crossed out twice for new addresses and numbers. She got an answering machine after five rings.

"This is Carey James," Maureen said. She read from a script she'd scribbled on the back of a real estate flyer. "I'm a producer with Trojan Horse Films in LA. We're opening a Vancouver office because we're putting together a new video series and want some local girls in the production. We're on a really tight schedule—I'm flying back to LA tomorrow. Give me a call. This is a serious project with big time exposure." She left her cell phone number and hung up.

She waited to catch her breath before dialing the next listing. She was in the *D's* when the line failed and her phone flashed *No Service.* She jammed the phone into its charger and stuck the end of the cord into the cigarette lighter. She locked the car and hiked the stairs to the upper decks.

She resisted the urge to call Carole, to let her know she was going back to Port. She'd waited as long as she could for a call from Inspector Legare. It never came. She left a message at Helen and Anne's and locked her house and raced to the ferry terminal. She was actually looking forward to being in Port; to having something tangible to do.

The ferry reached open water. The smells from the cafeteria reminded her she was hungry. It was standing room only, so she bought a cellophane-wrapped bagel and a carton of orange juice in the snack bar and wedged herself into a seat with its own plastic side table. She surveyed the crowd. Not the usual tourist mob. The ferry overflowed with young people. They occupied every flat surface and congregated in the corners. Some slept, others played music, and the ones on the outside decks basked in the evening sun when it appeared through shredded clouds. At the rear of the lounge, where the foot-passengers boarded, more youth leaned into a mountain of piled backpacks and bedrolls. Two small children played Hide 'n Seek in the heap.

Maureen peeled the cellophane off her bagel. She tossed a dart of a smile to the older couple sitting side by side across the aisle from her. They chewed their sandwiches in slow-motion synchronization—chew, chew, pause, chew, chew, swallow. The couple watched her as they ate. Her eyes skipped past them to the expanse of battleship grey water beyond the outside deck.

"They've taken over the ship," the woman said, loud enough for Maureen to know she was being spoken to. She brought arthritic fingers to the corner of her mouth as she spoke. Her fingertips brushed at strands of coarse, grey hair sprouting from her upper lip.

"They're all goin' to some festival, I figure," the woman's husband chimed in with a grunt. "Every day's a damned holiday to the likes of them. Bloody lawbreakers, every one. Not one's ever worked an honest day in his life."

Maureen smiled gamely and tried to eat.

"If it were up to me they'd be up working the mines in the Territories, or plantin' trees, doin' something useful."

"They smell," the woman said. She glanced worriedly at a huddle of youth near the doorway.

"They got no respect for the law." The man yanked off his ball cap with his right hand, scratching a liver-spotted scalp with the two remaining fingers. He caught Maureen's look and grinned. He wagged the hand in front of her face. "Lost 'em in the mills, I did. Goin' on forty years ago. Left ol' Mr. Ring and Mr. Pinky in Powell River. Was back at work in a week, eh Hon.'

The wife smiled matter-of-factly, nodded, then turned to Maureen. "Never lets me forget it, neither. Do I go on about delivering four children without anesthetic while he drank himself potty in the waiting room?"

Maureen shot them another weak smile, gathered her wrapper and juice carton and slid out of her chair.

"Watch out for those troublemakers," the husband said. "They'll buttonhole ya for money, too, the lazy So-and-So's."

"Why can't they just take a bath?" The woman wondered aloud from behind her fluttering fingertips. "Once a week is the least they could do."

"Why are you trying to keep me away from my daughter?" Maureen rubbed away a fresh flood of tears with the back of her hand.

"We're not," Helen said. "Besides, she knows where to find you."

"I can't sit home waiting. Wondering."

"You've never waited for anything, Mo," Anne said.

"She's in as much shock as you," Helen said. "Give her time."

"I tried to give her a life," Maureen said. "A head start."

"And you did," Helen said. "What she did with it is not your fault."

"I don't believe that."

"You have to get on with your own life," Anne said.

"We came to take you home," Helen said. "We'll carry you if we have to."

It was dark when she arrived in Port. She resisted the siren song of fast food and cold beer and drove into the Queen Anne Hotel parking lot and dragged her suitcase from the car. She stopped at the front desk.

"There's a message for you, Ms. Cage. It's from Ms. Cohen in room one-sixteen," the clerk said as he handed her a slip of folded paper. "It's urgent—she said so."

Maureen unfolded the bond paper. It was her morning meeting schedule. Across the top, in heavy pen strokes, was a short, direct order: *Call Me!*

"Thanks." She wadded the page and tossed it at the wastebasket behind the clerk. It bounced off the rim and landed on the carpeted floor.

"Memorized it," she said to his worried expression.

She slipped into her room and set the deadbolt. She opened her suitcase and removed two bottles of red wine. Not as cheap as her first purchase: these ones came with corks. She set them on the dresser next to the television and returned from the bathroom with a glass and a corkscrew dug from her suitcase. She filled the glass to the rim. As the first swallow warmed her throat she caught the blinking red light on her phone. The voice mail recording told her it was a Washington State area code. Billy's cell phone. She took another drink, dropped onto the edge of the bed and kicked off her shoes. She was going to have to apologize sooner or later. Might as well be sooner. "Who am I kidding," she said, and drained the glass. The wine was already loosening the muscles in her arms and legs. "I'm as old as his mother."

She punched Billy's number. He answered on the second ring of a bad connection, clouded with static. Heavy equipment roared in the background. She winced, pulling the phone away from her ear. "Billy, it's me. Maureen," she shouted.

"Cage?" Billy shouted back. His voice sounded hoarse. "This is un-fucking-believable! Do you know where I am right now?"

"In the middle of a construction site," Maureen said, and reached for her wine glass. It was still empty. She stood and took the phone with her to retrieve the opened bottle. She refilled her glass and sat on the bed. "Are you going to tell me where you are?"

"They're tearing it up, Cage! Hear that? They've gone Bushido."

"Who?" Maureen tensed. She stood and began to pace at the foot of the bed, her glass sloshing wine dangerously close to the rim. "What are you talking about?"

"The Tse Wets Aht. They've closed the highway. The NFDI are here, too."

"A blockade? Are you insane? Billy, what have you done?"

"Me? It was Templeton what started it." Billy spoke quickly, his voice hoarse. "He called Josephine to warn her about the Heritage League. She called me right after. Said that the RCMP is part of it. See, Cage? Sometimes it pays to be paranoid."

"Chief David ordered you to occupy the highway? Why? You already knew about the Heritage League."

"Can you say *Cover Up*? Why didn't the RCMP warn them that they're being stalked by white fucking supremacists?"

"That's why *I* called RG. Why Templeton called Chief David." She pressed her fingertips into her eyelids. This couldn't be happening.

"Jo went ballistic. She figures this is the only way anybody's going to listen. You should see this, Cage. Port McKenzie's Finest have arrived and they're scared shitless. Haven't a fucking clue what to do next—they've never seen so many pissed off Indians with rifles." Billy's laugh ended in a coughing jag. "I need a smoke," he said, and coughed harder. "The RCMP has set up down the road, at the farmers' market. They're not letting anymore of my NFDI brothers and sisters through. Jo's called the Federation tribes. They're gonna kick a lot of vanilla ass tonight."

"Don't do anything crazy," Maureen said.

"Too fucking late," Billy howled. "Cage, you coming to the party? I'll save you a good seat." He hung up as another coughing jag filled her ear.

Maureen felt nauseous. She reached for the phone and began to dial Carole's number. "Get a grip," she said and dropped the handset. She turned off the room light and went to the window. Trucks and cars passed by the hotel—one turned into the fast food chicken place directly opposite the hotel. Routines hadn't changed. Maybe they didn't know? But wouldn't people still need fast food, gas for their trucks, rented movies? It was *her* world turned upside down, not theirs. She turned her back on the night and stared at the wine bottle. Opened, almost half full and completely defenseless. She gripped the bottle by the neck and turned it over, filling her glass again. She set both aside and lay on the bed and stared at the ceiling. It wasn't alcohol she wanted, it was company—and she'd settle for a friendly voice at the end of the phone. As usual, she was going to have to deal with this alone.

When they'd put her mother in the ground she'd stood by herself and watched the men lower the coffin with ropes while her father wept into her aunt's shoulder. Two weeks shy of her fifth birthday she'd walked away, unnoticed, her fingertips trailing across the frozen, marble headstones. The priest's muttered incantations were a vague hum in her ears. After it was over her aunt had come looking for her, finding her at the far end of the cemetery, her bare legs nearly blue from cold as she pressed her spine against a frozen grave marker. Her aunt scolded her for missing the service. For missing her mother.

There was only one thing worse than being alone: tricking herself into believing that someone else might care. Maureen scrubbed her face with her hands and sprang off the bed. She hurried through the hotel hallways, down the stairs to the lobby. She stopped in front of the vending machines that guarded the entrance to the restaurant. How long since a deck of smokes cost two bucks? She poured eleven dollars down the machine's throat and thumped the button over her old brand. A familiar white box dressed in a red band and fancy coat of arms tumbled into the tray. She crouched to snatch it up. Ten years wasn't long enough to forget what it was like. Her fingers closed tightly around the box. She grabbed a complimentary book of matches from the open tray on top of the machine and sprinted back to her room.

Anne and Helen went topside, but Maureen stayed in the car for the ferry ride from Victoria to Vancouver. She sat in the shadows, her face and right knee throbbing. She reclined the passenger seat and stared at the ceiling of Helen's SUV, rationing each indrawn breath to spare her bruised ribs. She let her vision relax, blur and the pattern of tiny, grey diamonds stitched into the upholstered ceiling dissolved into an endless sea.

Closing her eyes was worse: she saw Frances on the floor; gloved fists and polished night sticks crashing onto her back, her head, her arms. Before Legare's revelation it had been a disturbing vignette, grist for next winter's nightmares. It had been the Raven-exotic dancer by day, white supremacist by night—beneath the blows. Now it was her Frances: her baby, her lost and impossibly found daughter. She pressed her fingernails into her eye sockets. She longed to claw the images from her head before they drove her mad.

Mad or sane they chased her from the car. She limped to the side of the ferry. It was awkward, maneuvering her crutches between the tightly parked cars. The outside walls of the upper car deck were open to the water. She set her crutches beside her and leaned over a wide steel railing. Four stories below, where hull met waterline, a thin crease of foam danced on the wave tips. The ferry slipped between the Gulf Islands. Bare rock cliffs so close a strong jump from the top deck might reach them. The waters in the narrow passage morphed from bright, jade green in the shallows to crow-black near the hull. The ship's wake surged against the shore, momentarily submerging a jumble of rocks at the tide line. They shrugged off the waves, emerging sleek, wet and dazzling in the sun. Ribbons of foam broke on the cliff and receded, swirling, into deep pools. Gulls the shade of crushed dreams circled over the roiling waters, crying, hunting for food.

Maureen closed her eyes and leaned out to catch the breeze. She was suspended above the water, weightless. The vibration of the ship's engines traveled up her arms, resonated inside her skull, a murmured secret.

"Gone-gone-gone-gone-gone-gone."

She recoiled from the wind, folding her arms tightly across her chest. She swayed with the motion of the ship as it turned in the channel, a mother rocking her restless baby. The ship's whistle sounded. Three baritone blasts as it acknowledged an oncoming sister vessel in the widening channel.

"Hooooooooome. Hooooooooome. Alooooooone."

A reminder—no, a warning—of past crimes.

She woke to hotel room-darkness, save for the fiery seam where opposing rafts of curtain collided. A lightning bolt warning that morning had come. She lay on her back—she'd kicked off the sheet and blanket hours ago—and slid her hands flat onto the mattress to steady the bed. It still rocked. Her stomach hurt and her throat had been scraped raw. Somebody had stuffed her head with needles. There had been a time when she felt like this every time she woke up—except that it had never been so soon after sunrise. She approached the brightening scar in the curtains and tore it apart, shutting her eyes against the sudden brilliance. She groped for the handle that opened the window. She pushed it all the way forward and squinted into the sunshine and expelled the dry, hotel air from her lungs.

Port McKenzie was immersed in a golden fire: the sun had scarcely cleared the fringe of the eastern hills and it burned, beneath an umbrella of haze, like a torch above the valley. Colors emerged—dazzling greens and vivid blues and the rich, dun tones of brick and stone—unfiltered by emissions from the mill. But the sun climbed into the ring of pollution and the light changed, like a dirty lens had been set before it. Maureen gulped two breaths of outside air and began to cough: it was no cooler or any fresher than the hotel's air conditioning. She reached for her deck of smokes and matches and pulled a cigarette out of the pack. With trembling hands she lit it and watched the sun beat against the murk. Still no fires on Vancouver Island. But the air in Port resembled the newspaper photos she'd seen of the Interior fires that burned unabated under smoke-smeared skies. By the time she flicked her butt onto the street two stories below the landscape had been restored to the listless, drab view she recognized so utterly well. She staggered to the shower: she had a TAC meeting to run.

It was a large room, many-windowed, on the second floor of the Port McKenzie Community Centre. Used as a pre-school classroom during the school year. Children's artwork covered the back wall. The yellowed and curled edges of their paintings and crayon sketches—requisite samples of stick figures swimming or playing soccer, bright flowers in green meadows, square-cut fish boats and nets and sharp chiseled emerald forests—rippled in a hot cross-draft. The stubby desks and sawed-off chairs had been pushed out of the way to make room for an adult-sized table and chairs. Whether the result of some custodian's diabolical intent, or a pattern adopted by the members as they arrived, the TAC were lined up against her. Eight pairs of eyes watched her from the further side of the table as she picked her way between knee-high desks and deposited her briefcase on the meeting table.

"I hope I haven't kept you waiting," she said, rechecking her watch.

"No worries." A small man, too small for his brown tweed sports jacket, half-rose and extended his hand. "We got here early on purpose. To chat amongst ourselves. I'm Bob Gilliam, McKenzie Valley Chamber of Commerce."

"Maureen Cage, *Dee-Faz*," she said, shaking his hand. Strange, hearing that combination of words again. Her left hand pressed into the front of her business jacket where it could keep tabs on the poisons bubbling in her stomach.

They introduced themselves, each one standing in turn, leaning forward to shake her hand across the table. Sally Brackens, heavyset, with straight, silver-grey hair that fell to her shoulders: VP of Corporate Services for Western Pulp and Paper. John Conconi, the Mayor of Port McKenzie, with a fisherman's leathery hands. She'd met him once before, at the AIP signing, but his eyes stared blankly at her reminder of that day. There was no memory of her in those bloodshot depths. Sheila Chapman, housewife and part-time city Councilor wore a loose, peasant-style dress cancelled out by a prodigious layer of dried-on make-up. Tom Owen, consultant and chair of the Forest Products Alliance, was dressed in a new gray suit, pressed white shirt and bright, Frank Lloyd Wright tie below a neatly trimmed Van Dyke beard. Mike Hogan, the largest man on the panel, an ex-logger in a tight sport shirt and golf slacks and president of the

173

International Wood Workers Union Local 156. Phillip Deutsch, gray from his socks to the wild fringe of hair above his ears was the chair of the McKenzie School District. Lastly, John Jared, pastor and President of the North Island Interfaith Society. He perched, cramped at the end of the row in a collarless tee shirt and faded jeans and from beneath a shock of white hair eyed the space next to Maureen with a look very close to envy.

"You're it?" Conconi said.

"I'm it," Maureen said as she broke out her notepad, pen and closed her briefcase. "Are we ready?"

She was met by a general nodding and twitching from the other side of the table.

"Let me start by welcoming you—and by stating the obvious," Maureen said. "*Dee-Faz* has never met with a TAC directly."

"And look where that's gotten us," Tom Owen said. He smoothed his goatee with one hand as he spoke. "Road blocks and rifles in our city."

"Regardless of how well—or how badly—things have gone, your authority in terms of treaty settlement exists by extension of Victoria. That's why your proposals are bundled with the Province's. Leonard Thorne's team looks after you."

"Not very well. And it's bloody not good enough," Conconi said.

"We got loaded logging trucks sitting at the Sleeping Man Bridge," Mike Hogan said. His face turned red. "If they don't get through real soon, there's gonna be Hell to pay."

"How much is it going to cost us?" Gilliam said. "Tourists won't come if there's blocked roads and protests every time they turn around. It'll kill this town. Hell, it will kill the whole Island."

"The only solution is a Final Agreement, signed and ratified," Maureen said. "You need to let Victoria, Ottawa and the Tse Wets Aht know that you're behind them."

"Fine by me," Conconi said. He pushed a single sheet of paper out from beneath his hands and slid it toward Maureen. "Let's call this Step One," he said.

Maureen swept the page into her hands. "*Manifesto of Rights?*" She looked up.

"Are natives the only ones who can issue demands?" Hogan shouted.

"Unless the highway is re-opened within twenty-four hours, and unless our demands are formally accepted as an action plan for future negotiations, the City of Port McKenzie will withhold all taxes, license fees and other revenues which it collects on behalf of other governments," Conconi said. "I've talked to our Council, to other Island mayors. We're firm on this. You can expect more cities to follow."

Maureen glanced from the page. "I'm sorry, but I-"

"That's not quite all," Sally Brackens said. She settled a narrow pair of glasses across her nose and read from an index card tucked into the curve of her palm. "The ownership group of Western Pulp and Paper will close its doors and cease all operations in the McKenzie Valley unless the West Coast Highway is reopened immediately to commercial traffic. In addition, negotiations must restart with the full Pacific Coast Tribal Federation and will include sincere discussions of forest resource allocation. There will be no further consideration of transferring title of Crown Lands, upon which Western Pulp and Paper maintains paid, *legal* and working forest licenses, unless there is adequate and timely representation by Western's shareholders, through its duly elected Board of Directors."

"With all due respect," Maureen said. She set down her pen and held up her hands a foot apart. "There's the blockade." She motioned with her left hand, "and there's the Final Agreement." She raised her right hand. "I can negotiate and carry terms for one, but not if you're connecting it to the other."

"*You're* here to listen," Conconi said, jabbing a ballpoint pen in her direction. "So listen to this: the survival of this town is the *only* issue. Get rid of that road block."

"The blockade is now a police matter, Mr. Mayor. Bundling land claims negotiations with civil disobedience will not work," Maureen said. "I sincerely hope the sides will be negotiating soon. I think I can truthfully say that more threats won't help."

"*You're* responsible for this mess," Gilliam said, pointing at Maureen. "Between you and this Ottawa Special Investigations pencil pusher telling natives that our town's full of Nazis we're lucky things aren't worse."

Conconi pushed out of his chair. He sidestepped the corner of the table to open space and leaned toward Maureen. He was breathing hard. The shelf of stomach protruding over his belt rested on the table. "City staff are reviewing legal action against *Dee-Faz*, Victoria, Ottawa, the Tse Wets Aht First Nation, the Pacific Coast Tribal Federation, this NFDI group and even against you, *personally*, for damages resulting from the loss of jobs and commercial opportunity in this valley. We're not going to sit idly by while terrified governments afraid of offending every Indian with a microphone give away our birthright and ruin our town!"

"My members need paychecks to pay their mortgages. Their earnings keep this town going," Hogan shouted. His face was red.

"I understand the economic realities, Mr. Hogan," Maureen said. She grasped her pen at both ends and squeezed it tightly. "And I don't see how shutting down the mill will solve anything." She met Conconi's glare head on, willing her stomach to cooperate. "There will be no taxes for the city to withhold."

"Council backs me on this one," Conconi said, glancing to Sheila Chapman who nodded her support. "A little pain now beats being bled to death over the next twenty years."

"You signed the Agreement in Principle, Mr. Mayor. I was there."

The mayor flushed. "I never agreed to all this." His thick arm gestured toward the window.

"People!" John Jared raised his arms. "This is not helpful in the least. Miss Cage," he said, "we most respectfully ask that you forward our concerns to your superiors. Whether they belong in the treaty process or not will be for others to decide. They will, I am quite certain, be taken quite seriously."

"Mr. Jared," Maureen said, "I intend to do exactly that. But I must warn you-"

"There are hippies and freaks camping on the edge of town!" Gilliam's shrill voice cracked. "How did all these Nutbars from the mainland find out so fast? They're Tweeting and Facebooking 'til their thumbs drop off! There will be videos on *YouTube* any moment now. If it weren't for the RCMP they'd have *all* joined up with the natives and who knows what would be happening now."

"Except now we have *two* illegal encampments instead of one," Brackens said.

"But the RCMP have both contained, thank God," Gilliam said.

"We want things back to normal," Councilor Chapman said.

"We're still being too generous," Conconi said. He pulled his jacket off the back of the chair and draped it over his arm. "Ms. Cage, if you can't do anything for us—if we've heard nothing by noon today—we'll take our manifesto to the media. If professional negotiators can't settle this, maybe television cameras will." He swung open the door so violently it smashed against the wall and shivered halfway shut on its hinges.

"The trucks will roll, one Goddamned way or another," Hogan growled and stalked out at the Mayor's heels.

The remaining six TAC members stood and filed through the door in silence. John Jared winced as he coaxed the door shut in a gentle arc behind him. He paused long enough to nod his mane of thick, white hair in Maureen's direction.

Maureen placed the Mayor's single sheet on top of her stack of notes, and with both hands dropped the folder into the open briefcase. "That went well," she said, and exhaled wearily.

She threw her pen like a dart into the briefcase, its point marking the leather pocket where it struck. She slammed shut the case so hard it fell off the chair. She ignored it, pressing her face into her hands. Behind her the children's forgotten artwork crackled like nervous applause in a gust of hot wind.

"Take these, Anne uses them all the time," Helen said. She uncurled her fist. Three small, blue pills lay in the leathery creases of her palm. In her other hand was a glass of water, just filled from the kitchen tap. The rising air bubbles gave it a milky, Alka-Seltzer appearance.

Maureen took the pills and chased them down with tepid water. She coughed and settled back into the sofa, trying to find a position that eased the pain in her knee. "I'm good now," she said. She wanted them gone.

Helen made a face as she retreated to the kitchen. She came back moments later with Anne. "The groceries are away, there's milk and bread and eggs. Coffee for the morning," Anne said. "Call if you need anything." The tone of her voice turned each sentence into a question.

Maureen barely acknowledged them.

"We'll come by tomorrow, after breakfast, so don't be doing any gardening or furniture stripping," Helen said. "You can shout orders from the deck, I'm good at pulling things up by the roots."

"We're not done, yet," Sarah said. Her knuckles rapped the table top as Maureen rose out of her seat to leave.

"I think we are," Maureen said. She dangled a copy of the TAC demands over her gaping briefcase. "These need to be addressed, and fast, or there'll be more trouble."

"We're working on more important issues right now."

"Like what?"

The air was dry and irritated Maureen's sinuses. The meeting room Sarah had dragged her into was small, cramped and—like its spacious cousins down the corridor—suffered for want of functioning air conditioning. Maureen wanted a cigarette, didn't care that her stomach would make her pay.

"Like never mind," Sarah said. Her hands splayed across the table. "Trust me, we've got it covered."

"*We*? Who? You and RG?"

Sarah smiled and leaned back in her chair. "This will be over soon. TAC will get its answers. And they'll be thrilled, that much I do know."

"Riddle me this, riddle me that, it's all bullshit." Maureen said. She closed her briefcase and slid it off the table. "If you won't act I'll take the TAC demands elsewhere," Maureen said.

"You'll do nothing," Sarah said, climbing out of her smile. "You're job's done. Sit tight and wait. Period."

"Sorry, Sarah, no time for that. They're not bluffing when they say the mill's going down."

"They're panicking," Sarah said, "and I don't blame them. *You're* supposed to reassure them—to restore their confidence."

"Stall them, you mean. Feed them crap. We're way past that. Sarah, you can see the RCMP checkpoint from half the town." Maureen moved toward the door.

"I mean it, Maureen. Walk out now and you're really done."

Maureen leaned into the door knob. "Good luck, Sarah. You've the one quality essential to all great negotiators: you're a terrific listener." She pulled the door closed, peeled her fingers off the knob and hiked toward the lobby. Her free hand was already rummaging for the matches in her purse.

The highway was jammed. Cars were pulled over onto both shoulders to wait; others whose drivers were less patient or less tolerant executed U-turns, some leaning on their car horns or tossing obscene gestures through the windows. In front of the farmer's market the highway had been transformed into a street fair. There was music, dancing; a festival to the unwary eye. Some of the waiting drivers read newspapers or slept. A few gave in to their curiosity and milled at the fringes of a crowd that overflowed across the highway. Maureen watched from the driver's seat, unwilling to pull over. She nudged her Subaru into the throng.

"You'll never get through!" The driver of a stranded commercial rig called to her.

Other drivers laughed or cheered her on from the highway shoulders, where they leaned against their bumpers and smoked cigarettes. "Take a load off, Sweetie, I got enough cold beer for two."

Maureen tapped the gas pedal and the Subaru vanished inside a wall of shifting bodies. She'd driven onto their dance floor. She locked the passenger side doors, rolled up her windows and gripped the steering wheel. Her calf muscle tensed, her foot teasing gas and brake pedals as she insinuated her way into the crowd. The crash of music coming from the road edge made it hard to hear, and in the press of people she lost the road. She strained to find the painted yellow line beyond her hood. The bodies in her path moved or stayed, in their own time. They laughed at her through the windshield, giving ground only when the car brushed against them. The smell of pot was strong, even through closed windows.

She drew level with an old travel trailer that had been dragged to block the driveway to the farmer's market. Bob Marley and the Wailers' *Freedom for the People* blasted from roof-mounted speakers. Tents filled the parking lot behind the trailer—a sea of blue, grey and orange domes jammed into every open space; they jumped the highway to litter the bank of the Slough. A pair of Volkswagen camper vans nestled bumper to bumper next to the travel trailer. Their fenders had been hand-painted with yellow, red and green flowers, like they'd been dragged intact out of nineteen-seventy. A clothesline leashed the vans to the trailer, and a *STOP THE GENOCIDE!* banner hung limp in the space between.

She rolled down the window. "I need to get through," she said, and the closest dancers dove onto her hood and jumped on the roof. The metal bulged under their weight. They pressed their faces against her windows. She laid on the horn. The pair on her hood stomped, creasing the lid. Maureen killed the ignition and opened the door. Before she could begin her rant a young woman with violent, purple hair and a silver nose ring stuck a piece of green paper into her hand and floated away, smiling serenely.

Maureen glanced at the handbill. *DO YOU SUPPORT APARTHEID IN CANADA?* She crumpled the paper and tossed it through the open driver's door and slammed it shut. She followed the girl with purple hair in the direction of the trailer. She felt old and foolishly corporate in her business skirt and leather shoes, slipping between baggy army pants and peasant skirts and spaghetti-strap tops and rainbow-painted vests. The sun burned the back of her neck. She wanted a smoke and a drink. She would have taken a pull on a joint if anyone had offered.

An old Bingo hall table had been set up in front of the travel trailer. The letters *N.F.D.I.* hung on a painted sheet taped to the front edge of the table. The girl with purple hair dropped into a chair behind the table and began eating an apple. The silver loop in her nose jiggled as she chewed. She stretched her heavy black boots across the table and tipped her chair onto its back legs. A couple rolled on the ground beside her, entangled in a thrashing embrace that threatened to upset the table. She ignored them until one of their legs knocked her chair. She turned, aimed a kick at the nearest body and took another bite from the apple. As Maureen approached the woman stuck a sharpened, black-painted fingernail between her front teeth to dislodge a wedge of apple skin. Her eyes ran up Maureen's body with deliberate slowness.

"Narc," she said.

"I need your help." Maureen had to shout over Bob Marley and his wailing.

The woman snorted and the couple on the ground stopped wrestling. They stared, grinning.

"I need to get through," Maureen said.

"Relax. Enjoy the music," the woman said, between bites.

"I have to get to the Tse Wets Aht. I have something for them."

The woman sniffed and the nose ring jumped. "I'll bet." She stuck out her chin. "You're the first one who hasn't bitched about missing Jeopardy," she said. Her boots scraped across the table top as she straightened in her chair. "You gotta be a cop. They won't let anyone else through."

"Does it look like I'm getting through? Your friends are trashing my car. I'm with the Directorate for Aboriginal Settlement."

The woman choked. She twisted toward the couple on the ground. "Hear that, Rach? Ya know this one?"

The female half of the couple stood and brushed off her bare legs. She pulled her tee shirt down to cover her lowest rib and swept a strand of coral hair out of her eyes. "You're Maureen Cage, right?"

"Rachel? Rachel *Braithwaite*?"

The girl with RG's dazzling, glacier-blue eyes grinned.

Maureen dragged her suitcase from the hall where Anne had left it and rummaged through the bag. The address book was near the bottom. She leafed through the pages to the letter *E*. The entry for Elektra was on the first line. The street address matched the address Helen had given her. So this *was* the Raven's address book.

She phoned from the kitchen, the receiver jammed against her ear as she lowered herself into a chair. She glanced through the window, onto the deck. The shade of late afternoon had inched to the railing. She couldn't see the garden below. She didn't need to: her roses and daisies would have long since withered in the heat.

She began speaking the moment the line connected. "Frances, call me. It's Maureen. We've got a lot to-"

It was a recording from the phone company: "The number you have reached is not in service."

The purple-haired girl laughed. "She knows you, Rach. Too wild."

Rachel slapped dust off her denim shorts. A jagged, sun tattoo encircled her navel. Its starfish arms disappeared below the waistband of her shorts and radiated toward sharp, suntanned hip bones. A jewel flashed in the recess of her navel, at the centre of the tattoo. She ran a long finger around her ear, pushing a strand of hair out of her face. "My dad mentioned you. Several times. You sleeping with him?"

Her companions laughed over the music.

"No. But thanks for asking."

More laughter. Rachel stuck out her hand. "Hey, I wasn't trying to piss you off. When my dad mentions his female staff by name, my sister and I always bet on which ones he's doing."

"And you bet on me?" Maureen did not take Rachel's hand.

"I bet on all of them," Rachel said. "Women have been victimized by the *WMPE* for too long."

"Okay, I'll bite. W.M.P.E?"

White Male Power Elite," Rachel said. "Some of us call them *WiMPEs*, but I think that's dangerous. Makes them sound all cuddly and stuff. They're not. I don't blame you or any other woman. You have to develop survival skills according to the environment you're in."

"I'm not a victim," Maureen said. "I'm just trying to save my job."

"What a hero," the purple haired girl said. "It's time you aimed higher. Why not try saving the world?"

"Can I get through or not?" Maureen said.

"If we can't, you won't," Rachel said.

"I'll deal with the RCMP. I have business with the Tse Wets Aht."

"Take me with you," Rachel said. She tugged at her top, straightening the narrow straps across her shoulders.

The purple-haired girl squealed. The boy on the ground thrust his fist into the air and howled. He lit a joint and passed it to the girl with purple hair. Dancers closest to the table stopped, moving closer to listen.

"No," Maureen said, "I can't take you."

"Then you're stuck here with us," Rachel said. She grinned at Maureen and took the joint as it was passed around. "Hope you brought a tent."

Maureen shook her head. Her scalp itched from the heat. "I can't get you across."

"You're a professional negotiator, aren't you?" Rachel said, jamming her fists onto her hips.

The NFDI supporters hopped off the roof when Rachel jumped into the car. They formed a corridor of pumping fists and peace signs as Maureen gunned the engine and shifted the Subaru into drive. Rachel twisted to rummage through a backpack she'd dumped on the backseat. She pulled out a blaze orange ball cap and waved it at the rows of onlookers. They shouted and thumped the car hood and roof as it passed. The purple haired girl leaned in the window to hug Rachel. She had to leap clear as Maureen touched the gas. She threw Maureen a middle finger salute as the car lurched into empty highway.

"What about your boyfriend?" Maureen said, watching the rearview as the party resumed in their wake.

Rachel ran her hands through her hair and jammed the cap onto her head. The logo on its brim read *Go Solar or Go Home.* "Who? Jason?" She waved one hand to a bark of sawed-off laughter. "He's a just a guy."

"They could as easily arrest us, as let us through," Maureen said. She motioned toward the RCMP checkpoint.

"I have every confidence in you, Maureen Cage of the Directorate for Aboriginal Settlement," Rachel said, grinning.

"Keep quiet, then."

Police barriers blocked the highway half a mile past the town limits, where the road started to curve west in its final advance on the bridge. Here the Slough narrowed to become a quick, nervous stream. The Sleeping Man River officially began on the upstream side of the bridge: exactly where the Tse Wets Aht reserve boundary had been redrawn sixty years ago, when the city expropriated the last sliver of native-owned foreshore and sold it for one dollar to an eager American pulp and paper company. Maureen had spent so much time poring over old maps since she'd been assigned to Lee-Anne Carlyle's team she could paint a line around the town from memory.

She accelerated toward the flashing lights. The sun was hot on the left side of her face. She stuck her head out the window as they neared the bumble-bee painted barricades that hunkered across shimmering asphalt.

"No one's crossing, Ma'am," the RCMP constable said. He bent forward at the hips, toward the car. "I'm surprised as hell those freaks let you by. They started dancing at sunrise and I-" He fell silent when he noticed Rachel in the passenger seat.

"Can we talk? Privately?" Maureen handed the constable her driver's license and business card.

He took one step back to allow Maureen out of the car. With one hand draped casually over his holster he nodded to his partner to watch the car. He stepped to the side of the highway, toward his parked cruiser, his boots clipping the blacktop.

"I have critical information for the Tse Wets Aht," Maureen said.

"Who's she?" the constable jutted his chin at the Subaru and its passenger.

Maureen rolled her eyes. "My CEO's daughter. Rachel Braithwaite. She's volunteered to be our messenger."

The constable raised one eyebrow. "She looks like one of those mix-ups from the hippie show."

"For all I know she might be, but I'm just trying to do my job," Maureen said. "She's a law student specializing in First Nations issues."

"And you need her to . . . ?"

"To answer any questions they might have about the information I'm delivering."

"Why can't you answer their questions? If we let you across, I mean."

"Because I'm not staying," Maureen said. "Look. Search my car. Call Mayor Conconi. Our meeting ended a little more than an hour ago. I need to get through. It's nearly eleven and there isn't much time."

"What's the hurry?"

Maureen inhaled. "Do I tell His Worship that one Constable-" she squinted to read the nameplate on his left breast—"Sawchuk is the reason that Western locked out five hundred employees? Do I tell him that because I couldn't get through this blockade is going to last for weeks and cripple this town, maybe for good?"

"One second," Sawchuk said, scowling. He swung behind the wheel of his cruiser.

Maureen walked back to the Subaru. The other constable took up position beside her as she opened the rear door and flipped open her briefcase.

"Well?" Rachel leaned between the seats.

"Just wait," Maureen said. The nugget of headache had spread from the base of her skull. It pressed against her sinuses and radiated into her jaw. Her mouth was dry and tasted of stale coffee and cigarettes. Her stomach had reluctantly agreed to a surly, wait-and-see compromise.

Constable Sawchuk emerged from his cruiser. "We're checking. In the meantime, we need to search this vehicle."

Maureen popped the tailgate. "Go ahead. Rachel, get out of the car."

The constables were thorough. They lifted, pulled, flipped and dug from front to back. Sawchuk used the toe of his boot to sift through the contents of the glove box once he'd dumped them on the pavement. Three maps, an insurance folder, registration, half a roll of forgotten breath mints and an owner's manual whose pages fluttered like the feathers on a dead seagull. His partner spilled Rachel's backpack and left it inside-out on the highway. He opened Maureen's briefcase, but she held his arm as he began to tip the case upside down.

"Those documents are confidential," she said.

He glared at her, but set the case on the roof of the car and fanned lightly through the papers and closed it carefully.

Sawchuk turned to Maureen and Rachel. "We need to search you too, Ladies," he said. He was perspiring heavily.

"I want a female officer," Rachel shouted.

"We don't have one so shut up!" Sawchuk's square face reddened.

"I told you she was a law student," Maureen said. She spread her arms apart and waited.

Sawchuk patted Maureen down as if caressing a cactus. "Okay," he nodded. "You're good." He glanced to his partner. "Her turn."

"I'm lodging a complaint," Rachel said, as Sawchuk's partner stepped in front of her.

"She's clear," the constable said. He stepped away after an awkward, hasty pat-down.

A dispatcher's voice squawked through the radio at Sawchuk's belt.

He pulled the mike off the clip at his left shoulder. "Go." He listened to the static, nodding at regular intervals. He reset his mike and stared at Maureen.

"They couldn't reach anybody at *Dee-Faz*, so Sergeant called the Mayor's office. He says you're good to go. I just need confirmation on the papers."

"They're here," Maureen said. She pulled a manila envelope from the briefcase. "But as I said, they're confidential."

"Those are my orders," Sawchuk said. "The Sergeant won't let you through otherwise."

Maureen broke the seal on the envelope. She pulled a single sheet of paper from inside. She handed it to Sawchuk.

"This is it?" He glanced up after skimming the page.

"KISS principle," Maureen said. She held out her hand. "Mayor Conconi's signature is at the bottom. Along with Western's VP of Corporate Services."

Sawchuk placed the page into Maureen's open hand. He gestured to his partner to move the barricades. "Right, you're fine. But the car stays."

"What?" Rachel stopped halfway through stuffing items into her backpack. "We have to walk?"

Maureen glanced up the highway, and back to Constable Sawchuk. "You know it's clean."

Sawchuk smiled. He used a handkerchief to mop the sweat off his face. "Sergeant's orders. They got enough equipment up there. Besides it'll only take five minutes, even in your shoes," he said. He allowed himself the barest of smiles.

"Fine." Maureen ducked into the car and fished out her cell phone, purse and keys and dropped them into her briefcase.

The constables dragged the barricades apart as Maureen and Rachel stepped through. The barricades scraped across the blacktop behind them. Rachel had to hurry to match Maureen's stride. Her backpack sagged on her shoulder blade.

"What you got in there? Hair dye? Plastic explosives?"

"Piss off," Rachel said. "Hey, what you said to that cop. *Kiss principle*? What's that?"

"*Keep It Simple, Stupid*," she said. She shot the girl a sideways look. "Don't they teach anything useful at university?"

Maureen set the phone down, blinking away tears. She pulled herself out of the chair, grabbed her car keys from their hook by the back door and slammed the front door behind her. It took five minutes to walk to her car and ten to drive to Frances' downtown apartment. She parked on the street, in a loading zone. She left the Subaru running. The directory listing for suite seventeen-thirteen was blank. She pushed the button next to it. No answer. After three tries, she hit the button for the Resident Manager.

"Yeah?" The voice blared through the speaker set into the directory panel.

"Suite seventeen-thirteen. Is it vacant?"

"Yeah. How'd you know? The ad don't come out 'til Wednesday."

"When did they leave?"

"On the weekend."

"Did they leave a number or address?"

"You a cop? Or you lookin' for an apartment?"

Maureen's hands closed into fists. "I'm looking for Frances."

"Can't help you," the voice said.

"Did they leave a number?"

"Look, they just left. It happens sometimes. I only seen the one and she didn't even leave no number, no address, no nuthin'. She told me to keep the damage deposit. Said it was the other gal's dough and if she wasn't coming back to Hell with her. I thought I was gonna have a bomb site clean up, but it's not bad. I can show you the place, if you're interested. It's empty."

"No," Maureen said. "No thanks. Not if it's empty."

She let her finger slide off the intercom button.

"He doesn't get it," Rachel said. "My dad." She spat out the words like a bad taste.

"Get what?" Maureen kept her eyes on the berm heaped across the highway as she walked. She felt naked walking the centre-line of the highway between checkpoint and bridge. They were close enough now to see figures in masks and bandanas standing on top of the piles of earth where asphalt used to lie. Their hunting rifles caught the sunlight and dotted the crest of the berm with tiny stars.

"All this." Rachel waved her arms to include the bridge, the highway, the river. "It's all a big schmooze to him. He doesn't get that it's people's lives."

"I think he might have, once," Maureen said. "Now it's just numbers and quotas. It makes you numb."

"Then I hope I die before I get old," Rachel said.

"You don't have to be old to be numb."

Rachel glanced sidelong at Maureen. "Was that supposed to be deep or something? You gonna confide in me how you beat back your demons to get where you are today?"

Maureen stopped. "What would you know about demons? Spoiled brat."

"Fuck you," Rachel said. "Who are you to judge me?"

"Eminently qualified," Maureen said. She shifted her briefcase to her other hand and marched faster. "I have a job to do. You're only looking for another fucking party."

"You got no right-"

"Hold up, 'kay?"

It was a command, but it sounded like a question, reasonable except for the rifle. He stepped over the top of the ridge of excavated earth and broken pavement. He wore a white tee shirt, faded jeans and a wide, leather belt. A hunting knife hung in a sheath off his hip. His work boots were scuffed and marked by the loose soil of the berm. The scope on his hunting rifle dazzled in the sun.

Maureen stopped. Rachel halted beside her, her face flushed as her protest died unspoken.

The warrior shifted his rifle from his right hand to his left. The butt nestled easily in the crook where elbow met ribs, his hand cupping the stock. "We thought you were cops, but when we heard the bitching we figured you're just lost tourists."

Laughter erupted from a line of men near him. Each carried a rifle or shotgun. Some wore army fatigues, but all wore bandanas tied over the lower half of their faces, so that only their eyes were visible.

"What do you want?"

"I'm here for Chief David. Tell her it's Maureen Cage, *Dee-Faz.*"

"*Dee-Faz?*" The warrior glanced toward his companions. "You think you're gonna talk us out of here? Okay, boys, go home and get your tools. Better start building. We're gonna be here seven years, anyway."

More laughter from the gathered warriors.

"I'm not here to say anything," Maureen said. "I have demands Chief David should see."

"Demands?" The warrior's grip on his rifle tightened. "The only demands on the table are ours, got it? You can turn around and tell whoever sent you to stuff them up his fat, white ass."

"Sam." Josephine David appeared on the berm. She looked as she did at the funerals: black jeans, black shirt, her hair tied into a single, graying braid that hung thick between her shoulder blades. Calmly untouched by the heat. "What's going on?" She said, pulling hard on her cigarette.

"This one's from *Dee-Faz,*" the warrior said, raising his chin toward Maureen. "Says she's got demands."

"I know Maureen Cage," Josephine said, exhaling smoke in their direction. "We heard you got suspended. Did they bust you down to messenger?"

"Something like that," Maureen said. "These are from the TAC."

Josephine snorted. "Perfect. Let me guess what they're asking for."

"You don't need to guess," Maureen said.

Josephine's lips thinned. "I don't need to do anything I don't want to. Who's your partner?" She nodded toward Rachel.

"Not my partner," Maureen said. "This is Rachel Braithwaite. She wants to join you."

"Braithwaite? Is this a joke?"

"RG's daughter," Maureen said.

"I've been with NFDI for a year," Rachel said. "I'm nothing like my father."

"She's a spy," one of the warriors said.

"Screw that," Rachel said. "I've been in the streets for every major demonstration since I was seventeen. Now I'm here."

"She helped me through the barricades," Maureen said.

Josephine glanced toward Sam, who shook his head. She chewed on the inside of her cheek, sizing Rachel closely. "You heard of William Last Man Standing?"

"Who hasn't? I've read all his stuff," Rachel said.

"Find him. If he can use you, you can stay. If not, you're out."

"Excellent-"

"Sam will take you." Josephine cut Rachel off with a wave of her hand. "Billy's in a camper on the far side of the bridge. But your backpack stays here," she said as Rachel started to move.

Rachel swung her backpack off her shoulder, punching the air with her empty fist. She shot Maureen a victory smile and ran to where the piled rock gave way to bare road. A steel gate had been dug into the gravel shoulder. In front of the gate were four rows of spikes, nailed into pieces of discarded lumber. The tips—like jumbled rows of galvanized orca teeth—guarded the only way around the broken highway.

Josephine waited until Rachel had passed through the gate. "Why would *Dee-Faz* bring us TAC demands? Or don't they trust you enough to tell you?"

"*Dee-Faz* doesn't know I'm here," Maureen said.

Josephine's hand stopped, halfway to her cigarette. "You did this on your own?" She laughed. "Never anything by the book with you, Cage."

"They're going to shut down the mill," Maureen said. She bent to open her briefcase.

"Slowly," Josephine said. "Come 'round to the gate."

Maureen retrieved the envelope and followed Rachel's path to the spikes. The trench across the highway was ten feet wide and over six feet to bottom. Just looking down made her dizzy. As she rounded the moat she saw the excavator, tucked behind the berm and hunkered below the highway shoulder. She recognized it from the funerals, from the unfinished Tse Wets Aht Medical Centre. The company decal on its cab door had been covered with a black, spray-painted fist. Runnels of over-spray had dried against the faded yellow door. Its windows were now completely smashed.

Chief David waited at the gate. Two men stood at her side. They were much older. The eldest wore his grey hair long; it streamed from beneath a weathered ball cap that celebrated a *Six Nations* lacrosse championship a dozen years ago. Faded, blue tattoos decorated his forearms. The second wore his hair short, cut flat across the top of his head. His eyes glittered. Neither spoke as Maureen approached.

Chief David snatched the envelope from Maureen's hands and tore it open. As she read, Sam re-joined her at the gate. He leaned forward, trying to read over Josephine's shoulder.

"This is Henry's brother," Josephine said, raising her head. She handed Sam the paper. "What do you think about them shutting the mill?"

Sam pinched the rifle between his body and arm and tore the page in two, then tore it again and threw the scraps onto the gravel. He ground the pieces under his boot.

"I guess you have our answer," Josephine said.

"Will you ask *them*?" Maureen said, nodding toward the elders.

Chief David smiled. "What? To surrender again? Thomas Henry, William German. They are two of our hereditary chiefs. They keep our stories, our language. They are our witnesses. If they thought badly of our actions, we would have never left our homes."

Maureen squinted against the sun in her eyes. Perspiration ran under her clothes and her feet were on fire inside her shoes. Dust filled her mouth and nose, carried on a breeze that chased after the Sleeping Man River. The bones of the highway were grit between her teeth. She needed to get out of the sun. She needed a drink and a cigarette. "You're still going to need a Final," she said, certain they could hear the conviction draining out of her.

Josephine laughed. The faded orange superstructure of the bridge arched behind her, framing her face like an oversized Mardi Gras headpiece. "Once hundreds of us worked the mills and canneries along this coast," she said. "Not just Tse Wets Aht, but every coastal First Nation. The white managers didn't like it when our men left to fish or hunt or to set trap lines in the mountains. They hired Italians and Ukrainians and their towns grew from nothing. There were so many sockeye we were content to share. Now there aren't enough. No more easy trees to cut. The towns suffer. They want more fish, more trees, more everything to keep their people happy. They douse our forests with chemicals to stop them from burning, from renewing as Nature intended. When we begged to keep even a little of what used to be ours, they did nothing. But when *their* courts said we had rights—under *their* laws—finally they listened, started to negotiate. Even as we talk, they take what's left and leave us less. Always stalling. No, TAC will be happy only when we are gone."

"A Final will protect you."

Josephine expelled the smoke from a final pull of her cigarette. She crushed the butt under her boot. "Protect us? I like your sense of humor, Cage. Look around. *Now* we're protected." She pivoted on the soles of her black-heeled boots and vanished behind the berm.

From the top of the ridge of broken asphalt and earth, from the sides of the Sleeping Man Bridge, lines of warriors began to cheer. Thomas Henry and William German watched her, their dark eyes unblinking, their dry lips parted in half-smiles. The warriors' cries rode a sudden hot gust that flung sharp grains of dust into Maureen's eyes.

An evening breeze tugged at the leaves of the boulevard cherry trees. The swaying branches—and three of Anne's pills—inched her closer to sleep. Her living room was stuffy and she'd known this smell in Port—of sweat and heat, with a hint of cedar-bark. She'd never noticed it inside her own walls before.

She limped to the kitchen and found her cigarettes on the shelf above the sink. A brand new carton lay on top of a clean, green ashtray. Another gift from Anne and Helen. She grabbed the ashtray off the shelf and saw the pack of matches inside. Her fingers shook as they held the match to the end of the cigarette.

She blew smoke through her nostrils and tossed the dead match into the new ashtray. She glanced around the kitchen, remembering Alianna's ashtrays.

Maureen dropped her briefcase and stooped to remove her shoe. Another stone meant a fresh twinge of pain nipping at her heel. She hopped awkwardly to avoid setting her stocking foot on the scorched pavement as she fished out the pebble. She pictured laughing warriors on the berm—mirroring the pair of RCMP officers a hundred paces ahead. Her jaw clenched—she was sweat-stained, dust-streaked, her business clothes had wilted in the heat and the tops of her feet were raw inside her shoes. The glare off the pavement worsened her headache, and every dusty step blew more grit into her eyes. Her imagination conjured vignettes of Billy and Rachel alone together in Billy's camper. She stood no chance against a tattooed belly so flat, so taut, so young. The hands she imagined beneath Rachel's tank top were as rich and warm as burnished mahogany.

Her phone rang. She crouched and set her briefcase onto the double yellow line. She straightened with the phone pressed to her ear. She crossed her left arm beneath her right elbow and flared her hip. She should be charging for this kind of entertainment.

"Yes?" Her voice was weary, stretched too thin in the heat.

"Carey James? Carl Bender."

"Sorry?" Maureen's eyebrows collapsed into a frown.

"Carl Bender. You left a message yesterday. About Raven?"

Maureen's eyebrows arched. "Yes! Yes, I did. Thanks for returning my call."

"I'll cut the crap. She dumped me two years ago. Too big-time for a local agent like me." Carl's voice rang with bitter shrillness in her ear. "One fucking video goes international and suddenly I'm no good. Who got her the gig in the first place? I don't know where she is, but if you find her, tell her I hope she burns in Hell."

"Wait. Does she have any friends?"

"Friends?" He laughed. "She's got no friends. She's a user. She's possessed."

"So you've no idea where I could find her?"

Carl sighed. "She had a high school friend. Came with her from back east. She got into dancing, then dropped out. Her name was Candide—Candy—something like that. They shared a place awhile. I think she's in Victoria, but if Candy's grown some smarts she doesn't have anything to do with that bitch. Find somebody else for your videos, okay? Someday you'll thank me." He hung up.

Maureen dumped the phone into the open briefcase and snapped it shut. She moved as quickly as her sore feet permitted. The officers waited until she was a foot away before moving aside the barricades. They grinned as she stepped through the gap.

"Must be kinda warm on the highway," Sawchuk said to his partner as she passed.

"That stretch of road's gotta be over forty Celsius," the junior officer said, and whistled.

Maureen unlocked her car, dumped the briefcase in the back. She gathered her maps and other articles off the road where Sawchuck had left them and tossed them on the back seat. She rolled down the windows and collapsed into the driver's seat. It was as hot as a kiln.

"How were they?" Sawchuk stepped up to the side of her car. He worked a toothpick between his teeth.

"Thrilled to see me," Maureen said through clenched teeth. It was hard to breathe inside her car.

"Sergeant called. He finally got through to your boss." Sawchuk's lips parted into a grin. "If I were you I wouldn't answer your phone for awhile. Whoops. Guess I'm too late."

Maureen blinked. "You mean that call? Back there on the highway? That was Mayor Conconi. He was just asking me how to spell *Sawchuk*." She flashed him a syrupy smile and jammed the Subaru into gear. Her tires carved a smooth semi-circle from one shoulder to the other as she reversed. The car lurched ahead when she punched the gas pedal.

She hated the thought of slowing down for the NFDI street party. She was too tired, too sick to negotiate her way through. She wanted a shower, a smoke and a drink, in no particular order. As the sounds of reggae music reached her she accelerated, her hand on the horn. The crowd scattered in terror, momentarily opening the highway. They cheered when they recognized her, saw she was alone in the car. They closed ranks behind her, blocking the road to the stranded drivers lined on the Port McKenzie side. Maureen spotted the girl with the purple hair. Maureen laid off the horn long enough to stick out her fist, middle finger extended toward Heaven.

Stalled traffic stretched as far as the open mill gates. The police had set up a second barricade to detour cars away from the highway. She hit the double span of yellow *Do Not Cross* ribbon that spanned the highway. She dragged down a pair of sawhorses near each curb as the tape stretched, then broke and fluttered to the pavement. Two constables darted from the boulevard to right the fallen barricades. Drivers clustered near their cars looked up as she passed. They craned their necks toward the protest camp, not bothering to get out of their lawn chairs or stop what they were doing. In her rear view mirror the highway became a black, shimmering scar.

Alianna Agripolis kept her stack of ashtrays in the narrow space between the backsplash and the sink. Once a week she washed them and spread them to dry on a souvenir dish towel of Athens or Crete or Rhodes. It was her time to inspect them, to study each one in her arthritic, withered hands, and remember how each had come into her possession.

Considering how long and how much she smoked Alianna did well. It took sixty years for the cancer to turn up. During Maureen's time as a boarder she noticed how thin her landlady became. How her body, once lithe and mobile, became bird-like, frail and drained of color. Alianna kept smoking after the diagnosis. She refused to quit. She also refused chemo and radiation.

Her last morning in her house Alianna insisted on standing at the sink to wash her ashtrays one final time. Her son was minutes away, coming to take her to hospice. She'd barely the strength, but she refused Maureen's help. She banished her to the table by the window as she washed the ashtrays, turning each over in the sink, shaking off the water and placing it upside down on the waiting dish towel. Her wet fingers touched each in turn, like she was stroking the bellies of a row of upended turtles.

When she finished she dried her hands and limped to the table. She reached for Maureen's nervous fingers and until Michael's arrival they sat, bathed in a rare, February sunshine that bestowed a clean, cool radiance upon their intertwined hands.

Alianna Agripolis died four days later.

Her whole life had been an exercise in bad timing.

Meeting RG and Sarah in the hotel lobby was the latest proof. She'd fallen asleep in her clothes waiting for a call from the Mayor's office, from Sarah. Nothing. No messages, not a whisper. She showered, packed quickly and checked out, moving gingerly to mollify the pain behind her eyes. Sunstroke, she thought. A metallic taste filled her mouth and her body ached. At least her nausea had abated. She was about to protest the extra day's charge for late check-out when an arm closed around her arm. Must have been sunstroke, for she hadn't heard anyone approach.

"You took her right to them," RG said. His grip tightened. His face was so close to hers she could smell Sarah's perfume on his shirt. Something else was different: a lock of his silver hair was mussed, out of place.

"She gave me no choice," Maureen said. "You didn't return my calls."

"So you skulk out of town like a thief?" Sarah said. She stood a half-step behind RG, her carry-all strap on her shoulder.

"Let go of my arm, RG," Maureen said. She turned to the reception clerk. "Call the police." Her glance snapped back to RG. "This time I'm pressing charges."

"You bitch." He growled. But his hand fell to his side. "You drag my daughter into an armed camp and threaten *me* with the police?" Hooked fingers clawed his scalp.

"Those were her terms, not mine," Maureen said. She stepped back, set her suitcase between RG and herself. "I accepted. It seemed a fair concession, given the circumstances."

"*A fair concession*? That was my daughter!" He moved closer until the toe of his shoes knocked against her suitcase.

"She wanted to go. They all did. That's why they showed up in the first place, to support the Tse Wets Aht."

"Not anymore," Sarah said. She smiled. "RCMP cleared the camp this afternoon. Sixteen arrests and charges pending. Where have you been?"

"Asleep. Waiting to hear from you. I delivered TAC's proposals to Chief David."

"We know," Sarah said. "You nearly ruined everything. We've been doing damage control since."

"*Damage control*? What the hell are you talking about?"

"We don't have time for this, RG," Sarah said. Her hand settled lightly on his shirt sleeve, above the elbow.

"I'll see to it you'll never work in this business again, Cage," RG said. His fingers played with the knot of his tie, loosening it, unbuttoning his collar.

"Is that what you told Lee-Anne?"

RG reddened. "Get the hell out of Port, Cage. Right now *Dee-Faz* has more important fish to fry. I'll send someone to collect your keys, all *Dee-Faz* documents and anything else you have at home. You're fired."

Maureen inhaled, conscious of the pressure building inside her head. She let the air out of her lungs in a single, steady breath. "You brought me back to deal with the TAC. I did what I could to get their demands to the Tse Wets Aht. I thought it might inspire them to negotiate. Rachel helped make that happen."

"Negotiate? *I'll* do the negotiating from now on. You made my daughter part of the game. Big mistake. Sarah and I should have been out of here hours ago."

Maureen snatched her purse off the counter and stuffed it into her briefcase. She bent slightly to retrieve her suitcase. RG's large hand again closed on her arm, squeezing hard. An image flashed inside her skull of his lips bared, jaws parted, as if ready to bite off her ear.

"Hey, Buddy." A male voice interrupted.

Maureen straightened and RG turned, still gripping her arm.

He wore a washed-out tee shirt commemorating some long-ago Iron Maiden concert tour. His boots ended in riveted silver caps matching a square, silver belt buckle. His narrow face sported a cut below his right eye. The skin around the bandage was purple and black from bruising. Maureen recognized him from Canal Slats. Larry's friend. Rick Something.

"Let her go, Asshole," he said.

RG's grip loosened as he twisted to face the newcomer.

Maureen pulled her arm free and RG stumbled into Sarah, who put out her hands to steady him.

"Touch me again and I'll cut your balls off," Maureen said in a voice that made Sarah turn pale.

"So this is the kind of friends you keep," RG said. His upper lip curled as he brushed off his shirt. "Maybe they can find you a job you're better suited to. Like slinging beer."

"You got a problem with beer?" Rick stepped nearer and poked a finger into RG's chest.

"Get your hands off me, Friend," RG said. He leaned into Rick. He was shorter but thicker, heavily muscled. He forced Rick onto his heels. "Looks like you lost your last fight. Care to try again?"

"RG . . ." Sarah interjected.

Rick raised his hands, palms facing outward. "We're cool. No worries. Just go easy on the lady." He backed toward the hotel entrance.

"You're a piece of work, RG." Maureen grabbed her briefcase and suitcase and passed Rick going through the main doors.

"Don't even think of playing this out in court, Cage," RG called after her. "My lawyers will take everything you own."

"What a prick," Rick said, looking over his shoulder. "And his girlfriend's a frigid bitch. Young enough, though."

Maureen fixed her glance on her dented Subaru. The blood-tinged mist around her eyes began to lift.

"A *thank you* wouldn't kill you. I'm Rick St. Clair. We met at the strip joint awhile back." He crooked his neck to peer into Maureen's face as he walked. He was favoring his left leg.

Maureen stopped at the back of her car. She fished out her keys and folded her arms across her chest. "You here to return my lighter?"

"I didn't take your lighter, the Raven did." Rick stopped, his arms hanging loose in their sockets. He blinked slowly.

Maureen pivoted, opened the rear hatch and lifted her suitcase and briefcase into the back. "But you let Larry and Raven do it."

"Larry's a dick," Rick said. "Can I buy you a beer?"

"What?" Maureen stopped, her hand on the open hatchback door. "You showed up to buy me a drink?"

"Yes Ma'am," Rick said. "And since I rescued you, I figure you got double the reasons for joining me in a refreshment." When he grinned she saw the gap in his mouth where a molar used to reside.

"They worked you over pretty good. Where's Raven?"

"I got no frigging clue where the peeler went."

"Where's Larry?"

Rick's grin evaporated. "Who?"

"Stop playing games," Maureen said. "Raven's with Larry, right? Tell me where and I'll think about that beer."

"I wish I knew. I haven't seen him in a while." Rick kicked at a stone on the asphalt. The rock bounced off the Subaru's back tire and skittered back at him, striking his ankle. "Shit," he said.

"You're lying," Maureen said. "I have no time for this."

"Wait. I said I'd buy you a beer. C'mon. Seriously," Rick said. "If I knew where they was I'd tell. Honest. I just come here to help you out."

"Help me?" Maureen laughed. "You want to help me? Stop lying to me." She stuck her key into the ignition and twisted. The car fired on the first try.

"Warn you, then," Rick said over the idling engine. "That pencil-pushing prick from Ottawa, he won't leave us alone. He had me locked up two days, on suspicion I had something to do with that crash. He thinks I'm KKK. He keeps talkin' about you, too."

"Me?"

Rick shifted in his boots like a nervous teenager. "He figures old Adolf buried a chest of Nazi gold around here someplace, and he wants to be the first to find it. He's askin' a shitload of questions about Larry and Raven, you, everybody."

"Maybe he's spying on the mayor, too," Maureen said, but dampness formed on her hands where they closed around the steering wheel.

"Maybe. Said he's got proof, though. C'mon, let's talk about it over a beer," Rick said. "I know a great place."

"No. Thanks." A chill raced up her spine.

"For Chrissakes, what do I gotta do?"

"Tell me where Raven is," Maureen said.

Rick stared at his shoes.

"Right."

She slammed the door, stuck the Subaru into gear and fish-tailed out of the parking lot.

When Alianna's son left—late for his plane to London and taking with him only a small box of his mother's papers and photographs—he dropped his keys into Maureen's palm and asked if she wanted to buy the place.

"My mother really liked you," he said, rubbing his hand over his bald spot. A fine, Surrey accent had insinuated itself over his Kitsilano upbringing. "You were like a daughter to her. It was always *Maureen's got exams*, or *I'm worried about Maureen, she's working too hard*. Vancouver's so far for me, and I would be happy knowing the house is still in the family. You know what I mean. I'll do what I can to make it affordable," he said. He left his business card and hurried to his rented Lexus, idling at the curb.

After he drove away Maureen went to the kitchen and spotted the ashtrays she'd re-stacked next to the sink. She gathered them into the crook of her left arm and carried them to the living room. She opened the black mesh screen on the fireplace and took three steps back.

The first ashtray was porcelain, an oval saucer with serrated edges, toothpaste white inside a blue border with *Souvenir of Crete* painted in thin brush strokes across the bottom. Alianna had brought it back the year after Nick died. Like skipping a flat stone at the lake shore she side-armed it into the fireplace. Fragments like broken teeth ricocheted off the brickwork. She lifted the next ashtray off the stack. When it was over the living room floor was littered with broken china.

It was a week before she got around to sweeping up the mess.

She left Port with the early evening sun exploding into her rear view mirror. She tipped up the mirror and refused to look behind her. Traffic was light, and she pushed the Subaru hard up the side of the McKenzie Valley. As she dropped down the eastern flank of the ridge the glare vanished behind the trees and the throbbing in back of her eyes dulled. She counted yellow lines as they disappeared beneath the car.

Near Nanaimo her agitation returned, worsening at the approach to the ferry terminal. Her stomach protested. Her head ached and the skin across her face was hot with anger, replaying her last exchange with RG and Sarah. The edges of her vision blurred. What were they doing, skulking out of Port together, yet accusing *her* of running away? Why *was* she running home to hide? To a chorus of horns she cut sharply across two lanes to avoid the exit to the ferry terminal and aimed, instead, for the highway marker that read *Victoria—90KM*. Almost instantly the unruliness in her guts subsided.

She reached the Malahat an hour south of Nanaimo. The northern gateway to Victoria. A winding, narrow road through blasted rock that climbed three hundred metres above the sea before descending into the suburbs. At its summit Maureen made a darting, illegal left turn across the highway into a tourist rest stop. She had the parking lot and picnic area to herself. She shut off the engine and climbed onto one of the square-cut, timber tables. Cross-legged on the table top she stared over the tips of hemlock and twisted arbutus that shouldered down the steep mountain side. Shadows had settled for the night onto the forested, lower slopes as the sun slipped behind the high cliff flanking the highway. The calm waters of the Saanich Inlet, still too distant to surrender to shade, caught the lingering sunlight and, as if under the doom of a Philosopher's Stone, were transmuted into dazzling rafts of gold. The farther shore of the Inlet climbed out of the sea in the form of a forest-and-farm dappled peninsula, brushed with industrious yellows and diligent greens. Beyond it, the Straits of Georgia appeared: those same straits she had paralleled north of Nanaimo. It was as if the mass of Vancouver Island had been pushed west, carelessly shifted off its foundations by colossal hands.

With her chin cupped between her palms, she waited as the colors changed, then dimmed. Goosebumps emerged on her arms and with every breath an ache grew behind her ribs. She did not dare shut her eyes. Evening wove a web—a silken grey curtain that obscured the horizon—until the lamp standards that rimmed the pullout blinked on, and the water and the land vanished.

The ring of her cell phone resounded through the deserted parking lot.

"Hi." The voice was hard to hear even in this quiet place.

"Carole?"

Maureen slid off the table and began to pace. She stayed inside a circle of illuminated blacktop beneath the nearest lamp standard. Her skin turned a ghostly grey in the sodium vapor glow.

"Sorry, I've been so busy," Carole said.

"Busy. Gotcha."

"Please, I'm sorry, I've been stupid."

"Go on," Maureen said.

"I should have called. I really wanted to. I had the phone in my hands more than once."

"But you didn't."

"It's not *you*," Carole said. "It's *me*. I'm sorry if I said anything to get your hopes up. It was fun, it really was. But you're not who I figured you to be. I'm still trying to get my head around the dancer thing."

"There's nothing to think about. That part's done. Over. It ended ten years ago." Maureen felt the heat pour out of her skin.

"You don't just shrug that stuff off like you're changing clothes."

"I think you can. *I* did. Has it ever come up at negotiations?"

"You know what I mean. It's who you are. Give me some time, okay?"

The *Low Battery* alarm started to chime in her ear. "I'm out of time," Maureen said.

"I'll talk to you soon. Promise."

"I don't think so. I'm going to Victoria for awhile."

"What's in Victoria?"

"Nothing," Maureen said. She pressed the *End* button and exhaled into the phone. "That way I can't ruin it," she whispered.

She stepped out of the light and looked up at the sky. The glimmer from Victoria's skyline washed out the weaker stars that in Port shone bold against evening's backdrop. Still, compared to the milky emptiness of Vancouver's sky, this panorama of stars was impressive. Since she was small she'd loved stars, the reliability of their nightly appearance; how they winked happily despite their fixedness in a frozen, airless void. She didn't know their names or any of the constellations—except for the Big Dipper. She turned around and around until she found it; there, in the North West, barely clearing the cliff opposite the rest area. She traced the handle and the dipper with her finger as tears gathered in her eyes, blurring her sight.

She stopped at a suburban mall just off the highway to find a phone book and a map of Victoria. She wrote down six different motel numbers and addresses out of the Yellow Pages, tore out the map and her scribbled list and ducked into a cold beer and wine store. She bought cigarettes and a chilled case of *Kokanee*. Back at her car she unplugged the phone from its charger and started at the top of her list. She'd chosen outlying motels, because they were cheaper, farther from the tourist Mecca of downtown. She did not want to site-see. She needed only a place to hide.

She got lucky on the last try. The Green Gables Inn had one ground floor room with a small kitchen and bath for seventy-nine bucks a night. She told the manager she'd be there in a half hour. He told her he had to rent it to the first person who arrived, so be quick. Maureen cut across the mall parking lot, detoured to the drive-thru lane of the nearest burger stop and ordered two cheeseburgers and a side of fries. She stuck the warm, grease-spotted bag on the passenger seat. She pulled into the parking lot of the Green Gables Inn ten minutes later. Traveling distances in Victoria were not like Vancouver's.

The motel was a two-storey, brown stucco box. Only the floodlit sign at the side of the road was green and gabled. It was built into a steep-roofed shelter that resembled a Victorian cottage. The *NO* in the *NO VACANCY* sign in the office window was lit. Maureen cursed, swung into the last remaining parking space in front of the office and stepped into a cramped office. The smell of Indian cooking filled the room, wafting from a closed door with the words *Manager's Suite* stenciled across its painted brown front. A middle-aged man slipped through the door at the sound of her arrival. He was chewing, caught between bites of a late supper.

"I'm sorry," he said, pausing to swallow, his voice a sing-song baritone. "I have no vacancy tonight."

"I phoned ten minutes ago," Maureen said.

"You are the young woman from the telephone?" He arched one black eyebrow. "Very well," he sounded resigned as he spoke, "I am holding the room for you, then. I was making assurances to my wife that if you didn't show in five minutes the room is for anybody."

"Thank you," Maureen said. She opened her wallet and momentarily fingered her *Dee-Faz* Visa. She instead dug out one of her own credit cards and did a quick calculation based on two nights. The MasterCard should have room enough under its limit, but by month's end she'd be juggling balances.

The manager ran the card through his machine and grinned when he returned her card. "Room seven, along the back. Call me if you have any questions. My name is Ranjit, but you can call me Andy."

"Thanks, Andy."

"No problems. I'm sorry, you must leave your car out front. Don't worry, we keep a close eye on comings and goings, so you can be sure about security," he said. He had to raise his voice to speak over a surge of Bollywood music that blasted from the apartment. "That is my wife," Andy said, his smile vanishing, "always playing the music so loudly. Remember, Miss Cage," he glanced at the credit card receipt, "to call me if you need anything."

"Sure." Maureen took the key and backed out of the room. "I'll be fine." The office door banged shut in its frame behind her.

The room screamed cheap but it was neat: a double bed set against a mustard yellow wall crowded the tiny kitchen opposite the bathroom. A toaster-sized television perched on a stubby chest of drawers and between the bed and sagging sofa there was room for a small dining table and two unmatched chairs. Deep gouges in the table's surface betrayed the anger management needs of a prior tenant. The room smelled of stale cigarettes, evergreen air freshener and mildew.

Maureen dumped her briefcase on the bed, went back to her car for her suitcase and supplies. She put the beer in the fridge and lit a cigarette. She locked the door and set the safety chain, then stood in front of a dust-streaked window, pushing aside wispy, pumpkin-orange curtains. Street lamps revealed the gun-metal flatness of the road. She caught a glimpse of water between the apartment buildings across the street. It was as hard and grey as the road. She pulled the crumpled phone directory map out of her purse and turned it around until it matched her orientation. The water was the Gorge, a tongue of dead-ended, shallow salt water that pushed inland from the downtown harbor. She set down the map and let the curtains fall shut.

She ate a burger, most of the fries, and carried the ashtray from table to bed. She set down her beer and pried off her shoes. She picked up the phone and dialed Carole's home. No answer. It was well after midnight in Ottawa—Carole was either asleep or out. "I meant to tell you earlier—Billy told me what you said to him. Thanks, I guess. I'm sorry, too," she said, "more for me than for you."

She sat on the bed and immediately sank into a deep trough. She shifted her weight until her body lay diagonally across the mattress, two pillows wedged at her sides. It was like sleeping on a half-full water bed. She closed her eyes but did not sleep. The muffled traffic and creak of unseen bodies in the room above were enough to keep her awake. She sighed, sat up and lit another cigarette, inhaling deeply; breathing air that had never known the McKenzie Valley and its mill; air that had instead absorbed the pungent spices of Indian cooking, cigarettes, salt water and car exhaust. She felt brittle and sore and over-tired but at least she was safe, enfolded in this old motel mattress, stale pillow covers and mildew-tinged blankets.

BOOK FIVE

Old Habits

The light filling the living room came from wayward beams of street lamps: they dappled the walls with ivory and turned quills of exhaled cigarette smoke into pewter ribbons twisting like Baroque filaments toward the ceiling. Her stereo shelf hunkered in the shadows against the opposite wall, the sinuous grain of its shuttered doors reminding her of long-dead rivers on Mars she'd seen on some television documentary years ago.

The pine shelf had been doing penance in Alianna's basement when she'd found it. Abandoned in a corner with its back to the door, barely visible beneath boxes of canning jars. With Anne and Helen's help she'd wrestled it out of the corner. It had taken hours to remove layers of paint to reveal the original, buttery grain. When she'd finished Anne brought over a fridge dolly and they wheeled the shelf outside and up the front stairs to the living room, part of the action for a change. Maureen oiled its cupboard doors and shelves, its short, curved legs and fist-like feet, and used it to hold her stereo. The citrus tang of the oil hung in the room for days.

It took the sanctuary of a cheap motel room in Victoria to redefine home: Maureen knew it not as *somewhere* but as *someone*—as warm as a down comforter and as bright as a country kitchen in summer. When those red lips covered her with kisses Maureen knew she was home. The smile was proof enough; instant confirmation that within those loving arms nothing bad could happen. When she lifted Maureen off the ground, crushing her against her body, Maureen felt safe. She was beyond winter's grasp. Maureen would wrap her short arms around her mother's neck, squeezing as hard as she could, and still the kisses came; hot, breathless on her forehead and cheeks. This was home, no need to hold back, no need to pretend. Inside the circle of her mother's love she could be whatever she wanted.

She could be herself.

"The good Lord needs her more than us," Françesco would say from behind a glass tumbler as smudged as his eyes. She'd clean up while her father drank himself to sleep in his ratty chair. It was better when he slept; when he stopped sobbing about how wonderful she was, and how lonely life was without her.

Maureen had long ago forgiven the girl for running away, for leaving Françesco to fend for himself when he could barely remember his own name. The girl who tried to escape the bone-snapping cold that gripped the house after they buried the mother. The girl they always found and brought back to him, until his incapacity forced them to shuffle her from one foster home to another. The girl with the mother's features—except for the frightened eyes. And her nose was straighter, then, not yet broken by a fist in a frozen alley behind Maple Leaf Gardens. She'd run from the last foster home with new scars and a fresh anthology of bad dreams, the most horrific wormed deep inside her. She ran to the biggest city she knew, while the nightmare grew, until one early morning, on the basement level of the Dominion Parkade, the nightmare came to life, emerging in screams and hot tears and blood.

She kept it only until she could summon the strength to abandon it. Then her retreat into silence began. Over time the silence thickened and hardened to cold stone around her heart. The heat of her rage was walled off, entombed, and the numbness that began when her mother died spread unchallenged through her body.

Since its beautification the stereo shelf had been tireless in its servitude. She could not help but wonder if it had been worth the effort: the paint that had smothered it for nearly half a century had not impaired its abilities. If left alone it would still have functioned steadfastly for another century or longer. She had merely revealed its original identity, stripped it, repositioned it and put it to work. The shelf had become beautiful once more, but her efforts had not altered the fundamental purpose of the piece. What she'd done was superficial, incidental, done to satisfy her alone. It was Ego at work, and, notwithstanding the result, decoration was not to be confused with creation.

The house creaked. Maureen flinched, her thoughts checked. She knew every noise the house made—how the walls expanded in summer to tick like an oversized grandfather's clock; how they contracted in the cold with a groan or shivered in a flooding rain when the gutters plugged and overflowed. She knew the soft spots on the stairs and the forlorn howl of a Nor-Wester through cracks around the single-pane windows in the dining room. This was out of character—as if the house had shifted to make room for another presence. She held her breath, waiting. When the sound happened again it was different: half scrape, half creak.

It came from the basement.

After sleeping through morning and most of the afternoon she needed a lot of hot water to revive her. She spent an hour in the shower, once she got the hot water to cooperate. The motel bathroom smelled of wet wood: black bands of mildew flourished where the window pane mated to a rotting frame and sill. She gingerly dragged the shower curtain along the edge of the tub between her thumb and forefinger. Maybe the fresh cigarette tar she was depositing in her respiratory tract would trap and kill any microscopic mold spores before they infected her. Any excuse to rationalize smoking again.

It was six-thirty in the evening when she left the motel. She followed her map and pulled into a parking lot off Fisgard Street. It was a two block walk to Barclay's, the strip club wedged between blocks of government buildings. She'd danced there years ago—as Angel—under a pulsing black light that transformed the stiff, white shirts of deputy ministers and labor relations consultants into pale blue, riffling life-forms, like shy, misshapen species that resided at extreme ocean depths. Costume choices were dead easy: white bras and g-strings lured the glowing shapes nearer the stage to school appreciatively around her ankles.

She bought cigarettes and a lottery ticket from the magazine stand next door. An overbearing bass shook the frosted windows at the entrance. Her eyes took a moment to adjust to the artificial dimness. She slipped behind the first empty table near the back, on the way to the pool tables. She asked the waitress for an ashtray.

"No smoking," she said. She wore little more than the blond dancer on stage: cut-off *Daisy Dukes* frayed around the thighs and a sleeveless tee shirt stretched beyond modesty across her breasts. She waved her hand—her knuckles were spread wide with knife-edged bills—in the direction of a legal-looking sign plastered behind the bar.

"Anywhere?" Maureen asked. She searched the corners of the bar for evidence of co-conspirators.

"Not in this city," the waitress said, and leaned forward to shout in her ear. "It's killing the restaurant business."

Maureen jammed her cigarettes and matches into her purse and settled for a pint of draft. She hunched low in her chair, her arms folded across her chest. The place was half full. Busier than she remembered weekday evenings could be and that was long before any smoking ban. A younger crowd, college-aged, owned the tables nearest the stage. Half of those watching were female, and they were as loud and as appreciative as their male companions. The dancer surrendered her bra to applause and whistles from the front row. Her breasts perched above her ribs like baseballs on a plate.

"Tumors," Maureen said.

She unstuck a beer-soaked sheet from the shellacked table top and scanned the schedule of headline acts. Raven smiled promiscuously from a photo near the bottom of the page. *This Friday! Raven! Star of Adult Films and Magazines! Three shows nightly including one Spurt-tacular Duo with Special Guest Star Elektra! Book Early!!!*

Maureen picked up her beer and moved to the wall behind the DJ booth. The dancer on stage was halfway through the final song of her set, a slow, sugary, boy-band love song that cued her through her blanket contortions.

"Put your hands together for Cassidy, Ladies and Gentlemen! She'll be back again next hour!" The DJ cut to a pounding Heavy Metal track. He flipped a switch and a monstrous television screen at the back of the stage began to descend. The *Yankees-Red Sox* ball game filled the screen.

"I'm looking for Raven," Maureen said. She had to shout over the music. She leaned over the smoke-tinted plexiglass that separated the DJ from the crowd.

The DJ peeled off his headphones. "She's not here," he said. He stared at Maureen. "Not 'til Friday."

"Have you seen her? I hear she's been in an accident."

"Who're you?" DJ reached around Maureen to take a home-made CD from a dancer waiting in the shadows. She had the same, sleep-dulled look in her eyes as the woman quitting the stage.

"An old friend." Maureen dodged the transaction, watching the dancer make her last adjustments before going on stage.

"You dance?" The DJ asked.

"Used to." It came out easily, no hint of embarrassment in her voice.

"Here?" DJ squinted at her. He was younger than she'd first guessed.

"I quit ten years ago."

"Cool. I practically grew up here. Maybe I caught your act. What was your handle?"

"Angel."

"Sounds familiar. Long hair?"

"Didn't everyone?"

"Wild." DJ pulled off his headphones, leaned over the smoked glass divider. He rolled a peppermint Lifesaver between his teeth. "I'm kind of a collector. Some guys like comic books and baseball cards. Me, I collect peeler posters, flyers, you know,

215

promo material. I bet I got a picture of you around somewhere."
He grinned, showing her the nub of Lifesaver caught in his
molars. "You sticking around? 'cause if I find it I'll bring it in for
an autograph."

Maureen shook her head. "I'm looking for Raven."

DJ did a push up off the glass. "Now *that* one's wired." He
shook his head. "You should talk to the manager."

"Where is he?"

"Over there." DJ nodded toward the bar. "Big guy, the one that
looks like he doesn't want to talk to anybody."

"Thanks."

"Anytime. Hey, Angel. Care to make a comeback?" He held up
a CD. "We could improv a duo right now. What do you say, Wanda
Mae?" He leaned toward the dancer waiting in the shadows.

The girl gave him the finger and stalked to the stage.

"No thanks," Maureen said. "This business isn't well-suited
for comebacks."

DJ's laugh chased her all the way to the bar.

The manager was checking numbers with a calculator.
His too-tight golf shirt suggested an employment history as a
bouncer, professional wrestler, or both. He looked up as she
reached the counter.

"DJ said I should talk to you." Maureen put her beer onto the
terry cloth runner in the centre of the bar.

The manager frowned. His eyebrows met above the bridge
of his nose in a collision of coarse, black hairs. "You lookin' fer
work? We're stocked. Since Mandrake's burned down we're the
only girlie bar in town. No offense, but aren't you a little old to
be slinging beers?"

"I don't need a job," Maureen said. "I mean, I do, but that's not
why I'm here." She held up the soggy sheet of coming attractions.
"I'm looking for her. DJ said you might know where she is."

The manager squinted at the playbill, then at Maureen. "You
a friend? Tell me she fucking well plans to be here Friday."

"You don't know?"

His neck muscles thickened, released as he shook his head.
"Some psycho came in yesterday. Wanted me to redo my whole
schedule. Said she needed an extra week, that her arm was in a

cast. I told him to make it part of her act. He got pretty wacked. I hadda escort him outside."

"Thin guy, blond hair, tattoos?"

"Yeah." His thick eyebrows mashed together again. "You a cop?"

"No. But I was in the business, once. I need to find her."

"You used to dance?" His beefy jowls stretched into a smile.

"For too many years."

"Huh." He moved closer and leaned over the bar, allowing his glance to roam down her legs. "I woulda liked to see that. Anyways, if you run into her or that crazy front man of hers, tell'em she owes me a week starting Friday or she'll never work on the Island again."

"Did he say where they were staying?"

"No. So I calls her agency. They haven't seen or heard from her for days. They tol' me about her car accident, that checks out, at least. They promised me she'd be here, cast or no cast. Now how can they say that? They psychic?" He jabbed a thumb at the sheet in Maureen's hand. "I'm not reprinting my schedule. You know how much photocopying costs these days?"

Maureen pitched forward, away from the windows. Her heart raced, but not with fear. For a moment she imagined Frances had come home, but she dismissed this thought as she tip-toed into the kitchen. She passed over the knife drawer in favor of the cast iron skillet off the stove top. Her muscles itched for the swing of a blunt object. Her body replayed the sensation of the tire jack as it met Larry's skull; she could do it again if she had to.

She tugged open the door to the basement. The Port McKenzie smell was instantly stronger. It hung in the darkness. She flipped the switch and the scuffling repeated, louder this time. It was coming from the back corner of the basement, from Alianna's old pantry—the room where she'd discovered the antique pie shelf.

Maureen leaned on the railing, swinging her bad leg in front and keeping her weight on her arm. Her back ached. A red mist gathered in front of her eyes. "I haven't called the police," she called out. Her voice rallied her nerves as she spoke. "I aim to take care of this myself."

She whacked the skillet hard against the stair rail.

The back door was closed, its dead-bolt untouched. She felt it, before she saw it: outside air was entering through the broken window behind the furnace. Shards of glass glinted at the fringe of illumination. The pantry door was shut. She never shut that door, more afraid of what her imagination would conjure than anything on the dusty, shadowy shelves.

Maureen retreated to the back door. She grabbed a can of aerosol rust paint off the shelf near the door. She limped to the middle of the room and stood beneath the single, sixty-watt bulb. She threw the can against the pantry door. As it crashed against the planking, the door swung inward, pulled hard by an invisible hand.

Nelson Road dead-ended at a bird sanctuary: a marsh that—according to the information kiosk halfway up the block—in winter flooded deep enough to form a small lake surrounded by thickets of snowberry and wolf willow. Wild blackberry canes elbowed past the pavement's edge opposite the few older homes that lined the road. Maureen rechecked the address book.

The listing for Candy Hodgkin said nine-twenty-seven. A small house, mid-block, two from the end of the street. Its shingled roof was choked in black-green moss. The clapboard siding, once fire hydrant red, now was faded and streaked by years of rain. Had it resided in any 'normal' subdivision it would have stood out—a candidate for immediate demolition. But on this narrow lane, squeezed between dense thickets of alder and cottonwood it had a quaint, cottage feel—Grandmother's House. Despite the peeling white trim and the dusty, heat-stressed hydrangea bushes on either side of the front stairs the property appeared more quaint than dilapidated.

Maureen chewed her processed-cheese-sausage-and-egg in an English muffin and drank coffee from a waxed, cardboard cup. She felt better after the first good night's sleep in weeks. She'd returned to the motel from Barclay's with a fast-food meal in a bag and had fallen asleep after dinner, a beer and a cigarette before the late news. No nightmares, at least none she could remember. She'd awakened early, dressed, grabbed Raven's address book and locked the motel room door behind her.

She watched as a party of birders dressed in baggy shorts and long-sleeved flannel shirts disappeared through sweeping founts of brush marking the entrance to the marsh. She wondered if Leonard Thorne came here on his days off. The Chief Negotiator for the Province of British Columbia struck her as a bird-watching kind of guy: precise, bookish, a man of crane-like movements and quick, alert eyes. She finished her sandwich and coffee and got out of the car, wiping her hands on her shorts.

Three cars were parked in the gravel driveway. The car nearest the house was a 'seventies-vintage Duster with a faded paint job. It was on blocks, half covered by an equally faded orange tarp. A beat up Toyota Tercel parked behind the Duster. The last of the three, a sporty new silver Honda, angled behind the Tercel, its grill overhanging a neglected rose bed that bordered the drive. Maureen took down the license plate numbers. As she tossed the notepad and pen into her car another vehicle entered the narrow lane and rolled to a stop behind her Subaru. A pair of birders climbed out of their sensible sedan and smiled at Maureen as they rubbed sun screen onto their necks and faces and hung binoculars around their necks and slipped spiral notebooks into their vest pockets. With a final wave they tramped into the underbrush.

There was no sign of life within the house. No sports-jacket-clad husband emerged, briefcase in hand, on his way to the office. No lights, no sounds. It was as if the routines of a weekday morning did not apply here. Nobody responded to the ring of the bell when her thumb stabbed the button next to the front door.

Nobody peered through the curtains; nobody yelled at her to get the hell of the property.

Maureen returned to her car, debating whether to slink around the house and try the back door. After an hour's wait she put a heavy question mark next to the address and started the car. She eased the Subaru out of line and made a u-turn at the sanctuary entrance. Blackberry and salal smothered the four by four posts and black-and-yellow checkerboard sign marking the dead-end. In a year they would swallow the road itself. She passed the little red house with a last, nervous glance at the curtained windows.

A shape rushed from the room, hands blocking its face. It stumbled, as if it had expected to make contact sooner.

Maureen held the skillet like a tennis racket, ready with an overhand smash, but the figure stopped and spun around inside the circle of illumination. The Port smell surged over her in a wave.

"Billy." She said it calmly, as if she'd been expecting him.

He lowered his hands and blinked in the light. "Nice place, Cage," he said, and grinned. "Any chance a guy can get a hot shower?"

"You're mad at me," Maureen said. She stared at the ceiling from her sagging mattress.

"You're driving us nuts," Helen said through the phone. "And you're upsetting Anne. Come home. Stop this detective nonsense. Catch the next ferry and get on with things."

"What *things*?" Maureen shifted the phone to her other ear. The cord slapped her cheek, stinging her.

"Life, for God's sake," Helen said. "Come home where you're needed."

"You don't need me. I just worry you. Soon I'll be begging for money."

"Stop feeling sorry for yourself, Mo," Helen said. "You'll get another job. And we need you tons. Annie's missing you." She paused. "I miss you, too."

"Thanks."

After a long silence Helen cleared her throat. "Fine. We'll call you if those license plate numbers come through."

"Great." Maureen hung up and pounded her fist into the mattress.

Fifteen minutes later the phone rang. Helen coughed in her ear.

Maureen sat up. "What?"

"Anne made me call," Helen said. "I didn't want to bother you."

"What is it?" Maureen said. "Where are you? I hear traffic."

"I'm calling from the corner store."

"Why? What's happened? Is Anne okay?" Maureen twisted the phone cord around her fingers until they turned white.

"Anne's fine. We're both fine. That first license number you gave me? The silver Honda? It's her."

"What's her real name?" Maureen said.

Helen cleared her throat. "Listen. He's been calling, asking questions about you."

"Who?"

"That RCMP Inspector." Helen's voice trilled like a split reed. "He's called twice. Last time it was long distance. I did caller ID and it came up an Ontario number. Windsor."

"Windsor?" Maureen stood, ice water in her veins. She began to pace, one arm extended to fend off the phone cord. "What does he want?"

"Everything. He asked us if we knew where you grew up, where you went to school, who your friends are." Helen talked fast.

"Jesus. Rick St. Clair said he'd been asking questions. What did you tell him?"

"Anne hung up on him the first time. That was Sunday afternoon. He called back last night. He wanted to know where you were now."

"And?"

"We said we hadn't seen you in years."

"He'll get my phone records, if he doesn't have them already. He'll know you're lying."

"Why do you think I'm standing outside a crappy convenience store surrounded by criminals and car thieves?" Helen coughed out the strain in her throat. "Of course he knows. He's probably tapped our phone."

"Tapped? I'm no criminal."

"You're a good girl," Helen said. "Come home and put this behind you."

Maureen hooked the cord around her little finger, then closed her fist around the plastic coils. Her fingernails bit into her palm. "Jesus, Helen. He's gonna ruin everything." Her eyes began to water. "Why is he doing this?"

"What are you doing here?" She lowered the skillet, though her fingers gripped the handle tightly.

"Hiding," Billy said. "Best place to crash, don't you think? They'll never look in the home of a suspected Heritage League informant."

"Where's your car?"

"We dumped the jeep downtown, rode the bus here."

"Who's *we?*"

Josephine David appeared in the pantry doorway. She was gaunt, thinner since the fiasco at the house with Raven and Larry. She, too, averted her eyes from the light. "Got anything decent to eat?"

Maureen led them upstairs, turned off the basement light and closed the door at the top of the stairs. She showed Billy the fridge and sat with Josephine at the kitchen table while he fried eggs and bacon and shoveled buttered toast onto plates.

"Jesus, I'll have to restock," Maureen said as they ate.

"I gotta crash," Josephine said, between mouthfuls. "Can I clean up first?"

"Upstairs. I'll show you."

When Josephine was in the bathroom Maureen fetched extra bedding from an upstairs closet, tossed the bundle ahead of her and limped downstairs. She gathered the armload and dumped it onto the sofa.

Billy emerged from the kitchen, drying his hands on a dish towel. He stared at the pile of blankets and pillows, arched his eyebrows in question.

"It's here or back to the pantry," Maureen said, holding up her hand like a signal to stop. "Take it or leave it."

"It's perfect." Billy said, rolling his eyes as he grabbed a pillow and punched it.

Maureen turned her back on his grumbling and headed for the stairs. "Shower first. Josephine will be out in a minute. I don't want that Port McKenzie mill stink in my linens," she said as she padded upstairs.

The bathroom was empty. The air near the open door was heavy with steam. Maureen knocked on the door to the blue room.

"Yeah."

Maureen took the response as permission to enter. She pushed open the door and leaned against the jamb.

"Everything okay?"

Josephine was combing her hair. It hung straight, wet, to the middle of her back, soaking through the borrowed white tee shirt. She faced the window, its blind pulled open to the evening. "It's stuck," Jo said.

"I know. Painted shut," Maureen said.

"I need to go home." The hand that held the comb hesitated in mid-stroke.

The motel room was beginning to feel like a cell. She drove around Victoria for two hours, finally stopping at a fast food joint to buy dinner. She took it with her back to Nelson Road. A double bacon burger with cheese and fries, washed down with beer from her stash in the motel fridge. The burger tasted great. So did the beer. She found it hard to believe she'd gone ten years without either. She glanced into the rear view mirror. In two weeks she'd transformed from a non-smoking, non-drinking, straight-but-celibate vegetarian whose idea of excitement was curling up on the sofa with a cup of peppermint tea and Gershwin, to a chain-smoking, meat-and-woman-eating, alcoholic-in-training, ex-stripper-detective-wannabe.

Fuck all stereotypes.

The birders had gone; binoculars and notebooks packed away and sensible Volvos and Toyotas back in neat garages around town. The birds were silent, vanished into the spiny undergrowth. Evening deepened into raucous night. From the brush around the marsh invisible legions of frogs and insects sang to the iridescent moon. Maureen dropped the rear bench and lay in the back of the wagon. She was sure that someone would see her and call the police; sure that Raven, if she were inside, knew she was being watched and was ready to disappear again. She was sure, too, that Helen was right: it was foolish to stay here, wasting her time and skimpy resources playing detective. She was out of her depth. What would she do if Raven climbed in beside her and said: *Ask me anything. I'll tell you whatever you want?* She stared at the house and waited for inspiration.

None came.

The moon's milky light splashed the backs of her hands. They looked old, almost translucent, streaked with veins that veered around her knuckles like rivers sketched on ancient maps. She shivered and wrapped her arms around her sides. How had everything fallen apart so fast? Old habits—so arduous to break ten years ago—had surged back in a flood. The snug cove that was her life lay exposed, its protective breakwater swept away in the wake of the Pipeline Road accident. Alone, naked, she'd been unable—or too weak—to defy the tempest.

She woke cold, disoriented and cramped in the back of the car. It was almost ten. Lights were on behind the curtains of nine-twenty-seven. Raven's silver car was still there, trampling the roses. Maureen climbed out of the back and stretched the knots out of her back. The ache in her hip was killing her. She stuck the keys into the ignition and left the driver's door half open. A gentle 'ping' from the dashboard followed her across the street.

There were no streetlights on this road, but a single, halogen flood lamp mounted on the neighbor's garage shone bright enough to light a path to the front steps. Monstrous, square shadows, drunken geometric shapes, plastered the side of the house. Maureen scuffed the pavement, kicking the loose gravel with the soles of her shoes.

"Just knock," she told herself, "knock once and ask to talk to her." What she'd do next she had no clue.

She got as far as Raven's car when a chill encircled her like a thin mist from the marsh. She shivered, suddenly so frightened her body refused to move. She stood, rooted in the driveway, barely two paces from the front steps. Her knees shook and her stomach turned somersaults. A cold sweat formed on her arms and neck. The crickets and frogs in wolf willow and bog fell silent. A baleful light spilled from the front windows. Its glow touched her skin and Maureen knew that whatever was inside, she did not want to meet it. She pivoted slowly, twisting awkwardly at the waist. The grab in her hip coerced her into action and she flew to the car, legs pumping. The motor started as her foot hammered the gas pedal into the floor. She pulled a U-turn at the dead end and sped out of Nelson Road, not daring to cast another glance toward the house as she passed.

"They'll arrest you if you go home."

Josephine stared out the window. She exhaled, coughing over the rattle in her lungs. "I can't do this anymore. They can find somebody else to be Chief."

"What if they don't want anyone else?"

"What if I don't care?" Josephine turned, and Maureen saw she'd been crying.

"Then maybe you should resign. But you'll have to do it from jail."

Chief David sat on the edge of the bed, the blue comforter creased beneath her. She ran one hand across the fabric. "Cynthia's room was kinda like this," Jo said in a distant voice. "Taylor's using it now."

"Sorry," Maureen said. "We can switch, if you want."

Josephine shook her head. "Thanks, no. I'll be okay."

"I can help," Maureen said. Her grip on the doorknob tightened.

Chief David's eyes flashed, then looked away. "You drive me crazy, Cage. Always saying you know what it's like. You got no fucking clue, you in your fine, city house and your downtown desk job. But I'm too tired to slap you and I don't want to sleep outside."

She propped herself against the wall, surrounded by pillows, her face bathed in the television's flickering light. A lit cigarette rested between her lips and an ashtray balanced on her drawn-in knees. The bedspread covered her to the waist. The lump of fear had started to break apart when she reached the main roads, with their street lights and smoother pavement and increased traffic. Barricading herself inside her room had helped. An hour later she felt silly, hungry and tired, but mostly, she felt homesick.

"Maureen. Maureen! Open up!" The door shivered under a riff of rapid blows.

Fear came back like a seizure—until she recognized Billy's voice. She knocked over the ashtray as she scrambled out of bed. The pounding grew louder, more urgent. She slid the safety chain out of its bracket and unlocked the door.

Josephine David nearly fell into her arms. Billy raced toward her from the parking lot, carrying two bags away from his jeep.

"Hold her, I'm coming," he said and took some of Josephine's weight in his arms.

"What's wrong with her? Is she sick?"

Maureen backed up, allowing Billy to slip past her into the room. Josephine was limp in her grasp.

"Exhausted. She finally slept some of the way. Here, can you take her?" Billy ducked behind, shut the door and dumped the bags on the floor. "I got her."

He looped his hands under Josephine's arms. Billy guided her toward the bed. The Tse Wets Aht Chief nodded and spoke, but Maureen couldn't understand the words.

"What's she on about?"

Billy let go of Josephine and she fell face down onto the bed.

"Jesus, she's as limp as last night's noodles. You sure you didn't dope her up?"

Billy stepped past Maureen to set the deadbolt and safety chain. He peeked out between the curtains, then rearranged them, shutting out the parking lot. "This should work. They can't see the Jeep from the road. Got a beer?" He turned, threw Maureen a grin and dropped into one of the chairs. He pointed at the row of empties on the kitchenette counter. "Been entertaining?" He took off his ball cap and scratched his scalp. Several coarse hairs had pulled out of his pony tail and stuck out from his skull at crazy angles.

Maureen opened the fridge and pulled two cans from the plastic six pack holder. "Not 'til now," she said.

"Viva la Revolution," Billy said as he popped the tab and took a long, deep gulp of beer. "Ahh," he said, and raised the can at Maureen. "That's good." He set down the can and rubbed the dark smudges under his eyes with the heels of his hands.

"What the hell are you two doing here?" Maureen cracked open her can, retrieved her deck of smokes and matches and sat down opposite Billy.

"Running," he said. He watched her light a cigarette. He pointed, making a face. "I didn't know you-"

"Surprise," Maureen said, snuffing out the match with a sharp flick of her wrist. "Remember that time on the highway, coming back from Nanaimo? I took your advice. Know what my spirit guide told me? Drink beer, smoke your face off and eat all the junk food you can. So far she's right on. I feel great and it's cheaper than therapy."

Billy pried off his boots, toe against heel. "Disgusting habit, smoking," he said and wriggled his toes inside his work socks. "An experienced teacher should help you find balance without destroying your lungs and the atmosphere."

"Is the blockade over?" Maureen blew smoke in his face.

Billy beat the air with one hand. "Hell no. At least, it wasn't a few hours ago."

"Then what are you doing here? And how did you find me?"

"I asked Simons."

"You phoned Carole Simons? In Ottawa?" Maureen set down her can of beer.

"Didn't have to. She was right next to me most of last night."

Maureen blinked. "I talked to her on the way here. She phoned me."

"From Nanaimo," Billy said. "Cage, I was with her when she called you. We were just breaking from our first session."

"*First Session*? What the hell are you talking about?"

"Negotiations, Cage. All the heavyweights. We got it done."

"What *negotiations*?" Maureen exhaled a cloud of smoke and wrapped her arms around her chest. It was getting hard to breathe.

"Hargrove's boys set it up with Braithwaite. At some flashy waterfront resort outside Nanaimo. The Feds, Thorne and his team and us. Tons of security. Hargrove, he threw the dice. Almost won it all. He's toast, now. Come to think of it we all are."

Billy took another deep swig of beer. "Got anything to eat?"

Maureen glanced at Josephine, asleep nearly sideways across the bed. Her face was gaunt and the hair above her single braid was flat, shiny from neglect. Her black denims were grass-stained at the knees and her black boots were covered in a powdery dust. A rolling snore signaled each indrawn breath.

Billy returned from the kitchenette with an open bag of chips, his hand plunged inside to the wrist. He chewed noisily. "Good," he said, between handfuls. His eyes were bloodshot.

"You look beat," she said.

"Yeah," he said. "Haven't slept since Monday. Couldn't tell you when *she* last slept."

"What happened?"

"It exploded, went to hell like that. Fucking Braithwaite. Blew the whole thing over a woman." He tried to snap his fingers but grease from the potato chips prevented good purchase between thumb and middle finger. He nodded toward the television. "Find the news. They might have it."

Maureen stretched for the remote at the foot of the bed. She raced between channels. The local news channel was midway through its broadcast.

"Here. This is good." Billy dropped into the chair at the table.

"You're scaring me, Billy. What the hell is going on?"

"Wait," Maureen said. She raised her index finger and held it in the air between them. "I'm going fill you in once and for all."

Maureen hobbled downstairs and opened the door to her study. The room was little more than a collection of awkward shapes in the dark. She shuffled to her desk, sat down sideways in her chair and reached beneath, to the panel next the drawers. The wood was as smooth as polished marble and warm to her touch. A hand's span from the back she pushed. A sound—like the snap of a bird's bone—and a seam appeared in the panel. She pulled on the leading edge and a small tray sprang forward.

Billy held up his hands. "This was Premier Hargrove's baby. He wanted the blockade lifted. Wanted something big to take into the election. Jo wouldn't move, not without a coroner's inquest into the accident, and a guarantee that interims and the main table would happen simultaneously. They agreed. They fucking *agreed*, Cage."

"How did you get off the blockade? RCMP are swarming the highway."

"Braithwaite came with the proposal Monday night. Alone. We met in Jo's trailer, just us three. I gave him the keys to my jeep."

"Funny. I didn't think you were the trusting type. Rachel change your mind?"

Billy hesitated, glanced at Maureen from beneath a single, arched eyebrow. He shrugged and resumed chewing. "Braithwaite had it all worked out. Jo faked a heart attack. It looked good, she was drooling, turning blue." He grinned. "Don't know how she did that. I called the ambulance, but not 911, see? It was one of Hargrove's people driving. All fake. I got into the back with Jo and it took us all the way to the resort. My jeep was waiting for us there."

"How many know?"

"Just Thomas Henry, Chief of the Ot Kal Aht. Some of his people are on the blockade. He didn't want Jo to go. He was right pissed, but he knew the risk she was taking. Go big or go home, right? In the end he promised Jo he'd keep her secret. The other Federation Chiefs won't like this."

"Jesus Christ. What were you thinking?" Maureen smoked her cigarette down to the filter.

"Jo figured it was too good to miss. A home run shot. But if it worked—it'd be the deal of the century. She wanted it all: blockade lifted, accident investigated and a Final. Done and gift-wrapped by the Premier."

Maureen lit a third cigarette off the embers of the second. "What about Rachel?"

"You should quit," Billy said.

"Quitting's easy," Maureen said through clamped lips. "Done it hundreds of times. Did RG find her?"

"She made sure he did," Billy said, smiling. "She's smart—one hard worker. She was front and centre when he drove up to the gate. After the deal was done he wanted five minutes with her in private. He busted out of the trailer all red in the face."

"He tried to get her out?"

"Yeah. Rachel said he's still blaming you. Typical case of Father-Blindness. Probably thinks she's still a virgin."

Maureen's expression changed and Billy laughed.

"Relax, Cage. I kinda have a thing for older women." He wiped his hand on his jeans and leaned across the table to snatch the remote out of Maureen's hand. He pointed the remote at the television. "I haven't even got to the best part," he said, scrolling through the channels. "It's *gotta* be on the news by now."

It jumped open when she was refinishing the desk, her first summer as a homeowner. She thought she'd splintered the wood. She pushed it back into place, relieved that it looked as good as original. The next day she pressed the same spot, accidentally, and saw the tiny hinge. She tugged and found the tray. A small book lay inside. It was hand written, mostly in Greek, in a cramped, compact script. Even the later parts, the English entries, were too blurred to read. Alianna's name appeared toward the end, on every page. Michael's name appeared only once, on the last page, dated July nineteen forty-nine.

She nearly phoned him, long distance, to tell him of her discovery. Michael hadn't wanted the desk—or much else—and he took nothing back to London save a banker's box full of papers. What he didn't take with him he set at the curb with the rest of the recycling, or included as part of the sale. She put the diary back in the tray and to it added her miserable collection of treasures.

Lying flat across the top of the diary was a small cloth bag. Purple, the kind that held a bottle of premium Canadian whiskey. She lifted the bag out of the hiding place, then pushed the leading edge of the tray until it disappeared into the desk. With the bag clutched in both hands she retreated from the study. She detoured into the living room and stood next to the coffee table. Her ashtray and cigarettes lay under Billy's socks. She tossed the socks onto the floor and gathered her cigarettes and ashtray. Billy slept with his back to the room, his shoulder rising out of the dark like a single, smooth peak, steep on its north face, falling away gently to the south, toward his hips. The smell coming off his hair was fresh, clean. He was splendid, there was no doubt in her mind about that.

"G'night, Billy," she whispered.

She limped upstairs. Her bad knee throbbed. No way to take the weight off her right leg, but she refused to compromise the security of the purple bag. She always carried it carefully, in both hands, mindful of any bump or unnecessary pressure. She re-entered the blue room and moved to the opposite side of the bed from Josephine. She backed into a seated position, her bad leg stretched out in front, the cloth bag at her hip.

She glanced at Josephine. "Smoke? I know I need one," she said.

"Here." He waved at Maureen. "Listen." He fiddled with the remote to bump up the volume.

"*. . . but what we do know is that at approximately nine-eleven this evening, fifty-five year old Robert Gordon Braithwaite, Chief Executive Officer of the Directorate for Aboriginal Settlement and former defensive star of the Boston Bruins, suffered an apparent heart attack. We have no official word on his condition, however witnesses at this exclusive, ocean-front resort tell us he was not breathing when paramedics arrived on the scene. RCMP sources say they are investigating events before and after Braithwaite's collapse, and they are not ruling out any possibilities at this time, including foul play or an act of terrorism. Though information is scarce, it is believed that high-level negotiations were taking place on the property. There have been unconfirmed reports that members of Hargrove's cabinet, perhaps even the Premier himself, were in attendance. RCMP have begun an intensive search for Tse Wets Aht Chief Josephine David and other members of her entourage-*"

"Hey, they're talking about me."

"Shh!"

"-believed to be at large on Vancouver Island. More details as we get them. Back to you-"

Billy shut off the television. "You'd be aiding and abetting, now."

Maureen blinked. "RG's dead?"

Billy nodded. "Went into cardiac arrest right on top of her. And they say missionary style's boring."

"I don't-"

"It's the truth, swear." He placed his hand on his heart. "We were on recess, I heard the screaming. She was curled up in Braithwaite's room, wrapped in a sheet, looking like some fucked-up Grand Vizier of the KKK."

"RG was doing Sarah Cohen," Maureen said.

"Every chance he got, by the looks of things."

"Bastard."

"Jealous, Cage?" Billy grinned. "Everyone got the hell out when the sirens started. They just booked it out of there. Except Cohen. She was running around, wrapped in her sheet, begging anyone she could find to stay with her. Scared shitless. I dragged Jo to my jeep, she didn't want to leave without the papers, but Hargrove's people and the security teams swept them into boxes and stuffed them into their cars. Jo got into a fight over one of the boxes. They knocked her down. She wanted proof, something to take back. But they took everything."

"So nothing will stick?"

"I know how this goes. Jo's solo, now," Billy said. "They'll disown her for this. Hang her out to dry. Everyone's in full denial." He sighed. "We were *that* close," he said, his thumb and index finger an inch apart.

"What about Carole? What did she do?"

"The Feds left in the first wave. She got to Jo, right as the screaming started. I don't know what she said, she was gone by the time I got RG's bitch off me. We were the last out. We headed south. After a half hour of driving I remembered Simons saying you were in Victoria, so I called her. She was already at the airport. Before she'd give me your hotel she made me promise to tell you something." His teeth gleamed like wet pearls behind his parted lips.

"What?" Maureen shifted in her chair.

"*Sorry.*" Billy tipped his beer can and drained it into his mouth.

"That's it?"

"That's it, Cage," Billy said. He wiped his lips with the back of one hand. "She made a fair deal out of it, though."

Maureen played with the pull tab on the top of her beer.

"It's none of my business, Cage," Billy said as he swung out of his chair and pulled twin cans from the fridge. "Hey, you're out of beer." He straddled the chair, one beer in each fist. "You two—you know—*friends with benefits?*"

"You're right. It's none of your business," Maureen said, snatching a can from his hand. "We're going out for more, soon. What's happening in Port?"

"Dunno. Getting off the blockade was one thing. No way they're letting us drive back in."

"Shouldn't this end it now?"

"Uh-Unh." Billy cracked open his beer and drank deeply. "Blockades are busting out like Springtime, Cage. From here to the Alaska border. Jo keeps saying it's the *Raven Effect.* For all the clans, wolf, bear, salmon and raven. In her talks with Hargrove she kept going on about how, at the beginning of things, Raven tricked the Sky Chief into letting him see where the sun was kept. Then he stole the sun from the Sky Chief and put it in the sky for all our people, so they could see their world for the first time. So we could finally be warm, be free. Raven has come back to show us the way, to take our power back; to take the right to make decisions away from the white chiefs and return it to First Peoples everywhere. This is Raven's time. Our time. Aboriginals are looking to the Tse Wets Aht for inspiration. Nobody's gonna settle for leftovers anymore."

"I wish you luck," Maureen said. "I really do. But there are lots who will resist that vision of reality."

Billy set down his beer and yawned. "Maybe, Cage. But that highway's shut tighter than an eagle's arsehole in a power dive. It won't re-open until real concessions are made. Lasting concessions. Unless the police do something stupid. Then it will get extremely ugly."

"What's Josephine going to do?" Maureen glanced at the rumpled shape asleep on the bed.

Billy shrugged. "She's screwed. If she's caught it'll be jail time for sure. Her own Council will crucify her for what she tried to do. There's something about secret talks that makes people suspicious."

"Because, like, they're *secret?*"

"Yup." Billy took another deep swallow of beer. He belched softly.

"Then why participate? To save Hargrove's ass? It doesn't make sense."

Billy sniffed, ran the back of one hand across his nose. "It did to her. Hargrove was desperate. He was ready to gold-plate everything she wanted." He rested his forehead on his crossed forearms.

"But Braithwaite couldn't keep his dick in his pants."

"Amen, Sister," Billy said. His voice rose out of a well, little more than a muffled whisper.

"Did Sarah say anything? After RG went into vapor lock?"

Billy looked up. "Sarah? The *Recess Priestess*? I was the first one there when the shouting started. She was in a corner of the room, screaming *Omigod, Omigod.* When I saw how small his dick was I knew why."

Maureen laughed until foam ran out of her nose. "We need more," she said, coughing, stumbling to the sink to wipe the mess off her face and hands. "A lot more."

Her fingers trembled as she lifted a freshly sparked match to the end of the smoke.

Josephine refused Maureen's flame. "I want to smoke, not blister my fingers," she said, taking the matchbook out of Maureen's hand. "What's in there?"

Maureen tipped the bag into her open palm. Tears collected in her eyes—a reflex after years of habit. Holding the bag was enough to start her crying. "Ancient history," she said, sniffling.

"How's any of this gonna change *my* opinion of *you*?"

A gold crucifix, a set of rosary beads, a small, creased photograph and a bent, faded Polaroid tumbled into Maureen's hand. She twisted her wrist and what lay in her palm slid onto the blue bedspread. She raised the purple cloth with faded, yellow stitching to her nose and, with her eyes closed, inhaled.

"This is my first trip to Victoria," Billy said.

They had locked Chief David in the motel room, her deep, regular snores loud even outside the door. Maureen sped through nearly deserted downtown streets. She aimed for the nearest pub with off-sales, trying to outrun closing time. Limp figures of the city's homeless punctuated random doorways and alleys. Their booted feet stretched across dusty paving stones and cement sidewalks. Brindle dogs curled against their legs, occasionally raising their heads to sniff the warm, breathless air. Scraps of paper collected in drifts against curbs, like stubborn patches of filthy snow.

"You got 'em here, too," Billy said. "Byproducts of the system. Capitalism's great, ain't it? We can't afford to clean up our ghettos and slums and reserves, it'd be against the Almighty Free Market System, but we can impose the state's will on indigenous peoples halfway around the world. And at home the rich get richer. We call that democracy. Crazy, huh?" Billy craned his neck to catch glimpses of water as it appeared between old, stone buildings. The passenger window was open and his right arm rested on the door frame. He strummed the metal with his fingers.

"If you want I can take you to a pub for Cornish pasties and warm beer," Maureen said. "You can sing English drinking songs and play Keno with the tourists and lay off with the Karl Marx for awhile." She glanced at her watch.

"No need to be harsh," Billy said. "I met some people from Victoria once, in Seattle. Back during the WTO riots. They were right on. Very committed."

"Probably not the same people playing Keno." Maureen pulled to the curb, left the engine running and dashed through the side door of a pub. She returned with a brown bag under her arm. "Put them under your seat," she said, and jammed the gearshift into reverse.

"You didn't drink like this in Port," Billy said.

"You keep giving me reasons to."

Billy stuffed the six pack between his feet and leaned back in his seat. His fingers rapped against the Subaru door post, repeating the same riff as Maureen turned north. He hummed in time to the strum of fingers. "Buh, buh, buh, duh-duh. Buh, buh, buh, duh-duh."

"You're too young to know that song," Maureen said. She pointed the Subaru east, led him away from the main streets. "Paul Revere and the Raiders, right?"

"Too young? It's my theme song," Billy said. "I've been a warrior since I was born. Before, even."

As they left the street lights behind, the shadows around his eyes lengthened, connected, shrouding his face. The dim glow from the dash accentuated the angular cut of his chin. His fingers continued to strum on the door.

"My grandfather was shot at Wounded Knee," Billy said. He turned his face away from Maureen, toward the open window. "Sniper's bullet. The FBI still deny it was them. My mother swears it was. She was only four years old. I grew up on those stories and I've been fighting the Red Man's War ever since."

"Jesus."

"Furthest thing from him," Billy said. "You like Paul Revere?"

"You're kidding."

"No, I'm not. Weird, huh? I might be the only Aboriginal who does. Besides my mom. She wore out that record. Played it night and day, more when she got stoned. I remember back in university, we were trying to get the administration to change the name of the football team. I found a copy of the album in a pawn shop and we played it in the Student Union building and broadcast it over the campus radio station every day for a month. They called the team *the Fighting Sioux*."

"They sued for cruel and unusual punishment?"

"Better," Billy said. "The esteemed alumni beat up five of our brothers and sisters, put them in hospital. The Dean nearly called out the National Guard, things got so tense. I held on 'til end of term, then bailed."

"Why?"

"Too many death threats. I decided that if you're willing to die for a cause, at least make it meaningful."

His tired eyes returned Maureen's stare. "It's only a fucking football team and they were crap. Couldn't win a game unless the other team didn't show. Anyway, I'll always love that song."

Buh, buh, buh, duh-duh. Buh, buh, buh, duh-duh: his fingers tripped across the door frame.

"What are they called now?"

"Who?"

"The football team."

"*The Fighting Sioux*," Billy said and laughed. "We lose a lot of battles, but we'll win the war."

"Which one?"

Billy leaned his head out the window to look at the stars. "All of them, Sister. Like the prophet J-Master Mick says: *Taa-ah-ah-ime Is On Maa Saade. Yes it is.*" He sang into the night air with a loud, clear voice.

"Amen to that, Little Brother," Maureen said. She braked, swerved and steered between the high concrete curbs of an all-night burger drive-through.

"My dad's," Maureen said, wadding up the cloth bag and tossing it aside. "He was a useless sonofabitch." Maureen scooped the crucifix off the bed cover and dangled it by its slender chain. "This was my mother's."

The crucifix glimmered inches below her hand. The gold was clean, unblemished. She took the clasp between her hands, and after three tries she gave up with a groan, curling her unsure, clumsy fingers into fists.

"Let me," Josephine said, clamping her cigarette between her lips and offering Maureen her hand.

Maureen poured the chain and crucifix into her palm.

Her fingers were quick and she spread the chain and leaned close to Maureen. "You should wear it."

Maureen hesitated, her eyes on the spinning gold cross. "I've never put it on. Ever."

"Why not?"

"She was thirty-one when she died. Went to church twice a week. Why didn't that make a difference?"

"Maybe it did," Josephine said. She leaned nearer to set the chain around Maureen's neck.

Maureen could smell shampoo in Josephine's wet hair. She turned, exposing a ridge of bare neck. Josephine fastened the chain behind Maureen's head. Her fingers were like kitten strokes, warm against the skin on the nape of Maureen's neck.

"Thanks," Maureen said and shivered.

She tucked her chin for a look, but the tiny cross hid in the hollow of her throat. The gold was suddenly warm next to her flesh and the warmth began to radiate under her skin towards her heart.

"You told me you had a good reason for coming here," Billy said through a mouth full of cheeseburger." You gonna tell me or do I have to guess?"

"Just like camping, eh?" Maureen said. The aluminum can made a loud pop as she pulled up the tab. She took a deep swallow and sighed. She pushed back the seat and stretched her legs until they hit the firewall between the pedals. She held an unwrapped cheeseburger in one hand and a can of beer in the other. The Subaru engine ticked as it cooled, its tires resting in familiar ruts off the asphalt on Nelson Road.

"I wouldn't know," Billy said. "But there's worse places I've been stuck."

"I'll take that as a compliment," Maureen said.

"You're full of surprises," Billy said between mouthfuls. "When I first saw you at the funeral I took you for a stuck up ice-bitch. All business. *NFA.*"

"What's that stand for?"

"*No Fun Allowed. Not Fucking Alive.* Or *No Fucking Attempted.* Take your pick. One or all three."

"That's harsh," Maureen said. She gulped her beer and only half stifled the belch rising from her chest.

"It's like you have this double life," Billy said. He drained the can and leaned over to stuff it under the seat.

"More like I finally woke up," Maureen said.

A surge of heat warmed her face. She stared across the street to the red house. The curtains leaked electric light through the fabric. A fourth vehicle, a dented and mud-splattered Ford pick-up, jammed the driveway at a sloppy angle, hemming in the other cars. Its rear wheels hung over the driveway, onto the street. Chrome mud flaps, each with the silhouette of a fantastically-breasted woman in sensual recline, sparkled in the light from the neighbor's halogen lamp. The sense of dread was still there—the hairs on the back of her neck had tingled as she'd pulled over to park—but it was contained, close to the house, like a vicious dog on a short, sturdy chain.

"That person you first met," Maureen said. "That wasn't me. I've been stuck for ten years in an oil painting of someone else's idea of me."

"The Dorian Gray thing, right? Whose idea? Your ex-husband's? Stockbroker boyfriend? I'd punch him out."

"No ex-, no boyfriend. I'm the guilty one."

"Any particular reason?"

"Lots. But mostly I had to get me out of my way."

"How?"

Maureen held up the beer can. "I gave it up. Beer, smokes, pot, meat, sex. All of it."

"Sweet," Billy said, "I never met a nun before."

"A nun?" Maureen took another deep swallow. The beer was making her warm, sleepy. "You don't go from dancing the *A* circuit for ten years to Senior Analyst for *Dee-Faz* without making a few changes."

Billy's hands jammed against the dashboard. "You were a stripper? Honest Injun?" He held up two fingers in mock salute, grinning.

"Honest."

"You got the legs for it, I'll give you that much, but I can't see it. You? Shaking it for a bunch of drunken photocopier salesmen?"

"Ten years, Billy," Maureen said. She toasted him with her beer can and drained it.

"Any chance of a comeback?" He winked.

Josephine returned to her side of the bed. The mattress creaked under her weight. "My family went to church. It was something we did. Even as our traditions came back, the church was always part of it. Birth, marriage, death—how could it not be? They're the things that keep us connected." She plucked the string of beads off the bed and laid them across her palm. "Your mother's?"

Maureen nodded. "Don't know why I took them."

Chief David's fingers moved across the beads, kneading them gently. They clicked together happily inside her palm. "Nice and warm," she said, smiling for the first time. "You make it sound like you were stealing."

"I was."

The beads fell silent.

"I ran away. More than once, but this stuff I took the first time," Maureen said. "I think I was ten, about five years after my mother died. My father hid all her stuff away. In boxes. He wasn't doing anything with it. He wasn't doing much of anything, except drinking and feeling sorry for himself. I found the Crown Royal bag and jammed what I could inside it and took off. Where, I don't remember, anymore. But this is what I wanted to show you."

Maureen turned over the Polaroid where it lay on the bedspread. It was crisp, as brittle as old parchment. The colors had long since faded behind a sepia film that blended the finer details into a uniform, amber haze. The darkness of the bedroom robbed what little definition remained. Maureen leaned sideways, turning the photo toward the light that shone through the window.

"You?" Josephine asked. She exhaled a plume of smoke, leaned close so that her head was an eyelash away from Maureen's face.

Maureen nodded. "One of the street kids stole the camera and started taking pictures. I just got in his way." She inhaled the just-scrubbed scent surrounding Josephine. "I was in front of the Eaton's store in downtown Toronto. He threw the thing at me and took off."

It looked like night, but she knew otherwise: the day had been hot, sweltering and blindingly bright in the crossfire of glare off glass-fronted skyscrapers. The girl staring at the camera couldn't have been much more than fifteen. Her face looked smooth, but that was a lie conjured by shadows and the ageing Polaroid: Maureen remembered the ratty, greasy hair, bad skin and hollow, runny eyes that—for only a shutter's blink—found a reason to sparkle. Maybe it was the bundle in her hands, the small, smooth forehead that stuck out past a thin, shapeless blanket as she raised her arms to show off her prize.

"You're not the first person to ask me that," Maureen said, but she smiled anyway. "And you completely missed my point."

"No, I got it," Billy put up his hands. "You're finding out that the only true path in this universe is balance. Does this mean you're not a nun anymore?"

She tossed the crumpled cheeseburger wrapper at his head.

"So why'd you bring me here, Cage, if you're not seducing me?"

Maureen pointed at the house, squat, half hidden in the shadows. "I found our very own *Raven Effect*, to put it in Josephine's terms."

Billy hunkered down to look out the driver's side window, his shoulder pressing heavily against her side. His scent was strong in her nose; a hint of cinnamon riding on the musk of his sweat.

Maureen shifted in her seat and swallowed, her mouth drying. A gentle, subtle warmth flowed into her muscles. "She's in there. My guess says the truck's Larry's. Her Heritage League boyfriend."

Billy made a clucking sound out of the corner of his mouth. "How'd you find her?"

"Stripper radar," Maureen said.

Billy laughed. "So what now, Boss?"

"Sarah used to call me that."

"Sorry."

"Never mind," Maureen smiled, as the warmth soaked deeper into her limbs. "She's going to tell us what happened to Henry and Kenny and their friends after they left the strip club. She's going to tell us about the note the Tse Wets Aht received and if it really was a truck that sent them into the ditch."

"You just going to knock?"

"Tried that before," Maureen said. "Didn't work. I thought maybe an expert in civil disobedience would have better ideas." She flashed him another smile.

Billy met her glance, held it, then looked toward the house. He let out a deep sigh. "I think we should sleep on it, Cage," he said, and his smile set her skin tingling.

"Only picture I have of my daughter," Maureen said, the bottom dropping out of her voice.

Josephine straightened. Her eyes locked onto Maureen's and for a moment Maureen glimpsed something besides impatience. It looked like pain, visible in the lines at the corners of her mouth and in the downward tilt of her head.

"Where is she now?" Josephine said, her voice a hoarse whisper in the half-light.

"I don't know," Maureen said, and she pressed the back of her fists into her eyes. "But now I know *who* she is."

Josephine's black eyebrows collided above her frown.

"Frances. My daughter. She's all grown up, now. Prefers the name Raven."

They sat up for another hour, filling the blue room with cigarette smoke and tears and laughter—once—at a joke Maureen tried to tell but messed up halfway through. Maureen talked until her voice was raw, about her life on the streets; about stealing and panhandling until her baby was born in the basement of a Toronto parking garage. How Welfare was going to take away her baby. About the free clinic around the corner from the Salvation Army and the nurse there that made sure the baby got her shots. The nurse who showed Maureen how to breast-feed and diaper Frances and put in a good word so Maureen could get a part-time job at a downtown drug store, but with nobody to watch Frances she had to quit after four days.

Three days after the Polaroid was snapped she hitch-hiked to Windsor, walked the two miles to her mother's kid sister's apartment and lifted Frances through the open window of their 'seventy-nine Ford LTD. She cried on the way to the bus station and when her aunt had answered the phone all she could do was shout: *look in your car, now!* and hang up. She couldn't bear to go back to Toronto. She hitch-hiked to Calgary, soon after to Vancouver, knowing that without three-thousand-plus miles between them she wouldn't be able to stay away. She needed physical distance, the space of miles, to fix her resolve. Time would do the rest, would make her forget her daughter.

While Maureen spoke Josephine stared out the window, her head and shoulders resting against the headboard. The rosary beads were locked in her fist. "You never had a clue she was yours," she said when Maureen fell silent.

"She's moved out, gone. I don't know where to look."

"She's a stripper," Josephine said. "If anybody can find her *you* can."

Maureen blinked. "How did You-?"

"Billy told me. When we were hiding downstairs. Said you worked as an exotic dancer to pay for school."

Maureen shook her head. "Uh-Unh. Not at first. I never thought that far ahead. It just paid the bills, got me off the streets. School came later, when I finally figured out I needed a future."

"You are one fucked up white chick," Josephine said, shaking her head.

"Like mother, like daughter," Maureen said. "If it wasn't for Anne and Helen, I'd have been dead long ago."

"Hey, I know worse. You sure you want to find her?"

"Maybe I deserve this for what I did. But I *have* to find out the truth." She laughed—a harsh laugh that erupted deep in her chest. "Funny thing, Legare thinks *I'm* one of them." She shook her head. "And he's kinda right, you know? Even if he doesn't realize why."

"You gonna tell him?"

"No. He'll figure it out eventually. Useless prick. But I will find Frances."

"Why? So you can apologize? You got a bad case of maternal guilt. Comes with the territory," Chief David said. She closed her eyes, her breathing slow and deep. The lines around her mouth were nearly invisible. "It never ends," she said, after a silence so long Maureen thought she'd fallen asleep. "And I get to go through it twice."

"Taylor?"

Josephine opened her eyes. They glittered, diamond-hard. "The phone's gonna ring, I don't know when, but it will. They'll tell me they got my Cyn's DNA in a jar, or some dish, for evidence. All that's left of her will be in a lab, under glass, under some microscope. Like a virus they just identified. *Cynthia Lourdes Medeiros, File number 31X000401.*"

"You don't know that-"

"I *know* it," Josephine said, her voice suddenly on edge. "*They* don't, yet. I knew years ago. Can even tell you the day—hell, the hour—I knew my baby was dead."

She sat up, her fingers curled into fists. "When they figure it out, they'll call, make it official. Meantime I gotta find a way to do better for Taylor than I did for Cyn." Josephine's fingers worked over the rosary beads as she spoke.

"These are nice," she said, her voice trailing away.

"Keep them."

Josephine started, her dark eyes narrowing.

"Better than keeping them hidden all these years."

"I'm not Catholic."

"Neither am I, but they seem to like you. I remember my father asking my mother why she carried them around, constantly playing with them. She liked how warm they got in her hand. Made her feel watched over, protected, she said. He tried, after she died, but they were always cold for him. She'd have told him: *It's not your hand that warms them, it's your heart*, or something like that."

"They're hot."

Maureen smiled. "See? Keep them. Please. They're like ice in my hands." She stood. "I have to get some sleep." She swept up the photos from the bedspread with one hand as the other reached for the crumpled purple bag.

"What about that one?" Josephine pointed to the creased black and white photograph. "What makes that one special?"

Maureen hesitated. "Nothing."

"Can I see it?"

Maureen blinked, extending her arm, the photo stuck between her index finger and thumb.

"It's hard to make out in this light," Josephine said, moving nearer. She gripped Maureen's arm and twisted, turning both hand and photo toward the window.

A woman, handsome and dark-eyed, smiled at the small child in her arms. This child was no helpless infant: she was tall, her skinny frame too long for the dress she wore. Spindly legs stuck out below the hem, ending in white ankle socks and shiny black shoes. She was four, possibly five years old. The woman's hair was pulled tight off her face and piled into a bun. She wore a knee-length wool coat, buttoned against the cold, its outline stark against the snow. She pressed the little girl tight to her body. The girl was unhappy, on the verge of tears. Her arms were raised, elbows high, her hands covering her face. Her bare legs were only partly shielded by the woman's encircling arms.

"Your mother?" Josephine said. "She's beautiful. That's you, in the dress, isn't it?"

Maureen cleared her throat. "Yes. That was me."

"When was this taken?"

Maureen turned her wrist, felt the pressure of Josephine's fingers on her arm as the back of the photo was revealed. "January nineteen-seventy," Maureen read the handwriting.

"*Angel and Theresa*?" Josephine read the rest of the inscription.

"He only ever called her that. Theresa's my name. My real name," Maureen said.

Josephine turned to face Maureen. "Then who's the real Maureen Cage?"

"She died a long time ago. She was seventeen. I lived in her house as a foster kid for nearly two years, after she died. They were nice enough people, but they were ghosts. When it was time to get my shit together I thought of the straightest, cleanest person I'd ever known. Getting her transcripts was dead easy. Driver's license, Social Insurance. I've been Maureen longer than she was."

"Jesus." Josephine squeezed Maureen's hand.

"That picture was taken on a Sunday morning, we were going to church. We didn't own a car and the Church of the Immaculate Conception was a dozen blocks from the apartment. That was the winter I'd outgrown my snowsuit. I loved that snowsuit. So warm, so safe." Maureen sighed. "She died six months later."

In the deepening shadows Josephine's arched eyebrows looked sleek, smooth as wet fur. They settled across the bony ridge over her eyes as she lifted the photograph and squinted into its depths.

"Right after this picture was taken," Maureen said, her voice a whisper in the smoky room, "she squeezed me so hard. She kissed me." Maureen covered her face to catch the tears as they spilled from her eyes. "Why couldn't he have waited? Why didn't he take the damn picture ten seconds later?"

Josephine's long arms encircled Maureen's shivering body. "Why does that matter?"

"Then she'd always be kissing me," Maureen whispered, her voice breaking. She lowered her face into the hollow of Josephine's shoulder and wept.

Chief David had not moved in their time away. Maureen turned off the light and groped in the darkness to the bathroom. She leaned against the wall, flicked on the light above the sink and pulled the door shut until only a sliver of light spilled into the room. Billy pulled off Jo's boots and socks and folded the bedspread over her narrow body. Her snoring subsided as he shifted her weight.

Maureen ducked into the bathroom and shut the door. She caught the thin, metallic creak of the sofa bed unfolding as she undressed. When she stepped out of the bathroom, Billy was already under the sheet. His large, slender feet stuck out the bottom.

"Don't stare," she said, clutching her clothes in a bundle in front of her. She dropped them onto the nearest chair.

Billy lifted the blanket, inviting her into the space beside him. Her eyes skimmed across the smoothness of his torso as his body flexed, making room for her. She leaned forward, resting her arms on the edge of the sofa bed. She kissed his mouth. The same hint of cinnamon she'd noticed in the car.

"Smoke," Billy said, breaking away.

"I brushed my teeth. Sorry," she said.

The wafer-thin mattress sagged beneath her weight. She lay on her side, pressed against his body. It was firm and warm. His hands were on her breasts, on her back, on her thighs. She stopped him only once, and she surprised even herself at how quickly the condom slipped over the fullness of his erection.

"See?" she said. "How long did that take? Stopping at the drug store, I mean."

"You're such an eagle scout, Cage," Billy said as he rolled onto his back. "You get a badge for this?"

"No. Just lots of practice, once upon a time," she said, but then his mouth was on hers and his arms pinned her to the mattress.

"That was great," he said, exhaling heavily. He rolled off the bed to a chorus of protesting springs. As the bathroom door swung shut she glimpsed the spent condom swinging like a pendulum off the end of his wilting prick.

Maureen groped for tissue, then for her underwear and tee shirt and stepped out of the bed to dress. She shivered, despite the overheated air. She wrapped the sheet and blanket tightly around her shoulders and curled onto her side, her back to the middle of the bed.

When Billy returned he stubbed his toe on the bed frame, cursed, then slid behind her, his arm on top of the blanket. "Great way to end a drought," he said, nuzzling happily into her neck.

"Yours or mine?" Maureen said, without turning around.

"Yours, of course," Billy said, yawning.

Maureen shivered. "Thanks," she said. "I really know what I'm missing, now."

BOOK SIX

Cremation

Maureen raised her arms, deflecting the blows as they fell from all sides. Her attackers' faces were shrouded in darkness, but she knew them. She awoke, breathing hard, into the grey light of early morning. The crashing continued. Someone was pounding on her front door.

She sat up, rubbing her eyes. The purple draw string bag was on her bed table. She leaned closer and pulled open its mouth. Everything was there, save the rosary beads. She swung out of bed, glancing at the clock. Not quite five. She grit her teeth against the pain that flared through her knee as she stood. Her clothes had been laid out across the end of the bed. She shivered as she dressed, her fingers trembling as she fumbled with the buttons of her shirt.

It was light enough to recognize Sarah Cohen on her porch.

"What the hell do you want?" Maureen stood on the threshold, leaning against the door frame for support.

Sarah stepped back. The week had added years to the flesh beneath her eyes. Her face was grim, her lips dry and chapped and bleeding where she'd picked at them.

"This is all your fault," she said. A thin sound followed, a whimper.

"O for Christ's sake-" Maureen started to shut the door.

"Wait!" Sarah rushed forward. "Please. I have to find out where it is. No-one will tell me. I'm as good as dead to them."

"Where *what* is?"

"The funeral. RG's. It's today. Or tomorrow. I don't know where."

"Jesus, you *want* to go?" Maureen kept the door half shut. "You need help."

"I-I need to be there." Sarah ran a shaking hand through her hair.

"After what you did? You destroyed their best chance of ending this nightmare."

"He said he'd leave her," Sarah said. Her shredded fingernails hovered near the flaking skin on her lips.

"Right," Maureen said. "I've no idea, and I'm not exactly on anybody's invitation list."

"But you know his daughter. Rachel. You can contact her. Find out where the funeral is." Sarah's voice trembled.

"She's on a blockade, Sarah. Christ, get some sleep. And get over him. He was an asshole."

Sarah's face collapsed, then, as quickly, twisted into rage. "*You're* the asshole, Maureen. You're *worse* than the rest. Always acting like you're better than me. I hate you."

"Tell me something I don't already know," Maureen said, slamming the door before Sarah could reply.

Through the living room window Maureen watched as Sarah's hands covered her face. Despite her anger she felt an urge to help. Was it Sarah's fault RG was such a prick? Before she could move Sarah straightened, raked hooked fingers through her hair and walked slowly down the porch steps to the street. She turned east and disappeared behind the neighbor's house.

"She's onto something."

Billy's voice at her shoulder startled her. He stood where the living room opened into the dining room. He held a mug of coffee in one hand, while the blanket she'd loaned him hung loose around his shoulders and his hair stuck out from his skull. He reminded her of Alistair Sim's Scrooge, newly awakened to realize its Christmas morning. He grinned, and the resemblance vanished.

"Coffee's on," he said.

"She better not have seen you," Maureen said.

"No chance," Billy said. "I am the night. I am the darkness. Besides, I was in the kitchen the whole time."

"I'll take that coffee," Maureen said, brushing past him. His scent was strong on the blanket.

"Great," Billy said. He padded behind her to the kitchen.

Maureen stuck a clean mug under the spout of the carafe and filled it. She leaned against the counter. Through the window her garage and the lane beyond it emerged out of a grainy dawn. The sky was the color of dust. It was turning hot again.

Billy slipped into one of the chairs by the window, the blanket still wrapped around him. "Nice place, Cage," he said, his glance darting about the room. "You were doing okay, I guess."

"Living the dream," she said, sipping her coffee.

"Then you must've got woke up pretty hard." He flashed a smile.

"Thanks."

"No worries. You'll get used to it."

"To what?"

"The fringes. Living on the edge. Scraping by. Billions do it, it's not so bad. Better than being stuck in a suburban rut. Making a living? Huh. Making a *dying*, more like."

"Let's skip it, 'kay?"

Silence wedged itself between them. Billy stared at her, his eyes as comfortable appraising her as any inanimate object.

"Refill?" She looked away, grabbing the coffee pot.

"Sure," he said.

"Milk?"

"And sugar. Thanks." Billy took the coffee with both hands. "I meant what I said about Sarah. She's onto something."

Maureen slid into the chair opposite Billy, twisting sideways to keep her right knee from bending. "What?"

"The funeral. All the brass will be there. What a place to make a showing."

"You're nuts."

"You got no bad feelings for him? After what he did?"

Maureen leaned back in her chair. "RG was a jock who scraped through law school on his name and looks and his wife's money. He was too stupid to know how lucky he was. Let his family bury him in peace."

Her glance drifted to the deck. The hummingbird feeder that hung below the eaves was empty, stained and smudged by the last rains. Her deck chair needed a fresh coat of paint. A lonely hanging basket of lobelia and petunia had gone stringy and crisp from neglect. Her thoughts zigzagged through the last two weeks. Someone—or something—had turned her life upside down and shaken. Hard. But it hadn't been RG.

"Maybe." Billy shrugged. "What *do* you say at the funeral of a married dude who dies boning some office gash the same age as his daughter?" He gulped down his coffee and set the mug on the table. His thumb strayed across the plain, white surface below the rim. "I mean, I wouldn't wanna be *that* MC."

"Another good reason not to go," Maureen said.

Billy's teeth flashed white through his smile. "Wrong. Cage, I know what your problem is. You've an underdeveloped revenge gene. Any normal person would be dying to go. Me? I wouldn't miss this for anything." He stood, rearranged the blanket around his shoulders and padded out of the kitchen.

"Where you going?"

"Out. Got some calls to make."

"Rachel?" Maureen called after him. "You're calling her, right?"

"You got it, Pontiac." Billy's voice drifted from the living room. "Her and others loyal to the cause. You ever stop to wonder why the Big Three car manufacturers use the names of *our* people on *their* cars? *Cherokee. Cheyenne. Dakota.* I could go on. How'd you like to drive around in a fuel efficient Chrysler *Scotsman*? Or enjoy the smooth ride of the new Buick *Caucasian*? How 'bout a high performance BMW *Aryan*? Or a fast, curve-hugging *Sicilian*?"

His face appeared around the corner of the dining room wall. "That was all rhetorical, Cage. And don't worry, I won't make any calls from here," he said. "Too easy to trace." He retreated to the living room to finish dressing.

Maureen limped after him. "You're serious about this?"

"Dead serious," he said. He turned to face Maureen, wearing only briefs and holding a balled-up sock in his hand. He hopped on his right foot on the discarded blanket as he unrolled the sock over his left. "Sure, you desire me now, but last night you had me at your will."

"My loss." She stooped and swept the blanket off the floor and began to fold it into a neat square. "Unlike RG, I think my destiny is to find true love among my own generation."

Billy finished dressing. He pulled a comb from his jeans pocket and retied his pony tail. "Love? Interesting concept, Cage. Got anything to eat?"

She drove Billy to his Jeep. He'd left it in a downtown parking garage shared by a major bank, small retail outlets and an art gallery. Maureen stopped at a corner to let him out, didn't answer when he said he'd be calling with the funeral details.

"You gotta be there," he shouted as she sped away from the curb.

She headed south, out of the heart of downtown, and at the fringe of skyscrapers pulled into a parking lot. She reached for the sticker in her glove box and set it on the dash. It didn't expire until the end of the month. It was early, still more than an hour before the start of regular business. She unlocked the front office and slipped past the vacant reception desk. The lights were on and a whiff of coffee from the corner kitchen told her she wasn't the first to arrive.

Her name tag had been pulled from the office door. A single box sat on the floor in front, a box the kind banks used: a neat, compact cube with a snug, removable lid. *M. Cage* had been etched onto the outward face in thick, black marker. Maureen opened the door. In the dimness it was difficult to tell if the office had been reassigned.

"Don't bother. It's all been packed." The voice was dry, efficient. "I wasn't sure what name to put on the box."

Maureen pivoted. She hadn't heard Lee-Anne Carlyle's approach. "Congratulations, you got it right first try," she said.

"Not according to the good Inspector." Lee-Anne stood at the end of a row of workstations, one hand gripping the corner of the fabric-covered dividers. She stared at Maureen over the rims of her glasses. Her hair was shorter than it used to be, angled sharply off the nape of her neck. The lines around her pinched mouth were deeply etched into her pale skin.

"He's having trouble with the facts," Maureen said.

Lee-Anne's nose wrinkled. "Sure. A truck's coming by your place for our reference materials. I've got a list, in case you forget what belongs to us."

"You're so thorough, Lee-Anne," Maureen said.

She stooped to flip open the lid. Every shred of her existence at *Dee-Faz* had been piled into one box, with space to spare. One of her sweaters, a *Garfield* coffee mug RG had given her last Christmas that she couldn't bear to take home, a magazine on finding and restoring antiques and a small plaque marking her contribution toward the AIP signing so long ago. That was all. The price one paid for bringing nothing to work that would attract attention. She crouched, inhaling sharply at the pain in her knee.

"For God sake, I'll carry it," Lee-Anne said. She grabbed the box and turned for the exit. She hesitated at the still-vacant reception desk. "There. On the desk. Sign it. Drop your keys here."

Maureen snatched a single sheet of paper off the desk. Her name had been scribbled across the top. It was a form letter, full of check boxes. *To Be Reviewed and Initialed By the Departing Employee and His/Her Manager.* Under the space for *Reasons For Departure* someone had written: *Position acquired under false pretenses. Dismissed with cause.*

"Our HR guy vetted it," Lee-Anne said.

"How could I tell?" Maureen said. She pulled her office key off her ring and dropped it onto the desk.

"You can't claim damages."

"You're making this so easy," Maureen said. "By now the whole world knows what kind of a boss RG was. I think your HR guy better think again."

"*You're* suing *us?*"

Maureen limped to her car, Lee-Anne following a pace behind. She popped the hatch and stepped sideways to give Lee-Anne room to set down the carton. When Lee-Anne retreated Maureen saw the box's side panel. "Jesus Christ."

The cardboard had been tattooed with black swastikas. She elbowed past Lee-Anne, yanked the lid off and dumped the contents onto the floor. She flung the empty box into the parking lot.

"You have no fucking clue. Neither does that shit-for-brains Inspector," she said. She grabbed the coffee mug and hurled it across the parking lot. It shattered, sending ceramic shards skittering off the tires of parked cars.

"I can't really blame the staff for reacting emotionally," Lee-Anne said. "Especially in our business."

Maureen dragged one of her crutches from the car. She held it like a sledgehammer and pounded the box into the asphalt. The top of the aluminum crutch bent and split. Drivers entering the parking lot slowed to watch. Lee-Anne retreated beyond the arc of Maureen's swing.

"*There's* reacting emotionally, Lee-Anne. Check out Victoria General Hospital. Ask that Nazi bastard whose head I caved in which side I'm on." Maureen stood over the battered box, her chest heaving.

"You're a fraud."

"I lied, sure." Maureen thumped her fist against her chest. "About *my* life, *my* daughter, *my* private things. Nothing else. I lied to protect Frances. To protect myself. *You* sleep with your married boss and come back *as* the boss. But *I'm* the criminal."

"You've done as much damage to Port McKenzie as the fires have done to the rest of the province."

"Only your opinion, Lee-Anne." Maureen flung the useless crutch into the Subaru and slammed shut the doors. She gunned the engine as tears filled her eyes. "The damage *I'm* responsible for was many years ago," she said, but her window was closed and the roar of the motor drowned her words. She shifted into gear and, blinking back tears, sped out of the parking lot.

"What's wrong?" Josephine looked up from the newspaper. Another front page story about the fires. The army was coming to relieve the exhausted fire fighters. Jo was sitting where Billy had sat, at the kitchen table, wedged against the window sill.

Maureen dumped a small, engraved plaque onto the table.

Josephine picked it up and extended her arms, squinting at the script. *"For your outstanding contribution at this historic milestone."*

"RG gave them to everyone on the team. I'd only started a couple of months before."

Josephine propped the plaque, gently, on the window sill. "That was historic, for sure," she said with a sniff. She shuffled through the newspaper. "Today the blockade is page three. Knocked off the front page by the army and another fire." She nodded toward the plaque. "Back then our agreement was splashed across every front page in the country. Like it was the end of the world."

"Too much happening, right now," Maureen said.

"And it's all bad," Jo said, turning her face away from Maureen.

"What's wrong?" It was Maureen's turn to ask.

Josephine cleared her throat. "Nothing."

"You're lying."

Josephine laughed, softly. "You're the career liar, remember?"

Maureen waited.

Chief David rose from her chair, refilled her coffee mug with the dregs from the pot. "I phoned the police."

"What?"

"I called the detective in charge of my daughter's file."

"They'll arrest you."

"I don't care," Jo said. "I can't keep waiting."

"What did he say?"

"Just that he was sorry."

"O God, Jo. Not that."

Josephine returned to her chair. "It felt good, you know? At first. No more second-guessing. No more questions. I can get on with things. Plan her funeral, finally. She's number twenty-nine, unofficially. They think it'll reach fifty by the time they're through digging. My Cyn's just a number now." Her voice trailed away.

"I'm so sorry," Maureen said.

"I was lying in bed, this morning. After Billy and you left. Something made me call. It was like I had to," she whispered.

"I understand."

Josephine looked up. Her eyes were wet, above a tight smile. "This time, Cage, I believe you."

"I thought you people are supposed to work in pairs," Maureen said through the crack in the front door.

Inspector Legare shrugged. "Sometimes," he said. He leafed through the pages of his spiral-bound notepad. "Can I come in?"

Maureen's grip on the doorknob tightened. "No. You can't."

"I can understand you're angry with me, Ms. Pistilli," Legare said, slipping his notepad into his pants pocket. He was dressed as if he'd just walked off a golf course. Save for the half moons of perspiration under the sleeves he looked calm, unperturbed by the afternoon heat.

"My name is Maureen."

"Fine. I'll just get an order. Bring a uniform over to watch the house twenty-four-seven. You've been charged with a crime. At least you're still here."

"Where's Frances?" She let the door swing open wider.

"Let me in and I'll tell you." He smiled for the first time.

Maureen stepped aside and he half-jumped into the hallway.

"Nice place," he said, turning a full circle to take in his surroundings.

"Here," Maureen said. "In the living room."

"You alone?" Legare asked as he sat down on the sofa.

"Yes," Maureen said. She willed herself to keep her eyes on the Inspector.

"Big house," he said, settling into the cushions. He freed his notepad from his pants pocket and pulled a golf pencil out of its binding. "Tough to keep up by your lonesome."

"Sometimes," she said. Her ears strained for the slightest creak from upstairs.

"One of the conditions of bail is to remain in the country," Legare said. "Amazing how many people forget that."

Maureen shuffled, sideways, to the dining room. "Something to drink?" She turned toward the kitchen without waiting for his answer. She hurried to the counter, cleared off the coffee mugs, had just closed the cupboard door when she heard him behind her.

"Sure," he said. "Whatever you got handy."

"Water," she said, her finger stuck in the flow from the tap. The water slowly chilled.

"Shouldn't waste it," Legare said. He moved alongside her. "I read in the papers today the city has only enough to last 'til mid-October. It's the driest summer since they've kept records."

Maureen shut off the tap. "Where's Frances? You said you'd tell me."

Legare stared at the water vanishing down the drain. "I lied. I don't know. Thought maybe you might."

"Bastard," Maureen said. "I haven't a clue."

"When I mentioned her name, back at the station, you got extremely agitated. You're doing it again. Why? What's the deal with her?"

Her skin was hot. A red wash fell like a veil in front of her eyes. She had to look away.

"We're pretty sure she's slipped through the border at Port Angeles. We've asked our American counterparts to keep their eyes open for her."

"Then why are you here?"

Legare shrugged. He stepped away from the sink, wandered to the kitchen table. His fingers traced the faint rings left by a coffee mug, then trailed over a second ring a few inches away. "Maybe to make sure you have no desire to do the same," Legare said. He spun to face her, folding his arms across his chest. "And to see, since they haven't actually *found* her south of the border, if maybe she came here?"

Maureen's throat constricted. "If she did, I wouldn't be asking you, would I? If she did, it wouldn't be illegal."

"Can I look around?"

"No," she said. Her glance settled on the heavy skillet next to the sink.

"If you are associating with a known hate criminal, things will be harder for you," Legare said. His voice dropped into a lower octave to begin his lecture. "You are charged with spreading and inciting hate. You may even be an accessory to homicide. Chief David is still unaccounted for."

"She's not here," Maureen said, "Get out."

"I'll take a quick look around, first." Legare pivoted, moved past Maureen into the hallway.

Maureen limped behind him, her pulse crashing inside her head. "No, you won't," she said, then stopped, suddenly, to avoid colliding with him at the bottom of the stairs.

He didn't notice her behind him. His eyes were fixed on Josephine David, coming downstairs to meet him. The knuckles on his hand turned white as he gripped the banister.

"You'd probably act the same way, Inspector," Jo said, "if you found out Raven was your daughter."

Legare stayed an hour, rooted to a kitchen chair while Josephine told him Maureen's story from across the table. He interrupted constantly, scribbling notes in his book, putting lines through earlier details with his golf pencil. Jo waited patiently for him to catch up, repeated portions when he asked for clarification. With Josephine his manner changed: he eagerly rewrote his notes, drew connecting lines and made footnotes from earlier pages. He couldn't have been more accommodating.

"He's reworking his notes," Josephine said, after Legare left. She settled herself on the sofa next to Maureen, stroking her hand. "It seems to me he wants to do the right thing."

"Bull," Maureen said. Her eyes were puffy. "He'll screw me. And you. I'm surprised he didn't take you with him."

"No, he won't," Josephine said. She smiled wearily. "He wants to hunt Nazis. Now he knows the truth about you. Now he knows how you're connected to Frances. He can now file an accurate report, not one built on conjecture and hunch. He smells a promotion, maybe a transfer away from Ottawa. Think of this as my gift to you."

She paused to laugh, her eyes suddenly sparkling. "He thinks he's doing the Tse Wets Aht—and all the First Nations—a glorious service. That's why he won't give me up. Yet. I told him I have something to do before I go home. He put his notebook away and shook my hand. He's flying back to Ottawa today."

"But he's *RCMP*," Maureen said.

"Funny, isn't it? After all this why should I believe him?" Josephine shrugged, still smiling. "I can't tell you. If I'm wrong I go to jail. So? Sooner this is done the sooner I get to go home."

"Jesus."

"You should be looking for your daughter, not worrying about him." Jo released Maureen's hand. "Here," she said, jamming one hand into her jeans pocket. "Proof that he's done with you."

Josephine opened her fist. A gold lighter shone in the middle of her palm. "He's been carrying it around. Weird way to treat evidence and I told him so. He couldn't hand it over fast enough."

She placed the lighter into Maureen's hand and closed her fingers around it. "If he still thinks you're a racist, then I'm the next Premier of BC."

At nine-thirty Maureen took pain killers and one of Anne's sleeping pills, stripped and eased into bed. She set her lighter on the bedside table and watched it through one eye. Compact and smooth, its edges gleamed red in the glow of the clock radio. Her eye traced its neat silhouette. It had been contrived, originally, to make fire easy—a beautiful item of portable convenience—but once used its makers took no responsibility for the conflagration their device might cause.

The fault was entirely the user's.

She rolled over and stared at the back of the bedroom door. Her feet were hot. She kicked away the blanket to find comfort. The restlessness beneath her skin itched like an invisible rash. She should have taken more pills.

She must have slept in spite of herself, for the weight of Jo's arm around her waist and her body on the mattress stirred her to consciousness. She started to climb a wall of panic, then exhaled as Jo pressed her forehead into the back of her neck.

Maureen stared at the far wall, her heart racing. "What's wrong?" The words lodged in the back of her throat.

"Too many ghosts." Jo's breath was an electric current down her spine. The smell of stale cigarettes merged with a musky hint of perspiration.

"Ghosts aren't the worst thing," Maureen said. Her voice was broken, the words separating, unstuck. "You don't know enough about me," she said.

"I do."

Maureen folded her right arm over top of Jo's thin hand. "Coming in here like this."

Jo wriggled closer. "I've read the signs," she said. "Like being on a trail in the woods, I know which turn to take and when it's safe. Now go to sleep." Her breathing deepened. The silence between each breath expanded.

Maureen stared at the wall, conscious of a gentle warmth that ran from her shoulders to her ankles. She heard music—Fats Waller—and saw Jo in her kitchen, humming, her hands caked with the crumbling soil of her garden, her long fingers clutching a pair of fleshy potatoes as the smoke from a lit cigarette curled lazily to the ceiling. A lifetime ago, it seemed, though barely two weeks had passed since that day. A warm, golden haze surrounded her. Maureen settled into the warmth and waited for sleep, surprised that, for once, it didn't matter how long it took to find her.

She lay on her back, listening, unsure of the sounds that slipped beneath the vestiges of sleep. Either Billy had come back or someone else was in her house. She slid out of bed, slowly, mindful of her knee and of Jo asleep beside her. She clutched at her clothes and limped to the bathroom. She was pleased to catch the aroma of frying eggs. Her stomach rumbled. She couldn't remember when she'd last eaten. She dressed and went downstairs, poking her head into the kitchen.

A stranger stood at her stove. Young, unshaven, dressed in camouflage pants and a dark green tee shirt. One hand stuck in his pants pocket, the other used a spatula to prod at a skillet full of eggs. Her spatula. Her eggs. Her kitchen.

"What are you doing?"

"Hey. Morning." He waved the spatula at her. Droplets of grease hit the floor. "Sorry." He stared at the splatters, but made no move to wipe them up. He scratched the dark smudge of hair beneath his lip, and turned back to the stove. "You like 'em Sunny-Side Up, or Over Easy? Make the call, seeing as this is your place."

"Who are you?"

She limped across the kitchen to stand at his shoulder. A pile of backpacks leaned at the corner of the kitchen door.

"Billy said you were okay. He's at the jeep with the others."

"*The others?*"

"Yeah. Shannon, Tanya, Mikey. I'm Sal. Short for Salvatore, but only my grandmother calls me that."

"What's going on?"

"The funeral, Boss Lady. We got a party to crash."

"Jesus. You're NFDI?"

"Hardcore." Sal raised his open hand above his head, as if expecting Maureen to meet it with her own. He lowered it, awkwardly, wiping the palm across the front of his tee shirt. "Right."

"How many others?"

"We're it, for now. B-man's been on the blower, so there'll be more. No doubt."

"I need coffee."

"Cool."

Maureen sat on the front porch, her injured leg resting gingerly across the top step. She had run out of arguments. Jo stood three paces off the sidewalk. She wore the ubiquitous black jeans with the silver belt buckle, boots and denim shirt. Her only concession to the heat was that her sleeves were rolled to the elbow. Her hair was once again woven into a single braid that hung to her waist.

"It's time," Jo said, as Billy blustered out the front door.

"I think you should go home," Maureen said. "I can take you, if you want. Leave them to their media event."

"No," Jo said.

"She can't miss this one," Billy said. "Neither should you. See? I got it." He waved a piece of paper above his head. "We're on." He hopped down the stairs and shoved it under Jo's face. "Win, place and show. Outstanding, aren't I?"

She grabbed the paper and held it at arm's length to read the wording. "Caterers? I have to dress up like a maid? Christ, Billy." She pushed the paper into his chest. "When do we leave?"

"Now. You too, Cage," Billy said.

"I've already told-"

"Hargrove is gonna be there, Cage," Billy said. "I got that from an excellent source."

"So?"

Billy rushed back up the steps to the front door. "*So* everything. The Premier and a Cabinet Minister and the NFDI. The perfect set up. The perfect photo-op. We expose them for the liars they are and it'll be on the Internet in minutes. It'll go viral. C'mon. We gotta scoot."

Josephine jammed her hands into her jeans and followed Billy up the front steps, avoiding Maureen's glance as she passed.

"Yesterday you were ready to resign," Maureen said.

Jo stopped in the doorway. "I may again tomorrow. But today Hargrove will remember his promises."

"Then I'm coming with," Maureen said, hobbling inside to fetch her car keys.

Maureen followed Billy's Jeep through downtown Vancouver, lost it in traffic on Georgia, caught up again on the Stanley Park causeway. Theirs was a two vehicle convoy: Billy, Jo and a hockey bag of supplies rode in the jeep while Sal, Mikey, Shannon and Tanya squeezed into the Subaru with Maureen. Traffic was heavy over the First Narrows to the North Shore. At the end of the bridge Billy headed east, then swung north on Capilano Road to the highway. The Chapel was close to the Second Narrows Bridge, where the highway dropped off the high table of the North Shore. The cemetery and crematorium had been carved into the woods between Lynn Creek and the Seymour River. Condominiums crowded the lower stretch of road, squatting in plain view of the highway off-ramp.

Billy veered into the Century Inn parking lot at the foot of a short, steep hill. Its stone facade and waterfall stood in jarring contrast to the unkempt brush of the last undeveloped parcel on the block. He leaned into Maureen's window.

"How's it hanging in here?" He grinned at each of the passengers.

"She drives pretty good for a senior," Sal said.

"This is where we split up," Billy said. "Maureen, you're heading down the low road, into the park. You got the map?"

Maureen nodded. "I gave it to Junior."

Sal waved the crumpled paper out the window.

"Good," Billy said. He glanced at his watch. "Two hours-fifteen to contact. You guys ready?"

"It's freakin' hot," Mikey complained from the back.

"You'll be in the trees, 'til Rachel's sister comes for you. Sal, you know the drop spot?"

Sal nodded.

"Good." Billy looked at Maureen. "You can stay, or go, but you can't leave the car at the drop point. Too risky."

"This place have a bar?" Maureen jerked her head toward the lobby. "I can get ice for my knee and wait for the sirens."

Billy laughed. "The world will still need recreational drinkers after the revolution." He trotted back to the Jeep, waved, and raced up the hill, vanishing over the crest.

"We go that way." Sal pointed through the windshield.

"Roger that, Junior."

Maureen swung onto the side street leading to the park. She leaned sideways, catching the breeze in her face. She was anxious, parachuted among these children, but it was as close to Josephine as she could get. She felt it was her job to keep her safe. The park road wove between ball diamonds and two tennis courts.

"This was a garbage dump, once," Tanya said. She gripped the back of Maureen's seat and pulled herself closer. "All this. I grew up near here. My oldest brother used to ride his bike at dusk to see the bears. They'd already closed it by the time I was old enough to go."

"There. Up there," Sal pointed to a gravel road leading north from one of the parking lots.

"How far?" Maureen asked.

"Go through the park. There's cut outs from when they built wells, years ago," Tanya said. "To track the poison coming from the rotting garbage. They're all around the old dump. The stuff's deadly toxic. Turned the river to rust, before they figured things out. When they built them they had to bring their drill rigs from the main road, instead of coming through the dump. It was cheaper to cut the trees than build roads over garbage. The paths are overgrown now, but one of them comes out right at the chapel courtyard."

"Didn't they just block it off?"

"No way," Tanya said. "That was done before there was a crematorium. From that side it's all natural. Looks like acres of forest. Hike in ten yards and the old path is still there."

Maureen followed Tanya's directions and after three minutes of kicking up dust on the dyke road she felt a tap on her shoulder. She turned into the tiny gravel pull-out. Her passengers dove out of the car, groaning with relief. Maureen popped the hatchback and Sal dragged out a second hockey bag and dumped it on the gravel.

"Okay, boys and girls, time to change," Mikey said.

Maureen put the car into reverse. "I'll be at the hotel," she said. "Don't know if I should wish you luck."

"Thanks, Mom," Sal said. He stood at the driver's door. "You know, for the food and stuff."

"Just make sure nobody gets hurt. *Junior*," she added with extra emphasis.

She returned to the Century Inn. She brushed the dust off her shorts as she traversed the lobby to the piano bar. It was less than half full, and better still it was cool, dim and spacious. She found a small table near the glass that overlooked the hotel pool and ordered a beer. Her fingers itched to hold a cigarette. She peeled the label off the bottle instead, rolling slivers of paper between her thumb and fingers as she watched a family frolic in the water. Father, mother, two children—one boy, one girl—playing water games. The father hiked his daughter onto his shoulders and the girl catapulted, dolphin-like, into the deeper water. She broke the surface, shaking the water off her glowing face. An average family, nothing special to look at, yet as distant, as exotic to her as the Taj Mahal.

"May I intrude?"

Maureen twisted in the direction of the voice. Keith Templeton stood beside her table with a highball glass in each hand.

"The service in here is extremely slow," he said, lifting the glasses. "We're enjoying a quick libation before the unhappy afternoon. A bit of fortification, right? We were wondering if you would join us?" He nodded toward a table of five. Three women, two men.

Maureen's pulse quickened. A table of lawyers and their wives. "I really shouldn't," she said.

"Nonsense," Templeton smiled. The last time he'd smiled like that he'd just finished dissecting her in front of three negotiating teams. "You look fine. I assume you're going to the funeral, yes?"

"I-"

"Join us. Please. Bring us up to date at *Dee-Faz*."

"I'm not with them, anymore," Maureen said. She hated herself for blushing.

"Exactly," Templeton said. He winked. "I couldn't rightly ask Lee-Anne Carlyle that question now, could I?"

Maureen rose from her chair, grabbed her nearly-empty beer and limped along beside Templeton.

"Hurt your leg?" He frowned, gesturing toward her bandaged knee.

"Twisted it. Working in the garden." She ran her free hand across her shorts, tugging at the hem of her cotton shirt. She caught a whiff of her own perspiration and cringed.

Templeton grunted and broke into a quick round of introductions. Maureen shook hands with Templeton's partners and their spouses and settled into an empty chair someone had dragged next to Templeton's wife.

"So. The Tse Wets Aht blockade did you in," Keith said. "Unfortunate business, really." He took a long sip from his drink. The ice cubes rattled as he set down his glass. "I wouldn't take it personally, Ms. Cage. Under such disgraceful circumstances. They required something to distract the vultures. You fit the bill nicely. I am pleased they at least invited you to the service."

Murmurs of agreement rippled around the table. Templeton's wife shot Maureen a moist, sympathetic look.

"Are the Chiefs coming?" Maureen cleared her throat.

Templeton and his colleagues shared dry smiles. Keith shook his head. "Most are firmly behind a police cordon now. I am surprised, frankly, how far this has gone. I wish Chief David had consulted with our office before taking such drastic steps." He glanced to his partners. "I hold out hope she will give herself up soon."

Maureen stared at her beer bottle, at the remnants of label that stubbornly clung to the glass. "Me too," she said in a hushed voice.

"The army's on its way," one of Templeton's partners said. "It was all over the news."

"Indeed," Templeton nodded as he sipped his drink, "with the fire situation and the forests so dry, they're desperately afraid of an inferno on the coast."

"Because the highway's blocked," Maureen said.

Templeton smiled, an elderly professor pleased that one of his slower students had finally figured out the problem on the board. "The blockades here, and up north, have to come down before the whole province burns."

"You're expecting confrontation?"

"Not expecting, guaranteeing. Minister Henderson has already appealed to Ottawa to invoke emergency powers where there is civil disobedience, even a hint of protest. They want the army to lock things down, arrest and detain as needed, so they can fight the fires. At least, that's the official line."

"The bands don't want the forests to burn," Maureen said. "They'll stand aside the instant there's a fire."

"Not enough, I fear," Templeton said. "After the debacle in Nanaimo the Premier wants all roads opened. He wants it to appear he's doing something. His office called yesterday. We're sending our team back to Port, to negotiate with the Tse Wets Aht to call off the blockade. But I'm afraid they won't budge until they speak with Chief David. Some think she's in jail, being held in secret. The rest think she's dead. Personally, I think she's run off with that American activist."

He emptied his glass. "Too bad, she was a good Chief. One of the better ones, in fact. If she had any fault it was being too passionate." He frowned. "Disgraceful, that mess in Nanaimo. I shall need another drink before I can even look at Braithwaite's casket without retching."

Perspiration blossomed on Maureen's brow. "I should go," she said.

"Parking is poor at the chapel, so I've heard," Templeton said. "Ride with us, we all came by cab. Shirley and I have them arranged for one-thirty. We'd love to have your company, isn't that right, Dear?"

Maureen scanned each face as she struggled through the crowd milling outside the chapel doors. She was self-conscious, surrounded by black dresses and skirts and dark suits. Her off-white cotton tee shirt and pale blue shorts were beacons of inappropriateness. She ducked through heavy oak doors, holding her breath, half-expecting to be met by security guards. There were none, or they were elsewhere. Music from an organ somewhere in the building bled through speakers recessed into the ceiling. She recognized the melody of the hymn, but could not remember its name. It seemed slow and heavy, as if the heat had insinuated itself into every note.

She slipped into the washroom and locked herself in a stall. She checked her watch: fifteen minutes until the service began. She slapped at the roll of toilet paper and dabbed the perspiration on her forehead and cheekbones and stared at the floor, trying to slow her pounding heartbeat. The music ceased and a man's voice over the intercom signaled the start of proceedings.

"The Braithwaite family thanks each of you for coming, for supporting them by sharing in their sorrow. Please stay, there will be afternoon tea served in the courtyard on the west side of the chapel. Despite our city fathers' desperate prayers for rain we're grateful for clear skies and sunshine on this sad afternoon."

The creak and sigh of the restroom door became less frequent. Maureen opened the stall door. The bathroom was deserted. She hurried to the sink and ran cold water from the tap, cupping her hands beneath the flow and splashing her face, soaking her hair. She peeled off a handful of paper towel and patted dry her face, sopping up the extra wetness in her scalp. With a quick glance toward the door she stripped off her shirt and applied wet paper towel to her armpits and stomach. The service broadcast over the intercom as she washed.

" . . . . *and sing, as you are able, Hymn number 256 in your insert, Guide Me, O Great Jehovah."* Organ music ramped to full volume.

Maureen held her wrist under the flow of cold water. "Fuck the water shortage," she said.

"Jesus, I hate hymns. Oh, I'm sorry." A woman barged through the restroom door as Maureen was half into her shirt.

"Carole?" Maureen turned to face her.

Simons wore a man's suit, broad-shouldered and sharply cut at the waist. The jacket and pants were charcoal grey, with a green paisley design stitched onto each wide lapel. It matched her emerald green shirt. A thin black tie hung loose around her throat.

"Christ, what are you doing here?" Carole clenched a tube of crimson lipstick in one fist, its cap already in the other.

"Billy Last Man Standing," Maureen said. "Have you seen him?"

Carole frowned. "Isn't he still missing?"

Maureen turned off the cold water. "He's here. With Josephine. And some NFDI."

"And you?"

"I'm not with them."

"That's right. You're supposed to be a Nazi." Carole moved past Maureen to the next sink and peered into the glass, rubbing the lipstick across her upper lip. "I just can't sit there, I'm not one for God talk. Against my religion, you could say." She laughed, pulled up short and avoided Maureen's glance.

"I must admit I wasn't expecting to find you half-naked in a funeral home bathroom," Carole said. She glanced quickly at Maureen through the mirror. "Not that I'm upset or anything. But you're really not dressed for the occasion."

"You trying to say you're happy to see me?"

Carole blushed. She jammed the cap back onto the lipstick. "Yes," she said, clearing her throat. "Yes, I am."

"Me too," Maureen said. She jammed the wad of wet paper towel into the waste bin. "But I'm not on the guest list." She smiled. "Do you even *know* what a conventional wardrobe looks like?"

Carole glanced down at her clothes. "What's wrong with this? I'm wearing a tie."

"It's leather. At least it goes with the shoes."

"Who says you can't wear *Doc Martens* to a funeral?" Carole stepped back from the counter to check out the black, bull-nosed shoes. "I spent a lot of time putting this outfit together."

"I don't know fashion," Maureen said, "but I do know the 'eighties when I see them."

Carole stuck out her hand. "Let's make a deal. I won't bring up your sequined g-strings if you don't criticize my leather tie collection."

"Deal." Maureen smiled weakly as she slipped her hand in Carole's.

"How did you get past security?"

"Templeton. Keith told me about the army, about Hargrove asking Ottawa to send them in."

Carole leaned toward the mirror and rubbed stray lipstick off a tooth. "It's the real deal, Kiddo. The Order in Council becomes effective at midnight. If the bands don't re-open every highway, every logging road in the province, the army will do it for them. Too many fires, too many acres of tinder-dry forest and still no rain in sight." She exhaled, her shoulders sagging. Genuine concern accompanied the weariness in her eyes. "Peace keepers in our own country. Christ, does nobody want to talk anymore?"

Maureen touched Carole's arm. "I do."

Carole held her gaze for more than a heartbeat. "Me too."

"But it'll have to wait," Maureen said, "the NFDI are in the trees beside the courtyard."

"Jesus. This way," Carole said, tugging Maureen's arm.

The courtyard was decorated for high tea: white linen tablecloths hung limp in the thickening air beneath silver serving dishes and crystal stemware. The space was bordered by arching white arbors covered with climbing roses. Daunting thorns erupted from their waxy, green stems. The catering staff lined the near edge of the courtyard, the men stiff in white tuxedo jackets while the women smoothed their short, black skirts. One of the waiters dabbed at his forehead with his cuff and stared at the sky, as if praying for relief from the heat.

"Pretty swish," Carole said as she slipped beneath the first arching trellis.

One of the staff moved to block them. "Please, we're still preparing," he said, his thin voice rife with complaint. He steered them back through the arbor, the corners of his mouth pinned in disapproval.

Maureen skirted the outside of the arbor fence in the direction of the parking lot.

"Stop," Carole said, "there's more security that way. One of them followed me all the way to the front door."

"Then I'll wait here. My leg is killing me."

"What are they going to do?"

"They want Hargrove. They want to remind him what he promised in Nanaimo. Then they want to post this confrontation on *You Tube*."

Carole's lips thinned. "That will cause a fuss," she said.

"You better go back inside."

Carole raised a hand to Maureen's face, withdrew it before it grazed her cheek. Her fingers curled into a fist. "We were made to sign confidentiality agreements." Carole's eyes held Maureen's. "Believe me, I'd help Josephine if I could, but I've too many years in to blow it now."

"Sure," Maureen said, and looked away.

"Maureen, wait. I want-"

The double doors swung open and a wall of organ music surged into the courtyard. The Braithwaite family was first through the doors. Maureen and Carole stepped back, stranded between the parking lot and the procession.

A woman in an expensive black dress emerged at an urgent pace, as if trying to outdistance the music. RG's widow wore her silver hair pulled off her face. It glistened in the sun. Her eyes were hidden behind expensive sunglasses. She hurried under the rose-heavy arbor to the nearest table. Her hands trembled as they poured the first glass of punch, too quick for the catering staff to intercede.

Audrey Hepburn, Maureen thought; she's just missing a silver cigarette holder and elbow-length gloves. The string of pearls below her throat dazzled. She crushed a white handkerchief in one bare hand as she downed the punch and refilled her glass, waving away the cringing server. The sinews in her long neck bulged. Check that, Maureen thought, an *angry* Audrey Hepburn.

A younger woman, mirroring Emily Braithwaite's wardrobe and brittleness, followed her mother from the punch table to a circle of chairs in the furthest corner of the courtyard; beneath the shade of a massive climbing rose that filled each square of the trellis with bunches of small white blooms. The younger

Braithwaite appeared anxious, her glance darting past the arbor toward the trees.

"There's Templeton," Carole said. "And the Ottawa contingent. I have to go." She met Maureen's glance, held it, then turned to insinuate herself into the stream of bodies less than eager to be leaving the air conditioned interior.

Maureen retreated toward the parking lot. At the corner of the building she veered right, following a narrow concrete sidewalk toward the trees. An outcrop of bare rock—its sharp edges still bearing scars from past drilling and blasting—heaved out of the soil to block her view of the courtyard. It formed a rough shelf eight feet in height; a bulkhead between forest and chapel. To her left the rows of BMW, Lexus and Mercedes ended abruptly. No sign of security.

The rock sank below grade at a thin garden lined with scrawny rhododendrons. She skirted their stringy, sun-starved limbs and hid behind the nearest cedar. The garden ended in the root-choked undergrowth of brown-tinged salal and the crisp tendrils of fiddlehead ferns. Maureen searched for Sal, Tanya and the others but the forest was quiet, dry and hot. Over her shoulder a collision of voices attempted conversation over strains of Bach piped from the chapel. They jumbled into an unintelligible buzz that rose and fell with the harpsichord's indifferent pronouncements.

Maureen scrambled near enough to distinguish shapes through the gaps in the rose screen. She lowered herself onto the dusty ground, unable to kneel or crouch. Her knee throbbed and her heartbeat pounded behind her eyes. Her fingers twitched for a cigarette to hold.

Movement through the trees registered at the edge of her vision. Mikey, wearing a dark suit and clutching a small backpack, was hunkered down in the shade. Sal followed behind, carrying a cloth bag. Tanya and Shannon pushed them out of the trees. They vanished behind the far side of the courtyard.

The chapel courtyard was peppered with black suits and dresses, salted with the white jackets of catering staff. The crowd parted without warning, as if the ground had opened. Premier Tom Hargrove appeared behind a screen of security. Kevin

Henderson, his Aboriginal Affairs Minister, walked beside him. They moved toward the corner to meet Emily Braithwaite. The music hushed, or maybe it was the tide of voices that receded. Hargrove bent at the waist, took Emily's hand between his own.

"I knew it was you!" A woman's hand grabbed Maureen's arm and spun her around. A stab of pain shot through her leg.

Lee-Anne Carlyle, flushed and panting, stuck one long index finger under Maureen's face. A security guard, baton in hand, stood behind her, sweating and unhappy. "Look at my shoes," she said. Her finger dropped to point at her feet. Her black pumps were coated with a patina of dust. "You're not on the list." She jerked her head toward the guard. "Get her out of here."

The security guard reached over Lee-Anne and rested one hand on Maureen's shoulder. "Let's go," he said.

"You've made me miss my best chance to talk to the Premier." Lee-Anne stepped around Maureen to peer into the courtyard, her lip curled in a pout. "See? He's leaving already. This is so unfair."

As Hargrove turned, a pair of caterers broke into the Premier's circle. They tossed aside the silver bells that covered their platters. The lids crashed to the concrete pavers as they raised their trays. A wave of oily brown liquid sloshed over Hargrove, splashed Henderson's sleeve and spattered Emily and Nancy Braithwaite. The overflow sprayed the ground with a sloppy declaration that instantly silenced the crowd.

"Liars!"

"Jesus Christ!" The security guard released Maureen and sprinted over the rock shelf toward the courtyard.

"What are they doing?" Lee-Anne shrieked. She froze, horrified.

Maureen hobbled after the security guard as the second tray flashed in the sun, blanketing the courtyard with feathers. Hargrove could only raise his arms and swat at the white cloud. Feathers stuck to every appendage; to every soaked and dripping feature.

"Liars!" Josephine David dropped her tray and peeled off her white jacket. Her braid fell down her back as she tossed away her cap.

"Promises were made! Signed promises to the Tse Wets Aht Nation for restitution and justice long overdue!" She brandished a single sheet of paper. "*You* promised an inquiry into the deaths of our men. *You* committed money and land for a Final Agreement. *You* think you can deny them? You expect to act like they never were?"

The security guard threw himself at the arbor. He cried out, pulled away his hands. They were bloody, pierced by the thorns.

Maureen stopped and watched him struggle over the screen. The thorns tore his pant legs, caught on his sleeves. She could not follow. A terrible smell rose out of the courtyard, as if a sewer had backed up below her feet.

"Jo!" she called, her knuckles white as she gripped the trellis.

"Alright!" Sal and Shannon waved at her from the edge of the courtyard as security rushed past them. Sal pulled a bundle from a small backpack and together they strung a cloth banner from the trellis. The mourners around them backed away, some shrieking, others stiff with fear.

"Justice for the Tse Wets Aht!" Tanya shouted. She jumped onto the hot food table holding a video camera above her head. It was aimed at Josephine and Billy and Hargrove.

"Jo!" Maureen shouted again.

At the sound of her name Josephine turned. Security guards set upon her at once and dragged her to the ground. They pinned her against the concrete and wrenched her arms behind her back.

"If the Tse Wets Aht can't keep their forests, nobody will," Billy shouted. "This whole province is gonna burn!" He vanished under a charge of sweating, fist-swinging shapes.

Tanya was dragged off the table and disappeared behind a screen of panicked mourners. Sal, Mikey and Shannon were mobbed by security guards as they rushed for the chapel doors.

"Maureen!" Carole hurried toward her from the parking lot.

Maureen's last glimpse, as Carole yanked her away, was of Hargrove in a chair, the one Emily Braithwaite had abandoned as soon the brown fluid began to spill. He sat straight-backed, hands gripping the armrests, blinking behind a thick mat of white feathers.

"This way!" Carole had to half-drag her toward the parking lot.

"Lee-Anne saw me," Maureen said, gasping for breath.

"I know. I saw her follow you. Look, she's already on her phone."

Lee-Anne paced beneath the fringe of cedars, her eyes locked on the courtyard as she shouted into her cell phone.

"Not this way," Maureen stopped, pulling Carole to a halt. "Into the trees."

"Too late. They're coming." Carole turned to face the lone security guard who pursued them. "Go. I can handle this guy."

Maureen did not wait. She half-ran, half dragged herself between the trees. Tanya was right, the forest wasn't deep despite its dense frontage. The ground began to slope away, toward the landfill. Shooting pains ran up her leg as she picked her way through the underbrush, praying that Billy had dumped his jeep with Sal and the others. Every step sent needles of pain through her leg. She turned before the trees closed completely around her and saw a security guard drag Carole into the parking lot. He seemed to be limping.

A black fender emerged from the undergrowth.

"Keys. Billy, did you leave the keys?" She pried open the driver's door.

The keys dangled in the ignition.

"Thank you, Billy."

The motor caught on the first turn. Maureen backed the jeep out of the pullout and flattened the accelerator as she hit the dyke road.

She slapped at the tears welling in her eyes. A dust storm chased her down the leachate road, past the ball diamonds and out onto the low road. There was no other traffic in the park. She passed the Century Inn, abandoning her Subaru. Police cars raced toward the chapel as she turned onto the highway, southbound.

Thirty minutes later the jeep bounced off the curb in East Vancouver and her machine-gun knock rattled the glass set in Helen and Anne's back door.

Anne pulled over two blocks shy of the bus station. "Take this." She pried open Maureen's hand and stuffed a wad of bills into it, pressing Maureen's fingers tightly over the money. "Helen doesn't need to know."

Maureen bit her bottom lip. "Yeah, she does, but thanks." She slumped onto Anne's shoulder. "I'll call soon as I can," she said, her arms wrapped around the big woman's neck.

"Where will you go?"

"Someplace they won't expect."

"Don't forget the suitcase." Anne unlaced Maureen's fingers and straightened out of the hug. She wiped her eyes with the heel of her hand.

From the sidewalk Maureen reached through the rear passenger window and pulled a small paisley case off the backseat. Helen had filled it with old clothes—*from before my diet,* she'd said. *They should fit pretty good.* Anne sped from the curb without a second look back.

Maureen paid for her bus and ferry ticket to Port McKenzie and found a hard bench that faced the open gallery of the depot, toward the side exits. Every noise, every scrape, every shout or sudden thump of a carelessly dropped suitcase was amplified under the vaulted ceiling. She hugged her purse to her chest and watched the sweep second hand race around the face of the clock above the departure gate.

Of all the possible places, Port seemed her only choice.

She breathed deeper when her bus lurched out of the depot. It was an hour's ride to the ferry terminal south of Vancouver. The passengers were only allowed off after the bus had parked on the ship's lowest level, nosed up against the heavy steel doors at the bow. Maureen rented a day room for thirty-five dollars and locked herself inside. She drew the curtains across the porthole. The sofa against the outside wall was flat, backless, but comfortable. She shut her eyes and tried not to think about Jo or Billy. Or Carole.

She had a two hour wait in downtown Nanaimo for the North Island bus. The same rustic station Billy had found her in after visiting Kenny Jacobs in hospital. She slipped into the dingy bar next door and ordered a beer and smoked the last of Helen's emergency cigarettes and listened to the twang of Country & Western music over the stereo. She told off the first guy that hit on her and he wandered away, shaking his head and talking to himself. After that she was left in peace to peel the label off her beer bottle and roll the scraps into tight, dry beads and flick them at her reflection in the mirrored pillars that ringed the bar.

It was dark when she reached Port. She was one of three passengers who disembarked, and the only one who didn't need the bus driver to open the luggage compartment. She hiked downhill, toward the Slough, grunting softly with every step. She inhaled the evening air. It took her a moment to notice the freshness: its familiar, acrid odor was missing. The mill's spot-lit bulk glittered under countless points of light. Its stacks were empty, its steam vents dry. From where she stood it could have been any warehouse or industrial park in any town.

It was a slow hike to the Timberman Hotel. She paid cash for two nights in a single room on the second floor and locked herself inside. The faint pounding of music from Canal Slats below her made the walls shiver. The bass leaked through the mattress, into her spine. She closed her eyes but could find no relief in darkness. She struggled into a pair of Helen's cotton pants and threw on a loose shirt and let it hang over her waist, hiding the stressed waistband. It took time to navigate the stairs to the main floor and longer to coax herself inside the bar. She hobbled to a table in the corner and sat alone in the shadows. Despite the crashing volume the music bothered her less than when it was a muffled thumping under her bed. Impossible to think, this close to the speakers.

"Wanna drink?" The waitress approached with a tray of freshly-opened beer.

"A cold beer would be great."

The waitress set the bottle onto a cardboard coaster, cocked her head sideways. "Hey. You're from that agency—the one doing the land claims. I'm Sandy, remember? You and that American guy came by my place."

"I remember."

"Four-fifty," Sandy said. "Or do ya wanna run a tab?"

"I'll pay as I go." Maureen slipped her hand into her shirt pocket and fished out a ten dollar bill.

"Aren't they lookin' for you? The cops I mean?" Sandy frowned. "No worries. I won't tell. And if I did, they wouldn't do nothing. They're all over at the blockade. They say the army's coming and the cops are right pissed. Turns out they like playing soldier more than breaking up bar fights."

Maureen passed Sandy the ten. "Keep it."

Sandy shot her a quick smile as she folded the bill in half, lengthwise, and stuck it between her fingers. "I know what it feels like, when the shit hits the fan."

"Screw the fan. I'm where the shit lands after the fan's through with it."

Sandy flung out her hip. She jammed her fist where a thin leather belt circled her waist. "That was really funny, them saying that you're hanging with the creeps. Shows how much they know. You? With Ricky and Larry? Now *that's* freaking hilarious." She laughed as she moved to the next table.

Maureen leaned back in her chair, one arm folded across her breasts as the other lifted the beer to her lips. The music stopped, the lights above the stage rose as the DJ introduced the next dancer. A girl in tight, white pants, white navy-style top and black spike heels climbed the steps and strode across the stage to scattered applause. She halted her routine to lean close to a group of middle-aged men cradling their beers at the edge of the stage. Maureen couldn't hear the exchange, but she knew what they were saying. Unless one of the three was her father, they'd be asking if she took Visa or MasterCard. The dancer laughed, waved as she backed into the centre of the stage and began to move to the music.

Maureen sipped from the bottle, forcing beer past the catch in her throat. Twenty years ago *she* had been that girl. The terror was still fresh: not of being naked, but of falling—tripping over a loose floorboard or slipping on sweat or spilled beer—anything that could shake an audience out of its reverie and goad them to ridicule.

Sandy returned with the ripple of applause that chased the dancer's shirt to the floor. She slid into the empty chair across from Maureen and waved her nearer. "Because if you *were* hanging out with Larry and Rick's crowd you'd already know that Raven's back."

Maureen's hand gripped the beer bottle tight. "Where? When?"

"Saw her earlier today. Manager said she was here to pick up her stuff."

"For how long?"

Sandy frowned. "Still looking for her, eh? They said on the news you got fired."

"I was," Maureen said. "This is personal."

Sandy shrugged. "She's hanging around, somewhere. They couldn't find her stuff so they told her to come back tomorrow. She was right pissed off. Told everyone she's overdue in L.A. for some hot-shot movie deal."

"I'm in room twenty-four upstairs," Maureen said, pointing at the ceiling. "Could you call me when she's back?"

"Dunno," Sandy said. "Apparently she's being a real bitch. Why'd you need to see her so bad?"

Maureen rummaged in her shirt pocket, retrieved and unfolded a crumpled twenty dollar bill. "Because," she said, yelling into Sandy's ear over a blast of music that rivaled the wall of noise inside her head, "I'm her mother."

The dancer paced from one end of the stage to the other, having shed everything but her disinterest. Save for the gaping onlookers nearest the stage, who applauded every glance, every hint of attention, she was not winning over the crowd. She had trouble keeping up to the music. She dropped to her hands and knees to arrange her blanket in the centre of the stage. She could have been setting a table or arranging a sleeping bag for a camp out. Maureen closed her eyes and the girl was Frances, then a rookie stripper named Angel in a bar not very different than this one. The stage vanished and the girl on her knees shivered in a cold alley in downtown Toronto. A hand brushed her leg. She jumped.

"Take it easy." Sandy stood and set a beer in front of Maureen. "On the house." She patted Maureen's shoulder and slipped back into the shadows.

It took her a moment to recognize the action. From the bed Maureen's fingers fumbled with the remote's volume button. Shouts and the sounds of chairs and tables crashing. The camera shook, swung erratically across a mob scene.

"*You're witnessing first-hand video shot at the scene of today's attack on the Premier,*" the television anchor said as the camera swept across the paving stone patio. Emily Braithwaite was seen diving out of her chair as the first tray's contents caught Hargrove from behind.

"*This was the chaos that occurred at the private funeral service for R. Gordon Braithwaite, former Chief Executive Officer of the Directorate for Aboriginal Settlement. Channel Nine received this file earlier this evening from an unnamed source, who claims it was shot by NFDI activists inside the funeral. Josephine David, Chief of the Tse Wets Aht First Nation, is in police custody for her role in the attack.*"

The lens caught Jo twisting, glancing toward the camera, then crumpling under the weight of uniformed security guards. The image wavered, panned skyward and turned blinding white. The head and shoulders of the news anchor filled the screen.

"*Equally shocking is the arrest of Carole Simons, a senior member of the Federal Treaty Negotiation Panel of the Department of Indian Affairs. Our sources confirm she was among those invited*" *to the funeral, but became involved in a scuffle with security staff hired by the Braithwaite family."*

Maureen needed air. She wriggled out of Helen's jeans and pulled on her own shorts and tee shirt. That they smelled of old perspiration didn't bother her. She lit a cigarette and stuffed her lighter into her shorts pocket. She tried to ignore the replay of Tanya's video but the confusion in the courtyard transfixed her. The phone next to her bed rang. She reached it on the fourth ring.

"She's back." It was Sandy's voice at the other end.

"Frances?"

"Raven. Frances. Whatever. Jerry just paged me. She's at the front desk. I told him to go slow, but he'd already got her stuff from the back and-"

Maureen dropped the phone and ran, ignoring the searing pain in her knee. She scrambled downstairs, leaning heavily on the rail, and stumbled into the lobby as a tall figure vanished through the main door. She followed, turning blindly toward the parking lot. The silver Honda idled in the handicap zone. A crouching figure backed out of the rear driver's side, straightened and slammed the door.

"Wait." Maureen caught Frances' arm as the she opened the driver's door.

Frances' eyes widened. "Fuck you!" She pushed Maureen away, favoring her arm as she pulled free.

"You can't go," Maureen said. She grabbed the keys out of the ignition as Frances' fist caught the side of her head. She was pushed backwards, onto the ground, Frances' knees knocking the breath from her lungs.

"You bitch. Give them back." It was Raven's voice snarling in her ear.

"Frances-"

Raven punched her in the stomach.

She couldn't breathe. She dropped the keys. She tried to roll onto her side as the first kick struck her in the shoulder. She raised her arms around her head, bracing for another blow. It never came. Frances seemed to float above her. It took several moments to notice the thick arms around Frances' waist, suspending her, screaming, above the sidewalk. Her feet beat the air, helpless in the bouncer's grip.

Sandy knelt at Maureen's side. "Easy. Take it slow." She put one arm around Maureen's shoulder and half-lifted her into a sitting position. "Deep breaths. That's it."

"You need these?" The bouncer pressed a set of car keys into Maureen's palm. "Can I put her down and get back to work now?"

Sandy looked at Raven. "You gonna behave?"

Raven's chin sagged and her body went limp. The bouncer set Raven onto the hood of her car and winked at Sandy. He moved toward the bar door, herding a small crowd ahead of him.

"Party's over, people. Nothing to see here." He turned. "Just holler if you need a hand, Honey," he called.

"Thanks, Randy," Sandy said. She turned to Maureen. "Thought you might need some help." She smiled and rubbed Maureen's shoulder. "You gonna make it? You look pretty rough." She turned to Raven, her expression darkening. "Fine way to treat your mother."

Raven's hands curled into fists, but she said nothing as she clutched her sore left arm and curled into a crescent moon on the hood of her car. Her eyes glistened like wet slate.

Maureen stood and reached for Frances, her hand trembling above the woman's bare forearm. As if summoned Frances slid off the car, and with her face turned away she buried her head in the hollow of Maureen's throat. Maureen raised her arms, hesitant, then let them settle around Frances' shoulders. She inhaled the faint, detergent scent of shampoo rising out of the roughly shorn, jet hair. As the first sob escaped Maureen's chest Frances pushed out of the embrace and stalked into the bar.

Frances slumped behind two untouched bottles of beer. She'd worn the same, sullen mask since Maureen had come inside to collapse at her table. Dewy beads crept down the sides of the bottles, colliding, merging, gathering speed until they soaked into the cardboard coasters, leaving clear scars on the brown glass.

"Here." Sandy slapped six pills onto the table. "Tylenol. Three each. For your knee. And for *your* shoulder," she said, pointing at Frances.

"Thanks," Maureen said.

Frances did not look up. She brushed a stray lock of hair off her forehead. The lightning bolt tattoo was cut in two by the thin strap of her tank top. As if sensing Maureen's eyes upon it Frances scratched at the arrow-tipped bolt, then rested her hand flat across the design.

"How's Larry?"

Frances glared. "Don't know."

"Word is you're off to California."

"Like I'd tell you."

"I'm not going to follow you. By tomorrow I'll probably be in jail. I've lost my job and I owe my friends a year's salary. I won't be up to much for awhile."

"Sounds like you got a million reasons to run away," Frances said. Her hand came off the tattoo and picked up a beer. She sipped, and the instant the bottle touched her lips her eyes met Maureen's. They were moist. "Like I want *you* chasing my ass."

Maureen shook her head. "My running days are done."

"Turning yourself in?"

"No. But I'll be here when they figure out where to look."

Maureen swept the condensation off her beer bottle. Three quick strokes of a fingertip and the shape of the letter *F* appeared.

"I'll call the cops for you," Frances said. "Make sure they know where to look. They can be so fucking dense."

"Thanks." Maureen gripped her beer in her palm and the *F* disappeared.

"No problemo. I'll just say: *I got that terrorist Maureen Cage for ya. Where's my reward?*" Frances took a deep swallow of beer, shifted in her chair. "You gotta be worth *something* to somebody."

"I don't seem to be," Maureen said, staring hard into Frances' eyes.

Frances tried to fling one arm across the chair back as she stretched her legs under the table. She grunted and rested her sore arm in her lap. "When you gonna go back to being Theresa?"

Maureen laughed, a short, weary bark. She shook her head. "Theresa's dead."

"I thought Maureen was the one who died."

Maureen shook her head. "Did I tell you I saw her, once, after the accident? After she died?"

Frances rolled her eyes. "A fucking *ghost?* You trying to tell me you believe in spooks and shit?"

Maureen shrugged. "She was wearing a dress, flowing, long. She sort of hovered at the end of the hall, at the door to her parents' bedroom. I could hear crying from behind the door. Then she turned and saw me and vanished. You don't have to believe me. For all I know she's still haunting the house she grew up in."

Frances blew air through her lips. "Loser. The spook, I mean."

Maureen shook her head. "Uh-unh. She was smart. Maureen was going places. *Theresa* was the loser. The foster kid nobody wanted. I come from a whole family of losers."

"Including me, right?"

"You came later." She lit a cigarette and set the lighter on the table close to Frances. She tapped the Zippo. "You should have been the best thing I ever did in this world." In the dimness of the bar the engraving on the gold case looked like a snail's aimless wanderings.

Frances picked it up, lay it in one palm, running her fingers over the gold case. "It's beautiful. My mom—my auntie—said it belonged to my grandfather."

"Françesco. I named you after him."

"The loser."

"Yes. He was. But he wasn't always. And maybe it wasn't his fault. Your grandmother wanted to name *me* Frances. At the time I thought I was honoring them." Maureen exhaled deeply. "If your grandmother hadn't died."

"Fucked him up that bad?"

Maureen nodded, blew smoke out the side of her mouth. "Both of us. But him especially. I hated her for dying, for leaving me with him."

"He didn't . . ." Frances cocked her head, her eyes narrowing. "You know. Diddle you or nothing?"

"No." She made a tired sound in back of her throat. "He didn't do anything. Except drink. No, the *really* bad shit started later. At the foster homes."

"Auntie didn't know too much about that."

"The only thing she knew about me was you. She found you in the backseat of her car."

Frances picked at the label on her beer. She rolled the scraps into beads between her fingertips and flicked them at Maureen's head. Behind her, to a dusting of applause, the DJ announced the last dancer of the evening. Frances looked over her shoulder, snorted, and turned away. "You're un-fucking-believable. You danced for how long?"

"Over ten years."

"Ten fucking years. Then you go back to school, become this straight-edge, picture-perfect, ice-queen-she-bitch. Running three thousand miles away wasn't enough, was it? You had to re-invent yourself. Turn inside out."

"That was later. Much later."

"*You're* the fucking ghost." Frances dragged her chair nearer the table, leaned toward Maureen. She jammed her elbows onto the table top and rested her head between her fists. "It's like you did everything you could to kill me without pulling a gun."

Maureen stared at the end of her cigarette, at the glowing red ash. "It was about surviving," she said.

"Bullshit. You did a one-eighty on me. Christ, when you walked into my hospital room I was sure I was looking at a cop. I wish you were. Anything's better than this."

"When Legare told me your real name it was like a nightmare. I thought the earth had opened up and swallowed me."

"That makes two of us, Bitch."

Maureen slapped the lighter off the table. It landed in Frances' lap. "Keep it. It's yours."

Frances slid it back across the table. It deflected off a beer bottle and spun to rest near Maureen's hand. "No thanks. That's bad luck. Nearly got me killed."

Maureen's fingers touched the cold metal case. "I don't understand."

Frances laughed. It was a cruel bark. She took a deep pull on her beer. "How the fuck do you think I knew who you were? That prick detective didn't have to tell me. I know that lighter better than anything I ever owned. It's in half the pictures in the photo album Auntie gave me. Grandpapa and Granny together. Grandpapa and my mother. Christ, they smoked a lot in those days! Want more? That crucifix around your neck? It was Granny's," Frances said. She smirked as Maureen's hand strayed to the cross at her throat.

"So what am I supposed to do? The DJ introduces me, I got nothing but a dead easy set in the capitol of Jerkwater BC when I see that fucking Zippo not ten feet from me. Then those Indian boys wanted to pay for my time, if you get my meaning. I thought, *why not, I can use the extra cash* and then one of them grabbed it out of my hand, they started passing it around the truck, tossing it like it's going out the window. I grabbed it out of that one guy's hand—Kenny, I think—but the truck swerved for a fucking deer or something, and I dropped it. He got it back, tossed it into the cab and started feeling me up. I hit him one, reached into the cab. I musta grabbed the wheel. I was so fucking pissed off, they were laughing at me, so I gave it a good yank. Next thing I know me and the skinny one are in the air and the truck's in the ditch and I wake up in hospital with my hair cut off and my head in bandages and my arm and ribs busted up." Frances leaned back in her chair and folded her arms across her chest. "No thanks, you fucking well keep it."

"Kenny said there was another truck."

Frances sniffed. "Coulda been. Larry told me they followed us. I don't remember. I remember waking up in hospital."

"So if there was another truck it didn't cause the crash," Maureen said. "If you knew I was your mother, why didn't you say something—anything? At the hospital, or at Candy's house?"

Frances laughed again and drained her beer. She slammed the empty on the table. "Out of all the people my mother could have been, I never expected you." She leaned closer, so that her face was just above the neck of Maureen's beer bottle. "We got sweet fuck all to say to each other, *Mother*. Not now, not ever. When I was sixteen and ran away I'd have killed to know my real parents. Who they were, where they lived, why they ditched me with their lame-ass relatives. I wanted to kick your fucking ass. But now?" Frances smiled. "I got money, a career. *A future*. Sure, maybe you went to school. Look at you. You're *still* a fucking loser. Fuck you."

"You killed them, all of them. Did you send the note to the Tse Wets Aht?"

Frances grinned. "That was Larry. Wanted to make it like it was a big fucking conspiracy." Her eyes narrowed. "We were at your place, too. Larry wanted to bust in, beat the shit out of you." Frances held up her hand, thumb and index finger a whisper apart. "I came this close to letting him. I should have, you know."

"When was that?" Maureen shivered. She knew before Frances spoke.

"Week or so before you cracked his skull. The night after the big rainstorm. After your dyke girlfriend left. Yeah, we saw you inside. He was gonna leave another note, you know, crank up the hate thing. Too much trouble. Things were pretty fucked up in Port anyway, people pissed off and such. Larry said there'd never be a land claims deal or whatever. Anyway, the crash was no fucking loss. Couple of weeks work. It's the hair that really pisses me off." She ran one hand through the thick, uneven mop on top of her head.

"Four innocent men died."

"Big deal. It's not like they were real people."

Maureen raised a hand and rubbed away the wetness on her face. Her body began to shake. "You know," she said, choking back her words, "I should have left you with your father. Your *real* father. His name's Bobby—Bobby Cage. I never thought of him having a last name. He was always just *Bobby*. Maureen's brother. He raped me, beat me up. Kept it up for eight months before I made him stop. Call him up, next time you're in Windsor. Ask him what good ol' Theresa did to him with his favorite *Louisville Slugger*. Ask him how long he had to eat soup through a straw."

Maureen plucked the lighter off the table and pushed herself out of the chair. She set her jaw against the shooting pain in her knee. "I *am* sorry. The two of you probably have a lot in common." She staggered out of the bar without looking back.

The downhill walk to the waterfront was hard. She chewed her bottom lip raw. She crossed the deserted highway, passing by locked boutiques and an empty coffee joint who's brushed steel espresso machine served up monstrous shadows against the designer décor, skirting the historical marker paying homage to the birth of Port McKenzie, to the water's edge. She collapsed onto a wooden bench and leaned backward, breathing hard. She lifted her leg onto the bench, crying out as her leg fell across the varnished wood. She leaned back and stared at the sky, spilled sugar on black silk. Moon glow back-lit the mill. The far side of the fjord was a dark mass that blotted out the stars nearest the horizon. The Slough waters were deathly calm, catching and holding the lights of the waterfront in unblinking, oily circles.

"It's a good thing, to know when you're done," she said, and the sound of her voice startled her. She could have been heard across the Slough, but neither the trees nor the stars challenged her.

She swung her leg off the bench. She hopped to the timbered railing, planting her hands a little better than shoulder width apart. Using her good leg she pushed upward, twisting her hips, coming to rest in a sitting position on the rail, her legs dangling over the boardwalk. Her bad knee throbbed.

"Let go," she whispered. She pulled her lighter from her pocket and rubbed the gold case with her thumb. A dull smear filled the lines of the engraving, vanished as the heat of her body wicked into the metal. It shone, unblemished. She squeezed the lighter inside her fist and cocked her arm, but she could not throw it. She lowered her hand, inhaling great draughts of air until her ribs ached. The sharp tang of a working mill was gone. She breathed slowly, deliberately, imagining the Port McKenzie of a century ago when orca and grey whales were common in the fjord, even to the mouth of the Sleeping Man River. When salmon as large as small children schooled, waiting for the gush of October rains to carry them upriver to spawn.

"So clean," she said and raised her eyes until the mill vanished, and the congregation of stars wheeled overhead. Relief flooded through her. She felt her balance shift as her body followed the arch of her spine. She smiled to herself. Never learning to swim *wasn't* one of her failings, after all.

"I don't think you want to do that."

Strong, cool hands grasped her elbows, her head snapped like a whip and she tumbled off the rail onto the plank walkway on top of Aaron Chen.

BOOK SEVEN

Ashes to Ashes

Aaron's silhouette was blurred, in equal measure, by the light that blazed through the hotel window and the sticky stuff in her eyes. The fifty pound weight hammering inside her skull was making her nauseous. She groaned. "Go away," she tried to say, but her tongue was thick and useless and the muscles of her jaw refused to work. She rolled onto her left side, away from the light.

"Never been on a suicide watch," Aaron said. "And three weeks ago if you'd asked me to predict who it would be I'd have never picked you."

Maureen lay still, listening to her breath as it rattled through her windpipe. She remembered only stars—so many, so bright, so close—they had come to welcome her among them. One of them, its light warmer than the rest, seemed to know her. Then utter blackness, the pressure of hands on her body. The pain of needles in her leg. She pulled back the sheet. She was in her underwear and a tee shirt. Her leg had been wrapped in a new support bandage.

Where was her lighter? Panic peeled away an edge of the fog. She opened her eyes and raised herself onto one elbow. The Zippo stood on the night stand, next to an empty bowl and a full glass of water. She fell back, her breath hot with relief.

"Can I keep the TV on?" Aaron moved into the narrow panel of her vision. "Man, you gotta see this stuff. It's all over the Internet, too."

"Where did *you* come from?" Maureen groaned and wedged herself against the wall, as upright as her body allowed. The iron fists in her head redoubled their efforts. She was thirsty, but the thought of anything in her stomach made her cringe.

"Short memory, eh? I never left Port," Aaron said. His back was toward her as he fiddled with the television set. "Can't find the remote." He flipped through a dozen channels. "We're big time," he said, pushing buttons. "We made *CNN.*"

"How did-"

"Shh!"

"Aaron, what's going on?"

"Aw, missed it." He snapped off the television. "I can get my laptop and show you. Or for sure it'll be on the evening news." He twisted around to look at her. He grinned. "How you doin', Boss?"

Maureen closed her eyes. "Lee-Anne's your boss, remember?"

"She's the head cheese, now that Braithwaite's dead. Sarah's on leave—she's been suspended—and you're wanted by the RCMP *and* suicidal." He spread his hands apart. "And my family wanted me to become an accountant!"

Maureen ran her tongue across her chapped lips. She was going to chance it. "Pass me the water," she said. She took the glass out of Aaron's hand with both of hers. They shook, spilling a little of the water onto her shirt as she raised it to her lips. "Why didn't you call them?"

"Who? The RCMP?" Aaron ran one hand through his hair, brushing it off his forehead. There were dark smudges beneath his eyes. "Last night nobody else cared enough to. And you could walk into any store in Port and take what you want and never meet a cop. The store owners have organized their own street patrols until the army gets here. Me, I figure you got enough on your plate. If they want you that bad, they'll find you without my help."

"Thanks. What time is it?"

"Two o'clock."

"Jesus. How long did I sleep?"

Aaron shrugged. "Almost twelve hours, since the doctor left." He lowered his eyes. "He asked if I minded hanging around."

"How did you find me?" Maureen asked between small sips.

"I was in the bar. Don't usually patronize such establishments but I was bored out of my skull. You can only watch so much TV.

I saw you with that stripper. I wanted to go over to say *hi* but things were looking tense. When you took off for good I told the waitress you used to be my boss. She said she was worried, that you'd just got more bad news than the Pope in a birth control clinic. So I settled my tab and followed you."

"Thanks." Maureen stared at her hands.

"Hey, no problem," Aaron said, filling the silence. "Want more water?"

Maureen shook her head. "She's my daughter."

"No shit? The one from the accident?"

Maureen nodded. "Kind of a tough reunion," she said, and the trembling in her hands worsened.

"I never knew you had kids."

"It's a bad story, Aaron." Maureen inhaled slowly, trying to suppress a wave of nausea. She set down the glass and rested the empty bowl in the crook of her elbow. The metal was warmer than her skin. "Jesus, what did that doctor give me?"

"Demerol," Aaron said. "For your knee. He thinks you tore some ligaments."

"Makes me want to puke," she said. She watched her fingers interlace, untangle, then knit together again across her ribs. "The worst part was finally figuring out what kind of a person she is. I must be simple. It never, ever occurred to me she could turn out—you know—badly." Her voice trailed to a whisper.

Aaron moved to the window. "I think a lot of parents feel the same, but most never say anything. Especially mothers. Mine smiles, asks me how I'm doing, but inside? I know she's disappointed."

"With you? I doubt it. You must be the perfect son."

Aaron leaned against the window sill and jammed his hands into his pants pockets. "I *am* a good son," he said. "But a good son *and* a doctor or a stock broker—now *that's* a successful son."

Maureen stared at her hands.

Aaron cleared his throat. "Another dry one," he said, glancing out the window. "We keep breaking records. Worse than the desert." He tapped his foot and picked at the cuticle of his left thumb.

"What's wrong? What did I miss?"

"Dunno. Maybe the start of World War III."

"Tell me." She trapped the water glass between her hands.

"You sure you want more bad news?"

Maureen closed her eyes. Her stomach was the real wild card. "Why not?"

"The RCMP in North Vancouver called a press conference early this morning. They say Billy Last Man Standing died in police custody. Last night. Choked on his own vomit."

"O God, no." She retched into the bowl. A film of cold sweat coated her arms, her face, her legs as her stomach muscles cramped.

Aaron rushed to the bedside, held the bowl as she heaved over and over. "Here," he said, grabbing a small towel off the chair next to the window.

"I'm okay," Maureen said, gasping. She leaned back, limp, her arms were noodles, but the pain in her guts was receding.

Aaron dumped the bowl's contents into the toilet and rinsed it. "Maybe you should eat something. Soon," he called over the running water. "Or you'll be heaving up your intestines."

"You're sure. About Billy? How did it happen?" Hot tears stung her eyes.

Aaron emerged from the bathroom drying the bowl with a towel. "That's some of what I was looking for on the news."

"Put it back on," Maureen said.

Aaron gave Maureen the bowl and leaned over the television. He found a Vancouver news channel. "They were doing a special on Hargrove. *End of the Hargrove Era* they were calling it. Here." He straightened and backed into his spot at the window.

"That's Carole," Maureen said, watching Simons face the cameras.

"I was getting to that," Aaron said. "She called a press conference a couple of hours after she got out of jail."

Maureen squinted. "Something's different," she said.

It took her a moment, before she understood. Carole was wearing normal clothes: light grey casual slacks and a woman's pale blue golf shirt with the top button open. Her hair, still peroxide blond, lay flatter, softer. No outrageous make-up or spike heels or leather ties. When Maureen turned to Aaron he was grinning.

"Weird, eh? It took jail time to get her to lose the retro thing."

"'*I first want to apologize to my staff and colleagues,*'" Carole said to the cameras. "'*But I am speaking out today because to withhold the truth is as much a crime as telling lies.*'" The microphones suspended near her mouth blocked half her face. She glanced down to a scrap of paper that shook in her hands.

"'*I cannot remain silent after the events of the past few days. It is clear I must speak out, now that others who would, cannot. I was in Nanaimo, as was Premier Hargrove and Minister Henderson. Promises were made. To Chief David of the Tse Wets Aht First Nation in particular. In writing. The Premier committed the resources of his negotiating team toward reaching a Final Agreement with the member bands of the Pacific Coast Tribal Federation. Premier Hargrove also promised an inquiry into the deaths of four Tse Wets Aht youth on Pipeline Road, and to work with the Federal Anti-Hate branch of the RCMP to investigate activities of the Heritage League in Port McKenzie.*'"

Carole looked up from the paper. "'*I watched as Mr. Henderson shredded these documents in the minutes after Mr. Braithwaite's death.*'"

"She's getting to the good part," Aaron whispered. He was grinning wildly. "The last nail in Hargrove's coffin. Maybe the clothes are an act, you know, to get people to take her serious?"

"Doubt it," Maureen said. "She's not that good an actor."

"'*I realize the risks I take in coming forward today,*'" Carole said, "'*but I have learned, the hard way, that you have to fight to keep those things that are most precious to you. Especially if they're more complicated than you expected them to be.*'" Carole tried to smile. Her cheeks reddened and she dropped her eyes to the text in her hands.

Maureen felt the heat rise in her face.

"'*William Last Man Standing is dead. Josephine David is in jail. The Premier and his staff would tell you they have done nothing wrong. That's not for me to say, but I do know the truth, and they're not telling the whole story. The people of this province are entitled*" *to hear it all.'"* Carole crushed the paper in her fist and waded through the microphones. The video feed skipped as the camera followed Carole to her car. A press of microphones and cameras surrounded her as she ducked into the driver's seat. She hid behind one out-flung hand and sped into Vancouver traffic.

"Shit," Maureen whispered. She pressed her palms into the hot skin below her cheekbones.

"Hargrove and Henderson resigned this morning," Aaron said. "Would've probably had to, eventually, what with Last Man Standing dead, and Simons out on bail giving it up to the media. Too much to deny, and no place to hide."

The NFDI video of the attack at the chapel was now on the screen. Maureen's hands dropped into her lap. A crushing sadness made her bones ache. In those few seconds of uneven video were Billy's last moments outside custody. It was his last, maybe best, accomplishment. She smiled as he tossed the silver bell that hid the foul stuff on his tray. He was laughing as the brown fluid covered Hargrove. His fifteen minutes of fame locked in a thirty-second video clip. Many lived ninety years and never won so much.

"It's the least of what they deserve," she said. "I can't believe they killed him."

"Nobody's saying anything," Aaron said. "I've been on the phone all morning. Lee-Anne's been talking to the A-G. She says there was a struggle, they had to subdue him, you know the routine—Tazer first then textbook RCMP choke hold. When they checked him in his cell they found him on his back in a puddle of upchuck."

"What are the other Chiefs saying?"

Aaron shook his head. "It's ready to blow. Lee-Anne had me call every member of the Federation, every First Nation not on a blockade. Most refuse to talk to us. We're implicated. The ones who will talk are scared you-know-what-less. They've heard about the emergency powers Hargrove was looking for. They think martial law is coming."

"But Hargrove resigned."

"The Finance Minister has been sworn in as Acting Premier. She's been riding Lee-Anne hard. She's told the A-G's office to co-operate with *Dee-Faz* and do whatever it takes to get the blockades down before the Feds decide to use force. Priority One. Higher status than the fires."

"What about Jo?"

Aaron shrugged. "RCMP say she's fine, but they won't let the media near her. I doubt if *she* knows. The Federation Chiefs are demanding to see her, to know she's alright."

"Or?"

Another shrug. "Dunno. Rumor is that the Tse Wets Aht have been making Molotov cocktails."

"That won't stop the army if they decide to go in."

"They're not for the army," Aaron said. "They're hanging them from the trees, rigged them to go up if the army moves. Least that's what people are saying."

"Holding the forest hostage," Maureen said. "That can't be right. They'd never risk their traditional territories. They'd die first." She shivered, despite the heat in the room.

"I know, but those are the rumors. Like I said, it's war."

"I need to make a call," Maureen said. She stretched for the phone on the bedside table.

"Whoa," Aaron intercepted her. "I'll get it. You need to rest." He handed her the phone, tugging to free the cord from behind the table. "Who're you calling?"

Maureen wedged the handset between her ear and shoulder. "Shh, I can't think," she said. She closed her eyes and tried to quiet the pounding in her head. She punched a long distance number and waited. Images of Billy filled her vision: his smile, his hair, his . . ."Hello? Rachel?" She shot Aaron a triumphant look.

Aaron's eyes widened in fear. He paced between the window and the bed, chewing his thumbnail.

"It's Maureen Cage. I'm sorry about your father."

"Screw him." The voice was strong, so clear Maureen could feel the anger in them. "We need to know the truth about Billy," Rachel said. "This is fucking genocide."

"I don't know any more than you," Maureen said. "But we've got a call into the Attorney-General. For sure there'll be an investigation."

"Fuck the investigation. Didn't Chief David try to get an investigation when Henry and the others died? Where is she now? We'll *all* be dead by the time their lies are printed. We know why the army's coming."

"There's still plenty of time to talk."

"You think we're gonna wait here to be exterminated? It's time to hit them where it hurts. Time for Port McKenzie to go through open heart surgery—without the anesthetic." Rachel was shouting into the phone.

"Where are you?"

"Screw that. Payment is due, with interest. No more genocide. No more lies. No more games."

"She hung up," Maureen said, tossing the handset onto the mattress.

"Was that a good idea?"

"They're over the top."

"The trees," Aaron said. "Then the rumors are legit. They're going to burn the forest."

Maureen handed him the phone. "Better call Lee-Anne. Somebody's got to do something—fast."

The Timberman Hotel coffee shop was as far as her strength would take her. Aaron propped her crutches against the wall near their booth. He did it left handed as his right was occupied with his cell phone since they'd left her room. The one-sided conversation did nothing to improve Maureen's mood, but at least her nausea had passed. She was famished, despite the fog of pain and sadness that enveloped her.

Aaron wriggled into the bench opposite her, his mouth drawn into a pinched, bloodless circle. The waitress came. Maureen glanced wistfully at the *All Day Platter of Eggs* but played it safe and ordered brown toast and peanut butter. The waitress looked at Aaron, blinking, chewing gum, waiting.

"He'll have the same. And coffee."

The waitress tossed her a frozen smile and hurried away.

Maureen surveyed the coffee shop. Theirs was one of three occupied tables, this being *Tweener Time*—too early for dinner but too late for lunch. Maureen shifted so that her leg could rest lengthwise on the bench. There was just enough room for her foot. Their booth overlooked the hotel parking lot. No sign of the silver Honda. Not that she was expecting to see it. Her jaw and shoulders unclenched. It would have been worse if it *had* been there. Bad enough she had no choices to make, no second-guessing herself. No agonizing over consequences. Frances was long away, whether to L.A. or New York or Vancouver.

No more intimate mother-daughter talks, she thought, and bit off a caustic laugh.

Maureen leaned back as the waitress slid coffee mugs onto the table. She pulled the foil cap off a plug of *Cremo* and watched the coffee change from jet to oily nut-brown. She couldn't remember the last time she'd had an easy choice: when making a decision hadn't felt like sawing off a limb. She plunged a spoon into the coffee and stirred at the ragged edges where brown met black.

When Aaron folded his phone he looked pale. "The army's going in. Lee-Anne's just spoken to the A-G."

"When?"

Aaron shook his head. "She doesn't know. But she figures hours, not days. Maybe tonight. There's three more blockades just started up north. The Fraser River's full of Aboriginal fish boats. With the drought and extreme risk of fire the Feds have authorized use of force if necessary."

"It'll be civil war."

"It's spiraling out of control," Aaron said, "but if they can settle the Tse Wets Aht situation there's hope the others will back down."

The waitress set down two small plates of toast, two sets of cutlery rolled in paper napkins, and a chrome caddy filled with individual pats of jam and peanut butter. She refilled their mugs and hurried away.

"Settle how?" Maureen tore her knife out of its napkin wrapper and gripped it by the handle, ready to plunge it into the table top. "Do they intend to honor the Nanaimo promises? They'll turn this province into a battle zone."

"It already is, Boss." Aaron's hands shook so badly he had to grip the edge of the table to steady them.

"I'm not your boss anymore. We need Josephine. Call Lee-Anne back. Now."

Aaron blinked once, grabbed the phone and dialed. He handed it to Maureen. "It's ringing."

Maureen clapped the phone to her ear. "Get Josephine David out of jail," she said, before the voice at the other end of the line could speak.

"Who is this? Cage? Why am I not surprised? Did you beat Aaron senseless and steal his phone? Put him back on this line, if he wants to keep his job."

"Listen to me. I've spoken to Rachel Braithwaite. The Tse Wets Aht know about Billy Last Man Standing. They've planned something. If the army tries to go in, it will be very bad."

"Whatever game you're playing, you're going to jail for a long time," Lee-Anne said.

"There's no time for this horseshit, Lee-Anne. Park your humungous ego for a minute and listen. Get Josephine David out of jail. Bring her back to Port. If her people can see her, talk to her, they might negotiate."

Aaron cringed and glanced around the coffee shop. He held up his hands, motioning her to keep the volume down.

"At least we know where *you* are," Lee-Anne said. "You're insane. *She* was the one who convinced them to a standoff."

"Because of the Heritage League," Maureen said. She crushed the empty *Cremo* container in her fist. "She needed answers and nobody wanted to give her any."

"So what makes today different?"

"I have those answers," Maureen said, and the calm in her voice startled even her. "But the Tse Wets Aht and the rest of the Federation need to hear them from her, not from me or you."

There was a long pause at the other end of the phone.

"Grant her a temporary release. Has she even been charged yet? If she talks the warriors down then drop the charges and build some trust. She just wants to go home, Lee-Anne."

"I *cannot* call the Attorney-General of this province and tell him that our ex-Senior Analyst—an alleged white supremacist and a fugitive implicated in the assault on the Premier—thinks that if the Tse Wets Aht Chief is allowed to return to Port and rejoin an illegal blockade she will make it all hunky-dory. Even if he believes me what's to stop Chief David from inciting things?"

Maureen's knuckles whitened. "She won't. And tell the A-G it's your idea. Josephine knows I'm no racist."

"Then she's more gullible than I thought."

"Billy was murdered in police cus-"

"He *died* in custody, Cage, there's a big difference."

"Too fine a point for the Tse Wets Aht and you know it. Healthy people don't die unaided. Get Chief David out. It will earn *Dee-Faz* props and buy some time. Since Carole's press conference you know a truck load of public opinion is now on the Tse Wets Aht side. You can decide later whether or not to bring her to Port, but *tell* the Tse Wets Aht she's getting out. At least do that. Aaron can be at the checkpoint in ten minutes."

The pause was longer this time. "I'll call right back. Make sure Aaron answers. And Cage, don't bother running. The police will be there in five minutes."

Aaron's hand was shaking as he took back his phone. "What'd she say?"

Maureen, exhaled, dragged her plate of toast closer. She peeled open a container of peanut butter and spread it thickly across a slice of toast. Her stomach growled. "That you're in supreme shit for helping me," Maureen said, grinning between bites. "She's considering the other thing."

"How much trouble? I have a family."

"Don't bother me right now, Aaron, I have to eat before they arrest me again."

She'd been locked up less than three hours—barely time to get acquainted with the holding cell's amenities—when Aaron appeared at the shoulder of the duty officer.

"You're coming with me, Boss," Aaron said. He waved a single, limp sheet of paper in the air. "You're free."

Maureen brushed off the seat of her shorts and limped to the cell door. The officer handed her crutches through the bars and stepped sideways to let her pass as the door swung open.

Aaron thrust the page her way. "It worked," he said over a schoolboy grin. "Here's your hall pass. Chief David got one, too."

"Where is she?"

"Sharing a plane ride with Lee-Anne and the A-G himself. Seems like we got a negotiation to run."

"Do the Tse Wets Aht know?" Maureen stepped through the cell door and slipped the crutch handles into her armpits.

"As much as any of us. They're sending a delegation to meet Chief David and the other Federation chiefs. The army's agreed to escort them into town. Seems they're willing to hold back awhile. Great throw of the dice, Cage."

"What about Rachel?"

Aaron's smile vanished. "That's a problem. They think she's convinced a couple of warriors to help her. A car's been stolen off the reserve. They figure she's headed into the woods."

"But they're looking for her, right?"

Aaron followed her up the stairs, shouting up at her. "By land and by air. So far no luck."

Maureen was sweating when she reached the main floor. She used the rubber tip of one crutch to push open the station's front door. "Christ, as soon as there's good news there's worse waiting in the weeds."

"The army has a couple of zodiacs. They're on the Slough, looking for trouble. The Forestry people have a spotter plane in the watershed and a helicopter, but not for long. They're overdue to help with the fires."

"Give me your cell phone."

"Again?"

After six rings she was directed by a recording into Rachel's voice mail.

"Rachel, it's Maureen. I hope you're checking messages. Chief David will be in Port very soon. You'll have the chance to see her. Come back to the bridge. Don't do anything crazy until you call me. I'm at-" She paused to read Aaron's number off the side of his phone and realized that though she used to call it a half-dozen times a day, it was long gone from her memory. "Please."

An RCMP cruiser escorted them to the Queen Anne Hotel. The parking lot had been cleared. Army vehicles guarded the entrance. Soldiers in desert-brown battle uniform patrolled the sidewalks on both sides of the street. Tourists and townspeople watched in small crowds beyond the cordon. Constable Sawchuk was waiting under the awning of the hotel entrance. The dark, half-moons beneath his eyes gave his face a poached appearance. He sipped coffee from a Styrofoam cup.

"Inside." He gestured toward the hotel lobby. "You can wait for the others out of the way."

"The Federation Chiefs?" Aaron asked.

"On the premises." Sawchuk sniffed. "Most of them, anyway. They're waiting in the banquet room. Must be like one big, happy reunion for you two," he said, mopping his face with his sleeve. He squinted at Maureen. "Don't even think about leaving town. You're only out of jail because the A-G wants you out. After this bullshit is done," he waved vaguely toward the army jeeps and personnel loitering around them, "you're back in custody."

Maureen met his stare. "Where would I go?"

Sawchuk blinked, took another swig of coffee. "Whatever. Next subject. I'm told you spoke with NFDI people behind the blockade. My Sergeant needs that number."

Maureen shook her head. "I don't think that's a good idea."

"We'll have it ourselves inside the hour," Sawchuk said. "Not only will you save us some time, it will reflect well at your arraignment."

"Not that I don't want to cooperate," Maureen said, "but I don't think it would be good if the next voice Rachel hears is police or army. It has to be Chief David."

Sawchuk cleared his throat, spat on the pavement near Maureen's foot and strode into the full sunshine baking the parking lot. He took up a position midway between Maureen and the sidewalk fronting the street.

"Seems he's been made your bodyguard, Boss," Aaron said.

"Fine by me. We go way back," Maureen said. "And I'm not your boss." She followed Aaron through the double glass doors into the lobby. Cool air enveloped her.

"Jesus, the air conditioning's finally working," Maureen said, as the doors closed behind them with a sigh.

Two minutes later Sawchuk tracked her into the hotel, his face red from the outside heat. He slipped to the edge of the lobby, beside the elevator. He squared his shoulders, hands clasped loosely in front of his belt. He winked at her.

Maureen rolled her eyes and leaned against the counter at the Reception Desk. Her knee throbbed and the skin beneath the bandage itched. "It doesn't make sense," she muttered to Aaron. She pointed out the windows to the forested hillside in the distance. "If Rachel is serious, this whole valley—Hell, every timber stand from the west coast to Georgia Strait—could be ash. It will make every other fire in the province look like a Goddamned dress rehearsal."

The delegation from Vancouver arrived behind an armed forces escort. Maureen hurried to the lobby doors but could not spy Josephine or anybody else behind the dark, one-way glass of the lead Crown Victoria. Lee-Anne climbed out of the last car and walked alone into the hotel as the rest of the convoy moved out of the parking lot.

"Where are they going?" Maureen said.

Lee-Anne ignored the question. "Tell me what you know. Tell me what *you* have that will get the Tse Wets Aht to stand down." Her forehead was damp with perspiration; dark stains discolored her business jacket at the armpits. The skin around her throat and jaw was red and inflamed; the comet-tail of a rash vanished beneath her blouse.

Maureen hoped it itched like Hell. "That wasn't the deal. What I have to say is for Josephine alone. Where is she?"

"Freshening up. The army didn't think the front doors were secure."

"But they let you and me use them." Maureen turned and limped back to the overstuffed chair in the corner of the deserted lobby.

Lee-Anne followed. "Further proof of how expendable you are, Cage. Tell me what *facts* you have that can turn this around. What will make the Tse Wets Aht put down their rifles and re-open the highway?"

Maureen collapsed into the chair. "For Josephine's ears only," she said.

Lee-Anne's hands curled into fists. She stamped down the hallway past the elevator, throwing Sawchuk a look that could melt glass. Aaron gathered a sheaf of papers he'd spread on a nearby table and hurried after her without a backward glance.

Maureen waited in the lobby, elevator muzak oozing from speakers in the ceiling. Sawchuk remained at the periphery of her vision, quietly immovable. He seemed to be enjoying the air conditioning. She'd thumbed through every magazine, counted every leaf on the potted philodendron in the corner when Keith Templeton appeared, his reading glasses loose in one hand and a dazzling white handkerchief tucked in the other. Josephine David walked beside him, her eyes lowered. She was a shadow of the woman Maureen knew, more wraith than a living being. A bandage covered her left cheekbone and the loose strands of hair that had escaped her braid gave her a disheveled, half-crazed look.

"We're on recess. You have fifteen minutes," Templeton said to Maureen. He took a single step backwards. As Josephine stepped nearer to Maureen Templeton cleared his throat. "One thing, before I leave you two alone. Ms. Cage, I must go on record as being shocked by your conduct at the Braithwaite funeral." He puffed air onto the glasses lenses. "Shocking and disgusting, the behavior of those people." The look he gave Josephine made it clear this was not the first time the subject had come up.

Maureen started to speak, but Templeton reset his glasses and held up one hand, cutting her off. "I changed my mind, however, when I heard Simons' press conference. *Nanaimo-gate*, they're calling it. Simply abominable. Without precedent. I now understand why events turned out as they have."

"You're upset because you weren't invited?" Maureen said.

Templeton blinked. "I won't even gratify that comment with a response," he said. "What I mean to say is that I am sorry you used my wife's and my generosity to assist in your ham-handed efforts, but if this ends well I will be happy that I played a part albeit unknowingly. If you require professional services when the time comes, our firm will be happy to represent you. Unlike others, I have no doubts about your character, if not your methods."

"Thank-"

"Later," Templeton interrupted her. "I have given my client permission to speak with you, directly. Ms. Carlyle isn't happy, but then, my interests are my clients' welfare, not *Dee-Faz* preferences. As you well know." A mischievous smile tweaked the corners of his mouth. "Say nothing to upset her further. If you have information that will assist the present negotiation then please, make it known and allow her to carry out her function. Be swift—the army will not wait for us much longer." His upraised hand turned into a stiff wave as he walked away.

Josephine looked up, meeting Maureen's glance. She kept her arms wrapped tightly across her chest. Her face was pale, accentuating the lines around her mouth and eyes. "He's gone," she whispered. Her voice rasped, as if broken glass lined her throat.

Maureen's fingers tightened around the crutch handles. "They didn't hurt you?"

"Just bruises." She touched the round bandage on her cheekbone. "My neck's sore. But that's from the funeral."

"About Billy. I'm-"

Josephine held up one hand. "Don't tell me you're sorry." A steely light glittered in her eyes. "Everybody's fucking *sorry*. We were so damn stupid. He just wanted to hold them accountable."

"But it worked. Hargrove and Henderson are gone. You called them out for the liars they are. Countless thousands around the province support you. The truth has gone viral by now. Billy didn't die for nothing."

Chief David was close to tears. "They didn't even have the guts to tell me until last night."

"There'll be an inquiry," Maureen said. "The A-G has to agree to that."

"No witnesses. If there was video it will go missing. It will take years, and tell us nothing we don't already know. It'll be like every coroner's inquest or commission inquiry done before. No charges, no restitution for the victims. No truth."

"Which is?"

"Billy was murdered." Josephine's chin trembled. She scrubbed her face with her hands. When she looked up the tears were flowing down her hollowed cheeks. "Booze. Poverty. Police. Government. The Four Horsemen of the Aboriginal Apocalypse. For generations the biggest killers of our people. Every thirty years the federal government appoints a Royal Commission. Each one has the same answers as before: better education, better medicine, better living conditions: basic shit the rest of you take for granted. But nothing changes. Ever."

Maureen reached out and rested one hand on Josephine's shoulder. She felt the woman's shaking through her fingertips. "Your nephew Henry wasn't murdered. The Heritage League wasn't involved, even if they wished they were. It was a car wreck. Period. No conspiracy."

Chief David pivoted on her boot heels. "How-?" She pulled Maureen's hand off her shoulder and covered it with both of her own. Her glance implored Maureen to give her something of substance; something real.

"Frances—Raven. She got hold of the steering wheel. Turned them over. She killed them. Accidentally. She was after this." Maureen fumbled in her pocket and withdrew the gold Zippo. She rubbed the pad of her thumb across the engraved letters. "Take it."

Josephine released Maureen's hand, backed away from the lighter. Her lips compressed into a thin, grim line. "She may be your daughter, but do you think I can ever forgive her? And how does this lighter—this *thing*—in your hand make it all right?"

"Put it on Henry's grave. Or throw it in the river, bury it. I don't know what else to do."

313

The muscles around Josephine's jaw rippled. "*You* brought this thing to Port McKenzie. Unhappiness is as much a part of it as the words engraved on it. It brought your daughter here and she did evil trying to possess it. Take it far away. Every time you look at it I want you to remember what your family has done."

"Jo," Maureen said, aware of the heat on her face, "it was an *accident.*"

Josephine turned away. "It was no accident," she said over her shoulder. "It was the Raven, the Trickster, set loose among us. We have been tricked again."

They hustled Josephine, Lee-Anne, Aaron, Templeton, Thorne and the Federation Chiefs to a line of jeeps in the parking lot. Maureen watched them drive away. Constable Sawchuk stood at her shoulder. He waited until the jeeps had vanished from sight. "Don't go far," he said, his glance locked on the line of vehicles shimmering in the heat.

"They're off to the blockade?"

"Can't tell you," Sawchuk said. "Wouldn't even if I could."

Maureen waited until the parking lot was an empty patch of boiling asphalt. A pair of soldiers patrolled the sidewalk beyond the hotel. She hobbled back to the reception counter.

"A cab. I need to get to the Timberman Hotel."

"You'll have to pick it up across the street," the clerk said, "they're not letting anyone onto hotel property."

"Just call me a cab."

Sawchuk did not stop her when she limped through the hotel doors. He followed a half-dozen paces behind, then retreated to his cruiser and waited. It crossed her mind, briefly, to ask him for a ride, but she instead hurried across the parking lot to the sidewalk. The soldiers watched her from a distance, through reflective, wrap-around sunglasses. The afternoon sun beat mercilessly upon her head and shoulders. Her eyes ached. Everything had the same chalky, over-cooked pallor, done in by the unrelenting heat.

A yellow cab rolled to the curb in front of her. "Took you long enough," she said as she opened the rear door.

"There's check points all over," the driver protested through teeth clamped around a smoke. He cupped his hands around his lighter and stuck the flame to the tip of the cigarette.

"Timberman Hotel," Maureen said.

The cabbie stared at her in disbelief.

"Trust me, I'd walk if I could," Maureen said.

The driver blew smoke at his windshield. "All right, get in," he said wearily. When Maureen had settled her crutches across the bench beside her he tromped on the accelerator. "Any idea when this bullshit is gonna be done?" he asked the rear view mirror.

"Why would you think I'd know?" Maureen slid one hand gingerly under the bandage around her knee and scratched.

"You're one a them government big-wigs. I seen you on the news."

"You work at the mill? Maureen glanced out the side window as they turned onto the highway and passed the hulking superstructure. The stacks were dry and hollow in the heat. Squinting through the glare they appeared derelict.

"'til last week. Know how long before the fucking bank takes my fucking house?"

"Hopefully soon. That it's over, I mean." Maureen turned and watched Sawchuk's cruiser glide onto the highway behind them.

"Them Indians got it right. Kill the mill, kill the town," he said. He swung into the hotel parking lot. "But if the mill goes down, so do they." He shook his head and coughed through his cigarette. "No figuring some people."

"How much do I owe you?"

"Five-Seventy."

Maureen gave him a ten dollar bill. "Keep it," she said, swinging her legs out of the cab. It was Helen's money anyway. Her tab was growing faster than the national debt.

The driver grunted in appreciation and jammed the bill in the console separating the seats. Maureen adjusted the crutch handles under her arms and clomped across the narrow alleyway to the front door of the hotel.

It was an oven inside her hotel room despite the open window. She splashed cold water onto her face and neck and unwound the bandage around her knee. The flesh was red, creased by the seams in the tensor bandage. She soaked a wash cloth in cold water and draped it across her knee and half sat, half lay on her bed. She could not bear to turn on the television. She stared out the window at a rectangle of parched sky.

Three weeks, that was all. Three weeks of an August heat wave. Within the span of those twenty-something days she'd fallen so far she could not fathom the climb back. It didn't matter, now. She'd had her chances, made her decisions. Even her attempt to end it all had failed, but so what. Nothing inside hurt anymore. Maybe it was the physical pain, shoving aside her feelings, but maybe not. Maybe she was simply done with everything.

Her glance settled on one of the smoke stacks, just in view through the window of her room. Deprived of its billowing discharge it was just another abandoned chimney blocking the view. When a Pope dies the most powerful cardinals gather to choose a successor while thousands wait in St. Peter's square, anxious, watching for the thin spiral of white smoke from the Vatican. The smoke represents hope, security and continuity. Was it the same for Port McKenzie? Did the town need its own white smoke, its steaming clouds swirling in the wind, to signify that all was right in the world?

A sudden chill raced down her spine, making her queasy. She grabbed for the phone and dialed Rachel's cell. Rachel answered on the fourth ring, the sound of splashing water audible in the background.

"I know where you are," Maureen said. "I know what you're going to do."

"Maureen Cage? Why aren't you in jail?"

"The RCMP are heading your way. Don't do anything stupid."

"You're such a bullshitter. Just like my father," Rachel said, her voice cutting out across the phone connection.

"Leave the mill alone," Maureen said. She could make out waves slapping a metal hull just before Rachel hung up. She dialed Aaron's number with shaking hands.

"Jesus, Cage, your timing sucks," Aaron said. "The Chiefs and the A-G are going at it toe to toe and then my phone rings and everybody's looking at me and-"

"Shut up, Aaron! Rachel's on the Slough. She's going for the mill. The mill, not the trees!"

Aaron groaned. "How do you—never mind. Christ, what next?"

"Tell the RCMP, tell Josephine!" Maureen shouted, slamming down the phone and grabbing her crutches. As she hobbled through the lobby she called to the dozing reception clerk for a cab.

"He's in the bar," he said, rousting himself out of his chair. "I'll get him."

"Hurry," Maureen said, and pushed on the door that opened onto the parking lot.

Constable Sawchuk's cruiser was parked three stalls over from the hotel entrance. As Maureen approached Sawchuk got out of his car and leaned on the fender, hooking his fingers into his belt.

"It's the mill," Maureen said. "They're going to burn it down."

Sawchuk frowned. "Stay where you are," he said.

"Take me to the mill before it's too late."

"My orders are to watch you, not chauffeur you around," Sawchuk said.

"Then call it in," Maureen said, her temper rising.

The cab driver strolled out the side door, still clutching a bottle of beer. When he saw Maureen he saluted her with the bottle. "Goin' back to the Queen Anne?" He chuckled to himself and drained his beer.

"Take me to the mill."

"Shit, Lady, its right there." He waved in the direction of the Slough. The stacks towered over the foreshore.

"I can barely walk," Maureen said. "I need to get there fast."

"We're locked out, Lady, or hadn't you heard?"

"Forty dollars," Maureen said, tugging two of Helen's twenties out of her pocket. "To take me across the fucking highway."

317

"Done." He snatched the money and popped the trunk. "Stick 'em in here," he said, pulling her crutches out of her hands. He waved at Sawchuk and stood the empty beer bottle on the pavement beside the cab. "Do I got an escort, too?" He grinned at Maureen as he dropped behind the wheel.

"Through those gates," Maureen said, pointing through the windshield as the cab pulled onto the highway.

"I know where I'm going," the driver said. "Least, after seventeen years I *oughta* know." He braked at the gates. They were thrown open, no sign of Security or staff. They welcomed arrivals to the deserted property where ribbons of heat rose off the asphalt.

"Shouldn't they be closed?" Maureen said.

"Dunno," the cabbie said, raising one bushy eyebrow. "Maybe we settled and nobody thunk to tell me."

"Take me inside."

"Can't do it, Lady. I'm a union man."

"But the signs are down. Tell them I made you."

"Wouldn't that just tear it? We settle an' I get blackballed for crossing. What if its scab labor they got in there?"

"Look. There's RCMP right behind us." Maureen jerked her thumb in the direction of Sawchuk's cruiser. "I need to get to the administration building. Drop me by the front doors."

"Why's he followin' you?"

"I'm a celebrity. He's been assigned to protect me."

"From what? Jesus, Lady, this whole town's coming apart at the seams."

"Hurry. Before this place is burned to the ground and there's no work for anyone."

Muttering curses, the driver shifted out of park. The taxi lurched ahead. He swung the wheel hard and pulled up to the front doors. The frosted glass and polished timber panels were shut.

Maureen tossed the driver another twenty. "Pop the trunk."

She limped to the back of the cab, dragged her crutches out and settled them under her arms. "Tell Sawchuk back there I'm going in."

"What's the big deal?" The driver hollered out the open window.

"Because otherwise they'll think *I'm* responsible. This time they'll shoot me."

"This time?" The driver began to laugh, but at a look from Maureen he bit his lip and sped toward the gates. He veered to intercept the RCMP cruiser as it circled at the gate.

No sign of operations staff or security. The heat was oppressive, not even a breath of air came off the Slough. The whine of a boat motor rose off the foreshore. Maureen half ran, half vaulted with her crutches to the corner of the building, just in time to spot the open powerboat pulling out of the mill's private marina. It leaned on the throttle, speeding away from shore. Three figures were outlined in the boat, but the glare coming off the water washed out all detail. As Maureen watched the boat veered west, toward open water. She heard the zodiacs before she saw them. They appeared out of the east and closed fast. A helicopter dropped out of the sky to join the chase. She turned, grinning, and gave Sawchuk a *thumbs up* and as she retraced her steps to the main doors. It took all her remaining strength to pull open the heavy door.

A lone security guard rose out of his chair at the reception desk. He raised his hand to stop her.

"A phone. I need to use a phone." Maureen limped to the counter.

"You're not supposed to be in here, Ma'am. I'll need to see some ID."

"Call the Fire Department. You have to clear this building," Maureen said. She lunged for the phone.

The security guard held her back. His hand closed around her wrist. "Now Ma'am, whoever you are. Calm down. I'm not calling anybody until I get some answers. We got a service call just now, Joe's probably showing them around."

"Who?"

"The Feds. Weights and Measures folks. They're here to test our pumps. Not that it's any of *your* business."

She could feel her blood pumping through her veins. "Jesus, they're not the Federal Government! They're terrorists! Didn't you hear their boat? How many are in the building? I need to speak to someone in charge. Sally Brackens. Is she in?"

The guard hesitated. He glanced warily at his roster. "She is." He licked his lips.

"Get her down here. Fast."

The guard squinted at Maureen. "Alrighty, then. I'll call her. But if you're yanking my chain there'll be trouble." He picked up the phone and pushed buttons. "Sorry to bother, Ms. Brackens. There's a-" he scowled at Maureen. "What'd you say your name was?"

"Maureen Cage."

"There's a Maureen Cage here. Very agitated. Says there's terrorists on the premises." He set down the phone, puffing out his cheeks. "She'll be right down," he said. "She'll be needing some proof."

"She knows me," Maureen said. Her palms were sweaty. "Call your partner. Make sure he's okay."

The guard shook his head. He plucked the walkie-talkie off the desk. He hesitated, his thumb hovering over the button.

"You rather be embarrassed or out of a job?"

He growled and pressed the mic. "Joe. Hey, Joe. You there?"

"May I help you, Ms. Cage?" Sally Brackens hurried through a frosted glass door, a second security guard in tow. "What's this about terrorists?"

"Clear this building. It's NFDI."

"I'm going to need some sort of evidence," Brackens said. "The last news I heard said you were wanted by police."

"They're outside the door as we speak," Maureen said. "But there's no time. You have to clear this building. Call nine-one-one. We don't have much-"

Sawchuk appeared inside the front doors as the blast went off. It started small, like a rifle retort in the distance. Then a typhoon struck the building, blowing out windows, knocking Maureen backwards as if she'd been swatted by a titanic hand. Brackens and the security guards tumbled past her, to where Sawchuk had been standing moments before. Oily smoke and dust filled her eyes and mouth. A rushing black tide of sound filled her ears, deafening her. She struggled to rise, but her legs were useless.

She cried out, clutching her side. She couldn't breathe. She could not see. She was sure, as the roar crested inside her skull, that she heard sirens, but they were distant, perhaps miles away.

From her bed in Central Island Regional Hospital Maureen watched video clips and news reports of the mill fire. They'd set her broken leg and operated on her bad knee the same day, the day of the explosion. They could do nothing for her cracked ribs and concussion except feed her painkillers and prop her up in bed. When the duty nurse could be persuaded to open the curtains the glimpse of pale, sun-burned sky hurt her eyes, but with borrowed sunglasses the television news filled in the gaps between the moments the Administration building vaporized to the present, two days after. The Vancouver news broadcasts were thorough and recurring. From the Slough came images of the wrecked gas bar and marina, smoking under a cannon spray from a Coast Guard fire boat. From the news helicopter the Administration building looked like it had been swept away by a Tsunami. The cameras then showed a grim-faced Attorney-General, standing shoulder to shoulder with Mayor Conconi, Keith Templeton and Josephine David. Their photo-op was strategically established on the highway shoulder as army bulldozers worked to backfill the moat. Traffic control people in reflective vests waved the first convoy of vehicles over the bridge as the highway re-opened to cheers and applause.

"This is all thanks to the hard work of Chief David, the Tse Wets Aht and the town of Port McKenzie," the Attorney-General said, the hot sun coaxing beads of perspiration across his brow. "Without them this could have been much worse. Tragic, in fact. The Tse Wets Aht have lived up to their name: *The People From the Place at the Beginning of Things*. And we are at a new beginning. They have fully cooperated with us and all agencies. Armed Forces personnel have successfully recovered a cache of terrorist weapons and arrested the ringleaders. RCMP has taken Rachel Braithwaite, daughter of the late CEO of *Dee-Faz*, and five other known members of NFDI into custody. The civil disobedience is over. Damage to the mill, though severe, is not as incapacitating as first feared. Reconstruction will begin as soon as possible and the ownership group is pleased to announce that some operations will resume as early as two weeks from today."

"We've been given another chance," the Mayor said. "I know you don't get many, so we better not waste this one. It's time to mend fences with our neighbors," the Mayor said. "With the new mill there'll be a new start for everyone. New opportunities."

Maureen used the remote to turn off the television. She felt her eyelids getting heavy. She must have slept, for when she awoke the room was in shadow and Anne and Helen stood at the foot of her bed.

"*Now* will you come home?" Helen said. Anne waved over Helen's shoulder, grinning broadly. "Doc says you can leave tomorrow or the day after. You are very lucky. He told me the others, that woman from the mill and the security guard, will be in here a couple of weeks."

Maureen nodded stiffly. "Sure, but I don't feel lucky," she said. Her tongue was thick, her mouth dry. Her headache was back, radiating pain through her skull. She pushed her sunglasses up the bridge of her nose.

Helen handed her a glass of water, twisting the straw so she could reach it. "Good," Helen said, sliding the curtains closed. "Enough of this nonsense. You need a proper job, one that will keep you busy and away from lunatics."

"We've a business proposition for you, Mo, when you're ready," Anne said.

Maureen held up her hand. "Theresa," she said, surprised at how different her voice sounded. Clearer, despite the frog in her throat. "Maureen's retired, for good this time."

"It's time we retired, too," Helen said. She shot Anne a hopeful, nervous look. "You know the business as well as anyone. We know you better than anyone. You're like a daughter, only better."

Anne laughed. "We *like* lending you money."

"Anyway," Helen interrupted, glaring at Anne, "we'd like you to become a partner. Help us manage A&H."

"You'll be great," Anne added.

Theresa closed her eyes to dull the throbbing in her head. Manage A&H? Manage a booking agency for exotic dancers? She felt weightless as an urge to laugh bubbled behind her ribs. She groaned, pressing a hand against her chest. "Let's talk when I get home," she whispered.

Anne clapped her hands. "This calls for a celebration," she said. "Helen and I are going out for dinner. To work out the details and do up the paperwork. Sleep now, get better, Mo—*Theresa*. We'll see you in the morning." She shuffled close enough to kiss Theresa on the forehead.

Helen patted her foot and waved goodbye.

Theresa Pistilli, Manager. She exhaled carefully. Maybe they'd add her name to the company? A&H&T. *AHT.*

At the Beginning of Things.

She liked how that sounded.

END

EPILOGUE

February

EPILOGUE

February

The kettle's whistle summoned her from her office. She scooped a generous spoonful of loose tea from a tin box and dumped it into her teapot, filled it with boiling water and set the kettle onto the stove. Lazy curls of steam drifted toward the ceiling. Rain pelted the window behind the sink, a steady strumming of fingernails on glass that started before daybreak and showed no sign of letting up. The fires of August were now a distant memory, drowned in a continuous trail of storms that, since November, had been blowing in off the Pacific. Freighters clogged the sliver of English Bay visible from the window. Sky and sea were stitched together by slanting rain. Grey stacked on grey, stacked on deeper grey.

Theresa fetched a mug from the cupboard and waited for the tea to steep. She punched a button on the IPod that squatted on a corner of the table, vying for space with a neat mound of unread newspapers, a dozen potted African Violets on saucers and a wicker basket that brimmed with a week's worth of Carole's mail. An old Beatles song filled the room. *Yesterday.* She filled the mug with tea and brought it near her lips to blow across its surface. The music followed her back to the study. Her own pile of Friday mail on her desk needed attention and Carole would be home soon after dark.

With the sale of her house Theresa had paid off Anne and Helen's loan and bought into A&H Agencies. Just as she'd imagined it from her hospital bed they'd renamed the company AHT Entertainment and listed Theresa Pistilli as junior partner and Vice President, Operations. She'd hardly seen Anne or Helen since Thanksgiving: they spent most of their days riding air-conditioned tour buses between Vancouver and Vegas. Since Theresa had signed on as partner AHT Entertainment had grown into Vancouver's largest booking agency for exotic dancers. *It comes naturally to her*, Helen said with motherly pride.

After the election and the complete demise of Hargrove's government, compounded by the subsequent cessation of *DeeFaz*, operations, Carole had quit her job and moved from Ottawa to start a consulting practice in Vancouver. Her work filled the void caused by *DeeFaz's* dissolution, so much so that she had hired Aaron Chen to manage some of the load. Then they had made it official: together Carole and Theresa bought a small, one-bedroom-with-den apartment in the West End. *I want to be as high off the ground as we can afford*, Carole had said, when they commissioned an agent to find them a home. It took only a day to find their place: a small suite in an older, concrete high-rise a short jog from Stanley Park and a block up from Beach Avenue. Eight floors up was the best view of the water they could afford. It was a seller's market, their agent had apologized.

The study walls—the three lacking windows—Theresa had covered with eight by ten photos of current dancers under contract. *You best keep that door closed if I have to bring clients here*, Carole said, but it hadn't happened yet: Carole was the one who traveled, driving or flying into First Nations communities as far away as Haida Gwaii. The portraits of retired dancers were packed away or shredded, with one exception: Angel's portrait remained, framed, on the desk where Theresa could see it without having to swivel her chair.

She set down her mug and settled in her new chair—she'd sold Alianna's desk, chair and most of the furniture (with the exception of the pie shelf, Carole refused to let that piece go) and replaced them with smaller, modern versions, the kind always on sale at the big-box office supply stores. She liked their neat simplicity. She sipped her tea and skimmed through the mail: contracts, booking confirmations, demo DVD's and the bills she still didn't pay online. She came across an envelope: thin, smudged, postmarked ten days earlier from Toronto. There was no return address. She held it up to the light and slid a letter opener through one end. A folded newspaper clipping fell onto the desk. No note, no explanation. Just the article. She unfolded the page, cut from the *Windsor Star* with an early January publication date scrawled in ink across the top.

Police yesterday discovered the body of a man after neighbors complained of a foul smell coming from his apartment. When they broke down the door they found Bob Cage, 53, dead in his bedroom. Police have declined to comment, but sources say he was beaten to death with a blunt object. Police have taken several objects for forensic analysis, including, witnesses say, a baseball bat.
"He loved baseball. He was a bit of a nut," said one neighbor who wished to remain anonymous. Contacted in Toronto by reporters, Cage's estranged wife showed little emotion upon hearing the news. "Since he lost the family property he kept some pretty disreputable company," Karen Cage said. "You know, gamblers and bikers and strippers and the like. This doesn't surprise me in the least." Police Chief Barry Curran said further details would be released as they were obtained, but at the present time they have no suspects.

Theresa set down the article and moved to the sliding glass door that opened onto a small, sheltered shoe-box of a balcony. She flipped the catch and stepped outside. A careening wind stung her eyes. The chill was quickly inside her knee, rekindling a familiar, arthritic ache. The rain was coming down harder, now, emptying out of a sky so close she could almost touch the ragged clouds. The penthouses of the adjacent high rises were hidden; English Bay and its family-friendly beaches vanished behind a curtain of smudged and tattered gauze. The afternoon was hushed, the ubiquitous traffic noises muffled by the clouds and rain.

Theresa shivered and hugged her sides against the chill as she pressed a shoulder blade into the glass of the door.

"Frances," she said in a voice only the drizzle could hear, "you shouldn't have."